The Willow Branch

Book 1 of the Daermad Cycle

Lela Markham

Breakwater Harbor Books, Inc.
Scott J. Toney and Cara Goldthorpe, Co-Founders
www.breakwaterharborbooks.com

Printed by CreateSpace, an Amazon.com Company

Lela Markham

My Thanks!

To my Lord and Savior Jesus Christ.
1 Corinthians 10:23-31

To my husband and children who allowed The Willow Branch to happen. Thank you for putting up with my staring into space, burning dinner, and the mock sword battles in the back yard that really had the neighbors wondering about us. Without you, none of this would have been possible and most of it would not have been worth it. There's a little bit of each of you in some character in this book. I know – Writers are weird, but it is my gift to you.

Thanks to Black Dog, canine pirate, for making me believe that animals can think for themselves without being cartoon characters. Joy and Sabre owe their existence to you, you ungrateful beast.

Immense thanks to the Authonomy writers who acted as alpha readers and critics. You all know how invaluable that was and remains. Special thanks to Scott Butcher (author of the Stillwart Chronicles) and Scott Toney (Breakwater Harbor Books) for acting as beta readers and editors and going above and beyond the Authonomy call of duty.

Time Flow, Geography and Culture in

The Willow Branch

This book occurs in a number of time periods. The first quote in Fate explains why – the present is built on the past and when we forget the past we imperil the future. This is also why the larger series is called The Daermad Cycle – daermad meaning "forgetful" in Gaelic. Pay attention to the subheadings because they tell you whether you're in Founding Year 931 or 1028. There are two main stories. The past with the doomed princes Maryn, Perryn and Donyl follows the destruction of the kingdom. The present with Padraig, Tamys, Gregyn and Ryanna follows the restoration. Unless the present actors can figure out what went wrong in the past, they are doomed to repeat it. Yes, Talidd shows up in both time lines as does the Morrigan.

In writing The Willow Branch, I found that I had two separate stories that could run in different books or different sections of the same book, but really were not stand-alone stories. They need to be told together to arrive where I want to arrive, so please bear with me because the past really is the foundation of the present in reality as well as in Daermad.

I tried to make it easy for you by obeying my own rules. Each chapters starts with a quote from the literary history of the peoples of Daermad, followed by a scene from Founding

Year 931 (the past). The rest of the chapter focuses on FY 1028 (the present), though there are a few subchapters that follow Gilyn, who would be the destroyer of worlds. If you pay attention to the subchapters, you should have no problem staying oriented.

The people of Celdrya are the descendants of a Treverri tribe of Celts that somehow stumbled through a "portal" back in the 4th century AD, which was the early Christian era for parts of Northern Europe. They have been in Daermad for about a millennia and so they are not exactly European Celts anymore, but they share some common history. You will also find other familiar Earth cultures living in Daermad. Where did they come from? You'll have to buy more books to find out. Where did the Kin and dwarves come from? Daermad!

The Kin speak Elvish, which is rendered largely in American English. The Celdryans speak some form of Gaulish, which accounts for the lilting narrative voice in those sections. In a nod to my immense admiration for Katharine Kerr, writer of the Deverry series, I've tried to follow her language conventions as to spellings. I make no claims to perfection.

Those extremely long names for the Kin are their full names. Just as I would be Lela Amanda Davis Markham, Morynsionryanna is Ryanna, daughter of Sion from Moryn. Similar to Asian naming conventions, the clan name is given first. Because Ryanna's father is Denygal, his place of birth is listed rather than his clan, following the Celdryan fashion of common names.

Table of Contents

Map of Daermad

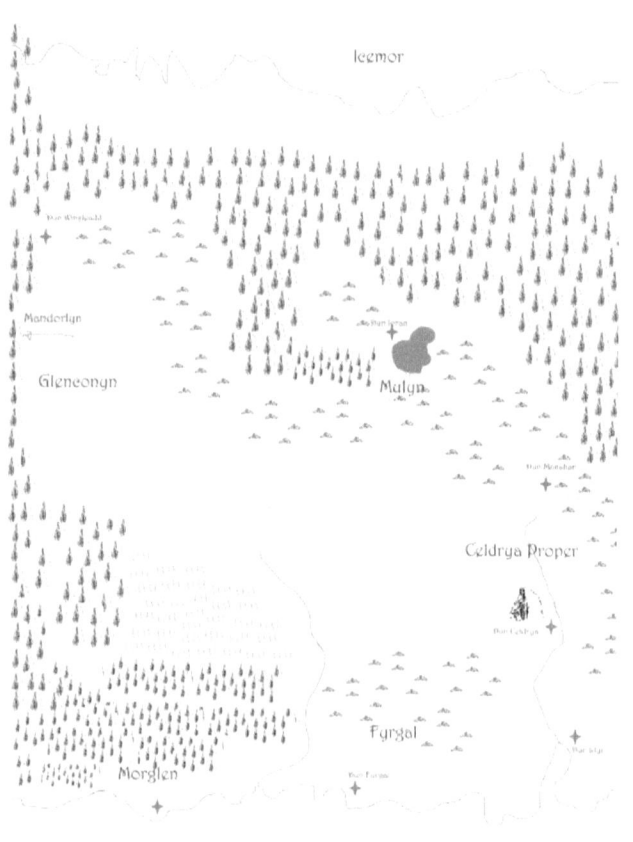

Denygal

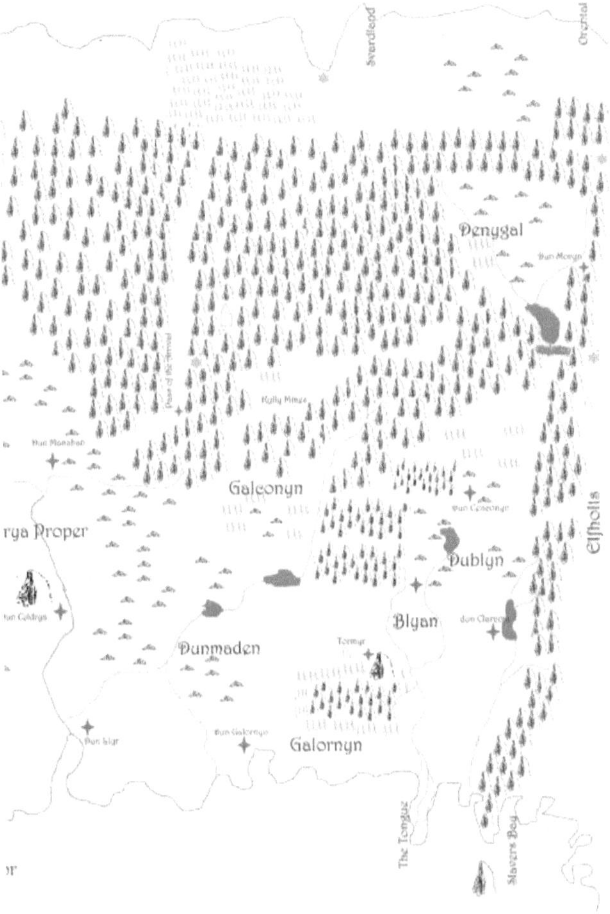

Dun Mongo

Peak of the Eternal

Holly Mittee

Galeonyn

Bun Manahul

rya Proper

Dun Canringe

Oner

Elfholts

Dublyn

dun Clareen

Blyan

Tennyr

Dunmaden

Bun Galomyn

Galornyn

Bun Isar

The Tongue

Mavere Bay

Fate

As a tree's leaves are nourished by the roots, the present is established in the past. The history of the kingdom is older than the lives of man. We are upon the land only a moment and then depart, leaving others to learn anew lessons our fathers grasped. The map of the kingdom overlays an older land, but none remember it so. The true king descends from God, not the king in High Celdrya. Celts, ignore that strong truth at all our peril!

Gwenedd, Druidess of the Christian Celts
(FY 448)

Founding Year (FY) 931
A Century Ago · Spring

Fate took Maryn ap Trevellyn, crown prince of all Celdrya, by surprise. Naught warned him that he'd been marked. Deryk ap Fyrgal camped with him in a wood off the King's Highway between the coastal city of Llyr and High Celdrya on a pleasant eve following a relaxing day of fishing.

They enjoyed cups of wine with fresh bread, soft cheese and rolls of thinly-sliced spiced meat.

"I do think that second marriages agree with a man," Deryk commented. He'd already had a bit too much to drink, as was his wont. Soon the tall blonde swordsman would settle back on his cot and sleep, leaving Maryn to contemplate the eve and his own thoughts alone. Twas always the way with them since boyhood.

"How so?" Maryn asked, leaning back in his camp chair, his darker brown hair and beard setting off his merry blue eyes. As heir-apparent to the High Seat of Celdrya, he craved the rare honest moment with a vassal who would speak freely.

"Do you not remember the first marriage, my friend? You were cockled for months before the ceremony. This time, you ducked into Llyr, confirmed the engagement and flitted away for the important things in life." Deryk demonstrated this by waving his wine cup about this den of manly comfort. Owing to his lighter hair, he had not yet grown a full beard, though his moustache had grown in nicely.

"She'll be in Dun Celdrya soon enough," Maryn assured his friend. "Aye, you are correct about Melynda. I was much in love. I'll not make that mistake with this one."

Maryn's first wife had died at childbed, delivering a stillborn daughter, at midwinter. He still mourned them both, but the kingdom demanded an heir, so his father had arranged a betrothal as soon as the official period of mourning was over. He would not lose his heart to this one, so it would not hurt so much if the gods were cruel again.

"Good for you." Deryk was on record as one more in favor of lust than love. "This one's already tried and found fertile, for all that she's a widow and childless. What more could a prince ask for?"

Gillian of Llyr, one year junior to Maryn's 23, had been married to a younger son of Galornyn and borne him a healthy son, but both the husband and child had perished in a fever last fall. With King Vanyn in ill health, it became urgent for Maryn to produce an heir and clearly Gillian could provide that. There were worse reasons to marry beyond political expediency.

"I liked her well enough," Maryn explained. "She's intelligent and being raised in court at Llyr made her wise. I won't love her, truly, but we'll enjoy each other, I think."

Deryk gave Maryn a searching gaze until the younger man set his cup aside.

"What are you thinking?"

"Did you sample the wares?"

"Oh, aye!" Maryn assured with a roguish grin. "She seemed as pleased with me as I with her. We're not children to mince about the issue."

"As I thought," Deryk said, draining his cup and yawning hugely. "I'm for sleep, my brother. And, you?"

"I think I will walk the pickets," Maryn decided. "Tis a pleasant evening and that cheese will disturb my sleep if I don't let it settle.

"Then good night to you," Deryk said.

Donning his cloak of red and silver plaid, Maryn stepped into the night. A few riders still talked round fires here and there, but most were retiring to tents and blankets. It must be nearing middle of the night, for a moon hung like a golden banqueting plate just above the southern trees and the cool air scented more of dew than spring flowers. Several fires burned down to coals, though the guards would keep one of the cook fires going through the night.

Maryn strolled along the horse picket first, knowing that there would be a guard stationed at the far end. He found Traegyr staring out into the quiet dark, standing at ease with his hand near, but not on, the pommel of his sword.

"Good even," Maryn called long before he approached. Traegyr, captain of Maryn's personal guard, knew his voice well and did not startle.

"Sir, is somewhat amiss?"

"Naught except for a belly of fine wine and good cheese. I'll walk tonight. Anything about?"

"I saw a fox at the start of my watch, but nay, naught else beyond a few night birds."

"Good then. I'll say good night to you."

The next sentry, having heard him chatting with Traegyr, greeted Maryn with good cheer. Leomyr, a grizzled man who had been with the warband at Maryn's earliest memory, expected not but a quiet night with a few mosquitoes and naught more to disturb the camp. Maryn moved on.

The alder wood seemed to shimmer toward the south as moonlight passed through fog. Somewhere nearby, a raven tek-tekked. Maryn thought he'd not heard many ravens at night. There must be a nesting ground nearby.

"Sir," the sentry at the south greeted. "I'm honored that you would review my work."

"Truly?" Maryn said with humor. He had learned from his pagehood that a liege lord should acknowledge the common-born men who guarded his back, so his personal guard were mostly comfortable with him in a respectful manner. This guard was new to him, having been part of the dun's war band until Traegyr had called him forth to the personal guard this winter. He was just shy of his middle years, with a lean unlined face and curiously slender through the hips. "You don't think that I am inquiring beyond what is needful?"

"Nay, sir, for I am employed in your service and good work should welcome attention."

"What is your name?"

"Pedyr, sir," the guard said.

"Unusual name," Maryn noted.

"Aye, my mam was from Dublyn."

"Dublyn, is it? My brother Donyl is at the collegiate there – or will arrive shortly, I suppose."

"The collegiate is up in Denygal," Pedyr explained. "My mam does hail from there, but I've never been. I did travel to Clarcom with your father once."

"Mayhap we can arrange for you to be in the honor guard to collect Donyl when the time comes. He'll not want to go, knowing him. Bit of a bookworm, you see."

"I have heard," Pedyr said with a slight smile, then jerked round as a raven scream split the night. Before he could draw his sword, there came a whistling and Maryn was thrown back against a tree.

Death took him by surprise as he looked down at the two feet of dressed wood protruding from his chest. He couldn't feel his legs, but he knew that he was staked to the tree like a squirrel.

I'm done for! I thought death would be more painful.

Pedyr bellowed for aid and the camp came alive as Maryn died, staring up at the moon with his life leaking away into the dirt by his feet and wondering why the shaft that killed him was the only one to fly.

Kindred Cycle 24573
Trading Grounds, Five Cycles Past

The moon shone out of time and dumped a shovelful of cold down Gil's back as he stared up through the smoke hole of the conical tent. He'd been contemplating the freedom of the Basketlands and hating the remembered stench of Celtmen as he dozed. Fully awake now, he rolled from under his blankets to pull on a pair of trews under the loose siarc he'd worn to bed. He walked out of the tent into what was meant to be darkest night and was as bright as day.

The silence had awakened him. A Kin camp was never silent, even in the dark of night. There was always someone singing, horses nickering, goats chewing on ropes.

Where is that cursed goat?

Nothing moved save the fires in a dozen rings scattered among the tall conical Kin tents. The goat had laid down asleep outside of Astralyn's tent. On the other side of the nearest campfire, Gil could see one of the dogs had also fallen asleep.

Where are the guards?

The female standing by the central fire must have something to do with it. Dressed in a black shift of breast-skimming fabric, her waist length dark tresses moved in a wind that he could not feel as the power of her golden eyes drew him forward.

The most beautiful female I've ever seen, he thought. She was not so tall as Ryanna, but here was a woman who was comfortable being a woman. *A female to make a man forget his woes and foes.*

"Do I owe the music of silence to you, my lady?"

"You owe all to me, Farenlucgilyn." She spoke Celdryan with an odd accent.

The silver-eyed witch was right, and that bitch I'm mated to did nothing to forestall my fate. Do I even care? Should I?

"You know who I am?" Gil queried. A fragrance of roses wafted from her white skin. When was the last time I scented a female wearing essence. They all think they don't need it.

"I know your soul, Gil. And, if you allow, I might be yours." Her voice flowed like warm honey. The cadence of her accent made him think of the old Celdryan texts his father read aloud.

"Many females have been mine," Gil told her.

"Have they? Lying with one such as me is not the same as possessing. Would not your mate agree?"

"What do you know of my wife?" he demanded.

"She is not here." It wasn't a question and the hair on the back of Gil's neck tingled.

"No," he agreed. *The bitch is Wise now!* "She chose another," he explained. *True enough!*

She had moved closer … or he had. He scarce remembered. Her hands lay upon his chest, heat radiating through his siarc.

"Do you love your people, Gil?' she asked.

Odd question! Does she know me so well?

Shanara's silver eyes filled his memory. *The seer foresaw this.*

"Both my peoples can burn in the deepest hells for my amusement," Gil admitted.

"Aye, you have anger enough to possess me," she announced.

"What must I do?" Gil asked. *A quality mare always comea at a price.* He felt himself, his will, falling into her golden eyes. "Shall I burn them?" His eyes scanned the rough circle of hide tents and he smiled.

"That would be a good beginning, but a beginning only. You will be rewarded as you serve me."

"What grand treasure does my goddess desire?"

This won a smile from her winsome lips.

"Very perceptive, Farenlucgilyn! And you willingly pay the price?"

"Oh, yes," he said in Elvish and then switched back to Celdryan. "Gladly, so long as my father's people suffer as deeply as they deserve."

"I think I can arrange that if you can give me a basketful of offerings."

"My mother's people in the bargain? What a rich treasure indeed!" Gil bowed his head, which was as much as he could do with her standing so close. "I'm yours, my goddess, but what weapon do I possess that will destroy both Kin and Celt?"

Her laugh was music.

"Not destroy – enslave. The dead cannot worship me and give me offerings. That is not to say there won't be streams of blood wherever we go. I envision many deaths and much blood, but we will preserve a remnant for my temples."

"Of course, my goddess."

"After you burn this camp, enter the byway to the north. You'll know where I wish you to go. Others have already laid the pyre. They need only your spark. We shall blaze across Daermad and your legend will be writ large and sung round the campfires for a millennium."

A lifetime, twice that for an elfling, and twenty-five for the Celt. That is reward enough.

A torch appeared unbidden in his hand, the flame hot upon his face. The tall conical tents caught easily as one by one they blossomed against the night sky. When the last was lit, she grabbed his braid in a strong hand and sliced it free. The heat from the fires beat the air round them as they kissed for the first time, but all was forgotten as she pulled him into his tent to lie with him. He climaxed to the smell of burning flesh. Only later would he wonder why no one screamed.

When Gil awoke from the dream, the Kin were dead down to the goat and dog and he owned a hundred strangely docile horses laden with a fortune in trade goods. He left his people where they lay, the beaded braid laid beside the central campfire. Due north was the opening to a long-unused byway. With confidence to which he had no rightful claim, Gil opened the portal and set forth north to claim the treasure he deserved.

Kindred Cycle 24578/ Founding Year 1028
Blue Iris Holt - Three moons past

The music swirled round them, driving hands to clap and feet to stomp. Padraig spun Ryanna round in a complicated reel of dancers, letting go, weaving, circling, rejoining. Ryanna laughed as the other dancers called the steps and feet tapped to the rhythm of the harp and pipe.

At last Padraig lost step and pulled Ryanna down on a ledge to watch the other dancers continue their revelry. Ryanna giggled, her eyes lake blue in the lantern light, twinkling with merriment.

"It's been so long since I laughed like this," she admitted. Some said he'd brought the light back into her eyes. Such was an awesome responsibility.

All round them the merriment of the solstice feast spun as they smiled at one another. Her full lips were pink and moist. He thought of kissing them, but she remained a married woman, as testified by the single beaded braid tangled in her loose dark tresses. Padraig straightened, putting distance between them, and her grin grew rueful.

"There's a council a half moon from now," she said in Celdryan. Although many in the crowd knew Celdryan, it provided them with a modicum of privacy, at least from the children. "I'll make my intentions known. It's been a five-cycle and I've done all I can. He removed his braid and left it. Even if he had not … done what he did … I am within my rights."

Padraig's Denygal upbringing rankled over divorce. It was Celdryan practice for men to set aside women to starve or be dishonored. The Kin and Denygal mated for life, but mates died without witness or fell to disaster. Farenlucgilyn had walked away apparently guilty of a horrendous act. Ryanna's petition was a formality and … yet …. Marriage was for life … unless your mate abandoned you following a horrific act of murder. When Gil sliced his braid off and left it behind, his intentions had been clear.

"You seem troubled," Ryanna noted.

"It's the clash of cultures," he assured her. *That must be it.* The Denygal, hybrid race that they were, lived shorter lives than the Kin. They had taken the lesson of mating for life, but not the pragmatic understanding that sometimes this was not true. "My love for you grows daily, but I would not love you against the One's will and miss His direction."

Ryanna nodded and moved to say somewhat, but a sudden gust of wind set the lanterns guttering as snow swirled through the high hall. The music stopped as the crowd turned to stare at the three men standing in the open doorway. Snow-covered and heavily cloaked, they stood amid the swirling ice of a solstice day. Goi'tan rushed to close the double set of iron doors that stood as tall as a dun's gate as the extinguished lanterns were quickly replaced by etheric light from a dozen sources.

The central figure of the three appeared sculpted in ice until he swept back the deep hood of his coat and focused bright purple eyes upon Padraig.

"Navaransenmador" Ryanna whispered.

Padraig glanced at her, confused, as Navaransenmador gazed about the chamber. His hair was silver, plaited with beads Padraig did not recognize, but his features were elven – furled ears, catslit eyes, slender face with high cheek bones.

"You besmirch the solstice with this celebration of your false god," he announced in flawless Elvish. Marsamonsynglysel stepped forward as he spoke for the Wise this five-cycle.

"You do not speak for the Kin," he said, as if reminding. "Please, join our celebration. You are welcome at our fire to eat our bread." He gestured toward the banquet tables.

Navaransenmador frowned, his silver eyebrows drawing down, accentuating his purple eyes.

"I've come to deliver a message, though why the One gives a message to heretics, I do not know."

His gaze fell upon Padraig once more. His frown deepened.

Yes, man, I'm Denygal, Padraig thought. *I am not the only one.*

Navararansenmador drew himself up and began to sing in a clear baritone that reverberated off the stone walls.

"Thus says the One Whose Name We Are Not to Know, hear Me, Kindred, and know that I am One God.

"A elfling shall seek the True King and find him in the aviary where no bird of a feather may rule. A chill wind from the north shall batter him before he climbs to the tower, but strong companions will lift his arms and bolster him until all bow before the dragon.

"The raptors fight over the aviary, but only one can rule and no bird of a feather will mount the throne. The dragon stirs and the One's King will arise. Go you then to find him and win him free of those who would exploit him. Who shall go? One who knows both worlds and can heal both the body and the rifts of men, one whose brothers rule, yet who would walk barefoot himself, one whose Companion shines like the sun.

"And how shall you know the One's King? He will be obscure -- near the rule, but not of it. He will be of the Kin, but not know the Kin. He will pass through tribulation. He will be plain of speech, heroic and thoughtful. The dragon will claim him.

"The raptors fight over the aviary, but all will bow before the dragon.

"Know this and hear the One speak."

When Navaransenmador was done, he sagged a bit, as if he had exhausted himself. One of his companions offered a steadying arm.

"You speak only to this elfling," Gly noted, indicating Padraig. "Why is that? Is this prophesy only for him?"

"The prophesy is for all of us," Shanara spoke from the shadows. A moment later an etheric light bloomed pale blue beside her, brighter than any other in the room. "The One's king is born, somewhere in the basketlands. Padraig is uniquely qualified to search for him and we are to aid him however we are able."

"How could the One's king be born among the Celt?" someone demanded from the crowd.

Navaransenmador seemed no longer interested in the topic. He and his two companions had withdrawn to a banquet table.

"Are they not God's children also," Barana, Gly's wife, reasoned.

Padraig groped for the ledge behind him, sitting down heavily, stunned. Ryanna placed a hand upon his shoulder. Many voices echoed past him, full of questions and awe, but he understood none of them. He felt the stream of history catch him up and drag him downstream, tossing and tumbling, helpless to stand against it.

He found himself holding Ryanna's hand as reality slowly shifted back into place. Gly was standing in the center of the hall; the Council of Wisdom stood near to him.

"The Council will call to order after the morning meal tomorrow. Padraig, we will require your presence. Shanara as well."

"What of Navaransenmador. Should he not speak?" Padraig whispered. Ryanna sat beside him.

"They'll be gone when we awake in the morning," she explained. "They come to chide us for violating the solstice. This is not the first time we've had prophesy from them."

"Who are they?"

"Winter people. That's what we called them when we were children. Gly's father, Marsamon, says they are the Sentinels."

"I thought the Sentinels perished in the Scouring."

"So did we, until we moved into Blue Iris Holt. Now they come and we listen, though often it is madness that they spout. This is the first time I've heard of any receiving interpretation."

"Shanara was not just speaking as Wise?"

"Nay, Padraig, she's not of the Council. The Holy Spirit does give her understanding."

A shudder shivered down Padraig's spine. *I'm trumpet-called. There's naught for it but to do as commanded.*

Easier said than done, he thought soberly, sadly, glancing sideways at Ryanna.

Would they let her go with me? Will she if they allow it?

Founding Year 1028 –
Southern Blyan – Spring · Present

The raven on the roof peak slept. The ethereal tides lay still as a shimmering lake. Tariq felt no fear, no outward encroachment as he picked up his stirring stick to scry.

Even pirates avoided the Tongue, a low pestilent peninsula east of Galornyn, where the Averblyan fanned out into the Stormor. Rumors of haunts lived among the mangroves, and pirates feared haunts more than rival pirates. That suited the inhabitants of the few islands of dry land amid mosquito ponds just fine; the folktales of murdering fogs and monsters protected their privacy without stretching their creativity. An ordinary man, possessed of an adventurous bent, would never survive the real dangers of the swamp to find Tariq's compound on one of the larger islands.

Thus protected, the greatest black mage in Celdrya tried to clear his mind, praying to Nudd that he might see the omens that the god of the underworld had for him. A month of ethereal fog foreshadowed anxiety in a highly trained mind that sought omens like common men seek water.

Amid the glimmering reflections in the black surface, a window appeared. After many decades studying the arcane arts, Tariq expected the vision to clear quickly, but mist had wrapped the occult for days. This one came just clear enough for Tariq to make out a young man riding through the hilly country of the north. From the snow still clinging to the craggy hills around him, Tariq guessed this a glimpse of now, rather than a true look on the metaphysical. A war horse, bearing a dark-haired rider who wore no plaid, trod a track near a road. *Why is a soldier off the road before the spring thaw?* The vision collapsed.

Muttering in consternation, Tariq stirred the ink, but no occultic window came in the settling surface. Growling, Tariq lurched to his feet to limp to the other work table. His workroom, one quarter of the ground floor of the rectangular main lodge, housed a fortune in furniture – two chairs, three stools, two tables, a shelf of books, and two cupboards stuffed full of materials and tools of his dark trade.

A quiet knock interrupted him midway across the chamber. Tariq frowned and opened the door. A journeyman stood without. Of middling height and slender, with brown hair and eyes, Sawyl looked no more interesting than a merchant, but was one of Tariq's stronger journeyman and a whoreson bastard in the bargain.

"Why do you disturb me at nadir of the astral tides?" Tariq demanded. Sawyl's 25 years under Tariq's tutelage kept him from quailing.

"My apologies, Master Talidd," he said calmly. "Eaddyn seized."

"When?" Tariq demanded.

"We worked on the stations ritual."

"How is he now?"

"It's been a watch. He remains unconscious. His pupils are unequal."

Tariq nodded, expecting the news. Pity. That lad had shown great promise.

"I will attend later, ascertain if there's aught to be done."

"As you say, Master Talidd," Sawyl assured as Tariq closed the door in his face.

Tariq, a thin, swarthy man of middle height, had more important things to investigate than a potential apprentice who could not withstand the rituals. Only an apprentice who could loosen the ethereal blockage would be of use. Tariq leaned on a crutch, dragging a leg, to reach a stool at the second worktable, where he began to mix the tiles waiting there. When satisfied they'd been thoroughly mixed, he separated five tiles and laid his hand upon the back of them, intoning in power:

"Nudd, god of the underworld and darkest night, hear my request. Show me the past, oh, Lord, that I might learn from it."

Methodically, speaking powerful words in the ancient tongue, Tariq turned over each of the five tiles.

The first rank showed the same combination he'd drawn for more than a year. The Fool, or important personage, might mean the true king. The Chariot, representing journey or change, and the Star, suggesting renewed hope, was followed by the Sun, representing success. The World, signifying true desire, finished the rank. The message seemed clear to the mage after long hours of meditation. The true king was born, somewhere in the land.

He considered the tiles with his highly trained mind. A constant message suggested stability. The king had to be growing somewhere in the kingdom, anywhere from a babe in arms to a young man with his first blush of beard. Omens had limits; the tiles didn't tell Tariq where to find the nascent king. He and his journeymen had scattered the seeds, but the harvest might be a long time off. If the king were found young enough to be influenced rightly, the outcome would be more than worth the effort.

The next rank of five depicted the near past, within the last month, most like: these tiles were not at all what Tariq expected. The Fool of Swords, the Emperor, Strength, Death, and the High Priestess. Oft you could only hope to make a story of the tiles and at this he was adept. A soldier important to the king had undergone a change or a trial and been set on a new goal. *What does the High Priestess represent -- wisdom, vision?* Even long thought did not bring clarity.

A tug upon his mind drew him to the ink once more. This time when he swirled the black liquid he saw another rider in unidentifiable mountains. Although the rider had no snow right round him, the stark mountains behind him were still white with it. This window too swirled and pulled like cloud shapes, but Tariq discerned a tall young man riding a sorrel mare, leading a dapple black pony, and wearing elven clothing. The lad had that tall, slender look that might mean a man of the Denygal. Curious, Tariq sent a line of thought out through the vision. The mind at the other end responded, replying with an equal curiosity. When he prepared to delve further, the rider's mind suddenly hardened and rebuffed him so thoroughly that the link collapsed. Growling with annoyance as he stirred the ink again, the black mage could not recall the vision. Too much effort failed, so he had decided to turn his attention to distillation, when a window unexpectedly appeared in the reflections.

A slender hand held a sword, working it with great skill. Knowing little of swordcraft, he could still tell the hand clearly knew its way around the weapon it wielded. The vision remained stubbornly small; against all his efforts to widen it, he could see only the hand, somewhat of the arm, and the sword, naught more. An attempt to send a line of thought out to the mind of whomever held the sword was turned aside as though by an iron shield and the link dissolved, the connection snapped like sewing thread from the other end.

Tariq shuddered in the spring warmth. Never in his long years of psychic workings had he encountered a mind that could simply repel him without even pausing in what the body was doing. *Who possesses such power?* Outside the open louvers, the raven shook its feathers, aware of its master's mood as he was aware of its.

Tariq returned to the tiles. The third rank represented the present. *The Fool, the Magician, the*

High Priestess, the Hierophant, and, the Star. Senseless omens! What ails in the ethereal?

The future, found in the fourth rank, remained closed to him, the tiles jumbled; he actually drew an empty one, somewhat that rarely happened as there was only one in the entire set. He set the fifth rank without any hope of spying the far-future. His expectations fulfilled, he prepared to put the tiles away when the raven cawed from the roof peak. He had seen Gregyn in the ink this morning and knew the lad neared. Heartened, he now sent his thoughts out and felt the lad's mind near to hand. The boy didn't respond; to become distracted in the swamp was a danger that he had trained his apprentices never to allow.

The stew he'd begun that morning neared perfection in a meal! Tariq set the table with a wooden bowl and spoon, cheese and a basket of bread -- a rich spring meal even in the swamp, for there was a limit to what might be grown in winter. The lad rode into the compound just as his master came to the porch. A tall, narrow-hipped young man with the wide shoulders and long arms of a man-at-arms, Gregyn rode a grey warhorse. Despite the sword at his hip, the old man saw an eight-year-old lad with a shock of dark hair shading wise grey eyes set in a half-starved face. He had to remind himself that his apprentice was no child now. Gregyn possessed great skill to go with a phenomenal power. What Tariq had done to prevent the squander of that power had been necessary; if the lad ever knew the extent of his power, the mage might wish that he'd been a less harsh master.

Gregyn, filthy, dismounted and led his mud-splattered horse to the porch.

"Master Talidd, may I have permission to bathe and care to my horse before I attend on you?" the lad asked, using the name Tariq presented to the world. He'd grown a bit more over the winter and his voice seemed deeper. His jaw was shadowed with stubble.

"Of course. There'll be a meal waiting."

The swamp could tire one who lacked what Tariq possessed to keep him safe. Was it the bravery of youth or did Gregyn possess skills that Tariq knew little about? An apprentice of his strength could write his own lesson book and therein lay the risk to the master.

Gregyn returned to the lodge nearly a watch later, shaved, washed and dressed. The man Gregyn knew as Talidd remembered when the lad walked the island in little more than a linen breech cloth. Now he'd donned blue linen breecs, probably left behind when he'd gone to Galornyn, and a white shirt blazoned with the dolphins of Galornyn. His feet were bare, though.

"Eat!" Talidd encouraged. "You may report later."

Gregyn hesitated for only a moment before setting to. After living on flat bread and hard cheese for a half moon, he naturally warmed to real food. Talidd thought he sensed wariness. At 17 or 18 (for truly none knew Gregyn's birth year) was a difficult age for apprentices. He'd been away at Galornyn all winter where there were many young lasses to turn a lad's head. That could bode ill if he'd decided the rituals were distasteful. Tariq needed his power in the rituals.

Gregyn finished his first bowl, got up and refilled, then ate more slowly, starting to give Talidd the information for which he'd taken the journey.

"Wergyn sends greetings," he began, speaking of the journeyman sent to Galornyn some years ago. "The Lady Peddryna seems pleased with him and she still has no idea of his true mission at the dun."

"Good. And what did you think of court?"

"From my view from the riders' table I found it entertaining. I think riders should not envy the nobles. They live life upon a stage and everybody waits for them to trip and fall."

Gregyn's intelligence and insight would serve Talidd's plans well, the master knew.

"Your status is appropriate for now. The day will come, though, when you will advance. Were you able to do as I asked?"

"I was able to get to know the younger members of the household. Two of the family members have the Talent."

"Not surprising. Did you begin preparing them?"

"Nay. One will not do because he's too old and because he's too honorable. Apparently Wergyn tried with him years ago. Tried and failed miserably."

"Aye, I know of that. Go on. The other?"

"He lacks the strength of mind to study the craft."

"Pity. That family should be mined. There's no reason for you to return there then."

"I found another," Gregyn reported. Talidd wondered if he had spoken too quickly.

"Tell it," Talidd encouraged.

"His talent isn't as great, but he's of a character and strength of mind to study and to – desire the power that comes with it." Gregyn's blue eyes twinkled for a moment. Talidd remembered the first lad he'd brought over. It truly warranted some excitement.

"A rider?"

"Nay, but he is noble-born and from a house you want roots in."

Talidd smiled. Gregyn shared a brief bit of information on this lad, who was young enough to worship Gregyn as an older friend. As a page, the lad would be in Galornyn for at least another three years and that would allow plenty of time for the initial training.

"I already set seals to control him, so that even once he's learned to shield himself from others I ought to be able to ensorcel him easily."

"Good, good. I wish that I were able to meet the lad and enforce your workings."

"I doubt much that I could convince him to come here. Not without thoroughly ensorceling him. I thought our plan was to leave the one we choose with a mind so that he might be useful in his own right."

Does he suspect that I can overrule his control if I get the apprentice early enough?

"True, true. An apprentice, though, might not be able to set the seals that truly control the lad."

"I got him to cut his thumb with his own table dagger," Gregyn reported. *My, but you are powerful for one whose potential is not fully realized.* "We've only just begun. Wergyn thought I'd done enough for one winter." *Good, Wergyn is trying to slow him down and keep him from making discoveries I'm not ready for yet.* "We want the lad to think this is all his own idea, don't we?"

"Aye. Have you done more?"

Was that a heartbeat of hesitation Talidd noted?

"Nay. He already has likes. If the time comes to crush him, I'll use it, but as long as we're keeping everything friendly-like, I don't think it's a good idea."

Gregyn seemed so reasonable, so logical. *Is it distaste that holds him back or mere prudence?*

"I will defer to your wisdom in this. Begin working on him to travel with him when he returns to his family. He can probably make you captain of the warband or somewhat."

Of course, with power like Gregyn possessed, his acolyte might well put him in a much stronger position and think it all his own idea.

"Done. Should I begin teaching him basic rituals?"

This was a tricky choice. Gregyn's power would only grow with practice and might, in time, outgrow Talidd's control.

"If you feel he's ready. I will rely on your judgment in this. Keep seeking a participant in the family at Galornyn. I prefer male, but I'd settle for a second female."

"Lady Peddryana doesn't seem to possess much of the Talent. There's a toddler lass, but any attention there by me would draw scrutiny." *He is wise beyond most acolytes.* "Lady Berdda prevents me from scrying as often as I know you would like."

"She's the source of the Talent that runs in the family. Are you certain you haven't missed any?"

"The vyngretrix himself or the heir and spare might be candidates, but a mere rider like me will never get close enough to find out. I thought Wergyn was supposed to worry about that aspect."

"Wergyn has been at court too long. I need fresh eyes." *Always spread suspicion and rivalry between the underlings whenever possible.*

"You have my report."

Talidd stared out into the jungle for a bit, then spoke.

"How long may you remain?"

"No more than three nights. The spring weather slowed my travel."

"I wish to work a ritual tomorrow night. See to it that you're rested and refined."

"Of course," Gregyn replied. His tone suggested no disloyalty, but Talidd sensed reluctance. He worried about the bond he and Gregyn shared. Was it weakening?

The lad stretched, rose and put his bowl and spoon in the pan for washing up.

"I am tired," he admitted. "I think I'll get some sleep."

"Of course," Talidd replied, giving him leave. Gregyn picked up the saddlebags he'd brought with him and looked from the ladder to the loft to the door to the smaller bedchamber.

"I've a full house right now," Talidd admitted. "There's an unoccupied bed in there," he indicated, pointing to the bedchamber. Gregyn hesitated.

"Who will I be sharing it with?"

"Sawyl."

This time Gregyn's carefully controlled features showed a glimmer of the dislike the lad felt for the man he'd grown up with. Talidd understood. As an elder apprentice, Sawyl had used his status to torment the younger, more talented lad. Gregyn had never voiced his hatred, but men in their craft rarely felt love for any but their masters, who liked it that way.

"It's warm. I'll sleep outside."

Talidd didn't argue. Gregyn's choice was not altogether unexpected. If he were to be the master that Talidd thought he could be someday, he would need to be strong in his hatreds.

Gregyn went out to the wide porch and walked slowly to the far side of the lodge. The night air lay moist and heavy with just a hint of orchid and lily fragrances. Here the morning sun would break through the trees, a time of day Gregyn particularly liked. Gregyn chose the widest and most stable of the many hammocks stretched from the overhanging rafters, found blankets in a cupboard, and arranged a bed for himself.

The year at court had proven to Gregyn what he had learned growing up on Talidd's island -- he was alone only in his own head. The freedom at court had taught him somewhat else. He hated Talidd, the rituals, and having to participate in them.

When he'd been an eight-year-old street urchin, scrabbling for crumbs in Dun Llyr's worst slum, Talidd's journeyman, a man Gregyn knew as Baddyn, had seemed quite attractive with his fine clothes and ample food. Initially, Gregyn had gloried in life in the swamp, away from the noise and confinement of the city. He'd not objected to the first simple lessons in the craft, excited by that first taste of power. Talidd's attentions had at first seemed odd to an orphan, but not terrorizing. The terror hadn't started until the night that Talidd had allowed Sawyl to have his way with the lad. Gregyn had been about nine. Seven years of first apprenticeship had followed. Sawyl had been allowed to do whatever he wanted with the younger boy. For reasons he did not entirely understand, the other apprentices and journeymen preferred Gregyn as a channel; thus he had never been the perpetrator of the terror.

A creak of the floorboards caused Gregyn to focus his eyes at the lodge. He saw Sawyl and Talidd walking across the compound. Gregyn wove Air and thought of Sawyl. It never worked on the master, but the journeyman had proven remarkably easy to work magicks on. Gregyn wondered that Talidd had not caught him out yet.

"He still breathes," Sawyl said as they crossed the compound. This spell made it seem as if he were riding Sawyl like a specter, privy to every sensation Sawyn encountered. "His eyes opened for a bit."

Talidd did not appear in the mood to talk. They entered the apprentice quarters. There were two boys sitting silently upon their narrow bunks and a third boy lying still on another cot, attended by a servant. Gregyn recognized old Jaryn from his crippled side. The servants were almost all palsied or speechless. Gregyn had only recently begun to wonder why.

Talidd leaned over the lad in the bed for a good while. Sawyl stood back, so that Gregyn could not see through his eyes, but he could smell urine through his nose.

"It's not worth the effort," Talidd announced. "We've enough imperfect vessels here. Take him to the swamp now. The beasts will make quick work of him."

Sawyl moved to look down at the lad then and Gregyn recognized Eaddyn, a young acolyte Sawyl himself had brought in. A surge of grief and rage roared through the journeyman before being quickly tamped down. Gregyn let the weave dissipate. He had no desire to feel Sawyl's emotions.

Since he'd found a possible apprentice in Dun Galornyn, he'd had to face what that meant. Being able to bring another over shortened the apprenticeship and Gregyn desired the power that would come with this arrangement, but he felt decidedly squeamish about being the master, if the master must do such distasteful things to the apprentice. The rituals galled, but the consequences could be deadly. *Do I truly want to leave a potential mage broken and unconscious for the swamp beasts to eat?*

Staring up at the night sky, Gregyn wondered if Talidd knew what he thought. The old man often seemed able to read the minds of his apprentices. He was doubtful that most apprentices guarded their thoughts as tightly as he, for he somehow knew that Talidd's respect was won by showing his dislike of Sawyl and his own death earned by showing his hatred of Talidd himself.

A year and a half into the second part of his apprentice, though not completely free of supervision, he was now allowed to travel and act somewhat independently from Talidd. He knew Wergyn reported to Talidd on him as he reported concerning Wergyn. A dark master must keep his hounds at heel or risk being devoured by them. There was advantage in that knowledge.

Gregyn wished he could simply run away, but as he prepared to return to the swamp, Wergyn had pointedly warned him that Talidd had power to draw Gregyn back and it would not be a pleasant reunion. Nay, better to bide his time. When the dark master died, the journeymen became free to set out on their own. Although other dark masters posed danger, a journeyman mage with strength could find all sorts of places in this world. Gregyn doubted he would enjoy being a noblewoman's lap dog as Wergyn was, but he might find better than that. If he could survive until Talidd died. If he could make it through the following night. If ....

Toward dawn, he heard a scream like a weak child out in the swamp and then birds exploded into the sky. Gregyn lay still with pent-up breath until he heard the distant grunt of a contented bull croc. Eaddyn was no more.

Gregyn returned to sleep.

Storm Clouds

Among the many curious groups of ardents to be found upon the land, I encountered a group in northern Blyan who call themselves "Chrystans". I thought at first that they were an Old Faith group that had wandered from the main, but soon realized that they worship but one god and hold it sacred above all others. They say they were thus when they came through the portal with us. Certainly they live like Celts except for a few odd religious practices that seem to color their daily living, but I am doubtful they ever trod the soil of Gawl. I believe them to be of Rune, since before we came here to tame the land. They are some form of wild folk, not true Celts at all.

Sedd of Odal, Scribe of Bel (FY 521)

Founding Year (FY) 931
Dun Celdrya · Summer

Celdrya's capital city lay shrouded in a days-long rain, as if in reaction to the death of the prince. The massive dun, home of the royal family, stood dark-grey against the stark light-grey stone of the Founding Rock, an imposing near-black fist thrust against a glowering sky. The Celdryan people bustled about their prosperous lives, muffled against the damp and wondering if there'd be war.

Deryk ap Fyrgal crossed the main ward of Dun Celdrya, shoulders hunched against the drizzle, casting a doleful eye toward the grieving heavens. The sky suited his mood and matched the black armband he wore.

Inside the door to the great hall, Deryk paused to shake water from his cloak, decided it was a lost cause and hung the sodden mess on one of the many waiting pegs among the myriad damp cloaks, quite a few of them plaid, but a notable number also striped. The merchants thought there'd be war and war was usually good for them, so they loitered about the dun to be the first to know, the first to get in at the trough. Merchants cared little that war meant death. They cared only for profits.

Deryk was expected upstairs in the King's greeting

chamber, but he could pause for a moment to gather his thoughts. A serving lass passed with a pitcher that wafted a scent of wine to him, reminding of all he would rather be doing. Maryn's death had torn a hole into the center of his life that would not be easily filled. Fun times of hunting and laughter sprang into his memory, only to be replaced with what had happened that night less than a fortnight gone. He'd been awakened by the raven's scream and sitting up confused on his cot when had come the shouting calls of murder. He'd rushed from the tent to find Maryn .... Deryk shook himself free of those thoughts and mounted the stairs to the upper floors of the main broch. It wouldn't do to keep the king waiting. Perryn had warned him that in the liege's current mood, Deryk could easily be accused of plotting to kill Maryn and take the throne. He shivered at the change of winds that had befallen the court. It never bode well when a lord loved his heir too much.

Deryk heard the shouting before he reached the chamber, even through the closed door. Vanyn was cursing a steady stream and demanding answers. His liegemen were trying to provide the latter, but he wasn't giving them much opportunity.

"Sire ...."

"I will not have my son murdered in my kingdom and not have the murderer brought to justice!"

"Aye, sire, but ...."

"I will not hear any cursed blathering!" he roared. Deryk thought it might be best just to duck back down the stairs, tell his honor guard to say they'd been delayed, but just as the thought solidified toward action, the door came open and he was left standing there with no opportunity to flee.

"Lord Deryk," Vanyn acknowledged. "Please, join us! It would be good to have the report of someone who was on the ground."

Deryk looked into the king's eyes and saw grief-madness, but raised a warrior, he stiffened his spine and walked into the room where Vanyn's councilors and several of his honor lords stood round the council table, mostly looking anywhere but at their king. Vanyn looked ill, grey of skin and tight about the mouth. Those who owed him fealty looked either angry or frightened and the anger of some seemed to mask fear. As they shifted to make room at the table for him, Deryk glanced round the room and a serving man brought him a goblet of mead.

"We were camped along the Avercelt after a day fishing. I turned in because the hour was late, but Maryn felt the need of a walk."

"And, you didn't go with him?" Burcan ap Manahan, the king's son-in-law, demanded. He must have ridden in from Mulyn straightway upon hearing the news. Even an ore boat down the Avercelt would have taken an eightnight.

"Why would I?" Deryk asked through ice-cold lips. "There were two honor guards each 15 strong outside the tent and we were in settled country. It never occurred to me, certainly, and I doubt if it ever occurred to Maryn, that he would be in danger there. We'd been there since the previous afternoon without seeing anyone outside of our own party."

He longed to take a sip of the mead, but he feared his hand would tremble, so he kept both fisted behind his back, one thumb hooked in his leather sword belt. He fixed his gaze on a portion of tapestry visible above the head of Councilor Dumyr who, while a man of great political skill, was short.

"Go on," Vanyn demanded. He set his own goblet of mead near Deryk's and seemed to steel himself for the report. Deryk had seen the look of confusion on Perryn's face when he'd told the complete story, so now he told the less detailed one he'd rehearsed on the ride to the capitol.

"I was just drifting off when the alaram was called. I rushed out and found – found Maryn staked to a tree by the spear that my rider brought to you yesterday. There was nothing to be done. It was not a survivable wound."

Vanyn began to cough, hands upon the table, his face turning from grey to red and then purple as he struggled to regain his breath. Amazingly, his mistress, Malona, glided up to his side and soothed him. He was soon able to take a sip of his drink and ask Deryk to continue. The king's mistress was a beautiful woman with lustrous black hair and large eyes of a golden brown color, but it was rare to see a woman in such a council and Deryk wondered at her presence and struggled to resume.

"Did Prince Maryn say anything before his death?" Dumyr, Vanyn's high councilor, asked.

"Naught that made sense. He was already close to death by the time I got there and in the death throes madness."

"What did he say?"

"Somewhat about 'she's beautiful' and a treasure that could not be his."

"Might he have been speaking of his betrothed," asked Lord Gerriant from near the border with Fygal.

"Mayhap, though I do not think they have yet formed a love-bond," Deryk answered. "Maryn was still mourning his wife. I think it was more likely he was dreaming of her in those last moments. No offence to Gillian of Llyr, of course," he added, suddenly remembering that Gerriant was a cousin of sorts to Maryn's betrothed.

"We know you mean the upmost respect," Gerriant assured, appearing to mean it.

"We searched the area and I spoke to all who were within earshot at the time of the attack. The guard he was speaking with at the time said they heard a raven scream just before the spear flew."

"A raven at midnight?" Burcan demanded. "And that far south this late in the spring? Most unusual!" Mulyn knew ravens, for they were a more northern bird.

"Aye, I thought so too until I found this."

Deryk produced the raven feather, laying it upon the hide map that rested upon the massive table top. Glossy black with a thick spine, it was almost as long as his forearm and as wide as his spread hand. The chamber erupted into loud exclamations as Vanyn began to cough again. This time, he brought up blood and withdrew from the meeting. With his son Perryn gone to recover Maryn's body, the councilor took the lead.

"This is no natural feather," he noted, which drew

no protests. "We all know what this is."

Deryk raised an eyebrow because he didn't know what it was any more than Perryn.

"We must deal with this immediately," Burcan agreed. "If the Assassin's Guild is once more operating in Celdrya, we must locate and eradicate them while the trail is still fresh."

The men around the table nodded and lent their vehement support to this plan of action.

"I will take this to the king as soon as he's had a bit of a rest and I'll have an answer for you by the evening meal," Councilor Dumyr assured the lords and left the room.

Deryk watched as the others slowly filed out, talking among themselves. A serving man began to clear the room of the various goblets and tankards. He glanced at Deryk's goblet and then at the young lord's face.

"I require a moment," Deryk explained.

"Of course, my lord. Do you want a fresh drink?"

"Nay, thank you, uh … I do not know your name."

"Talidd, sir."

"Thank you for your concern. I just need a moment's peace."

Talidd nodded, though his dark eyes still held concern. A good servant, he returned to tidying the rest of the council chamber. Deryk reached for his goblet of mead, distracted by his dark thoughts. As it neared his lips, however, he smelled somewhat to give him pause. Vanyn's goblet had been beside his and he'd picked up Vanyn's goblet by mistake. Like all younger brothers, he'd been trained to detect poisons lest he be required to act as taster to the heir. The pungent aroma of wolfsbane caused him to pull the goblet back before it touched his lips.

Gods, no!

"Poison!" he called, croaking, causing the serving man to pause in his duties and stare at him, throat muscles working. "Poison!" Deryk yelled again, louder this time, running from the room with the goblet in his hand to show the chirgeon. "The King has been poisoned!"

Founding Year 1023
Viking Date 741 / Kindred Cycle 24573/-
Hansorfjord, Northern Sea - (Five Years Past)

Hansorfjord celebrated the majority of their future kong by examining him for his physical and mental fitness.

His testing near-complete Erik Magnuson stood upon the testing ground, stripped to the waist in the summer sun, weighing his options. Hovdinkong Magnus Hansorsson watched from the reviewing stand, willing himself not to be anxious. The heavier spear would fly farther, but less accurately. Erik might only wound his prey, which would call his future rule into question.

Magnus watched the boy choose the lighter spear and tried not to be anxious. The spear might fall short of the prey and that would also call his future rule into question. The boy had had a near-perfect score so far over the last two days. He'd run a league in armor the first day and been only a quarter sector off Magnus' own time. Yestermorrow, he'd rigged a boat for sailing in record time. Hunting should have been the least of trials, but Magnus knew that there were those watching who would make much of the least.

No sooner had the boy made his selection than a flash of movement downfield drew Magnus' attention. The boy cocked back his arm and let fly. The spear flew straight and true and struck in the gorse-covered shield of a young warrior, who stood to salute the young heir-chief, tugging on the spear to show that the steel had stuck in the wood. Erik saluted him back with the spear he had just picked up and no sooner let the shaft fly, sensing movement just beyond the first warrior who dropped into the hiding brush to avoid being skewered. The heavier spear flew as true and actually toppled the warrior who wielded the shield it struck. The crowd laughed. The warrior stood slowly and saluted Erik in similar fashion, who saluted back empty-handed.

Magnus saw movement at the entry of the testing grounds and watched as a runner marked him and began a run round the pathway that marked the outer edge. The testing grounds occupied a narrow strip of valley with high rocky hills on either side and deep brush along the bottom. Magnus leaned over to consult with his hammer man, Jarl Barentson, who got up to relay the message to the guards.

Magnus had missed the third throw, but it seemed to have gone well for Erik. He knew he would miss others once the runner reached the reviewing stage.

Erik threw four more spears in the interim, all

accurate and powerful. He was starting to sweat and where his skin was not permanently kissed by the sun, he was starting to redden. This too was part of the trials. Magnus remembered his own sunbite with grim fondness.

"Kong, a runner comes before you with a message from Hovda Orma," Jarl announced.

"Bring him forward."

The runner walked boldly to his chief, aware that messengers were very valuable. He struck his sweat-stained breast with his right clenched hand. Magnus was first among equals, not to be feared

"Kong Magnus, there comes a merchant of Orenthal, bearing fine gifts and the seal of their king."

There were few things that would interrupt Magnus viewing his son, but the king of Orenthal or one of his envoys was among them. Magnus glanced at the sun. There were perhaps two more spears and then would come the field run, which could not be easily viewed at any rate.

"Return to Hovda Orma with this message. I will come within the half-sector. She is to provide the emissary with all comforts."

"Yes, Kong Magnus."

The runner turned crisply and began his run round the testing grounds to the exit and then to the five-mile track back to Magnus' fortress at the top of the fjord. Jarl awaited his orders.

"I must attend to this. See that Erik knows I viewed all the spears and that I will return after the midday rest for our contest."

"Of course, Kong Magnus."

Magnus signaled two of the guards to walk with him and struck out for the small harbor where his canoe awaited him. As soon as they were free of the narrow valley of the testing ground, they jogged toward the sea.

Hansorfjord, straddling the top of the fjord, hemmed in by spruce forests and slate crags, was merely a quarter-sector's hard paddle across the stunning blue water and Magnus lent his own considerable skill to the endeavor, so that they were soon upon the shingle below the fortress. There was a large Orenthal ship anchored a bit off the shingle here, the yellow-skinned sailors watching him coolly from the deck. *Would you be so haughty in the presence of your employer,* Magnus wondered. *Are you not servants to him?* Although in Svardin society, all men were free to come and go as they chose, Magnus understood that the servants of other rulers were not.

The ship impressed, dwarfing the fishing boats beached on the shingle.. The carved and painted masthead showed a beautiful woman of Orenthal features, her dark hair braided tight against her back. The Svardin had nothing like it. The death ferries were carved similarly, but no boat in all of Svardin was so large. Truth-be-told, they didn't need to be. The long boats were fast and cunning and, if many of them were amassed, carried more than enough men to overwhelm any community of land-lockers.

Magnus climbed the long switchback of steps hewn into the rock that brought him up to the fortress. Death awaited those who trod those steps unwarily, but the Hovingkong had no fear. He greeted each viking by name as he passed through their ranks in the guard house at the top of the stairs, then he crossed the courtyard where some husbandmen were shearing sheep and entered the great hall.

On this fine day, the window shutters stood open to allow air and light into the heavy-timbered room. His wife Orma, nearly as tall as he and with the dark hair common to her island, strode up to him.

"He's relaxing in the gardens," she announced, offering him the cloak of state. "Gilyn is his name."

"That's not a Orenthal name," Magnus noted, frowning, settling the sealskin cloak on his shoulders. It was too hot for such on this day, but appearances mattered to the outfolk.

"Nah. His hair is light, his features not slanted. But he bears the seal-mark of the Orenthal king and letters patent."

Magnus fingered the torc of braided gold round his neck, considering.

"Has he supped?"

"He accepted water only."

Magnus frowned at her. Tall, with a windburn face and sun-bleached blond hair, he was a man of action. Some supposed he was not given to deep thought. Their assumptions were occasionally their death. Therefore, he eschewed assumptions himself. He did not know what to make of this emissary. He checked the knife at his waist and signaled the guards to follow him.

The Orenthal emissary stood in the garden, at the wall overlooking the plunging river. His hands rested upon the ledge. Magnus did not try for stealth as he approached; still he was surprised when the emissary turned well before he'd traveled halfway to him.

"Hovdin Magnus," Gilyn said. Unlike Orenthal emissaries, this one was as tall as Magnus, though slender, with long arms and a thin face. His hair was light brown, his eyes an impossibly light grey shot with vines of ice-blue. Hovdin was a Svardin term for clan leader. The Orenthal did not recognize him as chief-king. For now, Magnus could not argue. Someday, he would crush them - or Erik would.

"Emissary Gilyn," Magnus replied. Orma had glided up beside him. Although her Orenthal was only passing, it far exceeded his. "Hovda Orma will interpret for us" just about exhausted his Orenthal.

"That will not be necessary," Gilyn said in slightly accented Svard. "I am conversant in your language."

Orma and Magnus exchanged looks, hers saying she had been unaware of this, and then she withdrew. By design, she would lie in the board and have a servant bring out a platter in the garden.

"Shall we sit then?" Magnus asked, indicting the table and benches that stood nearby.

"Of course." They took their seats. Gilyn wore black Orenthal silks, the lower garment cut in trews. His cloak, draped over the bench, was a fascinating grey that seemed to shift with the light. "You are no doubt confused, as I am not what you expected."

"You are not as the other emissaries, nah."

"I am in the employ of the Orenthal emperor, but I am Celdryan and Kin by descent."

Magnus knew of the Celdryans who occupied the

mainland to the south. He'd heard of the Kin who lived in the mountain fastnesses. Gilyn's appearance suggested the tales Magnus had heard were fantasy … the Kin were men like any other.

"And you have come to Hansorfjord for some business or to deliver a message?"

"For business. I understand your heir has reached his majority."

"Yah."

"He must undertake a great task to prove his worthiness to rule, yah?"

"He must."

"Has he selected it yet?"

"Not as yet." Truth-to-told, Erik had been fleeced of a great accomplishment by his own father, who had been all too successful in uniting the Northern Isles.

"Ah, good waters then." Magnus refused to show it, but he was impressed with Gilyn's command of the language. Usually idioms troubled speakers who were not Svardin. "I believe the continent to the south is ripe for the taking with a well-organized invasion. If your son is willing to attend an inspection with me, I believe he will come away with the same impression."

Magnus was familiar with the lands to the south. Now desert, there were signs of a great past civilization. A few vikings had followed a river up into the mountains, but the formidable barrier had not been surmounted by Svards to his knowledge. Then there was the matter of Gilyn's employers.

"And, what is in this for the Orenthal?"

Magnus knew well the Orenthal would always claim

the greatest portion of the spoils. A devious and rapacious race. The human face of his guest notwithstanding, Magnus trusted the Orenthal not at all.

"Of course, the spoils can be divided according to contribution," Gilyn said. "The Orenthal desire a partnership with the Viking."

"Hmm. The last emissary suggested subjugation might be in order."

"The last emissary had limited vision."

Magnus considered the offer.

"Erik's testing is not yet complete. Should he pass it, you may discuss the future with him. Is that acceptable to you?"

"It is." Gilyn held out a slender, but muscular hand to clasp Magnus'. Magnus held him firm.

"Just remember, Emissary. What a vikrus can count and carry is his by right and we'll not be playing any games of who owns what when the day is done. Yah?"

"Yah," Gilyn assured him. He laughed, a bit daft sounding. "You have my word as a Celdrya and a Kin that this will be above-board and honest."

"Against your own people?"

"My peoples turned their backs on me many cycles ago. I hold no affection for either of them. You'll learn to trust me on that."

"We'll see," Magnus replied. Magnus trusted few men, which was how he had become kong, but he knew an opportunity when one presented itself. Would Erik be so wise? It was time to find out.

Founding Year (FY) 1028
East Faren, County Dublyn · Spring

*N*ot to be too melodramatic, Lord, but did the ancient *Believers feel this way as they were forced to leave home to do Your work?*

Along a lonely mountain trail, a sorrel mare bore an elven-dressed human, his hair plaited with beads in Kindred fashion that identified his heritage to those who knew the meaning. Tall and slender with long fingers and strongly blue eyes that subtly hinted at elvishness, the man bore regular features and dark brown hair that showed rich in the sun; in most of the kingdom he would have been thought handsome and naught more.

Padraig ap Chenyn of Cenconyn traveled home, but he felt very much as though he departed his true home, for he left people he truly loved who would mourn his absence, to whom he hoped fervently one day to return.

He reined his horse to a stop at the top of a rise and caught his first glimpse of the Basketlands, to use its proper Kindred name Since leaving the camp at the end of the highway, he'd encountered some difficult trail, with washaway and downed trees, evidence of scant use in recent years. What he saw ahead looked more pleasant for horses' legs. This part of Dublyn was rolling hills of grassland broken by occasional copses of trees. Far to the north where the mountains began to rise round Cenconyn way lay a stretch of old forest between him and the dun he'd been raised in. He didn't think he'd be going there just yet.

In the broad valley below, Padraig could make out the road and a faint trail of smoke rising a half day gone. Being past midday, he faced a choice. Uncomfortable with camping in the open grasslands until he knew exactly where he was, yet recognizing he could not reach the first settlement that day, he decided to bide time and camp in a copse of trees within an easy ride of the mountains. He couldn't just ride there without preparation.

Padraig dismounted to begin stripping off his clothes. Good quality elven clothes consisted of a pair of leather trews and a coton tunic embroidered with flowers and vines. He folded these up and stowed them in the bottom of a pannier on the back of the dapple-grey pony he led behind the horse, replacing them with the traditional Celdryan clothing of loose woolen breecs and a shapeless linen siarc. He tightened the breecs with a draw cord and drew in the siarc with a wide leather belt. He'd have to wear his elven boots since he didn't have a Celdryan pair, but he supposed it wouldn't matter. Many a Denygal wore them and he planned to travel as a Denygalman. After four years of wearing the practical elven dress, Padraig felt near-to naked in the loose-fitting Celdryan garb.

Get used to it, man! he chided himself. *There's naught for it!*

As a final act, he removed the beaded braid from his hair with the edge of his dagger. That saddened him. Given different timing, he'd have given the braid to Ryanna against promise of his return. Sighing, he stowed the beads with his elven clothes, repacked the herbs on top and faced the kingdom.

As he mounted, he felt a tug on his mind. Thinking it one of his elven friends, he responded, then sensed the mind that touched his and recoiled at the filth encountered. With a sharp mental parry, he closed his mind and set seals against any unknown entrance.

"I suppose it might have been a dark one," Padraig said aloud, a bit breathless. "They are known to scry for those sensitive." Padraig laughed nervously then, and patted the mare's golden neck with an affectionate hand. "Listen to me," he scoffed, "spouting forth like I actually know somewhat about dark ones. I suppose I'll likely learn, don't you think, Joy?"

The horse's mind touched his, just the beginnings of communication, a sense that she understood what he was saying, or at least understood his tone and agreed with it.

"Well, I suppose you know more about dark ones than I do. They say animals are naturally attuned to what men ignore. I hope that's true, because one of us should know somewhat about things."

The horse, Joy, snorted, perhaps because a fly bothered her or, more like she found him ridiculous. He supposed that they were the same maturity level within their species and like any headstrong young lass, she found the folly of lads dreaming of adventure humorous. The Companion link allowed her to understand his species in a way horses usually did not.

Padraig reined to a halt at the bottom of the slope where a marker stone announced the border. The leaping hart on the kingdom side announced the vyngetrix of

Dublyn. On the mountain side the marker stone sported a hideously demonic face with peaked ears and evil eyes. He chuckled at the folly of man's mind that he would believe such nonsense. Still shaking his head, he clucked to Joy, continuing into the kingdom.

On the morrow, he awoke early to ride toward the chimney smoke he'd spotted on the horizon. He had dreaded the kingdom while in the mountains, remembering it more for crowded towns and bustling cities, yet as he rode along the barely discernable dirt track that passed for a road, the experience grew enjoyable. A faintly unreal color of gold covered the rolling hills, signaling they were about to burst into green. Leafless shrubs and occasional trees he rode past hovered on the edge of bursting into verdant life. Birds flitted from branch to branch and tree to tree in a riot of mating, their song filling the air.

The hard blue sky promised warmth, yet couldn't really produce it. He wore his good warm cloak, throwing it back on his shoulders. As he rode he began calculating the date as he had quite lost track of the wheel of the year in Celdrya while in the mountains. The Kindred kept their own calendar; by their reckoning it was about the spring equinox -- halfway between Imbolc and Beltane. The green would brighten the hills quite soon; already the grassland lay wet with run-off streams and many of the trees had water round their roots.

Padraig encountered a herd of sheep guarded by a watchful dog just before midday. The large black dog watched him with such suspicion that Padraig waited until he'd rounded a bend in the road before he dismounted to eat a bit of lunch.

He'd have to reach a farmstead or tavern soon as his tuck bag was nearly empty. The thought caused him to grimace, already wishing that he didn't have to give up some favorite elven foods. Naught for it, of course! He'd come home with a mission and no choice but to complete it, come what may.

He approached the first farmstead a bit after the meal. He topped a rise and looked down at the compound set behind tall stone walls. The chimney stood cold, but the thatch looked sound on the roof and he could hear chickens. He winced as at least a couple of dogs launched themselves against the wooden gate to announce his presence. He tried the latch, relieved it was bolted from the inside.

A wise farmer, then! Padraig thought. *Sensible, given that they're alone out here.*

Just as he noted the stones of the walls were dressed with a finery he wouldn't have expected from a farmer a face appeared at the opening at the top of the gate. Those blue eyes could only belong to a pretty lass.

"Hallo?" she greeted. "Are you wanting somewhat?"

"I'm a traveler on the roads," Padraig replied, slowly, his mouth unpracticed with Celtman speak after a lapse of years. "I'm hoping to buy some bread and per --- mayhap water my stock."

"Traveler?"

"Herbman. I've been foraging in the eastern mountains."

The blue eyes judged him coolly. Padraig waited.

Naught more would convince the farmwife to let him in or send him away.

"You be at Sion's steading, herbman. I be Sion's wife, Marya."

"Padraig of Denygal."

The eyes continued to weigh him. He waited again. This time the wait wasn't too long. The latch rattled and the gate swung outward.

"You don't look like a daemon anyway," Marya said, holding the gate open wide. Her smirk indicated she wasn't much afraid of daemons. The dogs slunk off as if shamed by their rudeness. They were the same large breed, one a buckskin and the other black, as their fellow guarding the sheep. "I baked bread last night and we've some dried apples left from the winter."

"Four coppers for two days' worth?"

"Five and I'll throw in a bit of jerked meat."

"Done." He released his tuck bag from a saddle hook and handed it over.

"Stock trough's over there. The barrel's by the door."

Padraig watched her walk away, noting that she just topped his shoulder and had blond hair tucked up under a headscarf. Her skirts hitched up into her kirtle in improvised breecs, she still carried the pitchfork she'd used for mucking the stables. She disappeared into the house, pausing long enough to scrape her bare feet off on a stone outside the door. She took the pitchfork with her.

That one's wise in the ways of men, Padraig admired.

Padraig allowed Joy and the grey pony, Earnest, to

make their way to the trough while he approached the barrel with his water skins. He drank long from the clear, cool water before washing his face and wetting his hair, careful not to let the waste water trickle back into the barrel.

That midden heap should be farther away.

Typical of a farm, every bit of soil in the yard turned to vegetables except for the composting pile, the walkways, and small spaces before the door and round the well. Padraig noted with surprise that the same stone built the cottage as the fence; he recognized the type -- had seen it oft in the basements of Dun Cenconyn, but never outdoors.

Pale pearly pink, almost luminous, it was not a common stone, dressed and in some places carved. Farmers would not have labored so hard on the esthetics of a cottage, much less a defense wall. The steading must have been built, as Dun Cenconyn, on the ruins of an elven city. There were a few scattered throughout the basketlands. He'd never known any humans willing to use the lumina stone; most considered it haunted, if not evil.

"Admiring our witch stone?" Marya asked, coming up behind him on silent bare feet. Padraig managed not to startle, though his heart thumped once. She held out his tuck bag. She'd left the pitch fork by the door.

"It's indeed lovely. Did Sion do the dressing himself?"

"Nay, nay, but the fields about here are filled with the stuff. Big blocks like that. Some say the Fey did leave it behind them when they moved on to the fairy realm ...

or, more like, the mountains."

"Aye? Do you see the Kin hereabouts?" Padraig asked, establishing immediately that they both knew the elves to be real.

"Nay, they don't come here anymore. Traveled to the Cenconyn faire long ago and we saw some. Beautiful people. Sion and I've been here five years and we've seen none."

"Then why the defense wall?"

"Tis a long way from the village and my Sion does worry about the troubles elsewhere, that those who are desperate may come someday. So far we've only seen the nobleborn, come each fall to the hunting track into the mountains. Still Sion built the walls. He used the stone because there's so much of it throughout the valley and, though there are some that call it witchstone, why throw away what is both beautiful and functional when you have need of it?"

Padraig nodded, impressed by her practicality. *Sion needn't have put the vines and stylized flowers where they'd be visually pleasing either.*

"Do they stop here?" She cocked an eyebrow at him in question. "The nobles?" He hoped for some gossip.

"Aye, to eat my bread and use our water without so much as a copper or a thank you very much."

Padraig laughed at her humored indignation, which won a full-mouthed grin from his hostess. She showed good teeth.

"The noble-born often show little care for those who fill their bellies and cellars," he agreed. "I'm a bit turned about coming from the mountains. Where exactly is Sion's steading?"

"Faren, County Werglidd. The village of Nalyn be about a half-day's journey west by horseback. Dun Werglidd is mayhap one day's journey farther. Lord Jarvys is rig there."

Padraig remembered County Werglidd within the Dublyner rigdon of Faren.

"How far is Dun Trevyllan?"

"Good four days by wagon. Mayhap two, two and half days on horseback."

"How are the roads?"

"The villagers in Nalyn have been repairing the road from the village to Dun Werglidd. I've heard that there's a proper road from Trevyllan to Clarcom. I suppose Cunyr wants his taxes more quickly."

"Cunyr is still vyngretrix then?"

"Aye. His heir, Bryan, be about 15 summers, I think."

The way Marya spoke she might just have been passing on information or she might hope for Cunyr's passing. Perhaps she hoped he wouldn't pass soon. After all, a cur like Cunyr was apt to whelp cruel pups. The elves said the hand that rocks the cradle held a stronger influence.

"Who is rig at Dun Trevyllan now? Still Beryl?"

"Nay, but Beryl did die in a hunting accident last fall. We got the news of Lord Geran's ascension just at snowfall. I suppose we'll be seeing what sort of overlord he'll be round Lughnasa."

Padraig knew Geran and decided to risk a bit,

though truly the risk seemed small.

"My master in herbs and I wintered in Dun Trevyllan several years gone. A good teacher, Geran's father. I think his son'll act honorably toward those who support him."

"Truly?"

"Aye. At least Geran never cheated at dice and he didn't quibble when he lost."

Padraig smiled inwardly at the lad he'd been back then, using his gift at guessing dice to win against the brash young lord. Geran might have suspected him of cheating, but he'd always paid his losings and he'd not used his position to call Padraig to justice.

"How long were you in the mountains?" Marya asked.

There was somewhat so open about her question that Padraig felt drawn by her human attractiveness. Her wide blue eyes set in a pretty face with a pert nose and a warm smile could make a man forget that she stank of the stables; Padraig reminded himself you couldn't muck out without smelling of muck. A tendril of blond hair had worked its way loose from her headscarf and it showed clean. The golden hair brought a response of longing from deep inside him.

He reminded himself sharply that he was not the sort of man who trifled with married women, but bitter truth presented itself. *Sin is sin and you've flown close to its flame your first contact back with humans. I repent Lord!* As soon as he thought that a small gust of wind wafted her scent to him. She stank of the stables and his desire stepped back into the shadows.

"I'd best be going if it's a half-day's ride to the village," he said. "Tis a lovely steading, Marya." He'd never know quite why he asked, but he did. Maybe it was to deny what he'd felt only a moment before. "Are your children with Sion, then, out tending the fields?"

She hesitated for a moment.

"Nay and you did say you were an herbman, didn't you? You've been in the eastern mountains. Among the Fey, aye?"

"I won't deny that I studied some of their lore, aye."

"I've heard that they've different sort of lore than we do, ways of healing our herbmen don't know."

"Some such, aye."

Marya hesitated again, considering some sad thought, then spoke quietly, but in a rush, as if she wanted to get the words away and have her answer before somewhat stopped her.

"Sion and I married five years ago. There's no children and I was wondering, well, if there's somewhat .... The herbman that travels through the village now and again said there's naught, but he did suggest the Fey might have a cure or two, then made it into a joke, like."

Padraig's heart went out to her. Although farm wives weren't likely set aside for barren, their husbands and the townspeople were sometimes less than kind.

"Sion wants children then?" he inquired.

"We both do. We even danced round the Beltane tree again last year to see if somewhat would happen, but naught."

Padraig understood this to mean that they had normal sexual relations. He opened his Sight to have a look at her, pretending that he considered his words carefully. It took only a moment to see that she was in perfect health. All the colors of a healthy young woman were present.

"I have some herbs that might help, but I have to ask some – some questions."

"Aye."

He queried about delicate matters like her monthly courses and whether her husband had ever had mumps. His healing Sight told him that Marya wasn't the problem. He couldn't Heal what wasn't broken. He asked God for permission to Heal Sion, but he wasn't sure of the response, did not feel anything that would tell him if God had granted the healing.

"I've some herbs I'll give you. Hold a bit."

He found what he was looking for in one of the pony's panniers and he quickly spooned somewhat out into two bags, one for each type of herb. Padraig swallowed hard at what he was doing. The red raspberry leaves were common enough, but the palmetto was a swamp plant and not so easily come by. Ah, well, he wasn't returning to the kingdom to make his fortune.

"The red cloth is for you and the blue cloth is for Sion. Make a tea of it every morning until it's all used up. I can't promise it will work, mind you. These things are often vexing. But, it does work sometimes."

"Thank you," Marya said, taking the bags and clasping them to her kirtle like a suspected treasure. "How much do I owe you?"

"Naught. Pleased that I may help you."

He caught Joy's halter and led the stock toward the

gate. Marya followed, kicking back the dogs who had come to say goodbye as if Padraig were an old friend.

"If we bear a child, we'll name the boy after you."

"Only if it pleases Sion," Padraig insisted.

"If it works, your name will please him well. What name do you favor for a girl?"

Padraig didn't have to ponder the question.

"Ryanna," he replied. He swung up into the saddle, nodded once to Marya and rode off down the road. He'd not gone far before he realized that he felt totally at peace with the encounter. He glanced back over his shoulder to view the farmstead one last time, and found himself staring in awe.

There had indeed been an elven city here in the long ago and its memory still lingered for them that are sensitive to such things. Though by no means a gifted seer, there was elven blood in his veins and he saw what there remained – the echo of the city.

Built of pale lumina stone that caught the sunlight and made it shimmer, the city rose in delicate spires and graceful towers throughout the valley where Sion's steading now rested. Broad avenues divided blocks of buildings, all in rectangles and squares, shaded by graceful trees. The stream flowing just east of Sion's steading was bridged by a graceful span of stone and there was not a defense wall to be seen.

Padraig blinked and the vision faded. He'd seen what had been there to be seen, almost as a beacon of light against the darkness. He'd come west with a mission and he must never forget that. Rescuing the basketlands was important not only for the society of men that now lived there but, for some unfathomable reason, for the Kin who had long ago fled those precincts.

Founding Year (FY) 1028
Blue Iris Holt - Spring Present

The community of Kin Padraig had departed from sheltered in the high mountains to the northeast of Faren. At one time, this elfholt had been a dwarven mine, but the dwarves had given it to the elves when the mine played out and now a thriving community of Kin called the caves home.

The beautiful half-elf Morynsionryanna sat beside a large stone basin, trailing an idle finger through the water to keep the visions active. In an ethereal window, Ryanna saw a tired-looking Padraig saddling the sorrel mare in a copse of trees somewhere in Dublyn. She didn't know how she could know that for certain, but she did know, beyond just the guess that he would still be in Dublyn. He looked hale enough and she supposed that after living in the holt for so many years, sleeping upon the ground would take some getting used to, thus explaining the shadows around his eyes. She wished that she could reach out to him and touch his mind. He could reply to a touch, though he was not able to scry in his own right. Alas, she'd been forbidden by Gly and to disobey would mean to lose these sessions where she might view Padraig. This was better than no contact at all, so she restrained her more rebellious tendencies.

Truly this must be love, she thought. *I never acted this way with Gil. I've scried often enough for him, but not with longing.*

The thought of Gil shifted the images in the basin to a faraway city that Ryanna knew she'd never visited. Dark haired people with almond-shaped dark eyes walked immaculate streets of the finest tile before white-washed buildings of a style she did not recognize. Their clothes were of the finest Orental silk. What she did not understand was why thoughts of Gil always brought her to this faraway foreign city. For five years she'd felt naught that would convince her that her husband was still among the breathing, yet thoughts of him always brought her visions of the Orental city. Had he perished there? She'd never heard that mage work could hone in on the last knowings of a departed soul, so perhaps it came from some human part of her abilities. Certainly no elf had ever claimed it as possible and none of her tutors could help her decipher its meaning.

As sometimes happened with her, her vision shifted, so that she now saw a Morikan caravan stopped in the desert, where a dark, turbaned trader haggled with a stout dwarf over some goods – nay, over human slaves. Not dwarfs then, but trolls. The dwarvish cousins were easily confused on first sight, but their ways had diverged in the millennia since their rift. From one of the little cottages on the back of a wagon, a woman completely covered in a veil watched the transaction. Ryanna supposed the desert-dwellers felt no compunction over keeping slaves since they kept their mates in virtual slavery.

Her irritation at that thought caused the visions to collapse completely. Ryanna paddled in the water for a moment more, hoping to return a vision of Padraig, but it was no good. Sighing, she sat up and looked around the Hall of the Wise. The large rock basin that she sat beside was filled by an artfully worked waterfall that fell in courses down the wall, yet somehow the surface was always reflective enough for scrying, tempting her to remain and continue her activities. The morning meal scented the air with warm yeast as acolytes, apprentices and the Wise descended from their chambers to the Hall. Her time of indulgence had passed. Time to embrace the day. In time, Gly would allow her more freedom, but only if she earned it. There'd be time enough for indulgences later.

As a farewell to her self-indulgence, she trailed a finger through the water one last time, though without any power behind it. She expected to see nothing beyond the ordinary sparkles of lantern light thrown off moving water, but a window opened unexpectedly in the depths of the pool. She leaned forward, curious, expecting to see Padraig once more, but espying instead a dark room lit by a steady low light that shimmered off scales of green and gold. While she contemplated the possible nature of those scales, a large brow ridge hove into sight. The head turned, dipping into a pool of darkness and then rose so that Ryanna could see the enormous eye with a vertically slit pupil surrounded by multi-faceted golden iris. Ryanna realized with a jolt that the eye saw her and in that moment, she lost the vision.

"Running a bit long on your scrying, yes?" a voice asked.

Flustered, Ryanna looked up at her tutor in wisdom.

Gly, like all full elves, was a tall slender man of undetermined years. His hair was a pale color, just a bit lighter than straw and his vertically slit eyes were violet. His ears were furled like sea-shells and rose in sharp peaks.

"I think I just scried a dragon," Ryanna gasped. Being a half-elf, Ryanna looked human. Her eyes were remarkable only in being beautiful and brilliant green and her ears were rounded.

Gly raised an eyebrow, but after a moment, a smile transformed his slender face.

"This is why I enjoy having you as a pupil," he announced. "You break all the boundaries. A dragon?"

"Yes, a dragon in its lair. She was beautiful."

"In its lair?" Now Gly frowned, the expression furrowing his unlined brow. Among men, Gly seemed a young man scarcely into his third decade, but he was near a half-millennium-old. "It would be a rare gift if you could scry into a dragon's lair. They have their own ways to prevent that, such as we protect the holt."

"And do I not have a rare set of gifts?" Ryanna asked. This elicited another grin from her tutor. She stood up from the fountain's edge, her simple cotan robe falling around her ankles to drape her lean frame. A tall elfling with a long braid of dark hair, she hardly rated a glance among the Kin. Elflings were not rare in the Kinholts, but they were still a minority. Her human eyes and round ears were odd-seeming to her mother's race, but in human society, many a man had chased after her like cat-mint. As she approached a half-century of life, she now recognized that her half-elven beauty had been part of the problem all along.

"I have not heard of any Kin in my lifetime who could scry a dragon," Gly assured her. "Not even Shanara is so gifted."

"Or she has chosen not to share," Ryanna suggested.

"Well, true. Shanara does prefer her privacy. When next she wanders this way, or at least scries to me, I'll have to ask after that ability. She is a connoisseur of historical lore."

They stopped at the long table near one of the two hearths that heated the enormous central chamber of the Hall of the Wise and collected breakfast – seed bread with eggs and dried berries soaked in goat's milk. They took their food around a corner to Gly's workshop. In the darkness, Ryanna smelled drying herbs and essential oils. She lit the lamps with a thought as Gly moved a tray from his work table. To protect the quality of his wares, Gly's workshop had no windows, so even on a cool spring day, the room was blackness without lamps.

"I had planned to discuss Scripture today, but I think rather we should investigate history," Gly said, selecting a codex from a floor to ceiling shelves of similar books and setting it before her. "Dragons are much on my mind now. What do you know of them?"

While Ryanna recited what she remembered of dragon lore, Gly ate some of his breakfast, not even looking at her.

"They are one of the elder races in the Basketlands, perhaps the oldest. Certainly they predate the creation of Kin and Dwarf alike, though there is question if the

Wardens might have walked the land before. They once lived in consort with Kin and were considered councilors of the Wardens, until the coming of the Celts. With the loss of the basketlands, we also lost contact with the Wardens and the dragons. Some still claim to see them flying in the high valleys, but they avoid the company of the other sentient races."

"You grasp the major understanding of the situation," Gly observed. "Please seek a deeper knowledge," he encouraged as Ryanna spooned a bit of berries and crème into her mouth.

Swallowing, Ryanna opened the codex, found the subject in the index and flipped to the pages. A line-drawing in colored ink showed a scarlet and black dragon that looked remarkably like the one from her vision.

"They live many thousands of years, it is thought. They live in caves on the sides of fire mountains. They're monogamous and bear live young that spend their early development in a mother's pouch. They are thought to have a language that is all their own, but they also speak Elvish. Ho, there, this writer believes they may all be gone."

"Garanthalgravynsyn," Gly identified. "He lived through the Scourging. That book dates from the last years of his life when he had not seen a dragon for four hundred years."

Ryanna swallowed a bite of seed bread before continuing.

"That's before we moved into the Dragon's Back," Ryanna said thoughtfully. "Could it be that dragonkind were wiser than we and simply moved away from the

Celtman early?"

"It well might be, though I have heard that the Celts hunted them where they remained in the basketlands. How we know that for certain, I cannot say."

"Yes, I remember the tales they told at Peace River. Hunting dragons was among them. The lives of men are so short, however, that they thought they were telling mere fancies. Except for those who lived with us there, most Celtmen thought elves a fancy, actually."

"They live short lives, men," Gly agreed. "Is there more about dragonkind there?"

"Not really. References to other books. He was writing from Moryn. I suppose these might be found in the collegium."

"No doubt. Perhaps I can scry to Tav, see if he can bring some of Garanthal's books back with him on his trip."

"You're excited by this topic." Ryanna did not form it as a question.

"Yes, yes, indeed. So much of this time seems so exciting. Winter People brought prophesy and prophesy ignites, sending Padraig to seek the king. After centuries of waiting, it feels as if the world turns once more on its axis."

"The Celdryans will not easily accept a king that unites both people," Ryanna reminded gently.

"They cannot stand against the One True God's choice," Gly assured her.

Ryanna flipped a page of the codex and gasped. Behind the dragon in flight, a fire mountain erupted, red ink enveloping a village far down the page. The artist's rendering seemed to suggest that the dragon was somehow responsible for the eruption. She pointed out the drawing to Gly.

"They are always tied to fire mountains in the lore. I don't know why the artist would suggest this, however."

"Could it be a gift of the dragons, such as I can call forth fire from wicks? They can somehow draw fire from mountains?"

"Perhaps. Our ancestors took dragons for granted and either didn't write about them or the books have been lost. We really know very little about them now."

"The Celts believe dragons can breathe fire from their mouths or noses."

"That sounds painful," Gly said wryly.

"That was my thought round the story fire. What am I to learn from all this?"

"I'm uncertain. What I know for certain is that the Gifted receive their Gifts from the True God as they are needed. If you can see into a dragon's lair, Ryanna, then God must have a purpose for it."

Ryanna sighed. Elves usually developed their gifts as children and their childhoods reflected the restraints needed. Powerfully gifted children were often apprenticed to the Wise. Ryanna, like many elflings, had exhibited only mundane gifts as a child, coming into increasing power as a young adult, already married and seeking her own life story. She had not submitted easily to the tutoring and the demands upon her freedom and she still did not seek to be a Wisdom.

"Why does the Council still refuse to block me from the Source?" she asked. "They know that I will never use my abilities in a position of leadership, so why do they not allow me to end my studies?"

"They do not owe you an explanation, Ryanna," Gly said. "Seems a shame to waste gifts such as you have."

"They could always unbind me if needed. I do not seek this life, Gly."

"No, you'd rather chase after Padraig."

"Not true," Ryanna insisted. "I accepted the restraints put upon me by the Wise. Even if I had not, Padraig would not have me until I had fulfilled my responsibility."

"And, you do not feel in the least rebellious about this?"

"I didn't say that," Ryanna said with a quick smile. "Of course I'm impatient. Elflings always are, by Kin standards. I have matured in my perspective, however. I will not go haring off to repeat the mistakes of my youth. Although I have never worn *goi'tan* grey, I understand why I earned it and would not earn it again."

Gly nodded.

"I think perhaps you are acquiring wisdom, pupil."

Ryanna smiled at him, warmed by a high compliment indeed. Then Gly pulled the codex from her and set another one in its place.

"What did Pol have to say about being content?" he asked.

Ryanna paused for a heartbeat, scanning the Scriptos before her.

"The letter he wrote to Filipai," she said, searching the pages. "Ah – here it is."

Before moving on to the next portion of the lesson, however, Ryanna looked at Gly.

"If Padraig is to find the king," she asked. "Are my gifts to be used in some way to secure the king's reign?"

"We have no way of knowing and thus the council chooses not to restrain that which God appears to find needful."

Ryanna shivered as a sensation like snow sliding off a roof washed down her back.

"I think you might speak truth," she said.

"The Wise always speak the truth as it is available to us," he replied. "Now let's get back to your lesson so that you are ready when God calls."

When God calls? Ryanna thought. *What if I see the trumpets being prepared right now?* And another shovelful of snow slid down her back.

Grief

The elves built with wondrous stone, strong and easily worked, but lit as if by witch light, excellent for foundations, but fearful to the eyes of men. The cities were well situated, so that our cities are built upon the remains of the elven kingdom. I call it a kingdom, though they never presented a king. How could they build such wonders without a king?

Aiden ap Shalar, Priest of Bel (FY 132)

Founding Year (FY) 931
High Celdrya - Early Summer

Perryn ap Trevellyn refused to weep as Maryn's favorite horse was led into the burial grounds. Had his brother's body arrived a day earlier, he could have indulged a bit of grief, but he would be crowned tomorrow and a sovereign did not cry in front of his vassals. Truly, what a bastardly tradition! He was burying his father and brother in the same day. Did that not explain tears? Surely, if there was ever an occasion …. Perryn placed his hand on the pommel of his sword and squeezed hard. The gemstones cutting into his palm dried his eyes and no doubt the slight grimace made him look appropriately angry. Being only 19 meant he had no lines on his face with which to affect a believable scowl.

The priests were going about their duties, invoking the gods and mumbling prayers. Perryn allowed himself to look round the circle of faces at the grave site. His brothers-in-law Burcan and Joran, both of Manahan, stood just opposite him, watching the priests with unreadable expressions. Joran had ridden in just this morning, though Burcan had been here when Vanyn died.

What do you know of all this, my lords?

Lord Gerriant of Fyrgal, his father's step-brother, might have had been holding back tears, or suppressing amusement. He'd always seemed companionable with the man he'd grown up with, but he'd been here when Vanyn died as well, so was suspect in Perryn's mind. Deryk's eyes were bloodshot with crying. Perryn doubted his foster-brother wept for Vanyn, but he'd been bosom friends with Maryn since childhood and no doubt grieved as much as Perryn himself. His tears brought thought of Donyl, no doubt riding toward Dun Celdrya even now, grieving their father and brother as Perryn was not permitted. Perryn envied him that.

Councilor Dumyr stood near Perryn's elbow, occasionally whispering words of reminder into the heir-apparent' s ear. Perryn murmured the requisite words without processing them. Did Dumyr grieve the loss of the king he'd served for a quarter century? Impossible to tell. Dumyr's wife, the Lady Wymffa, occasionally raised her handkerchief to her eyes to daub what might have been tears.

Malona, Vanyn's mistress, stood among the crowd gathered in the burial grounds, but not in the front ranks of the mourners, as that would be unseemly. Perryn had always acknowledged her beauty, but today there was something both alluring and repelling about her. He couldn't place his finger on it, but while her beauty drew him, somewhat also set his teeth on edge. Mayhap it was only that she was his father's mistress.

What indeed am I to do with you?

The sky was dark grey with clouds that promised more rain. It seemed fitting that the sky would be unable to cry, as Perryn was unable.

The priest drew a ceremonial sword and sliced the jugular vein of the horse, intoning words in the ancient language as the horse collapsed to its knees into Maryn's grave. The second priest sliced the jugular vein on Vanyn's favorite horse and the same ritual was worked there. Perryn tossed handfuls of dirt into each grave and then turned woodenly to walk toward the towers of the dun. The mourners followed him.

"You should withdraw to your private chamber, my lord," Dumyr suggested as they neared the main broch of High Celdrya. "It is appropriate and will give you time to school your resolve."

Perryn nodded and turned toward his own rooms. In doing so, he passed Deryk on his way to the ale barrels.

"Will you speak with me privately?" he asked.

Deryk blinked at him, swallowed tightly and turned to follow him. Neither man spoke until they reached Perryn's chambers on the third floor of a side broch. Deryk stood just inside the door, looking ill-at-ease. Perryn could not remember if Deryk had ever been in his chambers. He had naught against the man, but they had not been close, more by virtue of age difference than temperament.

"Please, do sit down. I would speak with you as kin."

Deryk took the seat Perryn offered. His greeting chamber had been handsomely appointed as the captain of the warband with cushioned chairs and a divan. Perryn checked the silver pitcher on the tray and offered wine. Deryk stirred slowly.

"Watered, aye." Perryn raised an eyebrow and Deryk sighed. "My mood is such that I might draw cold steel in your hall with the slightest provocation. Best to not dull my honor on the point of wine."

"Aye, I know that well." Perryn poured wine into two goblets and watered both. "I ask you this as friend, as I am not your liege at the moment. How did my father die?"

"He was poisoned. Surely the lords told you this."

"Why would they tell the spare heir anything at all?" Perryn said. "Burcan and Joran hope the vyngretres will find me wanting and raise one of them instead."

"Careful, Perryn. That sort of accusation can carry risks."

"This is in confidence," Perryn assured him. "Please take it that I just buried my father and brother. My father was poisoned. Are there any theories to who did this treason?"

"Nay, not that they have shared with me, but I am not without sources. My youngest sister is one of Lady Wymffa's attendants. The lords believe the Assassins Guild is involved."

"They're a myth."

"Someone makes the poisons that kill noblemen at the rule. And, I know for certain your father was poisoned. I almost sipped the mead myself."

"And, you are qualified to recognize poison?"

"My father believes that younger sons have an obligation to protect the heir with their lives. I recognized wolfsbane."

Perryn stood and stalked to the window. Deryk took a small sip of the wine, grimaced at the water, and set the goblet aside. He waited for Perryn to speak.

"What you described ... Maryn's death ... might it all have been a way to hide involvement with the guild?"

"Mayhap. I had always thought of them as mere poisoners, but I'm revising that opinion."

"Can you find out who might have hired them?"

"I can try, but it will have to wait until you are crowned because I will need the weight of the sovereign to wrest answers from those I question."

"I will name you the war band captain as soon as I am crowned."

"I thank you for the honor and I will accept pending approval by my father and brother. I'm 5th from the rule, so I doubt they'll object, but I must honor them."

"It is one reason I'm asking you for help. Maryn always said you are the most honorable man alive."

"Since Maryn's death that may be true," Deryk said soberly. He paused for a moment and took a deep breath, swallowing audibly. "I will do whatever is needful to bring his killers to ground," he promised in a husky voice. He drained the goblet and stood. "I'll start looking right now."

"Thank you."

Deryk nodded and left. Perryn stared down at the ward beneath his window. It had begun to rain since they'd come upstairs and the paving stones were starting to glisten. Just as Perryn was about to turn from the window, three riders clattered into the ward. One of them flung himself from the saddle and strode toward the great hall. The slight hesitation in his step identified the rain-soaked plaid as belonging to Donyl, Perryn's sole remaining brother.

Perryn paused briefly to set his untouched goblet on the table and moved to meet his brother before any others could speak with him.

Founding Year (FY) 1028
The Tongue – Spring · Present

Gregyn stood on a log on the far side of the lagoon, watching the sun make its progress across the sky. Due to the dense overgrowth, he couldn't often see the sun, but he tracked its glow filtering through the trees. Soon it would be sunset and time for the ritual. Gregyn shuddered.

Naked save for a breech cloth, Gregyn had perched upon the log for a quarter of the afternoon, pondering his near-future. A ritual of this import required three. Assessing the population of the island and who might reasonably be excluded from this particular ritual, and recognizing Talidd had never stayed his hand to spare Gregyn's feelings, the third in the ritual would be strong in the Power. Gregyn wished he'd known Talidd and the others desired his strength in the Power back when he'd been so eager to wield it and thus be included in the secret, and therefore, alluring rituals. He could have feigned weakness, or madness. Madness would have excluded him. Talidd would never believe it now. Weighing out the strength of those present on the island, and knowing two who would already be included in the trio, Gregyn accepted that Sawyl was powerful enough to bring visions on his own, so was the likely choice. There'd been a time when Gregyn had wished to be that powerful. Now he prayed he would not become so. The cavalier way Sawyl wielded such power frightened Gregyn, who did not frighten easily.

Even as he prayed to be found wanting, Gregyn swelled with pride for his skills, of the innate strength of gift that placed him apart from other mere apprentices in the Art. He might someday be a master and masters had naught to fear. No one could come against one such as Talidd. Gregyn wanted to know that sort of invulnerability in a way that only a former street urchin could.

The first bell rang, echoing across the swamp like a call to a burial. Gregyn shuddered. Time to wash. Time to prepare. *Don't dawdle!* he told himself sharply. Time enough for a ritual of your own. He paused as the gong's echo slowly died in the mangroves.

Seeing the croc laying low in the brown water under a mangrove root, Gregyn cast a hiding upon himself and set the nearby water shaking with a thought. The croc glided toward what it thought was a bird, though mayhap it knew he was upon the log. When it reached the phantom prey, Gregyn slapped Air around its jaws and lifted the struggling croc to the rock quay on Talidd's island. Diving in, he struck out to meet it. Pulling himself out of the water, he drew his dagger and slit the croc's throat. As the rich red blood flowed, Gregyn bent over the rift and sucked down all that he could stomach. He felt ethereal power flow into him, filling his entire being all the way to his toes. He felt as if he must glow with barely contained power. Staking the still bleeding croc on a pole, he left it for a servant to dress, rinsing the blood from his face and hands in the nearby swamp. Then he turned to the dock, ready to face the rest of his day.

Whichever servant had been given the task of watching him today had already left a basket of cleansing implements for him on the dock. Gregyn had always known he was being watched, had always been careful to be the dutiful student, the unwavering initiate. Since the day Talidd's agenda had first become clear, Gregyn had known that he must never let it be known how much he hated all of it.

Don't dawdle! Being late to a ritual was a killing offense, he knew. At the very least, the consequences would be unpleasant. Stripping naked, Gregyn sudsed with a scrap of soap and then rinsed in the bucket of settled water provided. He dried off and donned a clean breech cloth. The sun settled into the treetops. In the far distance, a bull croc roared. Gregyn wondered, not for the first time, if the death there might be preferable to the life here. It would be so easy to fail to take precautions when he killed for the blood power. With a shudder, he admitted to himself that he was not that desperate yet.

The ritual hut might have been deserted for all the activity Gregyn saw as he approached the stone structure and stepped into the alcove where the robes and other personal ritual items were kept. Talidd's black robe with the myriad of sigals was already gone, as was one of the journeyman robes in charcoal grey. Taking a deep breath,

Gregyn opened the cupboard where hung the robe of the apprentice. Color meant much in this ritual and tonight the robe was red. Gregyn gripped the cupboard door, fighting dizziness and nausea. *Red!*

Gregyn fought his mind to calmness, reaching deep down into the training that Talidd had so meticulously drilled him in, buoyed by the croc blood as it coursed through his system. Slowly, slowly, in the storehouse of his mind, he placed his fear on a shelf and covered it with a golden cloth, so he could don the robe without shaking like a leaf in high wind. He would come back to it later when it would be a useful tool and not an impediment.

Thus calmed, Gregyn entered the ritual lodge without so much as a quickened breath. His resolve almost crumbled when he saw Sawyl standing inside the door, but he had been well-schooled, trained as much by life as a starving street urchin as by life as Talidd's apprentice. Odd to realize that. Talidd's training had saved him from the streets and the streets' training had saved him from Talidd's training. *Where did I learn the trick with animal blood?*

The ritual lodge had been built without windows and the doors were staggered to prevent light from entering. *Light is the enemy of dark,* Talidd's instruction echoed in Gregyn's mind. The plastered interior walls and almost everything else were painted black, making the room seem vast. In sharp contrast, the floor sported an elaborate maze painted in vivid colors. Lore said only one with the knowledge of the stations could survive the crossing of the maze. Greyn knew the stations by heart and fervently wished he did not.

Tall stands held lit candle lanterns with the louvers almost closed. Talidd noted Gregyn's entrance as he threw a handful of herbs on a brazier. Gregyn took a slow, deep breath as the mind-numbing smoke billowed toward him. He held the smoke until he needed to breathe, feeling the magic relax his neck and calm his stomach. Tempted to take a few more breaths so as to feel naught, Gregyn schooled himself against it. The duties of the ritual demanded that he not drug himself too much. Gregyn thanked Nudd for the herbs and accepted what little he could afford to indulge.

He held by the door, waiting for Talidd's instructions. He had not done enough rituals of every type to know with certainty what would happen next; silence held the fewest dangers.

Talidd struck a small gong, starting the ritual.

"Nudd, we come to ask for wisdom and clarity in the seeking of omens," Talidd intoned. His mage's voice sent shivers down his apprentice's spine. "Gregyn, open the stations," he ordered. Sawyl handed Gregyn a bowl with some dark liquid within; Gregyn smelled blood. This meant a stepped increase in the ritual, beyond anything he'd done before. This was the ritual that had killed Eaddyn, though the young apprentice had worked at a much lower level. He had undoubtedly not known the intoxicating power to be found in killing a croc.

Gregyn steadied himself and stepped forward to the beginning of the maze. He took seven steps and bowed to the west, then spoke in a mage's voice, deep and commanding.

"Nudd, father of winter, ruler of night, come to stand with those who serve you."

Talidd struck the gong. Gregyn straightened and took seven more steps along the maze, then stopped and bowed to the east.

"Nudd, destroyer of summer, he who hangs a curtain across the sun, come to stand with those who serve you."

Gong! Gregyn took seven more steps, bowed to the north.

"Nudd, bringer of death, gatekeeper of hell, come stand with those who serve you."

Gong! It seemed as though the building vibrated with the resonance of the gong. Gregyn took another seven steps and bowed to the south.

"Nudd, God of the underworld, master of night, father of winter, come stand with those who serve you."

Gregyn's hands began to tingle as he felt somewhat enter the lodge. He didn't have time to wonder what Sawyl or Talidd might be doing. With the sounding of the gong, he had a fifth station to open. Seven more steps brought him to the steps of the altar, diagonal from the door.

"Nudd, we serve you and give you our blood to satisfy your hunger. Come stand with those who serve you."

Gregyn poured the contents of the bowl into a larger bowl to one side of the altar. The candles flared, scented smoke reached Gregyn's nose. The master and journeyman came to stand beside him, bracing him on either side. When they stepped onto the altar stage,

Gregyn stepped up with them, entering Nudd's realm for the first time. The tingling in Gregyn's hands had crept up to his elbows. His face felt aflame. His senses preternaturally sharpened, he realized with a shock that Sawyl, who had never seemed in the least emotional, was breathing raggedly. *Fear?*

"Kneel," Talidd ordered. The apprentice obeyed. As Sawyl stepped behind him, Gregyn took a deep breath, sucking in the drugged smoke until he drifted somewhere in a void. The journeyman pulled the back of Gregyn's robe up and reached in and under. Gregyn breathed again of the saving smoke; though it numbed him to what was going on, it did not make him unaware. His body responded to Sawyl's manipulations and a warmth flushed through his cold flesh. Talidd grasped his left wrist with a firm hand and drew his ritual dagger. Closing his eyes, Gregyn let the smoke take him as an image of the equerry's daughter rose in his mind. His breath came hot as a groan of near-climax escaped his lips. This ritual never ended in climax, for sexual gratification was not the purpose, but the power of the desire. Gregyn felt the dagger slice his skin, felt Talidd milk the wound for blood. Slowly, slowly, the blood flowed into the bowl. Through half-closed lids, he watched Talidd drink it down. Then the older man began to chant in the Old Tongue, invoking Nudd and Arrhodda. Gregyn felt tingling spread all over his body and the taste of coppers at the back of his throat. Suddenly his body was no longer his own and his mouth moved of its own accord.

"All is afoot. You need not know. You need not know. All is afoot. All is afoot. Wait, wait, until the turning of the tide. He lives. Wait, wait, until the turning of the tide."

As suddenly as the awen had come, it left him, causing his limbs to jerk like a string puppet. Gregyn collapsed forward onto the altar, gagging, bringing up the water he'd drank in lieu of a midday meal, intermixed with the undigested croc's blood. He vaguely acknowledged the sacrilege of vomit on the altar before he convulsed in a seizure that took his senses.

The dream world swirled with mist and shone with an odd light that Gregyn had never seen before. Gregyn extended his arm and could not see his fingertips, so he stood stalk-still, waiting for what might come to him. The dream world could be dangerous if one bungled about in it and Gregyn had not lived into his second phase of apprenticeship without learning not to bungle.

A tall young man with dark hair and bright eyes emerged from the fog and paused. He wore a cloak and breecs in a plaid Gregyn did not recognize. Most who came to the dream world were there by accident, having entered from their ordinary dreams. They didn't stay long … heartbeats at most. This lad, however, paused and looked at Gregryn as if fully aware of what he was about.

"Do you feel the storm coming?" he asked and then his clothes dissolved and he wore only a breech cloth and a slave chain around his ankle, a leather water bottle at his waist. "The storm will wash all away," the lad said, as if by explanation. Then he turned, donning his clothes in an instant and walking away into the mist.

A section of fog swirled and parted and Gregyn saw a beautiful woman with long dark hair dressed in breecs and a siarc, standing on a ridge line, her hand held out over an army as it marched toward utter darkness. A raven of incredible size winged toward her, black wings against the murderous sky.

The thunderous thump-thump-thump of wings sounded behind him and Gregyn ducked just as a dark winged creature much larger than a cow closed on the raven.

Gregyn came to himself still on the altar stone, listening to Talidd and Sawyl speaking behind him.

"He's too powerful," Sawyl was insisting. "That's the strongest awen I've ever seen anyone channel. I'd be dead if I drew that much. If he only knew, he'd be dangerous to us both."

"He doesn't know and I still have the power of the name. He'll not be able to harm me, or you, for a good long while."

"I'm not sure about that. I didn't cast the name spell. You did."

"My spell will hold for you, lad. I know it! More importantly, he must never know."

"What of this omen? He'll remember what he experienced."

"Will he?" Talidd inquired in a voice that struck fear in Gregyn so that he shuddered involuntarily. Talidd missed naught.

"Awake, lad? Good, good."

As Sawyl dragged Gregyn to his feet, the lad met eyes with Talidd, though he did not want to. Immediately, he felt the world spin. *I've felt this before. When?*

"You'll not remember this, Gregyn. Sawyl had the omen. You got sick and defiled the altar. Do you remember that?"

"Aye," Gregyn whispered, his will gone. "I was afraid of the omen and I got sick."

"Sawyl had the omen. Do you understand, lad?"

"Aye. Sawyl – omen."

"You'll remain awash until you wake up at the dawn. Do you understand?"

"Aye. Sleep. Need sleep."

Gregyn stumbled along beside Sawyl to be rolled into his hammock, where the journeyman muttered.

"You're a scary lad and you don't even know it. When Talidd dies, I'll have to kill you quick. I will kill you. If only I could harness the omens, but you're too strong. You're bound by his spell now, but that won't last, not after he dies. Kill you quick."

Gregyn felt the world spin off into a murky sort of grey. He awoke to the early dawn, fog enclosing the island. He sat up in the hammock, disoriented as the last he could remember was the knife slicing his arm in the ritual. Only a faint line indicated that he'd been cut there once. He never did scar, odd enough given the swamp's climate, and sometimes he healed quickly. He didn't know why and he wasn't about to ask Talidd for an explanation. Rubbing his eyes, he rolled out of the hammock and found a bucket nearby to wash the old vomit from his mouth. He'd bit the inside of his cheek during the ritual and it stung. Opening his eyes, he found an image in the dancing surface of the bucket. A hand holding a sword, working a sword. Gregyn stared, unable to identify the hand, unable to open the vision any wider. Then, as if by magic, Gregyn heard Sawyl's voice saying "I have to kill you quick. When Talidd dies, kill you quick."

Gregyn shuddered and the vision dissipated. Despite feeling like leftover porridge, Gregyn recognized immediately that his future plans must include escaping from Sawyl -- or killing him. Sawyl acted in fear and warned Gregyn, who did not question the reason, only plotted his survival. Returning to his hammock, he feigned sleep to plot the perfect plan to thwart Sawyl.

Founding Year (FY) 1028
Dublyn · Spring

Padraig traveled a leisurely pace toward Dun Trevellyn, realizing from his encounter with Marya that he needed a bit of time to get used to humans again. The Kin bathed regularly, especially after mucking out stables. If he couldn't manage to visit a farmstead without nearly retching, a town would be too much, and he needed to be able to enter towns for what he was about. He also needed time to remember the language and customs of his father's people. It had been so long since he'd spoken and lived among them that he made endless mistakes. Of little consequence in the smaller villages and towns, they might get him hanged in Clarcom. So Padraig stopped at the small villages along the way and hung out a shingle for his herbs. He was mostly paid in chickens and cheese, but his master in herbs had taught him well how to turn such into coin.

Thus he'd been traveling an eightnight. Trevellyn village had grown a bit since last he had passed through. Padraig sold the last of his wages in the village market and counting his coin. He had plenty, having saved a bit during his time with the Kin, who had little use for coin; he calculated he could afford to meet his obligation in Dun Trevellyn without impoverishing himself. He made a pouch of some cloth he kept for herbs and walked up the hill to Dun Trevellyn.

"Where are you bound, herbman?" the guard asked at the gate. His tone seemed friendly, helpful, not hindering.

Built upon an artificial hill in a broad valley populated with small farms and plenty of cows, Dun Trevellyn itself consisted of a four-story broch with two shorter half-brochs and the usual tumble of sheds and stables within the walls. The ward had been paved since last he'd been here.

"I've business with Lord Geran."

"Lad, run a message to the rig," the guard called to a passing page, a tall young man who might have been in his last year. "Tell him that this man is here to see him. What is your name, lad?"

"Padraig of D – Cenconyn."

"Be quick about it, lad."

The page nodded toward Padraig, though his eyes, the color of a tarn lake, narrowed in suspicion, or mayhap evaluation, though Padraig could not guess why. The lad strode off toward the dun and returned a bit later.

"The rig says you may attend him in the great hall," he said. "I'll accompany you."

Though Padraig knew the way well, he did not object. The lad gave him a long look sideways.

"Is somewhat amiss, lad?"

"Your accent is Denygal, not Cenconyn."

"I'm late from Denygal," Padraig lied. The language of the Kin still colored his speech as clearly as it colored the speech of the Denygal. Mayhap it was permanent. He didn't mind.

"I see. Family there?"

"Why do you ask?"

"My mam is from Denygal, or truly she was born in Cenconyn, but her mam was from Denygal and she spent a good deal of time there."

"'Tis a lovely place to spend much time."

They entered the great hall, a full round of the main broch. Padraig scanned about and saw a man who might have been Lord Geran standing near the honor hearth. He glanced toward the page, who nodded as if he had read Padraig's question from the air. Though this piqued Padraig's curiosity, he'd come for a duty and he meant to get it over with.

"Padraig of Cenconyn," Geran greeted cheerfully. The gangling youth had grown into a tall slender man with blond hair and a trim moustache. "You've become a journeyman, I see." Padraig assumed he guessed at his status as Lodiac was not with him.

"Aye. I've been free of my master about four years."

"'Tis pleasant news. What brings you to my dun?"

"I heard of your father's death and wished to pay my respects."

"Thank you," Geran said. He looked momentarily sad. "It was a burden I was raised to take up, but I still grieve that I must do so." He shook himself and brightened. "It is good to see you, though. I thought about you a bit last winter watching some of the riders dice."

"Aye, well, that's the other part that brings me here. I hope you'll not have me hanged for a common thief and accept this with the honor that I did not have that winter." He held out the pouch of coins.

"What's this?" Geran asked, honestly confused, testing the heft of the coin.

"I cheated you at dice those long years ago. Now I wish to make myself clean of that crime."

Geran stared at him, glancing back and forth between the herbman's face and the pouch in his hand.

"Aye, well, I did think mayhap you were cheating me, but I could afford it more than you and I could not prove it, mind."

"Nay, it would have been hard to prove, but I knew what I was doing. I ask you to take my payment so that I might be clean before you."

"Of course. And there will be no more said of this," Geran said, putting the pouch within his siarc. 'Tis an honorable thing you have done. Few men would have."

"Aye, well, stealing from you was not honorable. I thank you for your forgiveness."

"We'll speak no more of it. Will you stay for a meal

and a night under my roof?" For him to offer that meant that he had truly forgiven the crime.

"Nay. I've business in Clarcom. I'm pleased you were here for me to speak with you."

"I'll not delay you, but know this, Padraig. You're always welcome at my gate and by my fire. I'd stake you a winter if you have need."

"I thank you," Padraig said. "Currently I have no such need, but I'll remember your invitation if ever I do."

Geran walked him to the gate and waved him along. Padraig reached the town gates before he remembered the young page who'd piqued his curiosity. Naught to do about it! Padraig turned south for Clarcom. He'd left Trevellyn too late to make the next village by nightfall, but he found a copse of trees not far from a Temple of the Moon in which he decided to camp.

The dark night with only starlight for illumination meant naught to a man of the Denygal. Padraig gathered wood and collected water without hesitation, for the night seemed no darker than dusk to his eyes. He ate a scant meal of bread and cheese and watered ale, then sat by the fire sipping tea for mayhap a watch. He'd just rolled into his blankets by the dying fire when he heard a twig snap off in the trees.

Padraig's eyes immediately opened, but he didn't move more than enough to put his hand on the hilt of his long knife, which lay beside his blankets. He scanned the trees, at first seeing naught, but then he made out a figure crouched in the trees. He waited, unmoving. He saw the figure turn and trot back toward the Temple of the Moon. As he watched the figure of a woman, dressed in the cowl and robe of a priest, disappear into the shadow of the Temple, Padraig threw out his mind to see what he might Sense, finding merely curiosity and a satisfaction of that. He closed his eyes and went right to sleep.

In his dream, Padraig saw a room that reminded him a great deal of a cave, except that the walls were dressed stone, rather than living rock. He saw no windows and only a small door. In the middle of this cell, a woman sat on the floor. She wore a brown robe and cowl and her dark hair was cropped short like a lad's. On the floor between her knees rested a bowl of water and she stirred the water with a finger. As he watched he saw himself rolled in his blankets, sleeping. She smiled and Padraig awoke with a thud of his heart.

Sitting up in the darkness, heart pounding within his chest, Padraig fought down panic. He'd never known that there were seers, let alone female seers, this side of the border who could scry out a man they'd never met in the flesh. He swallowed agitation. As calmness slowly worked its way back into his soul, he heard something just on the edge of consciousness. He stared in the direction of the temple.

Is that screaming?

Padraig did not sleep well the rest of the night. When he rode out at dawn, he knew he would remember the experience at the temple for a long time to come, though he truly did not know what to think of it.

Kin Cycle 24578/ FY 1028
Blue Iris Holt · Spring

The horses and goats were restless. Ryanna could sense their alert. It might be the spring weather, exciting the animals with its promise of rain and warmth. Or it could be a predator.

"Are you feeling somewhat?" Melim asked. As a horse drover, he knew the herds better than Ryanna, but he also knew she had skills he didn't possess.

"There is tension in the air," she replied, keeping her voice dark and soft. The horses were used to hearing Melim's male voice and it wouldn't do to spook them with a lighter tone.

"Chela says you can do more than just feel excitement on the air. I can do that. Do you Sense somewhat I cannot know?"

Ryanna smiled at him. Melim was a half-elf like herself, tall and dark haired with human features. Well, so long as he kept his hair over his ears because those were a bit peaked for a round-ear. Among her father's people, Melim would be considered handsome, as she was considered beautiful, but here in the elfholts, neither of them was that remarkable except for being a minority. Among a race with godlike beauty that could last 600 years, they were barely attractive.

Ryanna relaxed into her saddle, casting out her Sensing, trying to find somewhat that wasn't goat or horse or elven drover. She'd been asked by the Wise to investigate what had beset the herds and stop it if she could. As she Delved, she bumped up against Sabre's consciousness, that bundle of energy that was often near, but rarely beside her.

"Do you smell aught?" she asked.

I'm not a nose hound, Sabre replied. She sent a thorn of annoyance down the bond and he sent back a mental growl. *I'm investigating.*

Ryanna returned to her Sensing. What was that she Sensed on the rise toward the holt? Something furtive and stealthy. She focused more tightly, but still whatever it was eluded her Sensing.

"Over there, where the mountain goes up toward the holt, I think there's somewhat there."

They were speaking Celdryan because it was a language they didn't get to use daily and they both knew it. It was good practice.

Melim scanned the darkness. Like most half-elves, he could see in low-light, but not near-darkness as full elves could. Ryanna was similarly handicapped, but she had resources Melim lacked. Sabre sent to her.

Move the herd away from the mountain. Then there came a fantasy of huge cats with fangs dripping saliva.

"Move the herd away from the mountainside," Ryanna suggested. While she prepared a spear for hunting, Melim signaled the other drovers. Ryanna urged her horse forward, spear held loosely in her right hand, scanning the lower slopes of the mountain for movement. At first she saw only brush and dark shadows, but then she spied movement. She Sensed that furtiveness again, but this time there was no aire of fear or trepidation. *These are big cats!*

With that thought, she cocked back her arm and threw the spear in a flat, expertly aimed flight. At the last possible moment, the cat she'd struck for flipped back into the shadows amongst the bushes and the hunt was on. Ryanna had lots of spears. She drew another out from under her leg and kicked her horse to a charge. The third dart she threw finally struck home – she saw a figure slump to the ground just as she swerved to chase another cat.

Her horse shied sideways, neighing nervously as Sabre sent a warning. Somewhere a cat yowled, cut short in an instant, but then one of the cats launched itself at the flank of her horse and Ryanna realized that she had become the prey.

The darkness made exact estimates impossible, but there were at least a dozen cats and they all seemed to have turned to stalk her.

These are no ordinary mountain cats, Sabre reported.

Ryanna's horse reared then, nearly unseating her. She smelled blood and then the horse bolted in terror. She jerked hard on the reins and turned, but this told her only that she was being followed by a pack. She heard the bleat of a nanny goat somewhere off to one side and then she jumped clear as her horse suddenly stumbled and fell.

Ryanna tucked, rolling back up onto her feet and pulling her hunting bow free of where it lay across her back. As cats raced toward her, she expertly braced the bow against her leg, pulled the string into place, nocked an arrow and let fly. One arrow for each cat, but they were still getting closer, springing in athletic bounds across rocks and open ground. Just when she thought she might run out of arrows, Sabre sent a warning – *Look up and to the left* – and as she did, a cat came down at her from the mountain side. She left off drawing arrows to use her bow as a club, drawing her long-knife in the other hand. Cats circled her, hissing, striking with huge paws and dagger-like claws. She returned the swipes with thrusts of the long knife, showing them that she had claws of her own. Cats circled in behind her, trying to take out her legs. She beat them back with the bow.

The cats suddenly broke off, scattering, as the drovers came charging up swinging torches and howling like something out of the Celtman legends. Ryanna ignored their work and turned to her horse. He'd been hamstrung and now lay on his side breathing heavily, having given up trying to rise. Ryanna patted his neck.

"I'm sorry, friend, but this is a kindness."

She drew the long knife across the horse's throat and the breathing immediately stopped. Ryanna patted his ears and spoke soothing words while all around her the drovers ran off the cats. The horse passed just as the drovers drew up around her.

"Dawn's almost here," Melim noted. "Thanks you for what you did. Now that we know what's taking the goats, we can fight them." He spoke in Elvish since the other drovers were Kin.

"Yes," Ryanna agreed. "Well, that was exciting. Not everyday you get to sympathize with a vole."

The drovers all laughed. Ryanna began removing tack from the horse preparatory to dressing the carcass. The meat would be a relief at this end of winter. Several of the drovers moved off to patrol the herds, but Melim and another elf stayed to help her dress the horse and provide protection should the cats come back.

With dawn's early light, they walked over to the place where she'd struck her first cat and found a large male with paws as wide as Ryanna's hands were long.

"It looks like an ordinary mountain cat," Melim observed.

"Except for being truly big and not acting like a predator around man."

"Yes. They seemed to know that you were the huntress and they all focused on you. Well, look at that."

The early morning light showed Sabre dragging a cat into their area. The large black dog had clearly severed its windpipe.

I see the perennial war between cats and dogs continues, Ryanna sent.

It tried to kill me, Sabre retorted.

"Have you ever seen wild cats act like that before?" Ryanna asked Melim.

"No, not ever. That was more the behavior of a wolf pack. Cats are usually solitary."

Ryanna nodded, feeling that shovel of snow slide down her back again. *What is walking in the world, Lord?* Her only answer was another shudder.

Green Eyes

Some say the Temple of the Moon came from Gawl, that women there were equal to men. Some say the practice sprung up here when women objected to the priests drawing us away from the Old Faith's raw worship to more civilized forms. I cannot say which of these theories is correct, but I must say that the Moon is at its strongest in its dark phase.

Dagvyn, priest of Bel, FY 834

Founding Year (FY) 931
High Celdrya · Spring

*R*ule isn't easy, Perryn ap Trevellyan recognized. Of
course, his tutors had mentioned it wouldn't be,
back when ruling had merely been a theory for the spare
heir. The men round the council table were acting not as
his liegemen, but as rivals, making decisions that he had
not authorized as if it were their right to do so. *How did
my father do it? Did Maryn know they would do this when he
ascended? Or is it that they know I am the spare heir or do they try
all new lords such?*

"You ordered the burning of an entire village?"
Perryn asked, just to assure that he had heard Burcan
rightly. The words invoked rage in him. He could almost
smell the burning flesh and hear the scream of children
as they were forced back into the flames by men wearing
Manahan colors. *Stay your hand! You can't kill him in the
council chambers. Even the king cannot indulge every fantasy.*

"Aye, my lord," Burcan answered smartly. "The
assassins were found in the inn. I took decisive action to
assure that all the assassins would be eliminated
immediately."

Burcan might be married to Perryn's sister, but
Perryn had little knowledge of him. He'd met the man

only twice before and spoken only ceremonial words with him. He couldn't tell if the man were lying. Burning an entire village to eliminate the killers, even of the king, seemed overmuch. *Maintain calm!*

"I did not authorize that," Perryn reminded him. He spoke in a mild voice, just loudly enough to be heard.

Burcan subsided into stammering while the other lords turned their gazes upon their young liege. Perryn could feel his cheeks growing hot beneath his soft, short-cropped beard. He remembered discussions with his tutors about establishing authority early in his rule, should he ever rule. He'd not paid sufficient attention, he realized. In his heart, he'd always accepted that Maryn would rule and he would be the war leader. Perryn felt as if he were lecturing his elders, but he was their liege and he had to establish that relationship early … now … before the day was done.

"Please explain to me why you would take such an extraordinary action against innocent people without allowing me to make the decision?"

"Sire, you were not the king yet," Gerriant of Fyrgal said.

"I was the apparent king the moment my father died," Perryn insisted, his voice controlled as his rage hammered against his ribs.

"Sire, I mean no disrespect. Prince Maryn would have been king the moment your father died, but you are untried," Joran of eastern Mulyn explained. He was Burcan's twin and except for a scar along his cheek there was no telling them apart. Both were bluff men, bold and loud, and both were married to Perryn's sisters. If Joran expected Perryn to look away in trepidation, he was disappointed. "You wear the crown only because the vyngretroix board had not time to vet you between deaths."

Perryn allowed himself a beat, the barest of breaths, before responding. A Trevellyn had sat upon the throne for almost a millennium. Every time the line of succession was broken, the vyngretroix deliberated and suggested a possible change in leadership, but they always ended up installing the next in line of Clan Trevellyn. The vyngretroix were a holdover from Gawl where each tribe had been ruled by their own village-king, but only one king had passed through the portal and he'd been a Trevellyn.

"And, yet, they installed me officially this morning," he reminded the vygretroix gathered here. This was not the full council, but merely those lords who were involved in the assassination investigation. He needed these men to conduct the business of the kingdom, but there was a fine line between mutual cooperation and treason.

Steady, man! You cannot afford to fling a spear awry just now.

"It is true that I am untried. However, I was raised with the possibility of rule and I am the king. We will move on because there is no way to recall the flames and the innocent lives lost.

"Innocent?" Burcan queried, his voice laden with shock. "Sire, that village harbored assassins. There are none innocent in such congress."

"Surely there were children in that village," Perryn

shot back. He timed it for Joran taking a sip of mead and was pleased when the vyngretrix choked on his swallow. Burcan turned a bit pale. Like many lords, he led from a distance and mayhap had not considered the possibility of innocents in a village where assassins might be found. All here had been elder sons, born to rule. None had been a war leader passing by the villages that bore the brunt of noblemen's wars.

"Are you absolutely certain that the threat of the assassins has been eliminated?" Perryn continued.

The men round the council table traded questioning looks. Perryn waited.

"We believe so, sire," Gerriant said. "It's hard to be perfectly certain with men of this sort, but the ones in the inn were the only ones our investigation revealed."

"And you took none prisoner, so did not question any," Perryn said. It wasn't a question. He knew the answer.

"Sire, these men would not tell the truth and allowing them to live would only have wasted time," Burcan insisted.

"Aye, of course. Questioning an assassin about who hired him wouldn't reveal anything of worth." The more clever of the gathered nobles shifted, made nervous by the quiet sarcasm in his tone.

"Sire," Dumyr said. "The assassins guild trains their agents well. You must recognize that among that training is the ability to resist torture."

"Of course," Perryn agreed, deferring to his chief council on that point. He did not allow interruption, promptly continuing his thought. "Still, it might have been worthwhile to at least attempt the questioning." He allowed himself a moment to seem to be marshalling his thoughts. "Given this misunderstanding, I am requiring that all of you report to me according to this matter and make no hasty decisions without consultation." They looked shocked. "I realize that my father gave you more free rein and surely I will do so once we've established things, but for now, all matters having to do with capital punishment must be brought before me in my court of justice."

"Even within our own lands?" Malik of Blyan asked, voice weak.

I've just been gifted by the gods!

"If that seems wise to you, then aye, within your demesnes."

They realized that they'd just been tricked, but what could they do but comply now that their liege had so ordered? There were murmured "of course, my liege," and large swallows of the drink at hand. The uneasy relationship between the vyngretroix board and the king had just taken on a less settled tone and Perryn thought that he might be emerging the victor here.

Easy, man. A war is won one battle at a time, but rarely does a single stroke win a battle.

"Are we any closer to discovering who killed my brother and the king?" Perryn asked, though he knew the answer.

"Nay, my liege," Dumyr the councilor said. "We will, of course, continue the investigation. Will Lord Deryk remain the war band leader?"

"Most like," Perryn replied, though he was sure

every man in the room had a candidate or two to put forth for the post. "Our arrangement is temporary at the moment, but I will have need of a war band leader."

"Donyl intends to continue his studies at the temple?" Burcan asked, then realized he had overstepped. "My lady wife will ask."

"Donyl is not a war band leader," Perryn said. "I'll find use for him and his skills, but he will not desire Deryk's position. Or yours," he added, just to assure his vassals that he was not the sort of king who would disenfranchise a clan simply because he could. He doubted the vyngretroix board would allow him that sort of power, but it never hurt to establish one's dominance early in the rule. "Are we finished, men?"

There were murmured affirmations and then the group worked its way out of the room. Perryn hung back, waving away any who might have lingered. He stood at the window looking down on the ward until he heard Donyl's hesitant step behind him.

"What did you think?" he asked. The youngest of Vanyn's three legitimate sons, Donyl had suffered a childhood illness that had left one leg a bit weak, so he'd naturally gravitated toward books and learning. That had suited Vanyn well since he'd needed a son to feed to the temple. His bookish nature suited Perryn well now because he was ill prepared to be king. Among Donyl's many and varied talents was a knowledge of every nook, cranny and cupboard in the dun where one might put an ear to a crack and overhear a private conversation. As Perryn had set him up to spy on the council, he did not fear what his brother might have heard.

"I think Burcan is lying," he announced. "He fired that village for some reason other than ardor."

"Aye, I think so as well. If he'd truly been interested in finding the assassins' hire, he'd have kept a few alive. Do you think he arranged all this?"

"That I cannot tell you," Donyl said. At 15, his face was thin, but his blue eyes were innately intelligent. His voice had just finished changing, but it carried sober thought in every tone. "What would he gain from that with two heirs still to eliminate?"

"Aye, it is a risky bit of business, to be sure. Mayhap I am merely reacting to their disdain for my leadership."

"You are untried," Donyl reminded. Perryn appreciated his younger brother's candor. Coming from him, it was simply the truth, not delivered to unsettle or belittle.

"What do you think of that?" Perryn asked.

"You have a lot to learn," Donyl said. "You can rely on Dumyr for a while, but sooner or later, you'll need to surround yourself with wise men you trust who can direct you."

"Aye. My next question may take you a bit by surprise. Do you truly want to be a priest of Bel."

Donyl blinked, opened his mouth to speak, closed it and blinked again.

"When Father recalled me from Blyan, I hoped I would be allowed to make a case to study as a councilor since I would become the spare heir and as a cripple I would need great wisdom since I could never gain battle glory. Sadly, I didn't get the opportunity and truth be told, you will need ties to the temples. Lugh would be better, but Bel would be more suiting to me."

"My betroth' s brother is a priest of Bel to be assigned to the Celdryan temple. There's no reason for me to give my best asset to the gods."

"Just like that, I'm free?" Donyl asked. Part of what made him a valuable asset was his ability to analyze and question. Perryn nodded and waited. "What about my studies?" Donyl asked.

"Of course, I encourage your studies. I'll need you to be learned in the years to come. I suspect there will be challenges."

"Father's murder is a challenge," Donyl noted.

"Aye. Prepare to return to Denygal, leaving on the eightnight. In the meantime, talk to Deryk and give some thought to both events. I do not believe they are unrelated, but I also do not believe the assassin's guild just suddenly decided to kill the king and his heir without coin having traded hands, yet that is the only option given me. I do not trust that."

"You are better prepared than they suppose," Donyl observed.

"Aye, but our father did assume Maryn might fall in battle, so he did get me the second-best education coin could purchase. Still, I am untried."

"You won't be if we find Father's killer."

This gained a huge grin from his older brother.

"Now you understand the way of it."

"Mayhap I should remain, find tutors here in the city."

"Nay, but I truly don't want you here for this." Donyl looked perplexed. Perryn explained. "If I should fall as well, you will be the only hope for the kingdom. I'd rather have the kingdom's sole hope safely in a library in Denygal than here where he might perish by my side."

"Perryn," Donyl croaked. "I cannot be king."

"Nay, but you can father a king and stand as regent." Donyl started to shake his head, but Perryn cut him off. "If need be. Hopefully, I will live long and produce many heirs and you'll stand at my elbow and aid my rule."

Donyl's young face had grown quite somber.

"It's hard to think of myself as the last line before the darkness."

"Aye, well, would you rather the rule passes in the female line to Burcan and Joran?"

"Nay." Donyl straightened. "I'll seek the answers you've requested and I'll prepare to travel."

"Keep your preparations small and tell others you'll be leaving after my wedding. I've set it for Lughnasa. I wish heartily that you could be there, but I think it wisest that you fly before expected."

Donyl nodded, the weight of the kingdom darkening his eyes.

"I've an appearance to make in the great hall," Perryn explained. He heaved a deep sigh. "My life will never be my own again."

With that, he strode from the room, leaving Donyl to follow more slowly. As the younger brother left the upper hall, a dark man stepped from the shadows. Talidd, the servant, walked quietly into the council chamber, closing the door behind him. With a whispered word, he lit a candle lantern, then focused his eyes on the flame. He had a report to make and commands to carry out.

Founding Year 1028
Dun Clarcom

L ady Lydya ap Chenyn of Clarcom and Denygal lived a busy life as the wife of the vyngretrix of Dublyn and found that she might go a whole day without visiting her children in the children's hall, except that she scheduled it and kept her schedule no matter what might try to intervene. Thus when the chamberlain tried to slow her progress toward that appointment in order to make a decision on what wine to serve with dinner, she brushed him aside.

"You are capable of making such a decision, Lord Ogrynnyn. Please, please, do so. I will back whatever you decide."

She mounted the circular staircase toward the upper floors as Ogrynnyn stepped away to go about his own duties. At the top of the stairs, she hesitated as a young woman in a grey silk dress started to come down, but the lass scrambled back, stepping into the hallway to give Lydya passage, even bowing. Lydya did not mean to smile with a little bit of wicked triumph, but she did. She swept on up to the third floor without even looking at the lass who remained behind.

The children's hall occupied the entire floor. The main room, occupying half of the area around the stair landing, stood empty though not silent, for the sound of a young banisedh could be heard from the tutorial room.

There a battle raged along simple lines. In the middle, two boys batted at each other as each was constrained by a woman. An older lad stood in a doorway, laughing at the sight. As Shyla had the harder battle controlling the smaller Danyl, Lydya lent her weight there until they finally pulled the boys apart. Still they struggled. Lydya put her face down to Glynn's, wagering that her third son was still a reasonable human being, and shouted.

"Back up now or you'll rue the day, lad, I promise that!"

Glynn allowed Macla, the young lass who helped the nurse, pull him out of Danyl's reach. He stood back, chest heaving, waiting for his mother's attention.

"Let him be. Help us here," Lydya ordered Macla. With the young nurse's help, Shyla managed to drag Danyl away to his chamber. Lydya straightened her kirtle and head scarf and looked at her third son with less than a pleased expression.

"What was this about?"

"He went amok, Mam," Glynn replied, straightening his own siarc.

"Oh, just like that?"

"You know how he is."

"Aye, I do, and I'll wager it didn't just blow in like a summer storm. Tell me the truth, lad, or you'll regret it."

Glynn knew full well that his mother had an uncanny ability to know when one of her children was lying. He spoke the truth when she demanded it.

"I teased him a bit, but naught that should have caused him to want to murder me."

Lydya drew a deep breath, for she did not sense a lie, though mayhap not wholly the truth.

"We'll speak further in a few minutes. You will remain here. Both of you."

She included her second son, Cullyn, in the matter because she suspected him of having somewhat to do with all of this. Home two days and already fomenting trouble! She went to the one person she could trust not to lie to her – Danyl.

The five-year-old sat upon his bed, arms rapped round his knees, shaking. Shyla leaned into the wall next to the door while Macla sat on the window sill. The nurse rose and left the room as soon as Lydya entered. Chyla waited for leave to go, which Lydya gave with a nod.

To see the proud strong warrior shaking with tears did melt a mam's heart, sure enough.

"Come, lad. Tell your mam what's about."

"Naught," Danyl muttered. "Glynn's a hound."

"Well, that's true enough. What's he gnawing at now?"

"Naught," Danyl insisted, but tears formed in his eyes.

"I would wager coin that there's somewhat behind this. Tell me, lad, for I hate it when my children lie to me."

"He ... he ... he called me .... an .... an elf."

Now Danyl burst into tears and buried his face in his mother's dress. Lydya held him, rubbing her hand up and down his back while she fought to keep her emotions from overwhelming her. *No!* This could not be happening! A few swallows and a couple of deep breaths and she could speak.

"There, there, lad. Glynn's a hound for sure, but there's naught to it. It's the green eyes, you see. They run in Shyr blood and you've come up with them. Glynn's merely finding a bone to pick, lad, but you don't need to be helping it along by getting angry. Next time just say 'Well, if I'm an elf, what make you, my brother?' He'll back off right then, or be the one angry, I promise that."

Danyl sniffled and rubbed at his cheeks, looking up at his mother with eyes that looked like an inland sea – a striking green.

"I did not mean to break my word to you, Mam. He just ... just ...."

"Aye, well, next time you'll do better, though I suppose he'll find somewhat else to tease you over. He'll be going off to page someday. Moreover, Cullyn will be going back to page in the fall, so he'll not have his chief advisor to goad him on. Trust me there, things will be better when Cullyn's headed off. Now, you just remember that your anger gives them what they want. You hold tight to it and they'll back off quickly enough. Do you understand?"

"I try, Mam. Truly, I do."

"There's a love. We'll have Macla bring you some warm milk and bread and a bit of a nap and you won't want to think a bit of it. I'll deal with your brothers."

Before leaving the chamber though, Lydya paused a moment to look out the window and get her own temper and emotions under control. She'd known when she bore Danyl that he'd be a trial and she'd trusted his distance from the rule to keep him from the notice of her husband, but she'd never suspected that children's teasing might come so close to home. She meant to nip this in the bud before it could come to full flower.

From this window in the children's hall, Lydya possessed a nice view of the kitchen garden and a section of the inner wall around the dun. A young serving wench embraced a rider by the well. They kissed passionately, then faded around the creamery hut, groping at the fastenings of one another's clothing. *That gets bairns and, like as not, the lad will claim he's not the father.* She smiled to herself, for she had seen well both of their faces.

Macla had anticipated Lydya's request for warm milk and bread and was just returning as Lydya came from Danyl's chamber. Lydya made a mental note that the lass showed promise and thanked her, then turned her attention to Glynn ap Riordan, third son of Cunyr, Lord Clarcom, Vyngretrix of Dublyn.

"Danyl tells me you've been teasing him in a most despicable fashion," Lydya began right away.

"Mayhap I should go for this," Cullyn said, straightening from the doorway where he lounged.

"Stay right where you are!" Lydya ordered, voice cracking like a whip. "Glynn, what possessed you to say that to your brother? There are many things of a hateful nature that might have been said, but that is far greater than should ever be spoken."

Glynn shot of look toward Cullyn, confirming Lydya's suspicions.

"I apologize, Mam," he said immediately. "And I'll apologize to him. You're right, of course. It was a despicable thing to say."

Lydya sensed his sincere repentance. Though Glynn had said naught, she suspected him ready to make a soul-defining decision. She could only wait for him to come to her.

"Where did you get such a notion?"

"Oh, easily enough," Glynn assured her. "There's gossip about."

Lydya's heart thudded in her chest. *Gossip?*

"Who is gossiping about such?"

"Some of the kitchen wenches," Cullyn spoke up. "They were pointing out that he's tall and thin, taller than Bernys' boy who is the same age, but lighter. He seems an elf. Glynn's just repeating what he's heard others say."

"And there's the green eyes," Glynn admitted.

Lydya laughed to hide her dismay.

"Green eyes run in Shyr blood. My mother had them as well. Truly, your brother is naught unusual in the least. Green eyes are rare in the rest of the kingdom, but not in Denygal."

"Elven blood in Denygal veins," Cullyn reminded her. "Your mother was born a good deal before the purges."

"If my mother be an elf, what make that you, lad?" Lydya countered.

She received the desired effect. Both lads winced. Lydya drew a deep breath and spoke with all the authority her station as their mother and the wife of Clarcom afforded her.

"You are not to speak of this again," she ordered them. "Glynn, if I hear of you teasing your brother again, I'll see you humiliated among the pages. You know I can."

"Aye, Mam. I've already said I'll apologize and you'll hear no more of this from me. I promise."

"Cullyn?"

"Aye, Mother, whatever you say," the older boy replied, his voice reserved. He always had a sneer for her, so much like her husband. Lydya wondered at that, truly.

"I mean it. Listen, you young whelp, you may think my authority worth flaunting, but remember that I do have authority. I love you, dearly, but I won't tolerate this teasing of your brother. He's but a young lad who deserves the right to grow unmolested by his elders. If you continue with this course, Cullyn, I'll see you flogged."

Cullyn blinked, for never had he thought her capable of that. Yet all in the family knew that his mother did not speak lightly. She was the soul of compassion and fairness, until it was time not to be compassionate or fair. Cullyn straightened his siarc.

"I'll do as you say, Mam. My apologies for my part in this."

"Well and good then. We shall see how the rest of the summer progresses."

Lydya left the children's hall then, for she did have pressing matters to attend to. In addition to being the lady of Clarcom, a great dun, she also had rigdon business that required her attention. There were days when she wondered how she kept all the details in hand.

There were days when she wondered indeed if she truly had them in hand.

Founding Year 1028
Clarcom

Padraig had become aware of Joy's thoughts as he traveled south toward Clarcom. At first he'd thought it just his own desire to understand what she thought, but now and again, he felt a fleeting touch upon his mind, as if the horse reached out to him. So far just horsey thoughts came to him. She preferred apples over carrots, for instance, and she thought towns a very bad idea.

She thought Clarcom, even on a bright sunny spring day, a very bad idea. Her ears weren't yet laid back, but as they neared the walled city, he could sense her unease. Since he shared this thought with her, he doubted he could be much comfort.

Did the elven cities of old smell like this?

The largest town in Dublyn, Clarcom covered six rolling hills with the dun upon the only near-mountain in southern Dublyn. The city of 80,000 comprised the usual hodgepodge of thatched round houses and curving streets. Joy laid her ears back as they came under the walls and nearly balked as they went under the first gate.

Clarcom's defenses had been hardened and strengthened since Padraig's last journey this way. He supposed it spoke of Cunyr ap Riordan's power that he could have so much work done on the city walls in what was really a short period of time and that the people already felt confident to fill in the area between the old outer wall and the new with shops and homes that fairly buzzed with activity.

Are things truly that bad in the kingdom proper now?

Padraig's goal lay just inside the third defense wall, in an inn off one of the market squares. There'd been many changes in this area since Padraig's last trip here four years ago, so that it took him a bit of effort to find the inn, but he recognized the sign – a red giant – easily enough. Neighborhood legend had that the giant – who held a tree in his huge fist – had once been doing somewhat obscene a long time ago, before the owner had been married. The tree suited the place more now, given that the area seemed to have gained in respectability. In fact, the inn had added a third story and was beginning to take on the appearance of a merchant's home with a broch of its own. The door stood open as any good inn door on a fine spring day. Padraig tied off his stock at the hitching post and entered the dim interior.

This time of day custom was slow and the sole person in the tavernroom was the tavernman himself, polishing tankards on a board at the back of the room. When last Padraig had been here, the tavern room had been but a half of the round main floor, but it now took the full of it, indicating that the owner and his family now lived in a smaller round house out back.

"May I help you?" the tavernman said and Padraig recognized the voice.

"Aye. I seek Annan, innkeeper of the Red Giant."

"I be Annan. And who might be seeking me?"

"Padraig of Denygal, more late of Cenconyn, herbman."

Annan stopped with a tankard midway to the cloth and stared, then set his work down abruptly to come round the board and slap Padraig on the back.

"Lad, you've come back!" he crowed happily. "I don't mind telling you that I thought you might have perished after hearing naught for years and years. Where have you been?"

"About. I had much to learn after I left Lodiac and I've done that."

"Lodiac? You know he died three winters past?"

Padraig, surprisingly, felt grief like a blow at the news. His master in herbs had not been a young man, but somehow Padraig had expected to see him again.

"Nay, I did not know. Was his passing good?"

"Aye. He was here when the last illness took him. Heledd nursed him to his death. He had words for you, lad."

"Did he now?" Lodiac and Padraig parted on tense terms, though Padraig remembered that he'd tried to apologize for what he knew he had to do. "Kind, were they?"

"Actually, aye. He said if you were to travel this way, I was to say that he understood why you traveled on. It were your time."

Padraig felt a burden of weight leave his chest, for truly that was what he had tried to tell Lodiac, though the old man had felt himself abandoned. He'd taken a starving street urchin and trained him in herbs and barely five years into the apprenticeship, Padraig had announced that he'd learned all that he could and needed to travel on. Lodiac had, no doubt, hoped Padraig would remain with him and work with him even as a journeyman so as to ease his master's old age. Padraig had been tempted, but he felt a higher calling. He had never truly regretted it, but he had been saddened that Lodiac had not understood.

"Did he suffer much?"

"Nay, not more than one might expect in old age. And he died with a bit of family about him. Are you staying for a while?"

"Aye."

"Tavern room or a chamber."

"I've a bit of coin. Chamber. Not your best."

"Third best. Top of the stairs on the right. Will you be wanting a bath?"

"Oh, aye!"

"We've a shed out back where we have it all set up these days."

"Custom does look good!"

"Oh, aye. Cunyr may not be a kind overlord, but he's good for custom, sure enough. Silver a week, copper for the bath. In advance."

"Did you think I'd cheat you, Annan?"

"Nay, but I always remember that you started on the top of things and might not remember what it's like for the rest of us."

"I've been free of them for nearly half my life now. I have your coin for you."

Padraig smiled because he knew that Annan had

good reason to be cautious of his money-handling skills. He shook out two silver and five copper from his pouch and dropped the coin into Annan's broad palm.

"I'll be here at least a fortnight and I plan to enjoy this bath of yours."

"Going up the hill?"

"Among other business, aye. I'll be down in a moment to care for my stock."

"The lad can do that."

"I'll do it, my thanks."

Shouldering his saddle bags, Padraig mounted the stairs to the second floor and the third floor beyond. The third floor had been built of stone with a full-height ceiling, evidence Annan was planning ahead. Good plan! It looked like custom would be strong for many years.

Padraig shuddered as an icy hand raked down his back. What he was about would not assure prosperity, only that the One's will would be done.

Founding Year 1028
Clarcom

On the morrow Padraig bought a fine pair of grey breecs and a matching cloak and went to pay his respects, and his dues, to the head of the herb guild. Resyn, whom Padraig had known as a high-level journeyman, had increased in his fortunes considerably and was more than willing to trade gossip with the ignoble brother of Lady Lydya, especially in exchange for elven herb lore. Thus armed with valuable intelligence,

Padraig eyed the tops of the towers as he walked toward the dun. It made sense to pay court, but he didn't want to walk into the lions' den unarmed. He checked the position of the sun and returned to the Red Giant for a bag of herbs. He was stocking the bag, using one of the tavern tables, when a figure filled the sunny doorway, ducking under the lintel, and resolved itself into a tall young man with a sword on his right side and the long arms and broad shoulders of a born swordsman.

"I'm looking for the innkeeper."

"Annan's out back preparing dinner. There's room, I know."

"My thanks. I'd find him outside that door?"

"Aye."

Padraig continued packing his bag until the young man returned with Annan just as Padraig closed the bag. The lad's siarc bore no blazons and the breecs he wore were a plain blue, but he carried himself like a soldier.

"Padraig, meet Tamys. He'll be staying with us for a few days. Padraig's an herbman, Tamys." Annan dismissed himself to return to the kitchen out back.

"Herbman, eh?" Tamys noted, which won a nod. Tamys turned to the ale barrel and dipped himself a tankard of dark. He sat down at the table and drew of long swallow off the tankard. Padraig noted his eyes over the rim, the lightest blue he'd ever seen, large and the color of a winter sky. Against his dark hair and skin that still held a tan after the winter, they drew a lot of attention to themselves.

"Where did you say you were from?" Padraig asked, curious because eyes like that were so unusual.

"I didn't say." Although that sort of answer usually denoted a warning to stay away, Padraig tried yet again.

"What brings you to Dublyn?"

Tamys didn't reply, just drank some more ale. The set of his shoulders said it was a subject he preferred to avoid. Padraig had other business anyway.

"I must be going. If Annan asks, I'll be back for dinner."

Tamys saluted him with his tankard and Padraig left to walk up the hill to see his sister.

Fourteen years had seen some changes at the dun; though Clarcom had always been built for siege, the two defense walls had been heightened and thickened. The main broch thrust like a fist against the sky, seven full stories, completely surrounded by half-broches and then joined to a secondary broch by a rectangular wing. Already this new broch had reached five stories.

Padraig introduced himself at the gate and waited in the great hall for the page to return. He hoped that his sister practiced discretion. He somehow doubted Cunyr would be glad to hear he'd returned. If he ever came to suspect the reason why, Padraig might find himself at the end of a rope.

The page returned shortly and said the Lady Lydya would meet with him in her greeting chamber.

Aye, she remembers who she's married to!

This chamber, a pleasant wedge of the second floor of the new broch, sported a real glass window and Morikan carpets on the floor. A shelf held three books, a wealth even by noble standards in those days. On a small cabinet there stood a glass flagon and a half-dozen glass goblets.

Lydya already sat with her back to the window when Padraig entered, noting the real wood walls that offered privacy beyond mere wicker. *What does she hold over his head?*

Examining the room couldn't keep him from looking at her eventually. This moment, so fraught with unknowns and risks, made him profoundly nervous. He couldn't see her face, backlit as she was, but he noted that she was still slim even after six children.

"Padraig of Denygal, is it?" she said in a voice like honey.

"Seemed a more appropriate title."

"It suits you. Even your manner of speaking is Denygal now. You've grown fully a man, Padraig. How many years has it been?"

"Near a dozen, I think."

"And where have you been?"

"Walking about," Padraig replied, using a Denygal term for the journey a lad took prior to being accepted as an adult in the community.

"And did you find yourself?"

"Aye, I believe so. And you, my lady, has your life been all that you might hope it to be."

"Life is both lovely and awful in its turn, somewhat that you will come to understand as you live a few more years."

"I already realize that, my lady. Truly, I can assume that marriage to Cunyr would not be all a bed of roses."

"Roses have thorns, don't they not? Are you married?"

"Nay, but there's a woman who may someday be my wife."

"Do you travel together?"

"Nay. And, you, my lady? Are your children a joy to you?"

"Children are much like life – joy and sorrow in equal measures, but overall, I am pleased."

"I hear that some believe Bryan will make a good vyngretrix."

"If he lives, aye, I believe so."

"Tis a dangerous thing to ascend to the rule, I hear."

"I think you did not want to know."

"I would never have known, Lydya. My position was a long way from the rule."

"You know that Father died?"

"Aye, nine or 10 years ago. I heard Gerraent became heir."

"Nay, but he died less than a year after his ascension and Radraig did follow. Then he died four years ago, about the time you rode east, I suppose."

Padraig stepped so that he could see her face. Beautiful in the Denygal way that seemed to attract men so easily, she looked much younger than her 47 years, with lustrous chestnut hair and turquoise colored eyes. Seeing her now, as a man would see a woman, Padraig couldn't understand why Cunyr would take a mistress, no matter how young and pretty.

"How do you know where I've been?"

"Your accent. There's only two groups who speak Celdryan with those tones – the Denygal and those who have lived among the elves. Besides, if you'd been anywhere in the kingdom I would have been able to scry you out and I couldn't. Only in an elf holt could I see naught of you."

"Truly?"

"Truly. Why did you come back west?"

"That's a difficult thing, my lady. The telling of it could be a great burden or a great joy."

"You may tell me anything, brother, as if I were your own dear mother."

Padraig felt a clench around his heart. Can I trust her, truly?

"I want to trust you, but I am not sure if I dare," he admitted.

"I too would wish to trust you, but I am uncertain."

"Well, that's a fine kettle of fish." She smiled at the Believers' symbol of secret identification.

"You're a Believer like Mam and I, then. Truly, I do love to hear that. When did you accept the One True God?."

"Before I went off to page, from Mam I did hear it. And you?"

She nodded. They smiled at one another, more connected than they had ever been. Then Lydya sobered.

"You know that she's dead?"

"Aye, she died about a month before I left page. I think her death had a lot to do with my leaving when I did."

"'Tis a pivotal thing, to lose a beloved parent. Why did you remain hidden after Father's death?"

"I fled page to avoid him. I had no interest in taking

up his legacy."

"You did not care for him. What did he do to you?"

"He was himself and that was enough. I walked away as much to stay clear of him and Berys as I did because I loathed the idea of a life spent waiting for my turn to die in some petty honor feud."

"Berys is dead as well." When Padraig blinked, she continued. "After Radraig's death four years ago, along with his wife and two children. Reyn's the rig of Cenconyn now."

"Is that how you came upon the rigdon of Denygal?"

She laughed. It sounded like bells chiming in a light breeze.

"We came upon the rigdon, my brother. He set the rigdon upon the both of us."

"Why would he do that since I had been missing for 11 years?"

"Only seven by that time. He asked me if you were alive and then he set the rigdon upon both of us. It solves all the petty issues of the rule passing in the female line. And sharing the rule is not unheard of in Denygal, though there are some who think it unusual down here."

"Is that why Cunyr shows you such deference?"

"I hold more over Cunyr's head than a vote on the Council of Electors."

"Truly? Are you able to tell me about it?"

"Nay – or, truly, I might, but I think we should talk a bit before I tell all my secrets."

Their shared smile gave Padraig a moment of thought.

"Does Cunyr treat you as well in private as he does in public?"

Lydya remained serenely beautiful, but she turned her violet gaze away for a moment.

"Few Celdryan noblemen treat their wives with true love, as you know. Once the bloom is off the rose, they look elsewhere."

"I have never understood that thinking, especially not with a woman as beautiful as you."

"Thank you," Lydya said with perfect aplomb. "I think I've put her in her place," she continued as if discussing the quality of cheese at dinner. "And truly, I don't resent her Cunyr. She may have him if she likes."

"That's a practical view."

"It was never a marriage based on love, Padraig. Father forced me to marry him and I come as close to hating him as I can come without violating God's laws."

Padraig nodded, understanding. He knew another woman who had been unjustly treated by a husband and she had made him understand what she felt.

"Tell me of your children," Padraig prompted.

"Bryan is 15 winters. He's a fine lad, Padraig. A Believer. Cunyr's betrothed him to the daughter of Dun Blyan. I'm wondering what we'll be getting. I know I can't expect him to be able to marry a Believer, but I was hoping."

"Maybe she'll be reachable. None of us is born Believing. Bryan doesn't sound at all like his father."

"Hmm," Lydya hummed, then paused before continuing. "He's nothing like Cunyr, that is true," she continued in a tone that caused Padraig's hair to stand on end.. "Cullyn's much more in his pocket." She paused as if thinking of somewhat. Whatever that be, she chose not to share it. "I love my children, truly I do, but it's hard to like that one. Then there's Glynn. He's a charming one! He's not come to Believe yet, but I hope. I think he will. He at least has a conscience."

"And Shyla? She's your eldest lass, aye?"

"Aye. She's going to do wonderful things, if her husband will let her, of course. She's betrothed to the fourth son of Galornyn. Teddryn. Do you remember him?"

For a moment Padraig's mind was blank. He truly remembered only the three older boys and a younger girl who died of a fever while he was at page. He didn't remember – or did he? There'd been Jaryn, Stevyk, Maddw and, aye, it might have been Teddryn, and there'd been a much younger brother as well.

"If it's the one I think, he liked horses. He was a young lad – 10 mayhap. I remember naught about him. Are you buying a pig in a poke?"

"Aye. It was Cunyr's idea, to secure the alliance, and I've felt a bit at a loss for knowing naught."

"I'm afraid I can't help you."

"I can only hope that he'll be besotted with her, enough to ignore what she believes. I'd hate for her to have to lie for the rest of her life the way I've had to."

"Aye, 'tis not an easy life. I'm sure it's hardest when you think of your children. Mam managed to tell some of us, but not others. Surely, you have the same problem."

"Aye. The time alone with each is precious. Mam managed that pretty well with us lasses. I suppose the younger boys as well."

"What of Reyn, since he's acted so honorably about Denygal?"

"He was at page in Denygal at Mam's insistence, if I remember it rightly. And, aye, he is a Believer."

"It seems the Belief always flourishes even in danger."

"Like the Denygal rose. So will you at least be staying about for a while?"

"Nay, my lady, but I must travel on. I wait upon the supreme commander, now don't I?"

"True spoken. And never would I deny your mission, my lord."

"I am not a lord, sister, and it is best you remember that."

"Oh, but you are! You're the rig of Denygal, after all."

Padraig chuckled.

"So, besides all the turnips I can eat, what will that afford me?"

"Safe haven if ever you need it, of course. My squire would take you in without hesitation. And coin. I've not much on hand right now, but I'll get you your earnings. I've been keeping some back for you."

"That's not needful, Lydya. I make a good living by the sweat of my brow and in these times there'll be lots of physicking to do."

"Aye, but I have an honor of my own, brother. You'll have your part of the rigdon, I promise you that. Now that you're back in the kingdom, I should be able to scry you out easily enough."

"Aye. Well, I'll be about for a bit – an eightnight, mayhap a fortnight. I hear your chirgeon's looking for physick of a strange sort. I believe I might have what he needs. You'll let him know?"

"Oh, aye. I'll be telling them that you're a distant cousin from Denygal who chose a commoner's life because you were the 10th child."

"Well and good, my lady. This is a sack of kitchen herbs with some exotic spices. That'll cover things for today. Your tale should cover the rest. I'm staying at an inn called the Red Giant. It's near the old market."

"I'm sure Traegyr can find it. Be careful, brother. What you seek, I sense danger may follow it."

"'Tis true, my lady, that danger will stalk this prey. I thank you for your prayers. One thing, though, truly, how did you know that I had become an herbman?"

Lydya laughed.

"Lodiac, your master, came to me a year after you'd disappeared. He wanted a prentice fee. I sold a fine brooch to get the coin."

"Truly? I suppose that explains why he didn't want a prentice fee from me." Padraig laughed. "Now I know why."

"I think he liked you well enough, Padraig. He was an old man just trying to keep food on his plate."

"That I know. I thank you for being able to provide what I could not."

"No thanks necessary. I did it for love of my brother. I'd do it again without hesitation."

Padraig glanced out the window, noting the position of the sun.

"I should go before there's gossip. Remember what I told you."

"Aye, I'll pass the information on to Traegyr as soon as soon."

"Let him know that I'm no fool and that I want solid coin."

"I'll do that," Lydya assured him with a mischievous grin. "Now off with you before someone does start waggling their tongue. I'll scry you out when I need to."

They embraced briefly and she ushered him out the door. Padraig left the dun straightway, though he made a bit of a show of looking up at the dun as though it were some marvel he'd not seen before.

He returned to the Red Giant just in time to help prepare the meal — spit-roast chickens and basted turnips with fresh baked bread and ale. Since he owed Annan for his help over the years, Padraig didn't complain about chopping vegetables.

"Did the lad decide to stay?" Padraig asked.

"Aye, though Heledd isn't at all pleased. She reminds me that freeswords attract trouble. She does not understand why I would take one in."

"You always have, though, haven't you?"

"Aye, since the day I opened my doors. The gods only know that I might have been one of them, but for a bit of luck on my first scrap after I was kicked out of the warband. I ransomed a lord's son and got a fair bit of coin. Heledd doesn't know that side of me, so she thinks we should be proper and safe and not take coin from the likes of Tamys of Mulyn."

"Is that where he says he's from?"

"Nay, he has not said, but his accent is from Mulyn."

"Where is he, anyway?"

"He went upstairs to his chamber. He'd had a fair bit of ale and needed to lie down for a bit."

Padraig nodding, knowing of what Annan spoke. Just as dinner was ready, the patrons began to trickle in in ones, twos and threes – young merchants, mostly, a scholar, a traveling priest, a traveling bard. The bard was a nice boon, for he sang for his supper and bed. For a man four years free of the kingdom, Padraig found himself hearing news that he'd not heard before. When Padraig had left the kingdom, there'd been two main combatants for the throne – the Eagles of east Mulyn and the Hawks of west Mulyn. They'd been the two main combatants for the near-century of civil war that had held the kingdom in its iron grip. Recently, the Falcons of Fyrgal had thrown in their claim, which the bard seemed to think might be a bit stronger than either of the traditional claimants. He wove a pretty story, singing in his strong bard's voice, telling of the kingdom's life which for the people at the inn was interesting news they might not hear again for years.

"Which shall it be, good people, which shall it be? Whether Eagle, or Hawk, or Falcon. Which bird of prey will sit the throne?"

Padraig smiled secretly to himself, for the Lord's own prophesy had promised that "no bird of a feather shall rule the aviary."

When the bard pled thirst a rain of coins followed and he sang another song, this one concerning the cormorants of the southern coast, suggesting the Maille of Dun Llyr might also have a claim to the throne. Padraig dredged around in his memory for a connection, but none came. Finally, when the bard could not be induced to sing another song, saying he'd entertain a bit later, Padraig followed him to the ale barrel.

"Good herbman, would you like a tankard of dark?"

"Nay, but I've had my fill for the evening. I'll stand you a tankard, though, for a bit of information."

"Of course, so long as I don't have to sing it. What do you want to know?"

"You were suggesting the Maille might have a claim, weren't you?"

"It's rumored, aye."

"Based on what?"

"The Maille's great-grandfather was married to a bastard daughter of the royal family. His claim on bloodlines is less strong than any of the others, but the fact that the city holds the river trade – well, it's a right good rumor and makes a lovely song."

"Has he made noises to the claim?"

"Not as far as I know, but the son who just ascended to the rule is a proud man."

"Son? Which of the sons?"

"The bastard was legitimized last year, barely days before his father's death. He'd like to shove it in the faces of those who have held him down, I'm sure. And, truly, there's even rumor that he might have a claim on his mother's side."

"His mother is common, isn't she?"

"She was, but there's apparently a connection. I

hope to hear of that connection when I journey to Dun Llyr this summer."

"You say the Maille is a proud man. What sort of man is that?"

"As his father's warband captain he was quite the hero, but one wonders about one who was not meant to rule becoming a vyngretrix. He was certainly never allowed at the councils until his father legitimized him."

"Why did he?"

"The legitimate heir died in one of the wars. Now there's a thing to consider. The Maille, Lord Howydd, was war leader against Fyrgal many times and his brother was killed in battle against Fyrgal. I have to wonder if he might throw in his bid simply to revenge himself against Fyrgal."

As he hadn't heard of any of this before, Padraig really hadn't formed an opinion. How does it affect my mission?

"Why do you ask such questions, herbman?" asked Tamys, who had come to dip a tankard.

Padraig startled out of his reverie.

"Just considering my options for hire," he replied. "An herbman makes his money best round war."

Sometimes the stock of sayings that Lodiac had bored him with came in handy like. Tamys accepted his explanation without questioning and moved away to drink his ale in solitude. The lad sat with his back to the curve of the wall and he looked toward the door whenever anyone came in. Padraig, watching from a discreet distance, didn't think the lad looked hunted. He seemed more like he was used to being the hunter.

Padraig doubted the lad had been a freesword very long. In fact, he'd be shocked to learn the lad had ever sold his sword. The very fact that he'd asked after Padraig's curiosity showed that he knew somewhat about politics. Few freeswords picked up that sort of understanding, despite the wars they rode and the many duns they tarried in.

The bard started singing again after a bit, but the mood of the crowd had turned bawdy, so Padraig retired to his chamber. He sat down on the comfortable clean bed and pulled a picture codex out of one of his saddle bags. The sound of music filtering up from the tavern room provided an eerie backdrop to the message the pictures conveyed. Drawn on stiff pieces of bark, tied at one end, the 10 leaves had four pictures each. To the unlearned observer, the pictures told a meaningless story, but to one who knew what they meant, they served as a memory device for calling up the Scriptos. Padraig scanned the first one.

The mountain of the Lord will be established as chief among the mountains. Many people will come and say 'Come, let us go up to the mountain of the Lord, to the house of the God of Jycib. He will teach us His ways so that we may walk in His paths

Go into the rocks, hide in the ground from dread of the Lord and the splendor of His majesty. The eyes of the arrogant man will be humbled and the pride of men brought low. The Lord alone will be exalted in that day.

Men will flee to caves in the rocks and to holes in the ground from dread of the Lord and the splendor of His majesty when He rises to shake the earth. In that day men will throw away to rodents

and bats their idols of silver and gold which they made to worship.
They will flee to caverns in the rocks and to the overhanging crags
from dread of the Lord when He rises to shake the earth."

Padraig hadn't the slightest idea how this scripta matched up with his prophesy, but the Wise Ones had been certain of it. Certain enough that they'd bound the codex and sent it with him. Padraig assumed that the One True God would reveal the meaning to him a bit at a time, as He did most things.

Padraig acknowledged how tired he was, his eyes beginning to tear and his head to nod as he prayed. Padraig closed the codex up in his saddlebag and lay down on the firm straw mattress with the clean sheets. He'd just dosed off when he heard rattling at his door. Sitting up in the darkness, his hand groping for his long knife, Padraig thought it ironic that trouble would find him so soon. Then the rattling stopped and Padraig heard someone muttering oaths under his breath. It sounded like young Tamys, though a fair bit past drunk. Padraig waited until he heard the lock on the door opposite his unlatch before he lay back down. The music had stopped downstairs, but there were still some sounds, as if the travelers were laying out their bedding and the like. Padraig uncurled in the heat his body had made under the blankets and started to dose off again. Human or elven, the sound of a community settling down for the night had a relaxing quality to it that Padraig doubted he might explain to anyone. Just as he was about to fall off into true slumber, a little voice inside his head asked him a rather interesting question.

How does a dishonored soldier like Tamys, a man most likely turned out of a warband with only his gear and two coppers, manage to afford the luxury of a private chamber at the Red Giant?

Padraig was too sleepy to wake up enough to answer the question, but he knew he'd have to deal with it in the morning.

Fog

Celdryans live short lives, so that they quickly lose the past in the fog of the present. They believe much that is questionable, yet they hold to their truths passionately. Among these truths is that Rune was not a settled land before they arrived. Such speaks strongly of their arrogance.

Saroynan, scribe of the collegiate (FY 102)

Founding Year 931
High Celdrya · Spring

Due to a childhood spent in bed, Donyl had exhausted the library at Dun Celdrya a long time ago. It remained his favorite part of the huge dun for the smell of old paper, ink and leather, but today he did not have time to linger for Perryn's soon-to-be brother-in-law was reported to have arrived and Donyl wanted to speak with him. One should always thank those who saved one's life, he thought.

His bad leg protested as he climbed the winding stairs to the outer broch that housed the library. He'd been too long in the saddle on his journeys this summer. Despite the pain, he needed to walk, to stretch out the thickened tendon and keep the weak muscles limber. He assured the librarian that he could find his own way, which the man well knew, and set off through the shelves to locate his savior.

Donyl found Blethry in the very back room, standing upon a ladder, examining a shelf of scrolls far above Donyl's head.

"You're Perryn's brother, then?" Blethry said when Donyl introduced himself. He was young, his head fresh shaven clean. In keeping with his order's traditions, as his hair grew out, he would maintain a small tonsure, which would be gradually widened as his status grew. "I suppose you want a word," he said, moving toward the floor immediately.

"If possible, aye," Donyl said, his cheeks growing hot. Both his elder brothers had taken advantage of the respect their titles commanded, but Donyl had never felt comfortable with such behavior wielded by himself. The thought that Blethry was climbing down just to speak with him proved embarrassing.

"Shall we walk?" Blethry asked, indicating the nearby rear steps. "I hear there's a nice view from the roof."

Donyl didn't much care for stairs, but had a good head for heights so agreed. Soon they were standing on the flat roof, overlooking a portion of the great city.

"What are those houses?" Blethry asked, indicating row upon row of tiled roofs just the other side of the dun's defense wall.

"Merchants quarter," Donyl said. He had not noticed before that many of the merchants houses had generous yards behind their dun-like outer walls and that these were often filled with crates and barrels. "I was meant to be you, you know," Donyl confided, looking over the city. A freshening breeze tousled his wavy front locks.

"I am aware," Blethry admitted. Donyl glanced at him. "A bookish prince is the one they'd offer to the temples," the young priest explained. "Though I would assume your father wanted you to be a Lughan."

"Aye. That I've no interest in the priesthood at all

and far less for the Lughan cause was not judged worthy of thought."

"Perryn explained such to me when I arrived. Truly, I am Old Faith and the Bel, though different from my experience, is a good fit for me," Blethry explained. "I will strive to serve your brother well. You needn't worry that I have been inconvenienced, for I have not been."

"Thank you. I did wish to thank you, and I do, though I am glad to hear that it is actually your calling. I think one should have that for the temple and I never did."

Blethry nodded. He might only have been a couple of years older than Donyl. His shaved beard was still soft and there were no lines about his eyes or mouth when he smiled.

"Did you have more to speak with me about? I think you might."

"Aye. My brother Maryn -- have you heard the circumstances of his death?"

"I have. Somewhat troubles you?" Blethry phrased it as a question, but his gaze was direct.

"All the witnesses speak of the full moon, but that is now, not two weeks' gone. At least, that is what I believe. I seek verification."

"The librarian …."

"Can verify the information, but not give me the Old Faith perspective on it."

Blethry cocked an eyebrow, then nodded.

"There are Old Faith legends that talk about the full moon out of time. The dark of the moon favors a goddess called the Morigan. Her power can become so great that it manifests itself in the sky as a chariot that men mistake for the full moon."

"Is this possibly what happened?"

"It is a legend, sir. Legends often have a basis in fact, but I cannot say with certainty that the prince was killed by an ancient Celt goddess. There are certainly other more reasonable theories."

"The Assassins Guild?" Donyl provided.

"Truly."

"They cannot cause the full moon to rise out of season."

"To my knowledge, nay, but they are allied with sorcerers, so mayhap ...."

"Sorcerers?!! Come, good man, you are not serious!"

"Prince Donyl, sir, I know that the Lughans deny such takes place, but the Bel are aware that these men work within the kingdom. All that arises from the Old Faith such as this is usually brought from Gawl."

Donyl's heart squeezed and for a moment it felt like an icy hand swept down his back. He shivered in the warm sunlight.

"Do you have more specific information?"

"Nay. I could send to my brother's councilor and acquire some," Blethry offered.

"Do so. I will share this with my brother as soon as I might and I thank you for your candor."

Blethry nodded, but then caught at the sleeve of Donyl's siarc.

"Understand that the Old Faith does not condone this. It is heresy. We just know of it."

"I do understand," Donyl soothed. "As soon as you

have more information, share it with myself or Perryn ... King Perryn. Do you understand?"

"I do." Blethry cleared his throat. "Mayhap I could ask you ... my sister ... will Perryn be an attentive husband?"

"Attentive? Are you asking if he'll have mistresses? Rumor has it my father never did until my mother's death. I don't much remember myself, but Maryn spoke of it. Will that be answer enough for you?"

"It assures me a bit. We're close, you see. I want what's best for her."

"I admire that. I want what's best for Perryn as well. You speak well for your sister."

Blethry smiled at the compliment. They would be friends if given a chance.

Founding Year 1028
Clarcom

Several days passed without hearing from the chirgeon of Clarcom. As luck would have it, a spring rain blew in and flooded the roads, keeping everyone indoors. Padraig found his mornings spent curing the aches and pains of the chilled and damp townsfolk and his afternoons spent in mind-numbing boredom. He began to wonder if his sister's influence reached as far as she thought it did. There was naught to do for it, as the roads were unpassable. He used his time to good end in gaining a new friend, for Tamys was the only patron who remained in the inn the whole time and he was as bored as Padraig.

Padraig found the young soldier a puzzle to study. His speech branded him a Mulyn man, but his features found Padraig sometimes wondering if he might have some Denygal blood. He had long, slender fingers and the full mouth that Padraig knew so well. He wore a rider's clothes, plain blue breecs and an unblazoned shirt, but his manners and way of speaking indicated some court training. He might have been a servitor's son, trained for the warband and turned out for some reason of honor. Certainly the lad had a taste for ale that might cause a point of honor to hinge upon his tongue, though he was laconic enough with Padraig. Padraig tried to puzzle out an age for him, but Tamys had the studied wariness of a seasoned soldier with the features of a much younger lad. Padraig finally guessed his age at 18, though he supposed he might be as young as 16 or as old as 20. From time to time, especially when he'd had a few tankards of ale, Tamys would let his guard drop with Padraig and let slip with a few bits of information about himself. Padraig though he was not so much taciturn as private and that deliberate silence intrigued him.

One day, while the rain dripped heavily from the thatch, Padraig and Tamys sat by an open window, dicing for splinters. Padraig wagered only splinters because it was against his principles now to gamble for coin and Tamys seemed not to care. Despite the friendliness of the game, Padraig noted an uncanny ability to guess the fall of the dice in his companion.

"Have you thought of what you'll do, soon as it

stops raining?" Padraig asked.

"Naught, truly," Tamys admitted, taking an automatic swallow of ale. "It's still new yet."

"Aye, but you can't remain here much longer. Caravans will be hiring soon and if you want a place in a warband, you'll have to find one in the summer."

Tamys flinched. Padraig did not stay his hand at honesty.

"I speak as one who knows what it's like to be suddenly upon the roads with no plans for the future. Starvation lays that way, my friend."

"No doubt," Tamys agreed. He sighed, then let go with the most honest statement he'd made since his arrival at the Red Giant. "There's just somewhat that galls about selling my sword."

"True-spoken. You're young enough you might find a place by saying your lord's been killed. Certainly there have been many of them meet their end in the last few years."

"You mean find an honor position by lying?" Padraig could sense Tamys' injured honor rising to a sharp edge. The lad had not yet accepted what his new life meant in terms of honor.

"Unless the truth will do, but I think it will not."

Tamys shook his head, admitting without words what Padraig had already known. The lad took a long draught of ale.

"I suppose I'm trying to ignore the situation. I know I can't do that much longer, but herding mules doesn't sound like much of a living, nor does lying, nor does selling my sword. Were you faced with the same at one time, herbman?"

"Somewhat. I ran away from page when I was 13. I wasn't ready to join a warband and I had no other skills. An herbman took me in. You could likely find someone who might take you in the same way."

"I'm a bit old for a prentice," Tamys objected. "And, I don't much fancy being a farmer."

"Selling your sword's a short life and a troubled one."

"I know that." Tamys' mouth tightened. Padraig let him work out what he wanted to say. "Sword's the only work I know. And it wouldn't do to lie my way into another warband. Sooner or later, I'd be found out and hung for a dishonored lout."

Padraig answered slowly, recognizing that a common rider, unless of unusual skill, could easily become lost in a warband a long way from the territory he'd come from. Tamys had all but admitted to being noble born.

"You'll have to make your own decisions, of course. Just remember that freeswords never have honor. No matter what glory your sword wins you, no matter how sought after that skill may be, you'll always be viewed as little more than a thief."

"That I know, which is why I languish here in Pedyr's hospitality. Soon enough, though, I'll need to make my decision."

The outside door opened and a man and a young boy came in with the rain. Padraig recognized the plaid of the man's breecs, where they showed beneath his cloak, as that of Clarcom. The lad approached them after a moment of shaking the rain from his wool cloak onto Annan's clean floor.

"I am looking for Padraig of Denygal, an herbman."

"Who might be asking?" Padraig asked, just to be surly.

"Lord Traegyr of Clarcom," the lad intoned as if speaking a prayer.

Padraig felt Tamys stiffen even from the other side of the table, so that Padraig glanced at him. Tamys stared at the man by the door, his pale eyes narrowed with suspicion.

"And what does Lord Traegyr want with this Padraig of Denygal?" Padraig asked.

The lad glanced at the man by the door. Padraig's eyes had finally adjusted to the change in light since the door had been opened and he saw Traegyr now. Of middling height and squarely built, it was difficult to tell with the cloak if he was merely burly or fat, but he had jowls like a temple dog and a double chin.

"Herbs," the boy squeaked. He stared at Tamys now, who stared boldly at the lord.

"Aye, well, I might be having what he wants."

"You're Padraig of Denygal, then?" The lad looked from Tamys to Padraig, unable to feign his relief that Padraig, not Tamys, was the sought-after herbman.

"Aye, I am." Padraig swung clear of the bench and walked the length of the room to the spiral stairs. "Let's discuss our business in my chamber, shall we, Lord Traegyr?"

The toil to the third floor winded the chirgeon, which was exactly what Padraig wanted. He closed the door and turned immediately to question the chirgeon.

"My cousin, Lady Lydya, tells me you're seeking herbs for congestion of the blood."

"Aye. Do you have such?" Traegyr wheezed, mopping his forehead with a finely made handkerchief.

"We wouldn't have come up here if I didn't," Padraig assured him. "How much do you want?"

"All that you have."

"Nay, I'll give you a year's worth, naught a jot more."

Traegyr's cheeks flushed red, but he stayed the hand he wanted to wield. It wouldn't have ever landed, for Padraig had trained enough for the warband to be able to protect himself against any mediocre swordman and Traegyr was not armed.

"I'm willing to pay in hard coin for all that you have," Traegyr clipped out.

"You'll pay in hard coin for a year's worth."

"Now, see here – ."

"I see perfectly well, thank you. I have somewhat that you need, somewhat that it is very rare and only available from a source that will not deal with you. I can command the price, I can command the amount. I can chose not to sell to you at all. Others may have need of what I have. You'll get a year's worth, if you get any."

Traegyr's pig eyes narrowed even more, but he puffed out his breath and agreed.

"How much are you asking?"

"Ten silvers," Padraig said calmly.

"Ten?! I could buy a cow for that!"

"No doubt, but you'll give me ten silvers or you'll

get naught."

Traegyr looked strangled and Padraig wagered the coin might walk out the door, but he didn't really care. The sooner Cunyr died, the sooner Lydya and her children would be free of his influence. Padraig could always make more coin.

"I've eight silver and enough copper to make two silver."

"I'll weigh it out," Padraig assured him, indicating Annan's scale, which he'd borrowed.

Traegyr sighed and began counting out the coin. Padraig began spooning up the various herbs that created a blend that soothed the nerves and loosened the blood within the veins. He held back the pouch of herbs while he counted out the coin.

"You understand that the herbs don't truly work alone. They require a change of life – quieter, less rich food, less drink."

"I have made medicine my life's study. I assure you I know how to use these herbs."

"I know herbs, Traegyr. It's my obligation to warn you of the side effects."

"As I said, I know what I am doing. Your advice is not needed, herbman."

The way he said herbman made it clear that he judged Padraig skills and training a poor substitute for his own. Padraig wasn't insulted. He merely handed over the pouch and opened the door to usher Traegyr out.

Standing at the top of the stairs, waiting for Traegyr to exit the inn, Padraig felt a chill hand run down his back like a warning. When the chirgeon of Clarcom had left, Padraig returned to the tavernroom.

"I like that man naught at all," Tamys announced when Padraig sat down at the table. He took a long swallow of ale. "The man creeped my flesh."

"Mine as well," Padraig admitted. "I'm moving on tomorrow," he announced. "Why don't you travel on with me? I feel the need of a sword at my back and I can pay a bit of coin toward your maintenance. It would give you a bit of time to decide what you want to do."

"Where will you be going?"

"Initially, Dun Celdrya. I don't know after that."

Tamys nodded slowly.

"Aye, I'd like to travel on with you." He shuddered suddenly. "Are you sure you don't want to leave tonight?"

"Too wet, though it looks as though the rain has blown over. The roads will be a bit better on the morrow. And, I have a bit of business to conduct before I move on. In the morning, at dawn."

Tamys nodded. Padraig excused himself, telling Tamys to let Pedyr know that he'd be back in time for dinner.

The ward of Dun Clarcom was properly cobbled, but all the side paths were a mucky mess and, despite the clearing of the rain, the denizens of the dun were still indoors. Padraig walked past a fort guard that remained huddled under the protective roof of the high walls. He contemplated whether he should go to the main hall and announce himself or try to find Lydya in her greeting chamber, when a side door of a side broch opened and issued forth his sister and a whirlwind of plaid and dark hair. The lad was chattering happily as he towed his mother toward the stables. He ran right into Padraig, so intent he was on his mission.

"Sorry, lad," Padraig said as Lydya laughed at Danyl's startled expressions.

"Who are you, sir?" the lad asked.

"Padraig of Denygal," Padraig replied gravely.

"Are you a cousin then?" the lad asked. His eyes caught the dying light and Padraig marveled at the green of them.

"Somewhat of the sort, aye."

Danyl frowned.

"My mam has a brother named Padraig as well," he noted. He hunkered down to watch some ants walking among the cobbles.

"So she does," Padraig replied, looking at Lydya for guidance; she merely grinned like a berserker. "What are you looking at there, lad?"

"My name is Danyl," the lad announced. "And, I'm looking at ants."

"What do you make of them?" Padraig asked, hunkering down beside him.

"They seem to know what they're about, very workmanlike and all."

Just then, Padraig heard the cry of a bird of prey on the hunt. They all three looked up.

"Bit late for that," Padraig murmured. He felt Lydya shudder.

"'Tis the night-hawk," Danyl identified. Padraig felt a cold hand grab his stomach and jerk itself through his body. "Mam, may I go feed the horses?"

"Aye. Here's the carrots we got from Cook. You run along now."

When he'd disappeared into the stable door, Padraig cleared his throat to make whispering easier.

"He's not Cunyr's child," he identified. Lydya's eyes widened as she stared at him, suddenly wary. "There's no judgment in that, my lady. I'm sure you have your reasons."

"I did not put horns on my husband's head," she assured him.

"Were there only time for us to discuss it," Padraig lamented. "When the night-hawk cried, I knew that Danyl might be important to both sides. Raise him well. Has the wild blood shown yet?"

"He's a handful," Lydya admitted.

"And likely to grow in that," Padraig agreed. "Is he half? Well, more, considering our mother?" Lydya nodded. "Much exercise, outdoors, might help. He's only a little lad, right now, so he needs to be a child for the time being. He's a long way from the rule, so it won't matter if he's a bit wild. Cunyr will likely want to keep him for the warband, but have him trained to read."

"Thank you."

"You'll not thank me when you learn that I'm to be on my way," Padraig admitted.

"Truly?" Lydya asked, distressed.

"It's time I moved on. I'll leave on the morrow. I've just come to say my goodbyes."

"Well and good," Lydya said with a sigh. "You were honest that you were not staying. I'll scry you out and get you the coin I owe you."

"No rush. My skills net me a good living."

"I'm sure they do," Lydya replied with a brilliant smile. When Padraig glanced at her sharply, she laughed. "Traegyr returned a bit ago. He thought if he waited a bit you'd be desperate to sell. Instead, you got him over a barrel and near broke his back. Fair job, Padraig!"

"I warned you that I was far less than noble these days."

"Aye, and I passed that news along to him, but he didn't believe me. His mistake."

"Mam!" Danyl cried. "The piebald has a new foal! Come see!"

"Be there in a moment, dear," Lydya called back. "I must go as well. Every new thing is exciting at that age, and you're certain it will fade away in a moment if you don't share it."

"I remember," Padraig said with a smile. "Go with God, my lady."

"You as well."

"Mam!"

Laughing, they departed from one another, Lydya to return to her life as the Lady of Clarcom, and Padraig to return to his life as a missionary of the One in the guise of an herbman.

Night settled round the city and lights lit one by one. Cows and chickens were penned, lovers met in the lanes, and meals were served in homes and taverns. A man in a tower lit a candle to scry to a man on the southern coast, to tell him of one he had met who might turn the world on its top.

Viking Date 741 / Kindred Cycle 24573 – Founding Year 1023
Northern Coast · (Five Years Past)

The pier Gil had departed from a moon past had settled into the sea, blocking the junque from entering the ancient harbor. The long boat had pulled alongside for Gil then slipped past the leaning block of salt-weathered dwarven flow stone to put in on the pebble shingle below the collapsed dome of lumina.

Nature had reclaimed the broken city to where it took a keen eye to see what it had once been. Trees grew out of the rubble of the dome, belying what lay in the cellars. Half of Erik's crew had been here before and the other half had sailed past it, deeming it not worth their effort. They were mature men, masters of the sea and sword, sent to keep the heir safe on his maiden voyage. Still, they did as told when commanded.

Gil did not much like the sea. It seemed a treacherous conveyance. He silently rejoiced to have his feet upon solid ground, albeit wave-washed pebbles. When he met the junque here, he'd felt the broken city echo with disapproving ghosts who liked his worship of the goddess not at all, but today the burial place of Kin society was just an entryway to his future, a place from which to stage their reconnaissance. *My ancestors hold no sway on me. I will crush them beneath my boots.*

"Where is your ship going?" the Svardin youth asked, hand casually lain upon the hilt of his sword. The Vik were as turbulent as the sea they traveled so easily. Tall men with long ropes of blond and reddish hair and blue eyes in wind-burnt faces, they were given to quarreling among themselves and drawing steel. Too like the Celtmen in Gil's estimation, but to carry out the goddess's desire, he must needs make alliances and the Vik were the strongest alliance he could make. The sea was strong too … and you learned not to turn your back on it.

Gil glanced to see the junque sailing around the eastward headland.

"They're about my employer's business," he lied. Perhaps the goddess was through with them. He'd left naught aboard, so no matter if it did not return. In comparison to the Vik, the Orental were quieter and more difficult to read. Gil had never guessed their thoughts and that worried him a bit. "We will not be needing it, as from here we ride."

"Ride? Over those?"

The mountains stood leagues back from the shore, but the Roof of the World could not be diminished even by distance. They were enormous, a colossal wall of rock on the southern horizon that stretched as far east and west as the eye could see. The tops of them were clad in snow even in summer and most Vik believed them impassable, as they or their fathers had tried to breach them. Magnus had been willing to consider this only because Gil had sworn he had a way through them.

"Not over them. Under them."

Erik's crew were detailed along the shore, two securing the long boat, the rest investigating the area. The rattle of pebbles as they ascended the slope would wake the dead … or at least the horse handler the goddess had provided.

"How do we go under a mountain?" Jarl, Erik's second, asked. He claimed to have thoroughly searched this city in his younger years and found naught but mice and trees.

"The Kin have a saying – 'The map of the world is laid upon the past.'" Erik and Jarl seemed less than impressed by old Kin sayings. "We see a shattered city, picked clean over the centuries, slowly crumbling to dust." He gestured around to make his point. Only the eye of knowledge revealed this as a city, for the ruins were well fallen. "The elves left something behind," Gil explained. "The city was a long way from the basketlands. They had a way to come and go and it has lain here dormant for all these centuries."

"And you know it's here?" Jarl demanded.

"I do, because it's how I came to be here."

He led the way up a ramp of broken stone through a twisting copse of trees that seemed to be growing out of a hill of rock. The citadel had not completely collapsed. Lumina only looked delicate. With effort, they wriggled through the boles and under the leaning curve of the wall until they stood in what had once been a massive open space that now felt about ready to bury them. In the dim interior, Gil picked his way through the scattered stones to touch one of the lumina globes on an inner wall. It slowly gained light.

Erik's eyes flared wide while watching Gil.

"How do you …?"

"I'm Kin and the lumina stone reacts to my touch. The Wisdoms can make it shine like a lantern, but this is about all I can do."

It was enough light to reach the next globe.

"Witchcraft," Jarl spat when Gil kindled the third globe. They were within a sloping corridor thick with dust, walled and roofed by cracked stone. No doubt his temper was influenced by the close quarters.

"I've no abilities that way. That's Wisdom's work. These systems were designed for ordinary Kin, including the byways."

"Byways?" Erik asked. His youth gave him a different view of this venture. His eyes sparkled with excitement.

"You'll see soon enough."

They were twelve globes in when the corridor opened into many. On the far right was the byway. Water seeped through the wall of the smallish chamber and pooled in a low corner. Two pillars stood before them with only a few feet beyond. The pillars were cast of a stone Gil had never seen before – blue and translucent, more gem than rock, decorated at intervals with lustrous orange stones set in bands. Gil placed a hand on each of the pillars and waited. As before, the byway opened slowly, but then the back wall of the chamber seemed to dissolve and a long highway corridor stretched into the distance.

Jarl took a step backward, his lips disappearing into his reddish beard. Erik gasped and gaped. Both Vik laid hands on hilts.

"Once opened, it will remain long enough to get a sizeable herd through. My presence appears to hold it open."

Erik had moved to the side of the leftward pillar.

"There's nothing on this side," he reported, his voice hushed in awe. "How does it work?"

"I'm not altogether certain. The Kin know of byways, but we were told they were inactive. I'm not interested in arcane knowledge, so I paid no attention until my employer showed me how they worked."

Gil saw Jarl's glance, warning the kong-heir in some way. *What aren't you saying?* Erik ran a callused finger over a beardless chin and shrugged.

"Taking the summer kingdom has always been impossible because of those mountains. If magic brings us glory, then so be it."

"It's not magic," Gil corrected.

Jarl moved to the right side pillar to see what Erik had.

"Looks like magic to me, emissary. And, magic always comes with a price, Erik. Your father sent me to follow you and talk sense when sense is needed. Be wary of what we walk into. That's all I have to say on it."

Erik frowned.

"I see a problem. No horses. Or is the journey truly short?"

"Nah, we'll need horses. And I have more than enough." Gil walked away from the pillars, leaving the two Vik to scramble after him, glancing over their shoulders at the still-open portal.

Founding Year 1028/Kin Cycle 24578·
Blue Iris Holt (The Present)

Belsynsarala lay upon the stone, panting in the humid darkness as steam rose from her body. On the edge of her hearing were other Kin, talking of their daily tasks or the ability to control the elements, perhaps both and everything in between. They were a long way off, near the entrance to the bathing caves and unlikely to find her secluded alcove up near the ceiling.

Yesterday had been her 21st breath day and Sarala's mother had not shown for the celebration. It was not unexpected that she would find other diversions. Sarala could count on one hand the numbers of time her mother had acknowledged her breath day. Still, the 21st … it was meant to be momentous and yet ….

The Wise who had essentially raised her had done their best to soften the blow. She'd gotten a fine mare from Gly's herd and been honored as a student and community member. It should have been enough. It was not. How could it be? The circumstances of her birth tainted every good thing. In the nearly two five-cycles since her mother's marriage, Sarala had hoped each breath day to lay aside the name that marked her with shame. Her mother's mate had kindly offered his own name several times since the marriage, but Maryanara had never initiated …

Calm down! You're an adult now. Your name is your own to decide.

The voice was Gly's, speaking through the years, reminding her that the Kin never held the circumstances of birth against her. Only her mother's shame had become her shame because she had clasped it to her chest. It was her burden only so long as she chose to carry it.

It was rare for a Kin to change one's name. It usually followed a period of repentance under *goi'tan* grey, but when the shame was not your own, the change was painless. It could be done on a solstice after a breath day. One simply stepped into the circle and announced the desire. There were several Denygal in the holt who had chosen their names. All that she must do is come up with one …

Sarala knew that she was drowsing. The stone fell away from her and the warm air grew heavier. Although the baths were public, there were few places safer to drowse. Her alcove was on the edge of the dark passage that led to the men's bathing area. She was essentially alone as she slipped deeper into sleep.

The winter sky resided in his eyes, framed by dark lashes. Below him an army amassed, more rolling in from the horizon even as she became aware. A dark spot moved above the roiling crowds, bobbing slightly as a flight of arrows raced from earth to heaven. A beat like a heart tickled her ears and then died as the blob came closer to view, wings outstretched, legs splayed forward to touch the earth.

Sarala's hand splashed in the water and she jerked awake, back in her alcove once more. The beating was her heart, made bold by the heat. She rolled off the ledge to stroke to the cooling floor. The massive iron doors stood open to summer sky, but the floor was empty. Sarala sprang from the water to walk barefoot to the basket of towels and barrel of rainwater. The water tasted deliciously cool. One of the elemental Wise no doubt had been here while she drowsed. She sat upon a bench by the open doors and stared out across the valley. Far below were the horse herds, but she could not see them without leaning out and they could not see her at all. She used a hand rag to wash the heat from her skin and waited for her heart to stop pounding.

The bathing pools occupied the lowest level of the kinholt, a watery subterranean cavern of warm water and low light. Near the entrance was a bathing station and on the far end the cooling floor, a place for the more adventurous to rest after a tiring swim through the steamy waters. Since you couldn't see the bathing station, it might have been in a different cave altogether.

Leaning back against the stone, Sarala drowsed again. A child lay limp in her arms. Not an infant, but a child old enough to walk and feed himself. Eyes as green as emeralds opened and then his body stiffened and flailed. His weight dissolved like crysal sugar in the rain and she saw him walking toward the winged creature, dwarfed by its massiveness. It lifted its horned head and opened its mouth. Huge fangs flashed white in the sun and ….

Sarala jerked awake as Barana sprang up from the pool. Her foster mother grinned at her and dipped a drink of water before wrapping herself in a towel and sitting down. Sarala pulled the towel she's been laying on across her torso to be polite.

"Some days the baths are busier than others. I did not mean to startle you. What were you dreaming?"

"Dragons," Sarala admitted reluctantly.

"Really? That's interesting."

"Why interesting?"

"Gly mentioned dragons – to do with Ryanna."

"If Ryanna saw a dragon it would be a real one and it would talk to her. I just dream them."

"Perhaps, but there is a feeling in the air – like something is holding its breath, ready to burst forth into life."

Silence lay between them for several heart beats.

"I don't feel anything," Sarala admitted. She rose to slurp water, holding her unbound dark hair out of the barrel. "What if I wanted to walkabout?" she asked.

Barana hesitated only a heartbeat.

"That would be your choice as an adult," she replied. "Perhaps it would settle your thoughts. Where would you go?"

Now there's the thorn bush!

"The basketlands."

Barana's purple eyes widened.

"That's a concerning choice."

"I look Celt."

"Yes and a beautiful Celt you would be – as your mother was."

"Ryanna walked among them."

"With a sword, posing as a lad. You've no skills like that."

"My herbcraft --."

"Will not protect you from wolves. Please pray and consider before you make this decision. We cannot stop you, of course, but I pray you remember that we love you and hope you will think of the risks as well as the adventure."

She tossed her towel into the basket and dove off into the water, leaving Sarala to contemplate her future.

Journey Begins

Some say the Temple of the Moon came from Gawl, that women there were equal to men. Some say the practice sprung up here when women objected to the priests drawing us away from the Old Faith's raw worship to more civilized forms. I cannot say which of these theories is correct, but I must say that the Moon is at its strongest in its dark phase.

Dagvyn, priest of Bel, FY 834

Founding Year 931
Dun Manahan, Mulyn · Spring

The babe stirred within her, actually visible under the thin material of her dresses. It wouldn't be long before her child would be born into this world. And what a world it would be. Dark and powerful, full of promise and pain. She smiled as she felt the limbs of her child move under her skin. Burcan had no idea what she had planned and she meant to keep it that way. That was easier with him gone to the High City. She could work toward her own ends and surprise him later with the outcome. Her child deserved the effort it would take. Aye, her child deserved the world.

Founding Year 1028
Clarcom - Spring - (The Present)

After Padraig enjoyed a hearty breakfast in the solitude of the family rooms, enjoying the fine company of Annan and Heledd, he and Tamys set out early from the inn and cleared the town gates before there was any warmth to the sun. Padraig paused outside the gates to look up and down the road. Here the town wall stretched along the roadside, forming one side of it.

This was a king's road, though long ago the maintenance had been taken over by Clarcom. As such, it was well-paved and higher than the surrounding plain. At Clarcom's gate it ran north and south along the wall, but the broad breadth of the road turned west at the southwest watch tower. A smaller, lesser used track continued to the south. Padraig had come from the north. The road west would take them direct to Celdrya, but there were more ways than one to travel to the High City. Tamys waited patiently in the road while Padraig formulated his plans.

"I said that I am bound for Dun Celdrya, and truly, that is my only destination this day, but I would not risk a man's life. Is there a concern in the direction of travel?"

Tamys raised an eyebrow in surprise before soberly pondering the question.

"West is better than north and both are better than south, if only because that road wants wear."

"Used to be lovely farms down that way until the pirates began to take the farmers' children," Padraig told the lad, turning Joy westward. "Cunyr, the rig here, managed to put a stop to it, but the farmers haven't truly returned as yet."

"I'm not looking for a farm," Tamys reminded him. Inherent, yet unsaid was that he would eventually need to sell his sword to survive. Padraig rather hoped they would pass a truly inspirational farm along the way, but he knew it a sad hope. The lad rode a bay gelding with a warrior's saddle which he sat with an ease that bespoke of many days of many years on horseback. Whatever his start in life, Tamys had been bred as a soldier and naught else. He would not find a farm to his liking. Padraig scanned the countryside ahead of them.

"We'll be traveling through a fair number of those," Padraig assured him. "But you may ignore them if you wish, so long as you aren't rude. Rudeness might cost me some custom."

"Aye," Tamys grunted. Again, Padraig wondered about Tamys' background, for the lad was more than a soldier, of that he was certain.

The days were lengthening and the ground was thawing, but the nights were cold enough to frost, thus, they could not travel very far in a day and Padraig was not driven to do so. He thought mayhap he was to take this journey to make connection with Tamys and he spent a good deal of time merely observing the lad and praying for him silently. Tamys himself proved easy with a jest, though not forthcoming with personal information, so that he made a comfortable companion upon the road. Padraig had already liked him, but he found himself enjoying his company more with each passing hour.

The road west from Clarcom was busy enough that they spent a good deal of time in the ditches as they passed farmers making their way to market with the young-born of Imbolc while shepherdesses with their dogs guarded the fields on either side of the road. The first night, they slept in a copse of trees a watch's journey from a small village without a dun of its own. Tamys showed that he'd been in the field often enough, gathering wood and building a fire while Padraig sought water and dressed the game cock he'd taken with slingshot in the afternoon. They sat quietly by the fire and rolled into their blankets when it became dark. They set out just after dawn on the morrow. Padraig had to continually remind himself that he mustn't travel too late in the eve as Tamys might object to not being able to see.

Initially, they traveled through a prosperous and protected area. No one seemed in great want, even after the winter's famine, and the folk didn't seem suspicious of travelers, merely curious. Padraig had to admit that Cunyr had done a good job protecting his demesne, even if his taxes were higher than most folk wanted to pay. They occasionally passed warbands upon the road wearing Clarcom's colors, testament to the provisioning that Cunyr had undertaken. Much as Padraig did not care for his brother-in-law, he had to admire his administration. His father had not done so well at protecting the countryside. Mayhap he had not thought it necessary. After all, they were mere peasants and not for a great lord to worry about. Cunyr, as vile as he might be, might actually have been an improvement over his father and Padraig was willing to accept that. Certainly, he wasn't going to complain about the safety of the roads in Dublyn.

Not that he thought it likely he need worry. He was traveling with a soldier and he himself was not untrained with the sword he wore, though truly he thought the long knife would be what saved him. While Padraig hoped not to encounter brigands (the only menace likely to bother them this far from the coast), he felt more comfortable with a fellow at arms riding near. There were times when Padraig wondered if he had truly left the warband as far behind as he thought. It seemed as if he were thinking like a soldier now and of that he marveled.

The second night, the pair camped off the road in yet another copse of trees. The early evening was pleasant, so that they sat up past dark and drank tea by the fire. Tamys spoke more freely of Mulyn, though without enough detail for Padraig to puzzle out from where in Mulyn he hailed. Padraig told him a bit about Cenconyn and Denygal, not truly keeping any secrets other than that he was a Believer. He even let slip that he had spent a good deal of time among the elves. It was well dark when they rolled into their blankets, not exactly tired, but growing uncomfortable with the cold. The nights were still chill and neither wanted to sit up shivering by the fire when they had good woolen blankets to snuggle in. Padraig had been having a pleasant dream of sitting by an elven communal fire when somewhat awoke him. Heart thumping with unexpected fear, he thought to see torches flaring against the night and hear the snort of warhorses. Tamys sat up into the darkness beside him, reaching for his sword.

"Somewhat comes," the lad noted in a hushed tone, turning upon his knees toward the east.

"Aye," Padraig agreed, reaching for his long knife..

Without discussion, in complete silence, they rolled up their bedrolls, stuffed their gear in the panniers and slung saddles upon horseback. Joy danced, stamping her foot impatiently as if she too sensed the danger riding their way, but she did not blow, as if recognizing the need for silence. A moment later Tamys' bay tossed its head, jingling tack, but also not blowing. A seasoned warhorse, it likely heard afar off what they could not hear, but only sensed.

"We'd best be going and quickly," Padraig said.

"Not by the road. Follow me," Tamys said.

He mounted and trotted his horse off into the darkness as if it were noon bright. Only Padraig's part-elven eyesight allowed him to keep track of his companion, for his pace was quick and his course sure. Tamys paused long enough to lop a broad leafless branch free of a tree with his sword and tie it to the pony Earnest's pack saddle to sweep the ground behind them clear as they rode. Tamys had apparently noted a lesser road due south that they could follow, for he set off down this. Occasionally he would stop, turn and stand in the stirrups, checking their back trail.

"They've reached the camp site," he announced. "We'd best leave this road altogether."

A moment later, their horses splashed into a stream. Tamys turned his bay downstream and they rode along for about a mile until he urged his horse up a bank beside a mill yard. He skirted the palisade and then dropped into a second stream that the miller had built for some reason of his own. A moment later, they swam into the mill pond. Across it, the bank opened onto a wood. There they waited, standing still in the dark.

Not a sound, lass, Padraig thought to Joy. He didn't know her thoughts yet, but he sensed her laughing at him. She was indeed quiet. Tamys held his horse's head and Padraig held Earnest's, trusting that Joy understood the gravity of silence. They were near-to the road, but far enough away to be hidden by the early spring leaves. They could hear riders upon the paving stones and the voices of men calling back and forth, meaning that they would be heard if they or their horses made noise. They stood there scarcely breathing until near-dawn, not speaking. Finally, Tamys relaxed visibly.

"I think they believe they missed us," he whispered.

"I think so too. You are indeed a soldier that you could sense that coming our way."

"Aye, well, I've been well-trained," Tamys said prosaically. "Do you think it was the chirgeon of Clarcom?"

It took Padraig a moment to reply, for he was shocked that Tamys had known this. True, the lad had complained of the man's manner, but Padraig would have thought him less astute than that. He is indeed no mere soldier.

"Traegyr, aye, that I do. We'd best stay off the King's road for now. There's a cart road to the south, leads through more of those farms you're not interested in. Any objections to traveling at night until we reach Blyan?"

"You're paying me not to have objections," Tamys reminded him. He glanced at the sky which might have grown a bit lighter than a few minutes before. "Still lots of night left." He unlashed his bedroll from behind his saddle, pulled his mess bag from a pannier, and wrapped himself in one of the blankets. "I'll take the first watch," he told Padraig, settling his back, standing, against a tree, drawing his dagger to cut himself a chunk of cheese.

Padraig wanted to protest, but he sensed that Tamys

was a better choice. The lad was used to such shortings of sleep. Padraig felt desperately tired and chilled to the bone. Accepting this, he rolled into his blankets and slept, comfortable with Tamys' guardianship. He awoke at midday to find Tamys eating a cold lunch of bread and cheese and watching the mill wheel across the pond. Night had given way to a beautiful, even somewhat warm day and Tamys had doffed his blanket, though he remained standing against the tree. The trees were newly green with erupting buds and Padraig's nose was suddenly quite aware of growing things under the dusty smell of leaf mold.

"I've heard folk upon the road when it's quiet, but I think Traegyr did give up," Tamys reported, storing his food. He looked candidly at his traveling companion. "Do you want to tell me why he'd follow you with a warband 10 strong?"

"I've somewhat he wants, but I wouldn't sell it to him. I hope Annan and Heledd are well."

"No doubt they reported that you'd moved on and he left them as he found them. It wouldn't do for the chirgeon of Clarcom to be abusing a prosperous merchant," Tamys assured him, proving once again that he'd had a nobleman's training. "Those must be some precious herbs," he said doubtfully, but then shrugged, retrieving his blanket from the tree he'd hung it in. "I'm for my blankets. We'll set out at sunset, aye?"

"Aye," Padraig told him. Tamys gathered his blanket, spread it under a bush and wrapped himself in another. Quickly, he was asleep, leaving Padraig to sit up and watch the mill wheel and wonder why Traegyr had pursued him. Was it just for the herbs or was there another reason? The second had a resonance to it that he could not explain. Traegyr would have counted the herbs as an added incentive, but he had another reason for pursuing Padraig. What was it? Padraig could not say, yet he knew in his heart that Traegyr had meant him harm and that he would not give up so easily. They'd best be on their toes for the next few days, wary as cats and twice as sly.

Founding Year 1028
Dunmaden · Spring

Gregyn stared at the clouds, trying to scry. It was difficult to do in the saddle, moving down the road, in the company of riders. Truly, he would avoid such, except that it be needful. Lord Teddryn had brought his war band north to hunt brigands and he wanted them found. Talidd's last instructions were to distinguish himself so as to gain the nobles' trust. Roprick, the tracker, hadn't picked up the trail yet (thanks to the wildfolk covering the tracks on Gregyn's request), but not finding the brigands wouldn't do what Gregyn needed. Finding the brigands was imperative, enough to warrant scrying in the saddle.

Gregyn had recognized that he had skills other apprentices did not. He could scry using clouds, for example, and call the wildfolk. He remembered their humor and pranks from his childhood in the city. They'd helped him find food and shelter and kept him from feeling utterly alone. He had grieved when they had stopped coming to him on the island and been quite surprised when they had reappeared at the dun. The longer he was out in the world, the more wildfolk seemed to flock round him, except for the few days he'd spent back with Talidd. He realized, as he had been too young to realize before, that ordinary folk and black mages could not see the gnomes, nymphs and sylvans. More than seeing them, Gregyn could command them in small and growing ways. This morning they had erased the tracks of the brigands that were near the road, but now they were seeking the tracks that would lead them to the camp.

There was just one problem – wildfolk were unreliable at complicated tasks and finding a brigand camp in the woods was apparently more complicated than erasing a few horse prints at a crossing. Having come this far by trickery, he must now rely on true magicks – in the middle of the warband, on the road, in the saddle. Would the apprentice prove his worth this day?

An etheric window opened in amongst the clouds. Gregyn could see his band upon the road. To the south lay forest as far as the eye could see. To the north, there were hills wrapped in trees. Reasoning that the brigands would seek shelter, Gregyn turned his attention toward the north, toward a granite tor thrust up from a round hill. Gregyn narrowed his vision and swooped down toward the tor, spying men squatting round a low fire, talking. Gregyn broke the vision by tapping three times on the saddle peak. A stream ran north to south at a ford they'd already crossed. It was very close to where the prints had been before the wildfolk had erased them. He turned his horse out of line to ride up to Teddryn, who was berating Roprick in a low tone for his inability to pick up the trail.

"A word, my lord?" Gregyn said to Teddryn.

"Aye, lad. What is it? You are in Wergyn's squad, aye?"

"I am. I think we missed the trail." Roprick, a thin dark man who reminded Gregyn of a whippet, subsided into his saddle, sighing. Gregyn couldn't tell if he was irritated by the interruption or grateful that Gregyn was presenting himself as a target for the lord's ire.

"That's obvious, lad," Teddryn remarked. "Tell me somewhat I do not know."

"I worked for a caravan before I came to Galornyn. One of the guards knew a lot about hunting brigands and he told me somewhat about streams and hiding their trails."

"There were no tracks near the stream. I checked wide," Roprick objected.

"If they walked in the water, there would be no tracks to see," Gregyn explained.

Teddryn looked at Roprick who shrugged, then nodded. Teddryn turned to stare back on the road.

"It's a short distance, my lord," Roprick said. "The lad is right, that we should take a second look. The water was deep. I judged too deep for men to walk, but mayhap horses could have managed it. They'd not have stayed to the water long. We should be able to pick up a trail if it exists."

Gregyn sent a picture to the wildfolk of a river bank. There was naught more he could do than that. Teddryn, Roprick and a squad of five, Gregyn included, rode in advance of the main vanguard. The stream crossed the road without a bridge, leaving a muddy mess at the crossing. Roprick didn't even bother to quit his saddle. Any prints left by brigands would have been destroyed by the passing warband.

"Lad, did this guard give you any ideas to look right or left?" Roprick asked, just the slightest hint of mockery under his tone.

Gregyn knew this was a dangerous game he played. If he didn't deliver brigands, he'd face mockery and a loss of status. Still, he couldn't make it seem too easy. The spring leaves were out on the trees, so that just the top of the tors could be seen above the forest.

"The tors might provide shelter," he suggested. "Caves and suchlike."

The water to the north of the road was too deep for horses, but Roprick said naught, for he wouldn't want to call too much attention if it turned out the brigands were indeed in the woods near the ford.

Gregyn dropped out of his saddle and looked about the ground as if he had some clue what he was doing. The trees nearest the road were not thickly grown, so leading his horse, he walked a bit off the road, still scanning the ground. Teddryn had used the search for brigands as a training exercise and ordered the war band to wear full padding and mail shirts. Sweat trickled down Gregyn's back as he searched the ground for clues. The wildfolk had done their job – else the tracks were left from before. Here and there, near the stream bank, he could see scuffs in the dirt that suggested horses passing. Roprick saw them too and moved to the fore to lead the squad toward the tors. Gregyn swung up into the saddle to follow as Teddryn dropped back to direct the rest of the guard.

The squad rode silently through the trees along a narrow trail that might have been made by deer. Green-dappled sunlight shone down on them. Gregyn felt a tug on the reins of his horse and looked down to see the green gnome that most often came to him pulling on the reins and pointing round the other side of the tor. Oh, clever brigands. They had gone off trail.

Gregyn knew they were far too many for one man alone, but Wergyn was right behind him, so he stopped his horse and pretended to be tracking.

"Lad?"

"I think they've missed the trail again," Gregyn whispered, pointing to what might have been a rabbit trail.

Wergyn made room for Lord Teddryn, who nodded as if he could see what Gregyn was showing. Gregyn considered ensorcelment to speed things along, but it seemed subterfuge would work as well. Truly the nobleman seemed not to understand tracking at all.

"Should we recall Roprick?" Wergyn asked.

"Nay. He'll meet us on the other side, catch them in a pincher. You may lead, Wergyn, with your clever young rider."

Gregyn managed not to startle when the green

gnome popped into existence riding on his horse's neck. Wildfolk were unreliable, but they could be very useful. The gnome had scouted the area and while incapable of speech or useful knowledge like distance, it did know the location of the camp. Before long, the gnome proved its worth, waving its warty hands and pointing with long skinny fingers. Through the trees, Gregyn could see a shed roof for sheltering firewood and a line with clothes hung upon it. Since he was second in line, he raised a hand to stop the guard. Wergyn recognized a gap behind him and reined to a stop. Gregyn gestured that he'd found the camp. Wergyn responded with gestures of his own. The men dismounted and spread through the trees, surrounding the camp in a wide arc. Gregyn scanned the band and marked the leader – a tall man with a coat of mail instead of stitched-together leather.

Gregyn drew a war dart and awaited Wergyn's call. For a moment, the forest held its breath. The signal came soon enough – two long whoops – and the war darts flew. Gregyn struck the leader in the shoulder and spun him round, but it was merely a graze. The war dart fell away, leaving a ragged tear in the mail which soon shone with blood. The man staggered back, then drew his sword and rushed straight for Gregyn as men throughout the clearing broke into fighting duos. Gregyn drew his sword and met the leader's charge. Steel clanged against steel and sparks flew. Gregyn slammed his shield into the man's face. The leader was as tall and heavier than Gregyn, but Gregyn had youth and vigor on his side. The leader stumbled back, trailing blood from his shoulder, then swung his sword again. Gregyn blocked it with the shield, slipped under and up and felt his blade turn on the mail. The leader's blade slapped into Gregyn's mail, stinging his shoulder. The heat and weight of mail were beginning to tell on Gregyn's fighting prowess. Gregyn slammed the shield forward, but the leader braced his arm against it and pushed back, bearing Gregyn backward into a tree. The wind driven from him, Gregyn landed on his back and cowered beneath the shield, realizing this was not going to be an easy victory. This fellow had been a soldier before he'd become a brigand. There were men dying round him and he'd best make quick work of this before the tide turned. The leader hammered on the shield, which was painted wood, and it began to split just left of the boss.

There is power in aethyr, earth, air, fire, and water. The blood flowing down the brigand's siarc glowed with ethereal power. Gregyn drew from the aethyr, felt it flow into him as pure energy. He pushed with his crumbling shield, kicked with a up-flung leg and sprang to his feet. The brigand stumbled back, surprised at the strength, and fell. Gregyn's sword cleaved the juncture of the mail twixt torso and arm. The man's eyes showed shock as Gregyn drove the sword deep into his guts. Gregyn lowered him to the ground on the tip of his sword, placed his foot against the man's chest and pulled the sword free. Blood welled and the man's eyes grew unfocused as life fled.

Another brigand roared and charged Gregyn who, in his aethyr-empowered state, merely parried, swept down and under and back up to gut the man with hardly an effort.

It was a rout. The brigands were no match for a trained band of riders. All round Gregyn lay bodies of men killed by his fellows. A few brigands had escaped into the surrounding forest, but they'd gotten most of them and that was enough.

Gregyn was wiping his sword off on the dead brigand leader's threadbare breecs when Teddryn strode up. The tall, broad-shouldered lord had apparently taken part in the fighting, for there was a spray of blood cross his face, globs of red hanging in his light brown beard.

"Lad, well done!" he announced. "Truly, you may well be a better tracker than Roprick."

"Nay, sir. There is much Roprick knows that I do not. But I appreciate the honor, sir."

"You'll make a fine rider, lad. Two kills and one against a trained swordsman. You've done well. I'm asking Roprick to train you as his second."

"Thank you, my lord," Gregyn replied. As Teddryn walked away, Gregyn turned and looked across the brigand camp and saw somewhat that pricked his heart. The wildfolk stood on the edge of the encampment, watching as the war band stripped the bodies preparatory to burial. If a word described what Gregyn saw there it would be sadness. The wildfolk were deeply grieved over the bloodshed here this day, standing off to the side, sucking their fingers, their mouths gaping with soundless mourning.

Gregyn felt anxiety swell within him. He'd killed many animals in his life and dealt his share of cruelty. A black mage's apprentice needed to be hard. Yet this was the first man he'd ever killed. He'd seen others kill their first. They always cried or retched. It was mayhap a rite of passage. Yet he had just killed his first and he felt, barely, sadness. The death itself did not truly bother him. And it was that lack that truly did needle him. If the wildfolk grieved the death of men this day, was it not human to feel grief at the taking of a life? And if he did not feel grief did that mean he was truly not human?

Shadowplay

The priests parted ways during the Time of Troubles. By all accounts, the archives show that there was but one sect of Celtic religion when our people came through the Portal. It appears to have looked a great deal like the Old Faith. I can understand why people moved away from that. So messy and time-consuming. Yet we had but one set of priests from the third century on until that time. Records are sketchy, but it would seem that the priests disagreed about how to solve the Troubles or mayhap which king should rule following those times, so they split and moved into two sects. The priests of Bel remain the wisest of the wise, but the Lughans do have the ear of kings.

Halidd, Royal Historian, FY 753

Founding Year 931
High Celdrya - Late Spring

Perryn saw Donyl to the bolt hole on the night of his departure. The man he had selected as journey captain had served bravely at Maryn's death and Perryn felt certain Pedyr would be a loyal honor guard captain for as long as needed. Deryk had recommended him and Donyl seemed comfortable with him. Indicative of his intelligence, Pedyr entered the bolt hole, saying he'd wait a bit in for Donyl. He'd already been given ample instructions by both Deryk and Perryn and understood that the brothers needed a moment of farewell. Truth be told, Perryn wanted a moment for more than just formality.

"Learn all that you can and come back to guide me," Perryn said while Pedyr's lantern disappeared down the corridor. It faded around a corner. Perryn dropped his voice to a whisper. "I'm entrusting you with somewhat of great importance." Donyl gave him a quizzical look. Perryn opened a chest he'd placed right at the bolt hole entrance just for this occasion. Inside were set five objects worked in elven gold – a key, a cup, a ring, a locket with a white stone, and a message tube. "It is said that the Fey king used these as the crown jewels – the symbols of his sovereignty. King Branioc took them and the power of the land passed to him. During the

Time of Troubles, the items passed to our line and secured our rule. We must keep them safe at all cost."

"And you believe they would be safer with me journeying to the wilderness than here in the treasure vault?"

"Aye. My gut says this."

"Then I am honored with your trust," Donyl assured him. He cocked an eyebrow as Perryn opened a tuck sack and began placing the items, wrapped in squares of cloth, within.

"It can't look as if you're carrying the most valuable treasure in the kingdom," Perryn answered the unspoken question. "Secure these in a pannier or better yet, this haversack so that they are with you at all times. Put clothes on top. Keep them out of view." Perryn worked to hide the tuck sack and secure it as he spoke. "When you get to Denygal, find someone trustworthy and ask after them. None know how they actually work."

"Aye. Denygal is said to still have the descendants of the Fey living there. Mayhap the secrets have survived in their collegiate."

"That is my hope." Perryn noted the torch light growing stronger at the corner again. "You should go," he advised, handing Donyl the royal sword in a plain scabbard. Donyl donned it with shaking fingers. "I wish you could stand for me at the wedding, but this is the better way."

Donyl nodded and they embraced. If Perryn seemed to hold him a bit longer than was ordinary, Donyl wished that they could stand there longer, but he knew that sovereigns must make hard choices and when

Perryn eased his hug, Donyl responded likewise.

"Good journey, my brother," Perryn said.

"Perro, keep safe," Donyl replied. Then with a wrench of will, he shouldered the haversack and limped toward Pedyr.

Perryn stood for a long time staring down the bolt hole. The tunnel actually passed under the river and came out in a village northeast of the city. There'd be horses and men awaiting Donyl's arrival. Eventually, Perryn swung the bolt hole closed and arranged the treasure shelves in front of it. Only the sovereign and his named successor could know of the bolt hole's location. The captain of the guard was permitted to know of its existence. It was a last means of retreat in the event of disaster.

Perryn felt tears well up as he finished his task and stood for a space of time gaining control of himself. He was truly alone. He wondered if the Fey depicted in the murals on the foundation walls surrounding him had felt this solitary as they had faced the armies of the Celts so long ago. The bolt hole was made of similar material. Did it date from their time? Mayhap Donyl would learn such at the collegiate.

The dun had grown quiet since they'd come down here. It must be past the second night watch. Perryn took a circuitous route so no one would note that he'd been to the treasure chambers. Deryk and he would cover Donyl's absence for a few days by claiming to have talked with him. Donyl preferred solitary pursuits, so like as not no one would notice they didn't see him.

Perryn had not yet gotten used to going to his

father's chambers at night. It had been less than a fortnight since the funerals, so it was understandable that he still wanted to turn toward the secondary broch where he'd been lodged since his majority rather than toward the chamber he'd thought would never be his. He remained unused to having servants stationed just outside his apartments. Tonight it was only the young page, Jortham, who sprang up from polishing a pair of boots that didn't need polishing and offered to do Perryn's bidding.

"Nay, but I am fine," Perryn assured him. "I think I'll withdraw for the evening."

It wouldn't do any good to dismiss the lad. He was there not just to serve Perryn's wishes, but to sound an alarm in case of danger. He no doubt had some skill with the short sword he wore. His father was a younger son of Galornyn, a house known to train their young early.

"If there's anything you require, sire, please do not hesitate to call."

Perryn assured the lad that he would and entered the apartment. When he'd begun the move into his father's apartment, Perryn had scarcely cared for furnishing it and most of the items belonging to his father remained. Vanyn's tastes were subdued and dignified. Perryn saw no reason to waste energy changing them. His bride would no doubt have her own ideas and that would save the young king the trouble of developing any of his own.

Perryn sat down on a bench in the ante room and tugged off his boots, leaving his socks atop them for a servant to deal with, then walked barefoot into the greeting room. The lights were low, so that it was the perfume that drew his attention rather than the sight of her. Malona sat upon a divan in the far corner, a book open upon her lap, her lustrous black hair loose about her shoulders. She looked up as Perryn froze in surprise.

"My lord," she greeted, her beautiful golden eyes meeting his with candor.

"Malona," he greeted. She must be 10 years his senior, but he'd never seen a more beautiful woman in his entire life. "What brings you here at this watch?"

She set aside the book, but remained reclined on the couch. Despite her age, her bosom was firm and her waist narrow.

"Your father's books are not enough?" she asked regally, too elegant to simper.

"If you'd simply wanted to borrow a book, the page would have been glad to loan it."

Perryn reminded himself sternly that he would have to find suitable punishment for the young page. Not somewhat severe, but sufficient to assure he recognized his regent's displeasure at not barring the door to intruders.

"You may have a point there," Malona said. "You may find me quite useful," she added. "Vanyn certainly did."

"My father obviously valued your service as his mistress. I marry on Lughnadsa. What have you to offer me?"

"We could arrange service as your father knew," she suggested, but then added quickly, "but that is for later discussion. What I have to offer you at the moment is of greater value."

"I'm listening."

She wore her gown cut low for a woman of her age, revealing the tops of her breasts and tantalizing him. The dark blue silk reflected the lantern light.

"I control a network of eyes and ears that Vanyn used extensively," Malona explained. "Sadly, they did not warn me of the plot against his life. I was focused on solving Maryn's death instead."

"And?"

She rose and walked to a table where a silver tray held a pitcher. She poured out two goblets. Perryn smelled Hanolan wine. She sipped from one of the goblets as she offered him the second. This was a sweet vintage he'd not tasted before.

"Maryn despoiled Gillian of Llyr," she explained.

"They were betrothed and neither was a virgin. Where are you going with this?"

"There's a child."

"How do you know this?"

"My eyes and ears are everywhere."

"She can't be even two months along."

"Aye, but it is a problem for you."

Perryn sipped at the wine. If there was indeed a child it was a complication, but not insurmountable. He'd already been crowned and Maryn and Gillian had not yet been married. A bastard child had never unseated a sitting king. Even the Troubles had required the death of the sitting king to seat the bastard heir.

"I'm still waiting for you to prove your worth," Perryn said.

"You don't think that news is valuable?"

"I'd have discovered it soon enough when her father showed up to request recompense."

"Aye, but now you can be prepared for it. Vanyn appreciated the advanced warnings I could give him."

"Hmm, there's a point there, no doubt," Perryn agreed reluctantly. As they were talking, she'd been moving closer to him until now her breasts almost touched his chest. A tall woman, her eyes almost met his on a level. "You're suggesting I keep you about for this service?"

"I am worth my keep on several levels. You're to marry Ylaena of Clarcom, aye?"

"I am."

"What do you know of her family?"

"They were thoroughly vetted by my father and it was a marriage my mother favored from Ylaena's birth. We were to be married next year, but Father requested the wedding early when Maryn died."

"What do you know of her father?"

"You've a point to make. Out with it," Perryn ordered.

"A very ambitious man, Jochryn of Clarcom. He's married his daughters well, but his jewel was going to a younger son. Mayhap you will not be able to trust your father-in-law, but more, you may not be able to trust your bride."

"Are you saying he had somewhat to do with Maryn's death?"

"Mayhap. I've my eyes and ears trained that way." She smiled at him and Perryn felt himself smiling back.

She laid a hand on his chest, just below the blazons of griffins.

"My lord, I can be many things to you, if you are willing."

Perryn's instinct was to step back, but he did not. Her hand was warm through the linen and her eyes huge pools of gold that absorbed him into their depths.

"What would you ask for your services?" he asked.

"Nay, only that you keep me as your father did. I keep my apartment, may commission clothing and art to my liking at a reasonable level and receive an allowance that I may pay my spies."

"Was Daumyr aware of these arrangements?"

"He is."

"Then I will speak with him and get back with you …."

She pulled him into her embrace just then and her full mouth pressed onto his willing lips.

"I promise you, you will enjoy every minute of my company," she told him.

With a groan, he swept her into the bedchamber, trailing garments behind them.

Founding Year 1028
Southern Dublyn - Spring (The Present)

Padraig and Tamys packed quietly just before dusk, securing anything that might bang about, then set out on the cart road in the night, passing farmsteads and meadows and the closed gates of villages. Because it was waxing half moon, they could see to travel, and Padraig counted it to God's bounty. Although he could see well in the dark, he couldn't see as well as day. Regardless, he knew that Tamys would protest if he betrayed how well he actually did see in the dark. For some reason, he felt that the moon did not favor Traegyr, but he could not have said why. Usually a moon in its bright phase made seeking easier, but he thought Traegyr, having missed them the night before, had spent the day searching and would rest the night, giving them time to travel far off.

They spent another day in a deep pocket of trees, taking turns sleeping. The following night, they traveled again. Come morning, Padraig did not stop, but pushed on to a nearby village where they reprovisioned their bread and then traveled on. By late-afternoon, he was drowsing in the saddle and Joy was starting to stumble. They found another wood and burrowed into it.

"I think it's safe to travel by day again," Padraig told Tamys as they built a low fire in a shelter of high rocks.

"If you believe it so," Tamys said, showing that he had never commanded a war band, but that he'd been close to the commander. He didn't question, even if he might wonder. He could measure the situation based upon the information he'd already gleaned. He didn't need to argue; mayhap knew when it wasn't worth it.

They slept long that night and neither kept watch, though Padraig knew Joy was sleeping lighter than usual and that Tamys awoke once or twice to listen to the night. Padraig himself sensed their watchfulness even as he himself slept. Morning dawned chill and bright and they began their journey a bit late in the morning.

By late-afternoon, Padraig had stopped at an inn to hang out a shingle for herbs and spent the rest of the day earning them a place to sleep in the hay loft and a bit of coin, some of which he tried to give to Tamys, but the lad declined, saying that he had coin enough until a later time. This again piqued Padraig's curiosity. Who had provisioned a lad fresh turned out of a warband? A lord's son might have had siblings or a mam with coin and that would explain it, Padraig thought. He knew it would do no good to ask, for men like Tamys valued companions who didn't ask uncomfortable questions. Still, he wondered about what had sent a son of a Mulyn lord upon the roads. Some point of honor lost to the bottom of a tankard, mayhap.

Watching that night as they sat in the common room, Padraig wondered that it might have somewhat to do with a lass, for Tamys was quite social, though merely chivying the lasses. He didn't seem interested in retiring anywhere with them. Still, that wouldn't entirely mean that he mightn't have lifted the skirts of a noblewoman. That would get one turned out onto the roads if one were a younger son. Somehow, Padraig thought it somewhat else. Tamys seemed the sort of young man who would brag about his conquests, not turn taciturn and brooding when anyone even came close to the subject. Nay, there was a mystery to Padraig's new companion and he meant, in time, to know what it was, not for any wont to gossip, but because Padraig more and more wanted to see Tamys come to the Lord and change his direction in life. He knew it would take time and he was willing to go where ever the Lord might lead.

Thus resumed their leisurely journey toward Averblyan. Some days they traveled a full day because the villages were that far apart. Other days, they stopped and sold herbs for most of the afternoon. If Tamys thought this strategy a bit nonsensical, he said naught. It was on the eightnight that they began to have their first true conversation beyond light banter. It was while scouting out a ford downstream from a fallen bridge over the Averblyan that it began.

"It must have been a beautiful kingdom once," Tamys murmured, looking toward the bridge. "Imagine what it must have taken to build that."

"Aye and it stood for some four hundred years," Padraig added. Tamys glanced at him, betraying shock. "What, did you not realize the age of the King's roads?"

"Nay, I suppose I did realize. It's just that when you think about how much of it has fallen apart in the last century, it's hard to imagine that the bridge stood for 300 before that. Was it just that it was old or did it want maintenance?"

"Oh, it wanted maintenance. Only the dwarves build bridges that can be trusted for centuries without care."

"Aye, well, dwarven engineering is indeed a marvel."

"So you know of the dwarves?"

"I spent some time at the Pass of the Arrival. The dwarves still come there to trade."

"So, you've actually seen dwarves?"

"Aye. Have you?"

"Aye. They trade with the elves and with the

Denygal. Quite a mysterious people."

Tamys nodded.

"Do you think we could just swim it?" he asked. The spring melt had swollen the Averblyan, but this wasn't a terribly wide spot. The water was cold, muddy and turbulent, but probably swimmable for two mountain-bred stock and a northern horse.

"Nay, no need if there's a ford," Padraig answered, sensing Joy's mood. Mayhap she had a different idea about the river's navigability. "I wonder if a new king would rebuild such as this."

"It seems worthwhile," Tamys noted. "Only the middle span is down and it looks as these farms would make use of it. This isn't a King's road, is it?"

"It was once," Padraig assured him. "There used to be a lot more King's roads than there are now."

"How do you know so much about history?" Tamys asked after mulling it over a bit.

"Denygal has long dark winters and there was a good bard there when I would visit. Did not your bards in Mulyn sing of the kingdom?"

"Aye, but I preferred the bawdies," Tamys said with a laugh. "I suppose my speech gives away where I grew up."

"Aye," Padraig agreed. "Now, you're from Mulyn, so you must have a thought or two about who will father the True King."

"I am little more than a soldier and not fit to make such determinations," Tamys said after an uncomfortable hesitance.

"No one else is about to hear, lad. It's somewhat I

do to pass the time – catalog what folks think about the True King."

Tamys looked skeptical just as Joy paused at the edge of the river and snorted. She'd found the ford.

"I don't know who he will be but I'm fairly certain that neither Corbryn nor Tren will father the True King. Both have too much ambition to whelp someone with enough strength of character to rule a whole kingdom."

Padraig had a theory about Tamys, based upon his manners and the few things he'd let slip, but he knew the lad would not give him the information without subtlety.

"Do you know their sons?"

Tamys barely managed to suppress a flinch, but answered after a beat of silence. Padraig now knew certainly that he was noble-born. It explained a few things -- his manners and clear intelligence, the occasional flash of leadership. A third or fourth son of a fairly high dun who would have leave to meet with the vyngretrix or at least his children. Apparently Tamys knew there was no use lying.

"Aye. I've met both heirs and know one well, but they are not the True King."

"Well, the Kin say that the True King will not bear a device of a bird, so that lets out many of the great clans."

Tamys frowned, watching as Padraig walked Joy up and down the edge of the ford.

"How do the elves know aught about our kingdom?"

Could Tamys was ready to hear that the kingdom had once belonged to the elves? Padraig decided that he would hold that information a bit longer.

"They are a mysterious people who know far more than makes sense to the mind of man. This is the ford. We'd best cross and continue our journey."

Tamys looked skeptical, but he didn't argue the point. The road on the other side of the river was in a poor shape until the first farm and then improved. Clearly the farm folk had given up hope of the bridge's repair.

"Where are we headed?" Tamys asked as they set camp for the evening with the sun dropping in the west. "I think we're not headed directly toward Dun Celdrya."

"We're at least a day's journey south of the king's road," Padraig agreed. "If I remember rightly, this road will enter Dunmaden in another day or so."

"Dunmaden is the north of Galornyn territory, aye?"

"Aye. Your travels have mostly been in the north, then?"

"You guessed the location of my upbringing correctly," Tamys answered circumspectly.

"Lad, I'm not prying. It's just that I've noted you don't seem to know this area at all."

"Mulyn controls the north. We come south to siege Dun Celdrya, but truly, the army goes no farther south."

"Not to Galornyn?"

Tamys hesitated.

"I don't truly have a side anymore in the conflict twix the clans, but I prefer to not share any secrets I know. Corbryn's daughter is married to a Galornyn son, but Blyan is allied with Dublyn, not either of the lords of

Mulyn. We've no reason to come this far south."

"I've heard the northerners might be buying horses from the Kin."

"I don't know anything about that," Tamys assured him. It was clear that the conversation was over. He grew taciturn after that and Padraig subsided into singing softly to himself. He paid little attention to what he hummed under his breath and truly would have been surprised if Tamys had heard him.

The southern part of Blyan was narrow, so that they crossed it in a day. Dunmaden was separated from Blyan by a small stream where they camped for the night. Padraig remarked that the stream had been bought with a lot of blood two lifetimes ago. Tamys didn't reply at first, just sat there staring at the stream as it went its way from north to south.

"Blyan and Dunmaden were once at war?" he asked.

"Blyan and Galornyn, aye! After the king died, it seemed likely we'd split into many separate kingdoms, each ruled by a provincial vyngretrix Nobody said that, mind, but it seemed likely. Dunmaden is a long way from Galornyn and the folk mayhap have more in common with Blyan than with the folk on the sea, so Blyan decided to press a claim."

"Galornyn must have won," Tamys noted.

"I suppose," Padraig replied. "Two clans died out completely, killed each other off, for the winning of this stream. I think there weren't many left to fight when Galornyn finally rode north and claimed it for themselves once again."

Tamys watched the dirty stream roll past.

"Seems like that's the way of it ever since the king died. Folk fight over that which is barely worth having and naught ever truly wins."

"Aye," Padraig agreed.

Tamys flipped the dregs of his tankard into the fire.

"Dark thoughts," he said over the crackle and hiss. He turned to his blankets then and said no more.

Founding Year 1028
Dun Llyr

The trumpets' blare shook Randodd from a reverie, gazing out over the bay where myriad ships bobbed at anchor. Across the room, Howedd fussed with his baldric. A tall blonde man with strong arms and sturdy legs, he was more at home in the saddle than standing before a mirror adjusting his clothing. He'd sent the pages away and now was regretting that decision.

"I don't suppose you know how this is supposed to rest," he asked his youngest brother. Randodd stared at the baldric, then shrugged, getting up from the window sill and approaching his brother.

"I'm afraid they didn't teach about such in the brothel," he admitted. "Mayhap you need those young boys more than you're willing to admit."

Howedd growled at him. Randodd laughed.

"I was a page once, you know," Howedd retorted. "Admittedly, it was in a small dun in Fyrgal. I don't recall the lord ever wearing a baldric." He sighed. "I suppose I do need them." Randodd turned toward the door. "Wait – wait a moment. I am not yet ready."

"As you wish," Randodd said. "What I wonder is … why am I here?"

"You are here so that I don't forget who I am," Howedd explained.

"You are the vyngretrix of Llyr," Randodd reminded him.

"I am the son of our mother as well."

"Seems a long time since you've been that. When Lord Bran came and took you away – you were – what – 10? I was just a babe in arms."

"Aye. He recognized that with only one legitimate male heir, there was likelihood he would need his bastard. Truth be told, Rando, he was a decent man. Our mother's house did well in part because of his patronage and he saw to my education and even to yours."

"I believe you," Randodd assured him. "Yet, you honor our mother on this day. Why?"

"I was born common and I never want to forget that. It gives me a fresh perspective on the world that the nobility does not know."

"And I remind you of that?"

"Oh, aye, my brother, you do. You see, the world for the nobility is all ease and intrigue. I sleep on sheets and eat fine food. You know that the world isn't really like that. For most, it's sleeping on straw and eating what they can find. You remind me that I could as easily have been naught but the bastard son of a whore who'd never wear such fine baldrics."

"What do you expect to do with that knowledge?" Randodd asked.

"Mayhap I will remember the common born in my rule. A man's not less because he was born without pedigree."

"Aye, I'd agree with that. Oh, I near forgot. Mam asked me to pass a message to you."

"Do tell."

"She wants you to know – and these are her words – that we've a fine line of bastards on our side and that when you're the lord, you should check the archives for Gillian of Llyr. Seems she was a grand-grandmam of ours."

"I've never heard of her," Howedd admitted. "Hold that thought and remind me when all the excitement is over. I do owe our mother that respect. Though why some common-born lass from a century ago would be in the archives is a question. Oh, get those pages back in here. I've less than a watch to prepare for the most important moment of my life."

Kin Cycle 24578 / FY 1028
The Dragon's Back

Ryanna drew her coat closed against the chill mountain breeze, methodically working the leather thongs over the hooks, then shoved her hands deep into the pockets. Unlike the horse meadows where spring was in the air, the gathering ground beside the northern highway faced a mountain pass that still held the winter's snow. A cold dry wind blasted across it, swirled around the gathering grounds and then continued up the ridge line that separated it from the horse meadows. It stung Ryanna's nose and cheeks as she stood overlooking the caravanserai below, where the dwarven band was settling in a sheltered hollow. Soon Ovrstahl would wend his way up to the gathering ground just outside the highway portal, but for now, they waited. Ryanna's brother Cai fidgeted with a knife and a bit of wood, carving some bit of statuary for the enjoyment of some of the holt's children. Ryanna wondered if he'd eventually ask for Sybillina's braid. She would say "yes", Ryanna thought, but Cai was hesitant to ask. They'd been smiling at each other for more than five years now, though late she'd also seen him casting attention toward Sarala, who was much too young for him. The girl hadn't noticed, but ….

Ryanna blinked as a scrying window opened in the mottled snow of the hanging valley. Padraig and a young man who was apparently traveling with him, squatting by a low fire built under a stone ledge. As this was violating her agreement with Gly, she dismissed the vision, but then found herself gazing into the dragon's lair once more. This time, a large head covered in glittering scales turned toward her and an iridescent eye of gold stared at her.

"Hoy, girl, what are you about?" The thought caused Ryanna's heart to thump with excitement. It felt like a Companion touch, but she already had a Companion. The vision slowly dissolved, until she found herself watching Ovrstahl wend his way up the pathway to the gathering grounds.

Ryanna was the squire of this caravan because she had been elected in Gil's stead after his disappearance. Cai, the true merchant of the two, was merely a guard at the beginning of the five-cycle, his Dwarvish had been considerably less than hers, but he could conduct his own negotiations now. This would be the last time Ryanna would officially meet with Ovrstahl.

In keeping with Kin tradition, Ryanna wore leather trews and a linen tunic under her coat. What a Kin wore in his or her personal time was their choice, but when acting in the capacity of a leader, men and women wore similar clothes. This spoke to the dwarves as well, who believed that women were the true leaders, but men were merchants. By dressing in men's clothing (from the dwarves' perspective), Ryanna was showing that she was equal to the men of her band.

Ovrstahl was taller and less broad of shoulder than his countrymen, but had the same broad cheekbones, large dark eyes and thick black hair. Although a full beard was a symbol of manhood in his culture, he kept his face clean-shaven in deference to those for whom he was emissary – the Kin, who generally grew only light beards which they shaved. Upon seeing Ryanna, he sketched a bow to her, then offered a shallower one to Cai. He clasped hands with each.

"How are you keeping, squire?" Ovrstahl asked Ryanna. "I trust your purse is full."

"My purse has fine coins in it," Ryanna assured him, though truth be told Kin society didn't use coins often. "And, you, emissary? Have you been walking in tall grass?"

Dwarves cared for metals and ores, not grass, but Ovrstahl had been emissary to the elves long enough to know their traditions.

"The grass has been very rich for me and mine," he assured her.

"Come, let us sit and drink a warm beverage," Cai suggested. They'd built a fire and set out low camp benches that put the tall Kin on the same level as the short Mountain Folk. Cai filled mugs with hot tea and offered Ovrstahl a metal plate with seed cakes, goat's cheese and dried berries in crème. Ovrstahl's wife was with child. Ryanna's studies were going well. Cai had led several caravans. Eventually Ovrstahl and Ryanna set aside their plates and faced one another. Elves had pelts, food and mine ponies. Dwarves had forged metal goods, jewelry and metal statuary. The desert folk did not like to trade with the elves because the Kin women were equal in authority, so the dwarven caravans kept the Kin supplied with rugs and Orental goods. Ryanna used her gifts to show Ovrstahl the inventory and to notify the warehouses what to bring to the gathering grounds tomorrow. They discussed the exchange rate. They negotiated a bit. Then they clasped hands to show that the negotiations were complete. The discussion had taken only part of the afternoon. Now they moved to the real reason Ryanna had agreed to the five-cycle.

"I appreciate all that you have done to try and find Gil," she told Overstahl. The dwarven man's eyes crinkled at the corners as he smiled.

"It has been a great pleasure of mine. However, I

must admit that I have nothing for you this time. In past years, there have been rumors of rumors that Gil might be here or there, but this year there has been no such. I am sorry."

Ryanna sighed. She had expected this. If Gil were still alive, he didn't want to be found and she suspected he was on the far side of the desert, not in dwarven territory.

"I understand, Ovrstahl, and I truly appreciate your care. You are released from any obligation to continue looking for Gil."

"I never felt compelled," Ovrstahl assured her. "I sent word to the Orental cities via several caravans. If I hear back, I will tell your brother." Cai had been elected squire of the northern and western caravans for the next five-cycle. "I will not give up until we find out what became of Gil. You should know, so you can be free." By this, Ryanna assumed Folk society did not have an abandonment statute. The Kin married for life, but recognized that sometimes spouses were not honorable or that they died without witnesses. Or worse, that they killed their companions and fled the crime.

"Thank you," she said.

"If I were to disappear on a caravan, I would want other men to act as I have to assure my mate of closure."

Just then Ovrstahl's eyes widened and he pointed behind them. Ryanna and Cai slew around on their bench to see a huge black shape against the white-blue sky. Huge wings opened on the wind on either side of a slender body that ended with a switching tail. The dragon swooped low and then leveled off and flew on. A powerful downward pressure sent Ryanna's braid twitching and coats flapped. The dragon banked and flew toward the north. Staring at it in shock, Ryanna felt her spirit move with it. She responded to the mind within the giant wyrm and the world of stone and cold dropped away as her mind took up position behind the dragon's crest. She felt the powerful whomp-whomp of the wings as they propelled the dragon forward. Trees flowed below like a moving carpet, intermixed with snow and moraine materials. Mountains hove up on both sides. Never in Ryanna's entire life had she moved so fast, so effortlessly. The mountains turned barren and grey, a brutal ring of teeth thrust up against the blue sky. Ryanna knew that somewhere her body lay entranced because she did not feel cold or wind and though her stomach twisted at the thought of the distance below, she felt no actual fear.

Whomp-whomp-whomp.

Now the mountains were passing behind as the world opened into a broad plain inclined toward a glittering sea. The dragon flew straight for the sea. Grey ocean with whitecaps fluttered below their passing shadow and Ryanna felt her ethereal fingers tighten in concern. The land disappeared from behind them and the dragon continued thrusting forward. Then an island hove up on the horizon; the dragon banked and slowed, circling the rocky cliffs. They rounded a headland and flew low over a sheltered harbor where row upon row of long boats bobbed at anchor. The dragon banked once more at the opposite headland and circled a high keep with red pennants flapping in the wind. Outside the main walls lay row upon row of barracks. The dragon banked again and they headed out to see where the same ships she'd seen before were now at sail, moving in a massive formation toward the great harbor on the northern coast where the Celdryans had first arrived before the Scourging. The image before her dissolved like soap bubbles and Ryanna tightened her hands to keep from falling.

Ryanna felt the cold of the stone bench beneath her thighs and realized that the trance, though it had seemed to last hours, had only lasted moments.

"We don't see many wyrms these days," Ovrstahl said. Cai murmured agreement. "Feels auspicious. Like one of those prophet stories you Kin like so much."

Ryanna watched the tiny dot that was all they could now see of the dragon disappear around a mountain and felt cold dread. An immense army amassed within striking distance and appeared to be preparing for war. The council should be made aware of this, for truly, if dragonkind had concerned itself with the existence of the Kin once more, it was more than auspicious. Something was upon the wind that could sweep them all away.

Wolves

There is somewhat dark about a sect of druids in Dunmaden. I encountered one at a feast on Lughnadsa in the city of Galornyn. He seemed most interested in my work with the king, but noted that troubled times might upset this. I believe this druid was more than a druid, but sensed that he might be wielding magicks of a wicked sort. The High Priest discounts my worries.

Sarcan, Priest of Bel FY 693

Founding Year 931
Galconyn Mountains – Late Spring

Donyl had never seen stars so large in all his life. Lying on his back, hands behind his head, he stared at up at the White Road and located the constellations he knew. The Strider, the small and large Bears, the Hounds. All around him, the forests of Galconyn whispered with insect sounds and hinted at deer and rabbits. He wondered if there were any predators stalking them.

Nearby Pedyr sat with his back against a rock, eyes on the forest. A low fire illuminated the camp. Four of the 15 riders walked the perimeter while the rest slept. If Pedyr saw that Donyl lay awake, he'd chide him. Still, how could one resist such a beautiful night sky? His fingers itched for charcoal and sketch pad, though truly he didn't know how he would express the scene if he tried.

The journey had been more or less uneventful so far. They'd come out of the bolt hole at a farm owned by Pedyr's family, given to his father for service as a rider for the king. Donyl and his honor guard had set out the next morning, traveling northeastward toward the pass into the Galconyn mountains. They'd traveled as a merchant band with Donyl wearing stripped leggings and Pedyr allowing Branaff, one of the younger riders, to do all the talking when they stopped at taverns. Branaff's father was a merchant back in Dublyn. Once they'd left Celdrya proper, they'd returned to being a noble band on a journey to Denygal by an unusual route. Perryn didn't trust the vyngretrix and so was sending Donyl through Galconyn, a mountainous region whose lords had rarely interacted with Celdrya proper since the Time of Troubles..

A screech in the forest split the silence and brought every rider bolt upright in an instant. Even Donyl reached for his sword as Pedyr rolled toward him while coming to his feet, drawing his own sword. One of the riders, named Neff, also scrambled free of his blankets to crouch near Donyl.

"I said the dark of the moon favored her," Neff muttered. Pedyr didn't react as Donyl wondered what the rider meant by that.

The screech came again, rising on a light breeze like the cry of the banshee. The riders had closed the perimeter, some with swords drawn, others with war darts prepared. The horses whinnied and pulled at their tethers. Two of the riders were checking ropes and hooding horses as fast as possible. The cry reverberated off the mountainside, keening, setting the hair on end. Anxiety began to rise in Donyl's chest as the sound washed over him from one direction and flowed back from another. He rose to a crouch himself.

"Stay down," Pedyr whispered. "Don't present a target."

Donyl stayed low, his bad leg aching at the strain. He fished his shield, that which Pedyr had insisted he keep nearby, up onto his left arm. He might have poor skills with a sword, but he'd been taught how to protect himself.

Pedyr's lips were moving soundlessly. On the journey, Donyl had learned that Pedyr was a Believer – an unusual sect known mainly in Denygal. Donyl suspected he was praying to his gods.

"…in Jesu's name, amen," Pedyr whispered aloud.

Eerie silence swept the mountain meadow. A few of the riders visibly relaxed.

"Hold, men," Pedyr called. "Don't let it fool you. Keep sharp."

Nothing moved out in the forest. Donyl could hear Neff's breathing. One of the riders at the perimeter whispered somewhat about "not natural". Then a bird twilled out in the trees and an owl hooted and that which is normal resumed.

"Hold, men!" Pedyr insisted. "Be steady. Naren and Jasyn, build up the fires."

Now Donyl understood why they'd gathered so much wood. It hadn't made sense at the time, but now it did. The light brightened the meadow and drove the shadows far back. He moved to stand, felt Neff pull him down and then felt the swish of a war dart brush his hair. The camp exploded into noise, but all Donyl knew was the ground cloth pressed into his face. The riders cursed as wolves howled from all sides. Neff rolled off Donyl and dragged him back against the boulder where Pedyr had made his bed earlier.

"Stay behind the shield and your back here," he ordered.

Donyl stared as a leggy wolf charged the circle of

light. The horses spooked, tugging on their ropes.

"Get more wood on the fires," Pedyr bellowed. "Hold the perimeter! You two, with the horses!"

As the light from the fires built, more wolves became visible in the shadows, sweeping in, growling, snapping jaws, spooking men back from the line. Occasionally, there'd be a lull, enough to make one think the attack was over, and then the wolves would start again, running up to the edge of the light, snapping jaws at the riders and then disappearing into the dark. Once another war dart flew straight for Donyl, but he miraculously caught it on his shield. The piles of firewood began to dwindle. The wolves continued to circle, howling. Finally, the forest above them blushed with a pale golden opalescence and the wolves seemed to disappear like mist. Birds began to sing, For a tense span of time, the riders stood poised for more, but then the meadow eased into morning and the they could see that they were alone and unmolested.

The riders checked the ground and muttered of witchcraft, because there were no prints in the soft soil.

"Neff, what do you know of this?" Donyl asked as the young rider and the journey captain approached him.

Neff glanced at Pedyr, who made a face of annoyance, but then nodded.

"I'm from Dunmaden, don't know you, and my da's a druid, mam's a grania. Do you know of such?"

"I've read about them."

"There's tales of the Celtic gods and goddesses. One's known as Morigan and she takes the shape of the raven when she's on the hunt."

"And, the wolves?"

"Wolves feature in the legends too," Neff said. "The dark of the moon favors the wench and there's somewhat that's given her our scent."

"How long is dark of the moon?" Pedyr asked.

"It's been the last two nights, so there should be a thumbnail moon this night," Donyl provided. Pedyr frowned at him. "I study," Donyl explained.

"Of course. So we've a month to get him to Denygal before we have to deal with that bitch again?" Pedyr asked Neff.

"Mayhap," Neff said. "The dark of the moon favors her, but I don't know that she can't act at other times. I'm not a druid myself, just a rider who knows about them. I do think we're safe enough during the day."

"Well, assuming that we've time, we should travel fast and get this lad to safety." Pedyr strode off to order the riders about. Donyl caught Neff's arm before he could move off.

"Why me, do you think?"

"Why Prince Maryn?" Neff returned. "I was there that night and I've been trying to tell Pedyr since that there's somewhat nasty after your family, but he didn't want to listen. If my da were about, he'd make you a talisman of protection. All I can do is help you get where you're going. I believe Pedyr when he says Believer faith will keep the daemon at bay. The Old Faith have heard of the Believers and they seem quite as powerful as our druids. You'd best get packed. The riders are spooked. They want to leave this light-cursed meadow as soon as soon."

Neff headed off to pack his own kit and left Donyl on his own. When he reached for the haversack in which he carried his clothes, Donyl froze for a moment. Could Fey artifacts lure a Celtic daemon?

Spring FY 1028
Dunmaden

The air smelled of rain as they rode into Tormyr village in northern Dunmaden. A prosperous farming village with a well-fortified dun, it sat near Tornoct, a tall, foreboding granite tor that stood up from the surrounding rolling hills. The village was close by the northern fringe of the Black Forest, reminding Padraig of somewhat he'd learned from Lodiac when he'd been traveling with him. More went on in the Black Forest than game hunting, to be sure. Moreover, he remembered the old saw about Dunmaden – "there's never been a dun called Maden" – and considered that Tornoct translated Evil Hill in Denygal, which was a hybrid language after all. This got his linguistic curiosity going, for at one time there had been an elven city somewhere nearbouts called Lindanmadan. The Celtmen might have taken the name for the area from the city. Lindanmadan had been renowned, but Padraig couldn't bring to mind why. Nor did the One True God give him any indication than that he rode through normal farm lands. Not for him this day the sort of vision he'd been granted in east Faren.

They'd just passed the dun, riding south of the tor,

when Tamys's horse came up lame. Swearing, he swung down to lift the front left hoof and complain loudly.

"He's thrown a shoe," he announced in tones that suggested rage just below the surface.

Padraig felt a touch on his mind – Joy thought it funny. She wore dwarven shoes, which occasionally needed to be removed for trimming the hoof, but never broke or were thrown accidently. It occurred to Padraig that not any blacksmith or farrier could care for her hooves. He hadn't really planned well for that.

"I can smell the forge in the village ahead," Padraig told the lad, picking that information up from Joy's thoughts. "We'll stop for the day, sell some herbs. You can get the horse looked after while I earn coin."

"I suppose I have no choice," Tamys grumbled. Padraig shrugged, since he really didn't have words of comfort. He swung down off Joy to walk with Tamys into the village.

"I'd say that's the forge," Padraig said, noting the stone round building near the edge of town that had a healthy draft of smoke coming from the chimney in what had proven to be a warm morning. He pulled his purse out from his belt and started to work the binding loose. "You might need this."

"I'm not that destitute yet," Tamys assured his employer, making a declining gesture. "Thanks for the thought though. I'll see you at the tavern."

Tamys entered the forge, leaving Padraig to turn toward the tavern. There was no true inn, but the tavern was large with a well-kempt yard and the well was far from the privy. This spoke well for the place and the entire village. Folks nodded as they passed Padraig, probably appreciative that he walked his horses through the village, which consisted of about 100 round houses with neatly thatched roofs.

Padraig tied Joy off at the hitching post and entered the dim interior of the tavern.

"Welcome, traveler," the tavernman said, setting aside the tankard he was polishing. "May I help you?"

"I'm looking for some food, mayhap a place to sleep the night, and mayhap some custom. I'm an herbman, you see."

"Herbman! Why, that would make the day bright as summer!" the tavernman said with a large smile. "My wife does have the change and there's others that need physicking. Have a seat, have a seat! I'll send my boy out to spread the word. The ale and bread are on me."

"I have a traveling companion. He's at the forge right now."

"He's welcome as well. It's been a year since this village has seen an herbman and we're glad to see one now."

"Did your herbman die?" Padraig asked, thinking that a settled herbman wouldn't move from so prosperous a village.

"I suppose he's gone off chasing the wars. He'd not be telling us mere customers."

"I see," Padraig said, though he did not. How could an herbman work a village without making friends with the villagers. "I'm only here for the day, but I've a bag full of herbs and plenty of knowledge."

After Padraig had settled Joy and Earnest, he set out

his herbs at a corner table. Tamys arrived just as the first customer – the tavernman's wife – finished telling Padraig all of her woes. They weren't much more than the complaints of any woman who had born five children and now was done.

"Every shoe loose or near worn through. And good Mulyn iron too," Tamys announced darkly. "I may need those wages after all."

"We'll see," Padraig told him. "Well, I'll be here all afternoon. Will your horse be done today?"

"Nay. On the morrow," Tamys admitted. "It's going to rain, so you might as well physick the village and make some coin. We'd only be spending the afternoon miserable under a tree."

"Rain?" Padraig asked, glancing out the window. "It looks clear to me. I smelled it earlier, but it blew off. How do you know it's going to rain?"

"I just do," Tamys said with a shrug. He dipped himself a tankard of light and settled onto a nearby bench. He'd dozed off by the time the first drops splattered the paving stones. Padraig noted it and remembered how well Tamys guessed the roll of the dice and how he had known that Traegyr had sent the hounds after them. He wondered if the three were connected in some way.

By evening, Padraig had made a fair amount of coin and livestock, which the tavernman, Bormyr, was glad to buy from him. Thanks to the rain, it had been a good day of custom for them both.

"Are you looking for a quiet place to settle, herbman?" he asked as he served them a fine meal in the early evening.

"Nay, I have business elsewhere."

"Of course, but should you change your mind, Tormyr could use an herbman of caliber."

"I'll keep it in mind," Padraig told him. Truly, this seemed to be a prosperous village filled with pleasant people who wanted only to have their cares physicked in return for what they could pay. If the One True God had given Padraig leave, he might have settled here, but of course, that would only happen if the True King was found in Tomyr. Looking about at the people in the tavern, Padraig could not say that any were the King. He would have to wait upon the Lord.

"May I ask?" Tamys inquired as they settled in the inn's bunk room. The room's walls were lined with bunks enough for six guests, but only they were present. Padraig looked at him by way of answer. "I don't think you need a guard to sell peptics to the peasants. Why did you invite me along on this journey?"

Padraig pondered the possible answers to that question. Lying was a sin, yet ofttimes Believer had to lie in order to survive. Padraid didn't think it a good witness to lie to a new friend and a potential Believer, but he also wanted to live to see tomorrow. He opted for vagueness.

"There was Traegyr, of course. I felt the need of a sword at my back. And, ofttimes you feel somewhat in your gut, saying to trust or not. I felt that you should come along with me."

Tamys frowned, uncertain. He said no more, lying back on the bunk and staring at the ceiling until Padraig blew out the candle lantern. Padraig waited for him to say more, but he woke to the morning without Tamys speaking again.

Founding Year 1028
The Tongue

Sawyl scrubbed his leg with a rough cloth and a scrape of soap, but he knew that he would not feel clean for a good long while. Being a journeyman dark mage meant accepting what came with it. When the acolytes cried, Sawyl remembered his own terror as a seven-year-old boy and he always felt besmirched by it. There were times when it was tolerable. The overflowing power of caressing Gregyn had almost wiped away the stench of his terror. Almost. That had been a long time ago, before Sawyl had realized what a danger that lad would someday be to him. Sawyl of Trevellyn planned to take Talidd's position someday and he needed no rivals to that rule, especially not one trained in sword craft who could channel twice what Sawyl could.

The lagoon beside him lay still. Rain from earlier in the day dripped from the moss. A distance away an egret made a soft cry as a croc came too close to her nest. The leaden-grey sky loomed over the island, turning all steamy and still. Mayhap Talidd wouldn't question his need to bathe before breakfast after a long night of working rituals.

The aethyr remained blocked to Talidd. That intrigued Sawyl. How could a master of the black arts be sealed from the source of power? Why? The God of Pigs and Goats did not answer the question. All the journeymen on the island worked rituals almost continually. They'd lost another acolyte two days ago. Sawyl thought Talidd would soon recall Gregyn just for his strength of gift. It would ruin his plans for Dun Galornyn, but truth be told, Gregyn had the right of it. The family there were immensely gifted, but problematic. Character and the black arts did not walk hand in hand.

Sawyl rinsed off the soap and tied a towel round his waist. He could sit here a while and …. He heard a grunt and turned his head. It wasn't a croc, but old Jaran, gesturing for him to go to the lodge. Sawyl sighed.

"I'll dress and then be up presently," he told the crippled servant. Jaran had once been a journeyman near to Sawyl's level until a ritual had gone awry. Traegyr had told Sawyl that four apprentices had died in that tragedy. Sawyl tried not to think of what pressing the boundaries of their craft and strength might mean. Usually the acolytes or apprentices were the ones damaged, but there were consequences to what they were about, even at his level.

Sawyl presented himself in Talidd's work room dressed in linen breecs and a sleeveless tunic. Pirate clothing! It was too hot for Celdryan woolens. The pirates understood that well enough.

"I've been waiting," Talidd observed.

"Sorry, master, but I was down to the lagoon, trying to cool off before breaking fast and trying to get some sleep."

"Humph! You can sleep tonight. You'll be leaving

on the morrow."

"Leaving?"

Talidd had recalled Sawyl from a quiet post in the countryside last summer for reasons he would not explain. Sawyl was both grateful and concerned to hear of the respite from the Tongue.

"I need you to transport somewhat for me to Galornyn."

"Aye, master."

Talidd opened a haversack and pulled a bag out of it. Inside were five smaller bags. He opened one of these and showed the stoppered bottle. Most of the coin for items that could not be produced by the servants came from the sale of poisons.

"There's an inn in the Bottom, called the Three Oaks. A tavern wench by the name of Sylia. You tell her you're looking for Waryk. Then take a room. Ask for the third room off the top of the stairs on the third floor. When the haversack disappears, there will be a sack of coin in its place."

"Aye, master. What do I do with the coin?" Coin was useless in the Tongue.

Talidd handed him a list. He would have to memorize it before leaving the island as the items on it were not for the knowledge of town guards.

"Are you recalling Gregyn?" Sawyl asked as he realized the import of the listed items.

"That is not your concern. Simply acquire the items and bring them back here by Lughnadsa."

Sawyl forced himself not to swallow with fear.

"Aye, master."

"You may go," Talidd dismissed. Sawyl summoned all of his courage not to run from the man's presence. Black mages set their hands at dangerous work and Talidd was a master of the dark arts, but still, there were times when Sawyl wished he'd never taken that scrap of crust offered all those years ago. He could be an herbman now, happily traveling the countryside, treating the ills of the common people …. Sawyl chuckled to himself. Foolishness driven by fearful thoughts. Talidd had lived a good many years and his skill was renown among such as them. All would be well. He hadn't lost a journeyman since … well, he'd never lost a journeyman himself, had he?

Founding Year 1028
Tomyr Village, Dunmaden

On the morrow, Tamys had already risen and stepped out when Padraig awoke to the smell of bacon and porridge. He stretched and rose, donning clothes, realizing that he had become comfortable once more with the feel of Celdryan clothes. He found Tamys in the tavernroom tucked into a bowl of porridge, bacon and dried fruit with a thick chunk of bread. There was fresh yellow milk and a pot of honey as well. Again, Padraig wondered at the prosperity of a place. In Dublyn, there'd been the warbands and the distance from the high city. Yet, Blyan had shown some hunger, village taverns selling meals that were mostly wizened vegetables and grisly meat. Here in Dunmaden, there was food aplenty and the folk did not seem afraid. Padraig wondered at that.

"Soon as I'm finished here, I'll go over to the forge and see if my horse is ready," Tamys assured him.

"I'm in no hurry. The folks I've spent the last few years with don't believe in hastening their journey unless hounds are on their tail."

"I think Traegyr gave up a good while ago," Tamys said, making Padraig grin because Traegyr had reminded him somewhat of a temple dog.

"As I said, we may travel at our own pace. It rained most of the night, so the roads are a bit soft."

Just then, the door swung open, letting in the grey morning light and four riders wearing Galornyn devices. Bormyr straightened from his duties and sized these new customers with shrewd eyes.

"May I help you, young sir?" he asked of the young lord with the four. As was keeping with noble tradition, he'd walked in behind his riders in case there be trouble within. Padraig gazed at the lad as if he were a countryman gawking at the city prince, but he was truly trying to see which brother he might be gazing at. Teddryn, he thought, by the age of him.

"I'm Teddryn," the lad replied, answering the question. "Come from Galornyn. We stayed the night on Dun Tornoct's lands, but the lord there didn't have room for us." Padraig noted Tamys taking note and turning slightly away from the young lord. Was it possible that he knew the clan at Galornyn? Padraig himself was surprised that a dun in spring would turn away any from a noble clan. "Mayhap we could get some breakfast. I've coin."

"Aye? Copper a piece will do you," Bormyr announced, apparently unimpressed by his lordship. He called into the kitchen at the back of the tavernroom. "So, what brings the vyngretrix's son this far north?"

"Riding the borders," Teddryn said circumspectly.

"May I?" one of the riders asked Padraig, indicating the bench across the table from Tamys and himself.

"Aye," Padraig assured him. This rider was tall and broad-shouldered, though still with the leanness of youth. His hair was light brown and his eyes were a grey that looked almost silver. Two of the other riders sat with him. The fourth one, a lean fellow with piercing eyes, remained with Teddryn. The grey-eyed rider before Padraig spoke with the tones of Dun Llyr.

"I still don't know how you knew they were there," the youngest of the riders, a lad no more than 16, said, apparently continuing a conversation from before.

"I would like to know also, Gregyn," said the older of the riders. They both were addressing the grey-eyed rider. "You've not been in the warband but a year, and you're able to do that which much more experienced riders can't do – spot a brigand outpost in the deep woods off the road."

"I've had a bit of experience before I came to Galornyn," Gregyn replied. "I guarded for a caravan the summer before. I learned a good deal," he insisted.

"Not even Roprick saw that and I've been five years a rider and missed it totally."

"Mayhap it's a gift," Gregyn said with a smile. "To

read in the dust of the road what others cannot see."

Padraig's true interest was not on the lads across from him, but on the band leader, Teddryn, for this was to be his niece's husband. Padraig could see somewhat of Maddw, his elder brother who was Padraig's bosom friend, in his face and the solidness of his build, but his coloring was lighter. Also, while Maddw's face often was set in mirth, Teddryn seemed annoyed with the world, frowning about him as if the world did not quite meet his expectations. Padraig lacked the gift of reading auras, so that he could not peek beneath the surface. As he was thinking this, he became aware of the stare of the rider Gregyn upon him.

"May I help you?" he asked, noting that the lad was not truly focused on him, but slightly askew.

"Nay. I'm sorry. I thought you looked familiar," Gregyn remarked, looking away. "We've never met."

"I think not," Padraig assured him. Tamys wiped his mouth now and stood, taking his trencher and tankard with him. "Take your time, lad," Padraig advised. "So, there are brigands upon the roads of Dun Maden now?"

"Not any longer," Gregyn said with a wicked gleam in his eyes. Padraig did not need to read auras to know this lad's heart, at least when it came to his sword's encounter with brigands.

"I suppose we should thank you for making the roads safe for honest travelers," Padraig told the young riders.

"Aye, well, tis the honor of the riders, you see," the eldest said. Gregyn's gaze slid sideways at his comment, so that Padraig wondered if he wholly agreed. He may only have been a rider for a year, but he clearly was not awestruck by the glamour of riding in the warband.

"Thank you," Padraig repeated and finished his meal in a bite. "I've a bit of business. Bormyr, do you need anything at the smith's?" he asked. "I'll be going that way."

"Aye, you can take these loaves over," Bormyr said, readily handing over a sack of bread. "Are you sure you won't like to settle here?"

"I've business elsewhere, but mayhap I will travel through again with a different mind. Thank you anyway."

Across the village, he approached the forge. Tamys had taken residence on the bench outside the door, his eyes closed and his face lifted to the sun, his back against the thick grey stones, typical of every soldier Padraig had known. Padraig didn't disturb him, but entered the forge's warm interior. Built of thick stone blocks, the forge was doubtless cool in summer when the forge was not used, but these were the last few weeks of forging plowshares and the like, so that it was quite warm within. This morning, the forge glowed dull red, having probably not been worked that morning. The blacksmith himself was shoeing Tamys' horse. He was bent over, positioning the shoe to a rear hoof. Like most horses, Tamys' had a few tricks and apparently didn't like his hooves handled. As the smith worked, the horse reached out to nip him on the upper arm, but before his teeth could close, the smith brought his elbow up into its eye. Stunned and bewildered, the horse paused to consider its next thought and the smith attached the shoe to its hoof.

"A farrier as well," Padraig noted as the blacksmith straightened. Dark-haired with skin browned by the heat of the forge, the blacksmith looked the type – not too tall, but heavy in muscle with shoulders like an oxen.

"Aye. The last farrier in these parts left three years ago for the wars. I learned a bit from my brother before he traveled on, though."

"I see that. That the last hoof or –."

"Two more," the smith told him. "You must be kin to the lad with the light eyes."

"His traveling companion. I've brought bread from the tavernman. Mind if I watch? I've always liked watching smiths."

"Be my guest. I'm Ganyn, as it be."

"Padraig of Denygal. Ganyn? Like Gabanyn?"

"Nay, but my father did want a god-blessed smith for a son. Gabanyn did bless my hammer, sure enough," Ganyn said with a glimmer of good humor. "You're the herbman, I suppose."

"I am," Padraig said. He settled onto a nearby bench as Ganyn moved on to the front hooves.

Padraig had spoken truly about loving to watch a smith work. In Cenconyn, he'd often been ignored as an unneeded heir. He'd have turned his hand to some useful pursuit, but it was forbidden, so he had snuck around, seeking somewhat to entertain him. He'd come upon the forge and spent hours watching the smiths (there were three in a large dun such as Cenconyn) make iron goods and horseshoes for the demesne. One of the smiths had been an armorer and that had been fascinating to a young lad bound for the warband. Watching Ganyn work, smelling the low-burning of the forge, brought pleasant memories to the fore.

Ganyn was just finishing the fourth hoof when a rear door to the forge opened and a boy entered carrying a bucket of water. Padraig glanced at him, then stared, for the lad walked with a significant limp, dragging his leg as he came across the stone floor of the forge. The arm on the same side tucked against his chest as he walked, the hand uselessly curled into a fist. Padraig could not help himself, but opened his Sight to View the lad.

Ganyn glanced up from his work and noted the lad.

"Coryn, thanks for bringing the water. Your mam will be wanting the bread there on the table and then you can bring back some oil."

"Aye, D-d-da," the lad stammered. He lurched over to the table and grasped the bag in his good hand. Noting Padraig, he smiled and lurched out of the room.

Padraig held his tongue as Ganyn finished the horse and turned to wash his hands in the bucket.

"Your son," Padraig noted. "How did he come to be injured like that?"

Ganyn looked at him. It was hard to read the face that was as muscular as the arms.

"Two years now, about this time of year. We were thatching the roof at our cottage. He climbed the ladder when he weren't supposed to and he fell. Two days, he did not move and then he awoke unable to move his right arm and leg or speak. He lived though, and he's grown better with time."

The lad entered the forge just then and Padraig followed his progress with his eyes.

"Do you know of these injuries?" Ganyn asked. "I've heard the Denygal have elven magicks."

Padraig wondered for a moment how he might know that Padraig was Denygal, then he supposed that his elven accent had not lessened since returning to Celdrya. Ganyn must have met other Denygal at some time.

"Nay, not magicks, but we do have elven healing lore. May I look at him?"

"The lad won't mind," Ganyn assured him. He came up beside his son, a boy of about nine with a shock of brown hair and pleasant blue eyes, one slightly smaller than the other. "Coryn, allow the healer to look at you. You might find the leg of some interest, healer," Ganyn suggested.

The lad sat down on the bench and allowed Padraig to roll up his breecs for a look. His boot was held between two uprights of flat iron. Just below the knee was a cuff of leather holding the uprights, but the uprights continued up to another cuff at mid-thigh.

"When he first awoke, he didn't even try to walk, but toward the end of the first summer, he would try. He'd stand up and fall over. I thought and thought about how to help him, and it came to me that his leg had no strength, so I fashioned that to help. Took a few tries, but eventually I figured it out."

"Can you walk without it, lad?" Padraig asked.

"N-nay," Varyn stuttered. "M-my knee b-b-bends and m-my f-foot d-drags."

"Take the brace off, lad, so that the healer can see," Ganyn encouraged.

The lad obliged and Padraig tested the limb, noting a strong desire of the foot to toe in and down. He was aware of Tamys entering behind him as he replaced the brace. He tested the arm, finding that the hand uncurled and the arm straightened if he worked down from the shoulder. Ganyn gasped.

"I've not seen his arm so straight since he awoke."

Padraig asked God for permission to heal, but naught came to him.

"Can aught be done?" Ganyn asked.

"I think the time for elven herbs has passed," Padraig told him somberly. "However, my training says to test the limbs to strengthen them. Try for part of each day to walk without the brace. Straighten his arm several times a day. You can do it thus," Padraig explained, showing Ganyn how to ease each joint in order. "Mayhap this will cause improvement."

"Thanks to you, herbman," Ganyn said, obviously touched by his interest. "If you journey back this way and wish to stay, I've a cottage for rent. I'd be honored for you to stay for a small fee."

"I'll remember that if I am led back this way," Padraig told him sincerely. "Tamys, your horse is ready. I'll wait outside while you settle with the smith."

"Aye," Tamys grunted.

"Ganyn, if not for your skill and imagination, your son would be lying in bed or crawling. You're the best medicinal he has at this time."

"We do our best," Ganyn said modestly.

Padraig excused himself. There were times when he could not understand why God wouldn't allow him to heal and this was one of those times. Although he always sought God's will, there were times when he needed a moment to reconcile his desires with that which is permissible.

He sat upon the bench when Tamys came from the forge, leading his horse.

"He wouldn't take my coin," Tamys announced, clearly discomfited. "Just a copper for the feed."

"Tormyr is a twice-blessed village," Padraig noted as they walked toward the inn. "They are decent, hard-working folk who honor the little miracles."

Tamys raised an eyebrow at that, but said naught. They saddled the horses and pony and set out with a small bag of provisions upon the west-running road.

Kin Cycle 24578 / FY 1028
Blue Iris Holt · The Dragon's Back

Ryanna refrained from calling fire from the council benches, but just barely. Surely, she'd never been called to task by so many idiots in all her forty seven cycles of life. *Absolute drooling imbeciles!* How often did dragons appear to mortal beings in the last millennia? Yet they were debating the vision it had shared with her as if this were a common garden-variety occurrence that simply needed wise men and women to understand it. *Unbelievable!*

Gly sat back as Melor, the leader for this five-cycle, droned on about the known limits of the northern sea.

They were all gathered in the Council of the Wise – a large, squarish room with a natural rock ceiling and a semi-circle of polished wooden benches. With spring warming the mountain air, someone had propped open one of the high shutters. There was plenty of wood and oxygen to call forth fire. All Ryanna need do was provide the spark. Gly, though physically relaxed, was staring at her. That might have been because Ryanna sat on the witness bench at center stage, or it might have been because he knew Ryanna's temper and her capabilities.

Apparently, others felt the same way about Melor's inane chatter, because when he paused for breath, Farana shot out of her seat to take the floor. A very tall, impossibly thin full elf with very long side braids of strawberry blond, her uncoordinated movement elicited a laugh from Gly and a couple of the other Wise who were thoroughly done with discussing the history of the situation. Farana drew herself up into some semblance of dignity, but her own pink lips twitched slightly in humor before she asked her question in a grave voice.

"Does anyone know how long it would take a huge army to march from the northern coast to the holts?" Farana asked.

Finally, someone asks a pertinent question!

Not that anyone, including Ryanna, knew the answer. The northern coast was technically dwarven territory, but the Mountain Folk avoided water like the plague. The general discussion around the council chamber was that nobody knew if anyone even used the northern coastal harbors since the arrival of the Celtmen, so how would they know how long it would take to march from it. That information had died with the last generation.

"Would your father know?" Melor asked Gly. Gly's father was the last Kin of the Scourging generation.

"My father was a mere toddler when the Celts arrived. He may know something he overheard from his parents, but how reliable that might be …?" Gly shrugged the rest of the question. "We could scry to the emissaries and ask them," he suggested.

Farana had not conceded the floor. She remained standing. Others were free to speak, but not to monopolize the discussion.

"Yes, we should do that," she agreed, looking pointedly at Melor, who happened to be a cousin. Rumor had it they did not get along, but they didn't really show that in public except for the occasional glance such as this. "There's also a question of logistics." Farana was a supply clerk, in charge of a portion of the holt stores. Being gifted did not mean that one got out of mundane work. Her job made her innately interested in logistics.

"The other question," Melor said, because as a librarian, he thought logistics was a ridiculous consideration, "is why this army wouldn't simply march through the northern pass into the basketlands as the Celtmen did. There's no direct route through the mountains to the holts and a lot of dwarven axes to get through before they reach us, but the basketlands are vulnerable from the north."

The chamber grew deathly quiet. Although no Kin living remembered the basketlands as home in their lifetime, they all saw it as their ancestral home. Ryanna watched and sensed their emotions. Their anger at the Celtmen softened a bit as they thought of them ravished by an unknown horde. The One True God taught forgiveness. This generation moved in that direction.

"Oh, God in heaven," Gly whispered. "It's the prophesy."

A elfling shall seek the True King and find him in the aviary where no bird of a feather may rule. A chill wind from the north shall batter him before he climbs to the tower, but strong companions will lift his arms and bolster him until all bow before the dragon.

"Perhaps, Morynsynryanna merely dreamt this while contemplating the prophesy that sent her heart's desire away." It was Tavoran, back from the collegiate in Denygal. Technically, Tavoran was not a Wisdom and should not have been in this meeting, but his vast inquiries into many fields of knowledge afforded him some latitude. He was here as a resource, as far as the Wisdoms knew, but Ryanna sensed his manipulation. He'd barely been able to contain himself when Gil had disappeared. He'd been quite flirty with Ryanna as it became obvious that Gil was either dead or didn't want to be found. He'd also been spiteful when she and Padraig had started smiling at one another. Ryanna suspected he would try to block her liberty when the time came. He might be Gly's eldest son, but he was proof that the nut did sometimes roll a long way from the tree.

"Don't be ridiculous!" Ryanna snapped. "I was wide

awake and Cai can verify the dragon sighting. So can Overstahl and Mountain Folk are not known for their fancies."

"Neither are you, Ryanna," Gly said, reminding everyone in the chamber that Ryanna had an immensely practical nature while at the same time reminding Ryanna to keep her temper in check.

"Why would a dragon, if it chose to break its solitude after all this time, appear before a young caravan squire rather than to a member of the Council of Wise?" Tavoran asked.

Behind all the debate, there had always been that unspoken question. The prophesy had been given by the Winter People before the entire holt, but the dragon had come to a half-elf who, while acknowledged to have great power, had consistently chosen to separate herself from the Wise. The Wisdoms in this chamber questioned the vision because they questioned the visionary.

The door opened then to admit Shanara. Shanara had the furled ears and cat-slit eyes of a full elf, but her hair was silver and her eyes dark rimmed with ice-blue irises. Among the Kin, children were not named bastards because of odd parenting – the sins of the father were never visited socially on their children – but Ryanna wasn't the only one who wondered at Shanara's parentage. Besides her exotic looks, she was probably the most powerful Wisdom in a 1000 cycles, possessing gifts that no other Kin even recognized.

"Step off the girl's back," Shanara said calmly yet firmly as she strode across the chamber to stand in the middle of the stage. Falana sat down without argument.

"Would it mean anything more to you if I said I'd seen the dragon as well?"

The chamber rumbled with mutters.

"Where?" Gly asked, voicing the question for all those assembled.

"With my own eyes over the horse meadows this very night."

Shanara's strength of gifts assured they believed her. Ryanna tried not to resent it. The good Kin within her argued with the rebellious Kin.

I'm as strong as she is, but a half-elf, so they distrust me. You've earned their distrust. You've encouraged it, really.

"Tavoran, don't you possess maps of the northern coast and the mountain passes?" Shanara asked.

Tavoran didn't exactly frown at her, but something in his eyes said he resented her direct questioning. An icy hand slid down Ryanna's back. One never brought a Kin's past sins up after the time of repentance was past, but Ryanna wished she knew what Tavoran had done back when she was a baby. Something that had required in *goi'tan* grey to make the community forget. She wagered it was something truly dark.

"Yes," Tavoran replied.

"Some of us should have a look at those. If there's a scale, we might be able to determine a timeline."

"And, once we've determined that, what do you think we should do about it?" Melor asked.

"Well, long term, but as quickly as possible, prepare defenses, building upon what Gil taught us to repel the Celts. Of a more short-term concern would be to send news to Padraig."

Melor did frown, but Gly spoke to prevent any sort of confrontation.

"We should contact the Mountain Folk before we contact Padraig. We need to have information to give to him. It's a grave responsibility to give a man, to seek the True King and to also try to warn the Celtmen of something an herbman should not know."

"That is true," Barana, Gly's wife who served as secretary, said. "It's not like in the holts, is it? He can't just speak at a public meeting and have the news carried through the larger community. How will he get this warning to those who should order the defenses?"

"Padraig was selected in part because he has familial ties to the nobles," Shanara explained. "Ulryen was clear on that. Gly, do you know if he's been in contact with his family yet?"

Gly glanced at Ryanna, who was in the process of taking a seat to the side in grateful deference to Shanara taking center stage. Ryanna shook her head ever so slightly.

"No. We're not watching him all the time. I do know he traveled to Clarcom, the capital of the most eastern region, Dublyn, and I believe that is where his sister lives. I'll scry to him later and directly speak with him."

"Shanara, if I may," Farana asked. "What, if anything, was communicated by the dragon?"

"Nothing," Shanara said. "I saw it at a distance; it appeared to have a deer in its talons."

"Why would the dragon give a vision to Ryanna rather than you?" Tavoran demanded.

"Glynansyntavoran, you must give up on this," Shanara snapped. "This is similar to you and others who wanted to reject the prophesy because of the one tasked with carrying it out. Ryanna is Kin. Dragonkind has, for reasons we do not understand, chosen to reestablish contact with Kin. Who are we to argue with them about their choice of contact? No, do not answer that lest you decide to argue the issue further."

She's defending me?! My goodness! Miracles do happen.

The conversation continued for a bit longer, but it was growing late and Gly wanted to scry to Padraig to ask him about his family while Ryanna was to scry to Overstahl's contact concerning the northern lands. Gly caught Ryanna as they were leaving the chamber.

"You chose wisely," he whispered. She raised an eyebrow. "Not to set them on fire," he reminded. "It would have been a mess and I might have been singed."

They smiled at one another and went in opposite directions to be about their distant communications.

Dragon Speak

The Believers teach curious customs. For example, the following property law exists in Denygal, established from the sacred text of their One True God:

In the year of jubilees (which is the 50th year), every citizen must return to the property that they own. They do not – indeed, cannot – sell property. They may lease the production of property up to 49 years, but in the 50th year, the lease closes and the use of the property returns to the original owner. Newcomers into the community may open unused and unclaimed lands and these become theirs by right of use after seven years. If a family die out, the land must remain fallow for seven years and then is added to the list of unclaimed lands. Those already owning land may not claim unused lands, but may for a period of seven years produce from that land. All produce owes a 10% tax to the sectarian temple, and a 5% tax to the common weal, typically administered by those selected by the majority for a period of service."

Curiously, this system appears functional within their society though how they maintain order without a stable nobility is a matter of some confusion.

Nolyn, priest of Bel, Dun Moryn, FY 978

Founding Year 931
High Celdrya

The city had a lot of strangers in it and most of the inns were filled with those from outside. Some were there for the wedding, some for the Lughnadsa celebrations and tomorrow's market faire, others were there because the whole country suspected there'd be war.

The Golden Tankard stood in the lower town, almost near the new wall that was being built round the houses that had overflowed the city and crossed the river in the last decade. This was a tradesman's tavern, not the sort with harlots, but there were games of dice and a barrel of cheaper ale at the ready. Most of the men gathered here worked on the wall or the portcullis that would protect the river. The rest were laborers come to the city for the work, seeking employment.

The man Deryk met with was neither a mason nor a laborer. He was a metallurgist from Mulyn who had agreed to speak with Deryk for coin. They'd taken a corner booth, a bit from the nearest dice game, and ordered better ale. They spoke in lowered tones, though nobody seemed much interested in these two men. Mayhap this was because Deryk had worn plain breecs and a siarc without blazons. Owing to the warm weather, he had forgone a cloak.

"What can you tell me of Burcan and his brother?" Deryk asked Llewys. "You said you know them."

"Aye, I do. Mine is a larger smelter, so they are there a good bit."

"What is all the iron for?"

"Weapons, of course. Swords, spears, shields. Nothing your army uses does not contain Mulyn iron."

"That I know. How many of these weapons go to Mulyn lords?"

Llewys narrowed his eyes. He had a wide face and a prominent beard of strawberry blond. His hair was light as flax.

"You're asking me if Burcan seeks war with Celdrya?"

Deryk nodded.

"Nay," Llewys insisted. "Burcan and Joran are loyal to the kingdom if not Lord Perryn himself and they will soon respect him as well."

"You sound certain," Deryk observed.

"I am, my lord. It's not just that he's their brother-in-law. It's that he's the king and they're loyal to the crown. They swore fealty to him."

Deryk sat back, drinking down his ale while mulling over the report.

Truth be told, Deryk was beginning to lose his own loyalty to Perryn. Somewhat had happened these few weeks since Donyl had slipped off to Denygal. Perryn seemed to have lost his interest in finding his brother's killer or his father's poisoner. It would have been well and good if he'd been distracted by the impending nuptials. Maryn had been quite beside himself before his wedding. Nay, but Perryn seemed hardly to care about his bride at all. Deryk would not be surprised to hear that he'd not actually spoken to her yet. Perryn instead spent a great deal of time in his chambers and did not communicate with anyone beyond what was absolutely necessary. There were rumors about that he was abed with Vanyn's mistress, but that seemed unlikely.

Deryk was still thinking these unsettled thoughts when he exited the tavern. He paused in the sweltering evening to look up and down the street. Torch smoke drifted lazily in the muggy heat. A group of men passed on the far side of the street. Deryk idly noted that he recognized a face. Where did he know that man?

The serving man from the day Vanyn died. Hmm, I'd forgotten about him. Why was he never questioned?

Deryk decided he should catch the man up and ask him to report to him on the morrow. Mayhap he had noticed somewhat Deryk had missed that day. It was well worth the question and a slight jaunt through the evening heat. He turned bout to catch up the man and saw him disappear round a corner into an alleyway. Upon reaching the entrance to the alley, Deryk hesitated a moment.

Odd place for a king's servant. Mayhap I've spied a similar face. But, nay, I saw the livery. He's the one I seek, if only I could remember his name.

Deryk eased his sword in its scabbard just to be on the safe side as he forged into the alley. This was the territory of harlots and footpads. The walls of the buildings were closer than he liked and there were doors that would open in those walls at unexpected intervals. He stepped round a pool of suspicious smelling spew and startled when a dog barked at him from a narrow space between two of the buildings.

Suddenly darkness moved and resolved itself into three thugs with short swords and cudgels. One swooped in and aimed a blade for Deryk's ribs. The captain slipped sideways and drew his sword in a single movement. He swung round and caught a blade on his sword. Another of the thugs moved in for a feint and Deryk smacked him hard across the shoulder and sent him stumbling. He swung his long sword in a flat horizontal arc and reminded these malcontents that he was a trained soldier with a quality weapon when he sliced the siarc of one of them and nearly scored flesh on the other. They stumbled back and, scooping their companion to his feet, fled the scene.

Deryk stared about in frustration, for he'd lost track of the serving man and now stood alone in the deep dark of the alley. Sighing, he resolved to return to the dun and leave his investigation to another time.

Deryk caught an otherwise unoccupied carriage to the dun and spent a pleasant half-watch enjoying the slight breeze as the horse carried them uphill through the curving streets, past the opulent houses. The fort guard on the evenwatch were use to his nocturnal journeys into the town, so that they simply glanced him over as he came in the mangate. He headed toward his chambers in a half-broch closer to the stables and barracks than the great hall. A lesser man might have resented the slight, but Deryk preferred to be where he could keep an eye upon his men. The other nobles could take care of themselves, he thought.

What was that man's name? He told it to me that day. I'm sure of it!

Deryk stepped up on the landing at his floor and was surprised to find Malona standing there. The king's mistress had always twisted his gut in the past, but now her smile filled his heart with such warmth that he scarce remembered the suffocating night. He thought he smelled narcissus as her beautiful golden eyes captivated him and drew him in.

"May I help you, my lady?"

"The question is, my young sir, can I help you?" she said.

And that was all he cared about for a good long while that night.

Founding Year 1028
Celdrya Proper

The journey through Dunmaden and into Celdrya proper was more or less uneventful. They stopped at villages for Padraig to nurse ills and then moved on. They slept under the stars and in haylofts, eschewing the taverns and inns with their dirty straw and flea-bitten dogs. Spring was slow to develop. They woke most mornings to ice on the bucket and frost on their blankets. Padraig mentioned occasionally that an herbman wouldn't usually be traveling so early in the year, hoping that Tamys might begin to recognize that he didn't want the life of a freesword soldier.

Padraig had hoped to reach the High City by Beltane, but fell short by one day. They spent the night in a hayloft of a tavern that had seen better days, with thinning thatch and thinner dogs. The hayloft was the cleanest part of the place and even Tamys didn't complain about sleeping there after seeing the tavernroom floor. Late in the night, well before dawn, Padraig had an odd sort of dream. He dreamt that he stood naked in the silver light of the moon in the same hayloft watching himself and Tamys sleep. As he stood there, he saw a woman lean over the sleeping figures in the straw. Somewhat about it made Padraig's heart start with fear and, with that, he awoke.

The chill air upon his nose cleared his head immediately and Padraig wondered why he was awake, the dream already fading. He lay listening to the night for a moment, but heard nothing that would account for his sudden awareness.

When his hearing couldn't ferret out the cause, Padraig sent a line of thought to Joy. The mare stirred drowsily against his mind and remarked grumpily that humans ought to grow fur so they wouldn't be so afraid of the cold.

He knew what that meant and reluctantly reached out of the blankets to drag his cold breecs into him. Carrying a blanket with him and ignoring the cold on his feet so he wouldn't waste time with boots, he crept down the ladder and let himself out of the stable. Standing in the tavern yard, cold mud squeezing between his toes, Padraig began to pray for the tavernman and his family, for the villagers and travelers, for his newly-found friend asleep in the hay above the stable. He didn't stand there half-naked in the dark for long, but he finished his list and waited on God to tell him more. When more did not come, Padraig returned to the hayloft. For a moment, as he stood in the hay wiping mud off his feet, he almost remembered somewhat from his dream, but it got away from him before he remembered any details.

His blankets had grown cold in his absence and he spent a few minutes arranging them so that none of his heat could escape. He found himself growing drowsy almost immediately after his toes warmed up and was soon as soundly asleep as if he'd never woke.

Padraig awoke again to the pearly gray of early dawn and the sound of bells ringing. Tamys groaned and pulled his cloak, which he'd been using as a pillow, over his head. The bells continued. Tamys rolled over onto his back, growling. The bells continued. Tamys began to swear like the soldier he was and he reached for his shirt, swearing more loudly when he felt the shock of the cold on his arm.

"We're in no rush," Padraig assured him. "I'm not moving from these blankets until it warms up." Tamys hesitated, thinking for a moment. "Unless you'd like to go to the festivities."

Tamys glanced at him.

"I – you wouldn't mind?"

Padraig felt hair tingle on his arms.

"Why would I mind?"

"I thought Believers wouldn't hold truck with such."

Padraig took a deep breath and let it out slowly. He'd not really been discreet with Tamys, hoping to talk with him of his beliefs, but he'd thought he'd been more careful than that. Tamys noticed his discomfiture and spoke hastily.

"There's no one about and I've my own issues with priests of Lugh, so you needn't worry that I'll run to the local lord and have you hung," he assured Padraig.

"I wasn't worried about that. I won't be going, but I'm not going to keep you from your worship," he replied. "I didn't think you were that devout."

"I'm not!" Tamys admitted. "My father – well, he didn't raise us to be devout, but the faire is usually somewhat interesting. I thought I could find a lass to spend some time with – after the dancing round the pole is through, of course."

"You're not interested in wedding then. There'll be a bit of excitement in Dun Celdrya, to be sure, if you care to wait." Tamys said naught. "Well, you can do whatever you want. I'm going back to sleep."

Padraig rolled onto his side and snuggled down into his blankets. Tamys sat there, his shirt half on for a moment, before stripping it off and sliding down into the warmth of his own blankets. The bells continued to toll. Tamys groaned.

"Now that I've decided not to go, I wish those cursed bells would stop."

"They will in God's good time," Padraig murmured.

Less than a breath later, the bells stopped abruptly,

as if someone had cut the ropes. Tamys lifted his head from his cloak, listening, waiting for them to resume. When they didn't, he laughed.

"Almost as if they were listening to you."

"Not me," Padraig assured him. "Go to sleep."

They drowsed off, finally awaking to the full golden sun of true morning. The day proved good traveling, though the road wanted repair badly. They reached a small village in the shadows of the walls at midday. Estimating they had at least another two hours of travel, Padraig stopped at the tavern for bread and ale so watery even he would drink it. This tavern looked even poorer than the one they'd stayed in the night before. Outside a man worked to repair a cart filled with children and goods. Padraig watched a bit as he and Tamys ate their lunch, then admitted that the man was never going to be able to set the cart on the repaired wheel by himself.

Padraig approached the man while Tamys was drinking ale. The man wore threadbare breecs and a much-patched siarc and the children were little better clothed. None of them looked like they'd eaten well over the winter.

"Greetings, traveler," Padraig haled. The man gave him a suspicious look. "You look as if you could use some help lifting the cart onto the wheel."

The man looked him over with as much suspicion as before. Padraig waited. The man rubbed his jaw and then shrugged.

"You're right enough in that, truly. What will it cost me?"

"Naught. I'm offering free help, which is truly the

only that a man can offer."

"Don't know if the two of us can settle this on our own, but I thank you for the offer."

Tamys wandered over at that point.

"I can help too," he said, surprising Padraig, who'd thought he'd not be interested in such.

"Well and good then. If you two can do the lifting, I can get the wheel on the axle."

"On your count, good man," Padraig assured him. He turned to put his back against the side of the cart on one side of the axle, gripping the underside of the cart with his hands. Tamys set his shoulder against the cart side on the other side of the axle and got ready for the signal. The man counted to three, the two heaved the cart up and the man settled the wheel on the axle.

The man smiled and began to crank on the hub, while Tamys and Padraig settled their clothes back in place.

"Thanks to you both," he said. "My name is Cenydd, a carpenter bound for Dun Madyn."

"I'm Padraig, an herbman from Denygal."

"Tamys," Tamys replied and immediately moved away. He wasn't yet comfortable with introductions.

"Are you from the High City?" Padraig asked Cenydd.

"Aye. We're getting out, like so many others. There's not much left for tradesfolk and the winter saw a lot of death." Cenydd's eyes misted for a moment, then he turned as a baby cried among the children. "You said you were an herbman. I've no coin and little to trade, but I've a babe with sickness and I'd thank you to look at him."

Padraig smiled.

"I don't need coin," he assured Cenydd. "I'll do it for my love of the One God. Let me see the bairn."

"The – ?"

"Oh, Denygal call babies 'bairns."

"Oh, aye." Cenydd did take the child from an older sister who held the child tight to her chest and handed it into Padraig's hands. Padraig found himself looking into the small face of an infant. He asked a few questions and found that the babe was two months old and had been born with the death of his mother. Cenydd was determined to keep the child alive and had even brought a goat from the city, but lamented that the goat wasn't giving enough milk to support the child. "I fear I'll lose him as I did his mother."

"He seems a good strong child for his age, though you're right, he's underweight. I'm not a midwife, understand, but he needs nourishment. Travel more slowly and make sure the goat gets plenty to eat and enough water. Where are you bound?"

"Dunmaden where my brother has a tavern and a farm for me to tenant. The city's done for. There's still some merchant trade, but the tradesmen are leaving -- those who didn't starve to death last winter."

"A truly sad ending for a great city. Well, you'll want to arrive in Dunmaden a bit late for the planting anyway. Your children are more in need of rest and good food than hard work. Slowing your travel will like get you there after the planting or to the end and all should be more healthy."

Padraig handed the child over to his father and went over to examine the goat. Although the One True God hadn't granted permission for healing the child, who had nothing wrong with him beside his mother was dead, Padraig asked God for a bit of help with the goat and received it. He thought Cenydd would be pleasantly surprised at the increase in his goat's milk production.

"I've some herbs for colic," Padraig told Cenydd. "Your boy should be keeping down the milk he gets."

He found a bag of chamomile and spooned up some. When he shook hands with Cenydd, he walked over to Tamys and suggested they ride on. He did not want Cenydd to discover the bag of food he'd deposited in the cart until after it was too late to return it.

"Will the child live?" Tamys asked after they were out of earshot.

"I'd say he'll make it to his uncle's farm. Will he live the winter, die in a fall at 12, be killed by some war at 21? Who can say?"

Tamys looked thoughtful for a moment, then shrugged. They were just topping the rise when they heard a yell from Cenydd. Padraig turned in his saddle to see the man waving at him. He waved back and turned to follow Tamys on toward the city.

"What was that about?" Tamys asked.

"Naught. We'll need to renew our stock of food when we arrive in the city."

"We had enough for three days," Tamys protested, then hesitated, then laughed with a hooting roar. "You are truly amazing!" he said. "Truly, truly amazing!"

Kin Cycle 24578 / FY 1028
Blue Iris Holt

Ryanna slapped the water, sending a spray of droplets across the apron and onto the floor. A *goi'tan* stopped her assigned task to deal with the spill as several other Kin turned to stare at Ryanna, who muttered in Celdryan under her breath, then turned back to the water, hoping against hope to reach Padraig's mind this time. She'd been granted permission to connect with Padraig since Gly and Shanara had both failed in their attempts. Unfortunately, although she could view him, the window was shrinking and she could not seem to gain his attention.

The *goi'tan* was mopping up her spill. Under other circumstances, Ryanna would have felt ashamed at her outburst and asked to clean it up herself, but today was different. There was something going on that she didn't understand and it worried her greatly. As the sparkles in the water settled out into reflections, the image she saw was not the one she sought. Again, the golden dragon with the green eyes looked at her.

How long before they get here? she asked. She didn't really expect an answer and the dragon did not exceed her expectations. Instead, she saw a Celt boy running across a cobbled ward. *What does he have to do with the army? Who is he?* There were no answers. Then Ryanna heard the soft cries and came to recognize that her dragon was a mother.

"What are you doing?" Gly demanded, shattering the vision and causing Ryanna to gasp with startlement.

"Trying to scry to Padraig and getting our winged friend yet again. She has pouchlings," Ryanna announced. She stood to walk with Gly. She wore Celdryan breecs and a linen tunic today. "Perhaps we should consider that someone needs to travel to Celdrya to get hold of Padraig."

"And that someone should be you?"

"There are few in the holt who could pass among the Celts as one of them."

Gly sighed. The argument was sound, but her timing was bad, even illegal. She was still Gil's wife and should not be haring off after other men for any reason. If it were not for the prophesy, she'd not have risked putting herself forward in such a bold way, not even with her mentor.

"Do you realize what this might mean?" Gly asked her as they entered his workshop. He closed the door. It was rare for him to close the door all the way during their sessions. She knew it was serious when he did. "If you do not handle this rightly, you will find heavy opposition when you ask after the settling of your marriage. You remember this, I know."

"I do, but what else can be done? Who else can travel into basketlands?"

"There are a few."

"There are some who look human enough, but none have my skills and you know that."

"I know that. The others may not. If you are

determined, then I will present it and we'll see where it falls, but do not think it a light thing."

"I don't. Gly, please, I know you know that Padraig and I are adults who will not dishonor my contract with Gil. Yes, I want to see him, but not for the reason that dirty minds will suggest."

"My son has the dirtiest, I know," Gly said. "He shames himself, you may be sure." He sighed again. He'd already brought their breakfast into the workroom. He gestured for her to tuck in. "I step lightly here, but you do have some on your side. Shanara has suggested you be allowed to go with the caravan to Amalaren and carry a message to the lord there."

"Amalaren? That's Cenconyn. Padraig did not go to his father's home."

"I know this, but his family there may be able to send to him. We cannot allow you to go traveling about the basketlands, hoping to catch up with him."

"Why not?"

"Ryanna, you and Gil had a history, do you remember that?"

"Gil is dead and I'm near 20 years older. Are you saying you know me so poorly?"

"No," Gly said with a smile. "I know you quite well and I believe that you and Padraig will be nothing but honorable, but I am not the only one to judge. Shanara's offer is amenable. Your brother could as well carry the message, but I believe you should be afforded the respect. I also believe you should do what you are given to do and no more."

Ryanna put her face in her hands and prayed for

patience. It was not Gly's fault. It wasn't even the assembly's fault. She had done the things she'd done all those years ago and she was the only one to take responsibility for the outcome.

"Let us proceed then. Should I prepare in any way?"

"Be ready with a statement if they ask it. Let the God your Savior be your guide in what you will say."

Ryanna nodded. That Jesu was her Savior was easy enough to say; to wait upon His guidance was much more difficult.

Do you know the Savior, wyrm? she asked to herself, since she was not scrying.

This is the name of the One, is it not?

The voice in her head startled her. She was familiar with the touch of Sabre on her mind and this was not what she expected. This voice had a distinctly female cast to it. Yet no Kin had ever had more than one Companion at a time. How could this be?

You are not my Companion, the dragon said. *You are a Sensitive, so I am able to reach you, but you are not meant for me and I am not meant for you. One like you is meant for my son.*

"Ryanna, what are you thinking?" Gly asked, his tightening grip on her arm bringing her back to the workroom.

"The dragon speaks to my mind, Gly," she reported. Her mentor stared at her for several breaths and then laughed softly, shaking his head.

"Of course a dragon speaks to your mind. It had to be either you or Shanara." He sighed, then chortled and turned toward the door. "I'll make those arrangements right now. You perhaps should continue your, uh, conversation. I'll be a while, I'm sure."

Yet try as she might, after Gly departed, Ryanna could not get the dragon to respond again. She wished she knew what that might mean.

Kin Cycle 24573
Pass of Arrival (Five Cycles Past)

A warm wind scattered pebbles down the sheer cliff below as Erik of Halforfyord sat with his legs swinging over the broken edge of the ancient citadel's plaza. While the seacoast city had been barely recognizable as a city, the citadel had held up better. Even portions of the curtain wall were still clinging to the cliff face, though the doors and windows had long ago rotted away, leaving only the dark rock. In this, it was similar to the citadel in the elven mountains that they had viewed yesterday. The elven society had passed from the mind of men for centuries, but the dwarven-built buildings remained if one did not dismiss them as caves with unusual regularity.

The emissary Gil outlined the canyon far below with his long forefinger.

"My father's people tramped up from the coast and met the trolls near here. That set off the troll rebellion that fractured the Dwarven empire."

"My father spent half a lifetime looking for a pass through the mountains and never found one," Jarl reported. "How is that it remained hidden?"

"A rock slide blocked the northern terminus when my father was a young man – some three hundred years ago. If you didn't know it was there, you could miss it."

"There's a garrison beyond that bend, yah?" Eric said, pointing south.

"The dun at the Pass of the Arrival, yes. It will be a perfect feint to draw people's eyes from the coast."

"How do we get to the south?" Jarl asked.

"We will," Gil said. Under his carefully arranged features, Erik caught a flash of something – irritation? – that made him wonder if the emissary was not wholly informed of their plans. *Who stands behind you?* Gil thought himself very clever, but Orma had taught Erik to listen between the words and the emissary had let by enough for Erik to be sure that his knowledge of the byways was recent and seemed even to be developing. Erik didn't know how that was possible, but he was on tenderhooks listening for what the man was seeking to hide.

"These byways are more extensive than you know," he added, tamping down the fire behind his eyes. "You should leave some men here to scout out the tunnels that lead to the canyon floor. That's a dwarven highway. There had to have been a way to access the citadel from there."

"Wouldn't the Celt have found it by now?" Jarl offered.

"No. The dwarves are very clever at hiding entrances. You will find it from the inside or not at all."

"Jarl, detail three men," Erik ordered. The byway in the Dragon's Back had been readily accessible to a highway. There'd been the remains of a caravanserai not far down the path, though damaged by fire. Erick felt certain they would all have such access. "Will we camp here or move on today?"

Gil looked at the sun. Erik was almost certain that he was older than he looked. His skin was unlined and his beard soft, but his experience spoke volumes toward years rather than youth.

"It's not quite the noon tide. We should continue to our next point and camp there."

"Jarl, detail the three. Leave them with sufficient food for …?"

"A fortnight," Gil suggested when Erik paused.

"Should they reconnoiter the highway if they find the entrance quickly?"

Jarl was used to command. He'd been a war leader for Magnus. He always thought ahead, which made him valuable to the young Svard.

"Nah, we do not want to risk the dun becoming aware of us until we are ready to attack. When we return, it will be with clothes for spying."

Jarl's eyes shone with pride, letting Erik know that he had used good sense.

"When do we depart?" Erik asked.

"As soon as your men can be ready."

"Sun's hand," Erik told Jarl. "Tell the men to eat before they mount, fill the water bags."

Jarl bobbed his head in assent and went off to do as bade. Erik rolled back from the edge and gained his feet.

"This must have been a lonely place even in elven times. What was it for?"

"Religion or academics. Maybe both."

Erik's eyes wandered over the openings in the face of the citadel, pausing as he saw movement in one. A trick of the eye. He thought he'd seen a woman there. A shiver ran down his back as a shadow fell over the sun.

"We should get ready," he said. "Where will we be going next?"

Gil paused, seemed almost to be looking at someone to Erik's left, then he smiled mildly.

"Into the heart of Celdrya, of course."

The shiver became a shudder that Erik could not explain.

High Celdrya Fallen

"Why do you insist on being battered? Why do you continue to rebel? Your head has a massive wound, your whole body is weak. From the soles of your feet to your head, there is no uninjured spot, only bruises, cuts and open wounds. There have not been cleaned, bandaged or salved.

"Your land is devastated, your cities burned with fire. Right before your eyes your crops are being destroyed by foreign invaders. They leave behind devastation and destruction.

"[Celdrya] is left isolated, like a hut in a vineyard, shoe is a besieged city. If the One who commands armies had not left us a few survivors, we would have quickly become like Sodom, we would have become like Gomorrah.

"Listen to the Lord's word, you leaders of Sodom! Pay attention to our God's rebuke, people of Gomorrah!"

From the Scriptos of the One, Writings of Isayah

Recorded by Brethry, Priest of Bel, Moryn
FY 941

Founding Year 931
Mulyn, Dun Joran

Burcan ap Manahan, lord of western Mulyn, rode into the ward of the new dun at Loramar, where his brother Joran was establishing his own demesne on the site of an ancient hunting lodge. Two grooms scrambled out of the stables to take his horse and spare as Burcan strode across the partially cobbled ward to the great hall on the ground floor of the broch. He could hear his honor guard sorting themselves out as he let the door close behind him.

Joran met him at the door with a slap on his shoulder. He called for mead as they climbed the stairs to his greeting chamber, which for now was just a generous slice of the second floor. Joran and his wife, Lady Cadda nee Trevellyn, had no children yet, so they occupied half of the second floor. The greeting chamber was smallish, with a single window overlooking the ward, a collection of stools and one chair, a small table, and a collection of shields leaning against the outer wall.

"Did your wife give you a son, yet?" Joran asked. It could have been a matter of competition with them, but Joran understood that Burcan was the actual heir, born 10 minutes before him, and his children would not rule except as lords. He seemed comfortable with that notion.

"Aye, Loryna gave birth to a healthy boy. How long before Cadda whelps?"

"Soon. An eightnight, mayhap a fortnight."

"And she's doing well?"

"Aye, she's not having the difficulties Loryna had."

"Well and good then. Now, for the reason I came. I think we acted too swiftly in Maddyn. Mayhap an assassin got away."

Joran's brow furrowed. Although others thought they looked almost exactly alike, Burcan did not see it. They had similar hair, eyes and beards, but he really saw no resemblance beyond that. Among their many differences was that Joran was more thoughtful. He'd cautioned that they go slowly in their judgment at Maddyn, but Burcan had overruled him.

"That mayhap be true," Joran said, circumspectly. "Do we know more?"

"He mayhap have been a serving man at Dun Celdrya. He's slipped free of there. I've got eyes-and-ears out to track him."

"Well and good then, Mayhap Perryn will forgive our haste in Maddyn if we bring the last to ground."

"He seems distracted by the coming nuptials," Burcan explained. "Will you travel with me?"

"Nay, but I will wait here with Cadda. Being as he's her brother, Perryn should appreciate my absence."

"I'll make the argument for you. He should be pleased to hear we've secured the line of rule in Mulyn."

"So your concerns have been assuaged?" Joran asked.

"Not entirely, but I did find him much better

prepared than I originally feared."

"He and Maryn were not close, but Maryn liked him well enough," Joran added. There was a knock on the door. Joran glanced at Burcan and then called, "Enter."

A serving man entered, carrying a tray with a flagon of mead and two pewter goblets, along with a platter of cheese, meat and bread.

"You may place it on the table, Talidd. We'll serve ourselves," Joran instructed.

"Of course, my lord," the young servant said. He was quite dark with brown eyes and hair of a close color. "Do you wish me to wait on the landing if you need somewhat?"

"Aye, that would be useful," Joran said. Talidd arranged the table smartly and then withdrew, closing the door behind him.

"Where did you get such a well-trained servant?" Burcan asked with a smile. "I've not seen him before."

"Oh, he came with Cadda from Dun Celdrya," Joran said, eyes focused on the door.

"Truly? I seriously cannot remember him." Burcan poured out the mead and handed Joran one of the goblets.

"He's waited on you many times," Joran said. He set aside his goblet after just a small sip and gathered bread, meat and cheese to nibble. "We have demesne business to discuss. Lord Rhemry is acting as if I do not have authority as vyngretrix."

"I'll speak with him. It's not unheard of, what we've done, but it's never been done in Mulyn before, far as I know. We'll have to find a way to direct our underlords with fairness and equality. What is the specific issue?"

"He's got rivalry with Donyn and asked for malover, but he didn't like my ruling."

"What did you rule?" Burcan now set aside his own goblet to partake of the food.

"It's an issue over grazing rights. Donyn has traditionally grazed their sheep in the high meadow every summer. Rhemry's demesne has no history of using it, but when he expanded his flocks, he moved into the high meadow. I ruled that Donyn has first use of the grass. Rhemry then said I am not the legitimate rule."

Burcan nodded thoughtfully.

"I'll speak with him before I travel to Celdrya. If he gives you more grief, I'll make it clear, he'll suffer penalty."

"Well and good then. And, the penalty?"

"What do you consider to be the acceptable penalty?"

This was the secret to their partnership. They traded decisions. It worked well. Eastern Mulyn's population had been sparse until their father's generation, but now that farmers were settling the land, it behooved to give them protection and splitting their effort when there were two of them made sense.

"We need to make an example so others will not be tempted. Half his demesne goes to Donyn if he fails to comply with my rule."

Burcan blinked. There were times, as with Maddyn, that they disagreed, but it was rare that Joran was more overreaching than Burcan. He was the brake to Burcan's charger.

"I'll make that clear to him as well. A penalty like that should lay aside any lingering doubts as to your fitness to rule. We should go on the morrow. We can do the trip in the day and then I can prepare for Celdrya. I'll send Mam from Manahan to wait with you."

"Aye, I'm sure Cadda would appreciate that. If we're done discussing our business, I should go see to the cooks. With Cadda in her confinement, I need to keep her eyes on things."

"That's what your chamberlain is for."

"Man's gone soft in the head," Joran announced. Burcan raised an eyebrow in question. "He's old, Burcan. I'd like to believe otherwise, but he forgets somewhat."

"Mayhap it is time to retire him, then. Do you want me to send someone to you or can you make the selection on your own?"

"I will handle this myself, thank you, brother. I need to be competent to rule."

"I'll see to Ygrevnyn's retirement. He served our father for many a year."

"Aye. And he deserves honor for his service. I'm off to check on the cooks. Would you let the grooms know that we'll be traveling at first light?"

"Aye."

Joran left the room, leaving the door ajar. Burcan finished his mead in a gulp. As he lowered the goblet, Talidd came in the door. Their eyes met and Burcan felt the room dissolve around them. When he came to himself, he was sitting at the board in the great hall, being introduced to Talidd, the man who would replace Ygrevnyn as chamberlain.

"I am so pleased that my brother has found a man with such impeccable letters of reference," he said.

Talidd raised his goblet and toasted.

"I simply want to serve this family to the best of my ability. I shall strive to accomplish all that my liege asks of me."

Founding Year 1028
High Celdrya

Entering at mid-afternoon, they probably saw the city at its most productive time of the day. Dun Celdrya sat on the west bank of the Avercelt which flowed from the iron-rich region of Mulyn, now in enemy hands, and the great Stormmor to the south, its mouth guarded by Dun Llyr. Directly to the west of the city was the massive monolithic stone mountain, the Founding Stone. The Stone was so unscalable that it protected the city from the west while the great river protected the city from the east. The many bridges that crossed the river and the harbor that supplied the city were actually within the walls of the city. Giant metal gates hung above the water course to be lowered in case of attack, but they had been damaged in the wars and could no longer be lowered. Beyond the river were rolling hills and what had once been prosperous farms that supported a thriving city. All mostly gone now.

There was a faire of sorts set up at the market square just inside the walls, but overall the area near the walls stood desolate, a place of burned-out round houses and rotten thatch clogging dirty streets. The city huddled behind breached walls and the massive iron-bound gates that allowed entrance into the walls hung askew. A squad of workers labored rebuilding a section of the wall, but even Tamys could see the material was inferior to the original workmanship. As they walked through the streets, Tamys stared around at what had been wrought by his countrymen, and himself, since he had been among those who had besieged the city the summer before.

"It seems almost empty," he whispered, as if speaking in a burial ground.

"This city could hold 100,000. If there's half now, I'd be surprised."

"Where'd they all go?"

"Have you ever entered a city after you sieged it?"

"Nay. I've sat under the walls, but I've never been permitted to enter."

"Hmm, well, most cities fall to disease and famine before they open their gates. Sometimes they fight before the army enters. I'd guess Mulyn used siege engines – catapults to throw fire over the walls, that sort of thing."

"Aye, they do at that."

"Houses aflame with families within. Disease and famine. People die in a siege long before the gates and walls are breached. The rest probably left for the country."

"Why?"

"Would you remain in a city you knew would be sieged again this summer or the next, a city with no king to defend it and no end in sight to the destruction. Nay, but folks probably thought the end would come sooner – a defender would come – but now they have begun to doubt, may well be far past that doubt. So, they load what they can count and carry into their carts and on their backs and they move to the countryside to become farmers, leaving behind the trades that supported them in the city. Their children will grow up to be farmers and not know how to wrought silver and weave fine cloth. They'll not return to the city because they'll not be fit for the city. And there will be fewer and fewer. When the true king does come, there may not be a high city worth defending."

"He'll have to fight for it first anyway, won't he?"

"Will he? Maybe nobody will want it by then."

"Will there truly be a kingdom if there's no king's city?"

Padraig shrugged, since he didn't feel qualified to discuss such a matter of philosophy. He was not a priest of Lugh – or would it be a priest of Bel – to discuss such esoteric matters.

Accepting that the area by the walls stood abandoned except for brothels and the lowest sorts of taverns, Padraig led the way up one of the hills that had been a middling neighborhood of merchants and craftsmen. By stashing their swords with their gear they were able to convince a suspicious innkeeper that they wouldn't burn down his inn if he rented them a smallish chamber up under the eaves. With so much destruction in the city, the inn was nearly full, but there were a few chambers on the fourth floor and Padraig paid a pretty amount of coin for one of them, though it smelled of old grease and urine. The ceiling was so low that neither man could stand straight, the plaster of the inside wall wanted white-washing and the mattresses roiled with bedbugs, but it wasn't a hayloft and Padraig wanted some privacy now.

"I think I'll go enjoy the city's sights," Tamys announced after kicking his mattress to life. "You sure you want to sleep there?" he asked, indicating the other mattress.

Padraig turned from digging in one of his packs and dusted both mattresses with a yellow powder that did not improve the smell of the room any.

"The bugs ought to be dead by the second evening watch," he announced.

"And the smell? When does that die?" Tamys asked, looking like he might retch.

"Sooner. Sorry. I might have warned you, I suppose."

"No doubt. If I find what I want, I may not be back until late."

"That's your choice," Padraig explained. There was a polite rap on the flimsy door of the chamber. Padraig opened it and accepted a bucket of warm water from the lad who stood there, handing over a copper for the lad's trouble. Tamys watched as Padraig spread a blanket on the floor in the corner and then began to disrobe.

"Would you prefer if I retired to the hayloft?" Tamys asked.

"Nay, but the chamber is yours as well as mine. I'll pray for you."

Tamys didn't reject Padraig's offer, but he fairly fled

the chamber at that point. Padraig stripped to his small clothes, then bathed with a scrap of soap and a towel, even washing his hair, then disposing of the water out the window, careful not to splash any passersby. Thus physically clean, Padraig lit a candle lantern and closed the shutters to screen out the street sounds. Softly, he began to sing in the elven tongue, not because he knew the psalm better in that language, but because he knew anyone overhearing him would not understand the words and assume he was just humming meaningless songs as men often do when they don't want to be alone with their own thoughts.

"Give ear to my words, O Lord. Consider my meditation. Listen to my cry for help, my King and my Od, for to You will I pray. My voice will You hear in the morning, O Lord. In the morning will I make my request to You and wait for Your answer.

"I will praise You, O Lord, with all my heart. I will tell of all Your wonders. I will be glad and rejoice in You. I will sing praise to Your name, O Most High.

"The Lord reigns forever. He has built His throne for judgment. He will judge the world in righteousness. He will govern the Kin with justice. The Lord is a refuge for the oppressed, a fortress in times of trouble. Those who know Your name will trust in You for You, Lord, have never turned away from those who seek You. Sing praises to the Lord, enthroned in Sion. Tell all the kingdoms what He has done, for He who avenges the bloodshed remembers, He does not ignore the cry of the afflicted."

Padraig spent much time praising his God, lifting

high – though in low tones – the One True God, the King of kings, who waited to give those who believed in Him the joy that only He possessed. When he'd finished with that, he moved onto asking for forgiveness for his disobedience to God.

"O Lord, do not rebuke me in Your anger or discipline me in Your wrath. Be merciful to me, Lord, for I am weak. As the deer pants for streams of water, so my soul pants for you, O God. Have mercy on me, according to Your great compassion, blot out my transgressions. Wash away my iniquity and cleanse me from my sin. For I know my disobedience and my sin is always before me. Against You and You alone have I sinned and done what is evil in Your sight.

"Surely I was disobedient from birth, sinful from the time my mother got me. Surely You desire truth in the inner parts. You teach me wisdom in the inmost place. Cleanse me and I will be clean, wash me and I will be whiter than snow. Hide Your face from my sins and blot out all my disobedience.

"Create in me a pure heart, O God, and renew a steadfast spirit within me."

Padraig named those sins he could remember – such as the desire to ride away from Cenydd in his difficulties and the haughtiness he'd felt when meeting the innkeeper who smelled of stale ale and dogs. He asked for forgiveness for those sins he did not remember and the Lord brought a few to his mind, like the superiority he'd felt toward Tamys when the lad had indicated he'd go out looking for harlots that night. For a moment he'd been proud of his ability to resist, but the

Lord brought to his mind that he'd noticed the innkeeper's daughter, though only glancing and he'd entertained a moment's thought about her. Padraig prayed a long time for his forgiveness.

In time he began to pray for those folk he cared about – Lydya, his elven friends, Tamys. He found himself praying a good bit for Tamys. While he still didn't know the lad's tale, he knew enough to know that Tamys had some weighty decisions to make in the next few months and that the Lord had put Padraig in his path to help him with it. He didn't know what was coming, but he knew Tamys somehow needed somewhat Padraig had to offer.

The night wore on and the chamber grew quite dark because Padraig allowed the candle to burn out. To keep from falling asleep, he knelt on the hard wooden floor and continued his prayers. At dawn Tamys stumbled in and collapsed on his mattress. Padraig paused in his prayers to cover the lad with a blanket and then returned to the dark corner and his entreaties to God. He fell asleep sometime after dawn, awaking to the sound of the door shutting softly and the recognition that a blanket had been drawn across his shoulders. The air was hot under the eaves, though the shutters had been opened. Padraig found a bottle of tepid water in his bags and drank it dry, then returned to his prayers. Having not eaten since midday of the day before, his stomach ached with hunger, but Padraig ignored it, acknowledging it only in the most perfunctory of ways.

"Lord, give me this day my daily bread," he sang softly under his breath. He sank back onto his blanket and began to prayer for Tamys in earnest. The lad had gone out into the largest city in the kingdom, a city that had lost its hope and might be full of folk who had nothing to lose, certainly not honor. Padraig knew there were dangers out there, though he couldn't have named the specific ones that might cross Tamys' path. He prayed and prayed some more, weeping to God for this new-found friend.

Toward dusk, Padraig stood with his back against the outer wall, praying about things he didn't even have words for, when suddenly there appeared in his mind a vision of a high road braced by higher cliffs in a dry and arid land. The setting sun shone at the end of the road. The vision faded into another -- this of a bit of Celdryan interlacement with elven symbols worked in and the smell of herbs. Peace flooded Padraig's soul and he suddenly felt exhausted. It was acceptable to sleep now, for he had an answer. It was an answer he didn't completely understand yet, but he knew that would come after sleep and a meal. He lay down on his mattress for the first time and pulled the blankets over himself.

True dark like the midnight smothered the room when the sound of the door opening awakened Padraig. He sat up, blinking at the pale light from the hall, to see Tamys creeping in. The lad closed the door and began to undress in the dark, apparently not wanting to disturb Padraig. Padraig's Denygal sight could make out the candle lantern on the hook by the door. He rose silently and struck iron to flint to light it. Tamys startled, then stared at him, standing in his small clothes, blinking.

"I did not mean to wake you," the lad assured him.

"I came round earlier, but I could still hear you whispering to yourself, so I went away."

"I'm finished praying and have been asleep for a bit. What have you been about, lad?"

"Naught. I talked with the town militia for a bit."

"Aye? Hardly a carouse, I'd say." Padraig wrapped his top blanket around his waist to cover his near-nakedness.

"Truly, I sort of lost my appetite for it after last night."

"Somewhat happen last night?"

"Nay, just that I found women selling themselves to me distasteful. I'm not sure why."

Padraig suspected his prayers had somewhat to do with ruining Tamys' carouse, but he didn't offer that as an opinion.

"Sex with a stranger doesn't sound alluring to me," he replied. "Every man has to make his own choice, of course."

Tamys nodded. He checked the mattress for bugs and then sat down on it. Padraig watched while he scratched.

"Did you get an answer from your gods?" Tamys asked.

"The One True God spoke to me, aye. Did you find any caravans hiring?"

"Nay. I did ask about, but apparently we're a bit early for the big caravans and the small ones don't trust the likes of me." Tamys scratched again.

"Truly? Well, I'll see what I can scare up on the morrow." Padraig narrowed his eyes, looking at Tamys.

"You itch, lad?"

"Aye and – well, somewhat burns tonight when I piss." Tamys' cheeks turned red with embarrassment.

"Aye, well, there's a price to pay beyond coin for laying with harlots. I've somewhat for it, though."

"Your elven lore is a marvel, truly."

"Not elven lore. Elves think you deserve what you get when you lay with harlots. Lodiac, my old master, he's the one that taught me this. I've just improved it with an elven herb or two. Put on your breecs and get me a small pot of lard from the kitchen and mayhap some bread for me while I prepare this."

Tamys arose immediately and did what he was told. By the time he returned, Padraig had mixed some of the yellow powder with some herbs to gentle the stink. When Tamys offered bread, watered ale and a chunk of cheese, Padraig set it aside to mix the medicinal with the lard. When he had it well-mixed he handed the palm-sized pot to Tamys.

"Smear the salve from your white belly to mid-thigh and make sure you get the back. Leave it on tonight and then wash it off in the morning. If the burning persists, tell me and I'll mix it stronger, but this usually works."

"You don't expect me to rub this stinking witch salve on myself, do you?"

"If you want to continue pain free urination, aye."

Tamys growled, but did as he was told, hissing as he slathered on the ointment.

"It stings," he announced, sounding a bit indignant.

"Aye, that's where it's touching the bites."

"Bites?"

"You don't just get bugs from the mattresses in this city," Padraig assured him. Tamys' shudder told him he understood Padraig's meaning. "It'll cool in a bit and you'll be able to sleep. In the morning, when you wash it off, it shouldn't be a bother at all."

Tamys looked skeptical, but he finished applying the ointment, then slid between his blankets and tossed his small clothes to the side. Padraig picked it up and dusted it with some of the yellow powder.

"I'd better find a fire mountain to replenish my supply of this," he murmured. "Thanks for the food," he said aloud.

He began to eat with a heartiness that he rarely exhibited. Tamys took a bit to get comfortable, so they talked while Padraig ate.

"The militia plans to hold the city next time someone wants to take it. They've grown tired of being like a piece of meat between wild dogs."

"Can they manage to hold the walls?"

"I doubt it. They're typical militia, poorly armed, poorly trained. They're determined, I'll give them that. My accent almost got me thrown from the ramparts."

"That's a vexed situation. Why'd they let you go?"

"Their captain knows a freesword when he sees one. Suggested I stay on and join the fray. Said I might win a place in some new lord's band that way. The fool doesn't understand nobility at all."

"Few commoners do. I'm for bed," Padraig said, stretching. "Do you mind if I blow out the candle?"

"Nay, it'll merely hasten my falling asleep." Tamys yawned as Padraig blew out the candle. "An army could just sail up the river. Those southern gates don't work anymore."

"That's too bad. The time I spent with the elves makes me rather relish the idea of commoners casting off the nobility, though I never did think it would work."

"Aye. The noble born have too much in their favor. And certainly the lords of Mulyn aren't going to give up their claim anytime soon."

"Not likely."

They tried to settle down, but Tamys apparently had somewhat on his mind.

"You know, I never thought I'd feel uncomfortable with a harlot. My father favors them highly."

"Some men do and then there are those who think with their brain rather than their baser parts."

Tamys chortled nervously as Padraig fumbled for his blankets.

"It wasn't my first time or anything," Tamys announced in the darkness as Padraig settled into his blankets. "I had my pick of serving lasses in the dun."

"Hmm," Padraig hummed non-committal.

"It never bothered me before."

Padraig took pity on the lad, since he sounded honestly bewildered.

"The serving lasses, you knew them a bit, most like. At least kissed them or traded a few jokes before you lifted their skirts. The harlot, you exchanged coin. Somewhat that's different from serving lasses. They at least fancied you a bit. The harlot fancied only your coin. Do you see the difference?"

"Aye, I see what you're reaching for, I think."

Tamys was quiet for a bit after that, long enough that Padraig almost dozed off. "So, why was the ale tasteless?" he asked.

Padraig remembered praying somewhat about that, but he knew that Tamys wasn't ready to hear that his friend had spoiled his carouse.

"Mayhap your life's turn has changed your view of things, made you more circumspect."

"Aye, mayhap. Aye, that could be."

Padraig waited for Tamys to say more, but the lad never did. When Padraig awoke with the light of the morning he realized he'd fallen asleep.

Founding Year 1028
Dun Clarcom

When the disturbing black shadow that followed his father everywhere developed the face of a daemon, Bryan ap Riordan of Clarcom knew he needed to have a private conversation with his mother.

Lord Darryl had fairy-like beings floating all around him that twittered at his jokes. They seemed harmless enough, though Bryan was not fooled. He didn't dislike his betrothed's father, but he was under no illusions that the spirits he entertained were as sweet as they seemed.

As Darryl finished a joke, Bryan looked toward Cunyr to see if he was laughing. He'd begun viewing auras last summer and understood that it was a gift of the elven blood that ran in the veins of almost every Denygalman. He'd seen the shadowy being following his father then. Tonight, as he looked at his father, however, the shadow took on substance and grew a face – beautiful and awful at one and the same time. Bryan sipped watered ale and tried not to look too closely.

"Then the lad fell over right onto his back, this deep in mud, toes to the sky," Darryl concluded. Bryan laughed as was appropriate, though truth be told, he'd not followed the story. This new gift was more than distracting in a room full of people.

Lydya was at the other end of the table, surrounded by her ladies and socializing with Lady Elora, Darryl's bride. Bryan had rather hoped that they'd bring their daughter Gwendolyn along on this trip, but it seemed that they were not to meet prior to the wedding. Well and good. He'd liked her well enough when they'd met many years gone, when they'd been mere children. And, he supposed they'd need to make the best of it, as noble heirs rarely had a choice in whom they married.

Elora had a pleasant aura shot with green, which was supposed to indicate that she struggled with jealousy. The streaks were faint; Bryan hoped that bode well. Lydya had met Gwendolyn last year and said her aura was pleasant with faint hints of red, suggesting (since she wasn't a warrior) a woman with a slight temper. Bryan couldn't read his mother's aura. She guarded herself from more than just his eyes. He wondered if she could read his aura. She'd sent a tutor to him in Trevellyn who had taught him shielding, but Lydya's skill at reading auras was apparently quite strong, according to the cousin who'd trained him.

Bryan blinked as a scantly-clad fairy appeared on the

shoulder of Elora's youngest lady in waiting. It turned and blew a kiss at Bryan. He truly needed to speak with Lydya, the sooner the better.

That proved more difficult than imaginable. Lydya of Clarcom was a busy lady, chatelaine to a large dun, mother of six children, rig of Denygal in absentia. For Bryan's part, his time at Clarcom was to be only an eightnight and his father seemed to think it wise to spend time with him. He didn't seem interested in teaching Bryan anything about ruling, but he made the lad follow him round the dun and demesne for three days. For that reason, Bryan and Lydya finally met late the evening before he was to head back to Trevellyn.

Lydya heard him out without outward reaction, simply just sat on the divan in her greeting chamber, eyes averted. By this time, Bryan had a whole host of visions to share with her and it took half a watch to tell them all. By that time, Bryan had screwed up enough courage to ask the truly important question.

"Just how much elven blood do I have?" he demanded. "And, don't lie because that's becoming a gift of mine too."

Lydya flicked a glance at the door and Bryan felt his skin buzz. She'd cast some sort of warding, he supposed. Two years ago, he'd not have felt it. Now it felt almost commonplace.

"You know my mam was secretly a half-elf," she told her son. That had been knowledge imparted when he was 13 and had begun to sense her gifts in use.

"Which would make you a quarter and should mean that I would have no appreciable gifts at all. Mam, it's time to be honest with me. I suspected it last year. If you're worried I'll not take it well, I'm just asking for confirmation of my long-held suspicion."

Lydya sighed. He hated having to do this to her, but he could no longer live with the question and was certain the answer would not hurt overmuch.

"The sort of honesty you seek does not lie with me, but with your father," she murmured, her blue eyes meeting his directly. "I can tell you that I've been faithful to your father in keeping with his wishes."

Noble families kept many secrets and Geran of Trevellyn had taught Bryan that the wise son learned to distinguish when a deep truth was being imparted obliquely. Bryan rubbed the chin where a beard refused to grow. Most lads by 15 had a soft downy beard coming in, but he didn't even have a shadow.

"He was married before," he noted. Lydya raised an eyebrow and waited to be judged. "And he put her away as barren." The bloodlines and marriages of the nobility were common knowledge to the women of the duns and Geran's mother, Ysolla, had shared it with him once in a very off-handed manner. "How many years were you married before I was born?"

"Three."

Bryan nodded, numb. Bryan had benefited from tutors from both Denygal and Clarcom. He had mayhap the most cosmopolitan education of any heir in the kingdom. He remembered a discussion of how noblemen sometimes had their heirs fathered when they themselves could not. With that memory, Bryan felt rising anger.

"There's six of us. Do we each have different …?"

"Nay. When it became clear that he was going to have me raped if he couldn't produce an heir, my Mam helped me find a surrogate – somewhat like a kinsman redeemer. He was a groom here for many years, until he married Lisbet and they moved back to Denygal. I suspect Culyn mayhap be actually Cunyr's."

"How?"

"The usual way between man and wife, Bryan," she said, her cheeks blushing pink. "Some men …."

"Nay, I am familiar with it from horses," Bryan assured her, sparing her embarrassment. "We're quarter or a third then?"

"Aye. Donyvan is more than I, most-like."

"Donyvan, who now lives in Denygal."

"He's the equerry at Dun Moryn now."

Bryan nodded. He doubted if he'd truly ever meet the man who had fathered him, but knowing that he could made him feel better. His fears that his mother had been unfaithful to the man he called father assuaged, now Bryan was curious concerning the man who had actually produced him.

"Is he a Believer?" Bryan asked.

"Aye. In Denygal, when a man dies without leaving heirs, it's common for a kinsman-redeemer to provide his wife with heirs and a living until the child is old enough to support her. On that premise, Donyvan agreed to come here and be Cunyr's surrogate. He is a kind man and he stayed until Cunyr had his fill of heirs. Do you remember him? You remember Lisbet, I'm sure."

Lisbet had become nurse to the children just as

Bryan had left the nursery. He did remember her, in the vaguest of ways. He remembered a groom who had been, come to think of it, unusually solicitous even with the heir of the rule. It might have been only his imagination in retrospect, but he'd had dark hair and a Denygal way of speaking.

"Does Father know?"

"Of course, he knows, Bryan. Why do you think he's so cold to you?"

"I thought that was just who he is, but I was asking after Culyn."

"Nay. If I let slip what I suspect, he'd have you killed in favor of the son of his body."

That thought had not occurred to Bryan. Fear struck him head to foot like a lightning bolt. He stood there shaking like he had the day before his first battle. He rubbed the back of his neck and took a deep breath. The fear stepped back, leaving only a mild anxiety.

"What if I abdicated?"

"Nay, it would not save you and Dublyn and Denygal need you. Some men are meant to rule, Bryan, and you are one. You're kind and compassionate, you understand the common man a bit, and you think before you do somewhat." She held up a hand, indicating he should wait a moment. He turned to the window to look down into the ward while she took a deep breath and released it slowly. He could feel the buzzing of her warding spell just a span from his face. "Also, it would be a red flag," she warned. "Cunyr is a deeply paranoid man and any unusual behavior by you will be suspected."

Bryan swallowed, mind racing, but trying to force

himself to quiet.

"I could abdicate and take the rule in Denygal. You've said you wished to send one of your children there."

"Cunyr would purge Denygal to punish us, Bryan." She stood, gliding up behind him and placing her hand on his back. Tall for a woman, she barely topped his shoulder. "Bryan, if it bothers your honor, I understand, but you must weigh it against the greater good."

Bryan continued staring out the window. The sky above the ramparts had just about lost all light, leaving just a sparkling streak of dark blue on the western horizon.

Lord God Jesu, help me to see the way through. What path would you have me to walk?

"You didn't think beyond your duty as a wife, did you?"

"Nay, I had no choice in the matter. He'd have turned me over to the warband and that would have dishonored me sorely. He'd have gotten his heirs at my expense. My mam thought clearly to avoid such terror. I did as was needful, as noble wives have done in the past. You are right, though. I did not expect that he would be so cold and suspicious of the heirs he demanded I produce. Cunyr is a horrible man, Bryan. You know what his father did to his siblings. Cunyr was a second son. Do you suppose his brother died of natural causes?"

Bryan shivered, took a steadying breath and turned to his mother.

"Can I cast a warding such as this?" he asked, indicating the window.

"Mayhap. With elflings gifts are often a matter of taking what your blood has given and enhancing it with practice. I will try to show you." She stepped away, indicating they should sit on the divan.

"Good, because if I'm to survive to be Cunyr's heir, I think I'll need to keep a lot of secrets."

Lydya managed a tremulous smile as he joined her to learn survival skills that Cunyr could not control.

Kin Cycle 24578 / FY 1028
Blue Iris Holt

Sarala dismounted in the small yard outside the cave her mother shared with her mate. Brennan looked up from some tack he was repairing. He stood up and came out from under the lean-to, smiling as if he were happy to see her. Perhaps he was.

"How's are you keeping, wren?" he asked. He had laid that play-name on her early in their knowing one another. She supposed it was for her brown hair, but she had never asked him.

"I came to speak with Maryanara."

"She's sewing. Do I need to take the young ones for a wander?"

"Perhaps," Sarala said. Despite his Celtic name, Brennan was more elf than not and looked thoroughly elven, with midnight black hair and striking grey eyes with purple vertically slit eyes. "I'm planning a walkabout." He said nothing. "In the basketlands," she added after a moment.

His breath caught.

"I suggest you and she go for the wander then. There's much misery in that news. I'll get her."

Sarala waited in the yard. This had never been her home. Her mother had raised her in the heart of the holt until she'd given her to the Wise when she was five. Brennan had come after and this was his home. Because he was a drover, he lived on the route to the horse valley, in a small steading hemmed in by mountains.

Maryanara knew Sarala had hard news when Brennan came to her, so her eyes were suspicious when she came out of the dressed cave that served as home. Sarala had heard all of her life that her mother was beautiful beyond what was normal even for an elf. She supposed it to be true. She'd born Brennan two children thus far, but she and Sarala looked an age. Her huge vertically slit eyes were corn-flower blue and her hair was spun gold.

"Sarala," she greeted, composed, reserved.

"Brennan suggested you show me your garden."

They didn't speak as they walked over to where Brennan had built up the ground above the stone to allow for planting.

"Strawberries are coming in," Maryanara said. "What brings you here?"

It's best to rip the bandage away and not lengthen the pain.

"I'm walking about in the basketlands after the solstice."

Maryanara's full pink lips tightened. She breathed in slowly and let it out.

"They kill beautiful women there."

"I know," Sarala assured her. "But it is something I must do."

"Why?"

"To know what my name should be."

"Then do a cycle as goi'tan. Don't go where men are wolves."

"I've nothing to be ashamed of, mother. I will do this and I will know both sides of me and then, perhaps, I'll be content."

"And if you never return?"

"Will you notice?"

"That's unfair!"

"No, mother, it isn't. I know you were traumatized, but I didn't cause that. I am the product of it. I am the victim of it. And, you ignore me to avoid the pain, but I will move on."

"I forbid it."

"I'm 21 cycles. You cannot forbid me anything."

"Gly will support me on this."

"Gly knows and while he doesn't approve, he is not standing against it. I'm a free female, mother. I will go as I see fit and I will discover what I must to know my name."

"And you will be destroyed," Maryanara cried. Her voice echoed off the mountainside.

"Or not," Sarala said calmly. Maryanara's cheeks were, surprisingly, wet with tears. Sarala felt a tug of sympathy that she resisted. "I just wanted you to know so that you could pray for me. It's a big decision, but it's a good one."

"No!"

"Yes! I will travel as far as Cenconyn with the caravan. There's rumors afoot that Ryanna may be going into the basketlands. I'll travel with her if I can."

"Ryanna's youth is legend. Be careful to separate the myth from the real woman."

"I will." Sarala wanted to run to her horse, mount and flee, but she was 21 – too old to act like a petulant child. "I love you, mother! I would the feeling were reciprocated, but it's what we have."

"You're wrong. It's not that I don't love you. I carried you inside of me for a cycle. There is no bond so deep. It is only that whenever I see you I remember and …."

"And you blame me for what I did not cause." Maryanara shook her head, but Sarala kept speaking. "Very well. It is as it has always been. Perhaps we can find common ground when I return."

"Please!"

This time Sarala did not answer, but strode to her waiting horse, vaulted into the saddle and rode away … lest Maryanara see the tears that flowed down her own cheeks now that the decision had been made and the chains of family shattered.

Confluence of Healing Streams

"Of what importance to me are your many sacrifices?" says the One. "I am stuffed with burnt sacrifices of rams and the fat from steers. I do not want the blood of bulls, lambs, and goats. When you enter my presence, do you actually think I want animals trampling on my courtyards? Do not bring any more meaningless offerings; I consider your incense detestable! You observe new moon festivals, Sabbaths, and convocations, but I cannot tolerate sin-stained celebrations! I hate your new moon festivals and assemblies; they grieve me beyond endurance. When you spread out your hands in prayer, I look the other way; when you offer your many prayers, I do not listen, because your hands are covered with blood.

"Wash! Cleanse yourselves! Remove your sinful deeds from my sight. Stop sinning! Learn to do what is right! Promote justice! Give the oppressed reason to celebrate! Take up the cause of the orphan! Defend the rights of the widow!

Come, let's consider your options," says the One. "Though your sins have stained you like the color red, you can become white like snow; though they are as easy to see as the color scarlet, you can become white like wool. If you have a willing attitude and obey, then you will again eat the good crops of the land. But if you refuse and rebel, you will be devoured by the sword. Know for certain that the One has spoken."

From the Scriptos of the One, Writings of Isayah

Recorded by Brethry, Priest of Bel, Moryn
FY 941

Founding Year 931
Dun Llyr

Gilyan of Llyr stared out over the harbor of Llyr at the many colored sails and odd shaped ships. On the opposite headland stood the fortress tasked with defending the most important harbor in the kingdom, the sealink through which Mulyn iron and Celdryan beef flowed. She found the commanding view to be soothing. It reminded her that her problems were small compared to the world round them. She would hear from Celdrya soon and all would be well. Prince Perryn -- King Perryn -- was known as the more honorable brother. Not that she'd been upset over marrying Maryn. He'd been nice enough and would have been an enjoyable lover. It's just that Perryn was known to act honorably above and beyond what his brother had been known to be. It concerned her that the message she'd sent had not been returned after a fortnight. Surely Perryn had received it and should have responded. Yet she still waited. Which was why she stood here on the top floor of the tower -- in what had once been the dun-jail for family members -- reminding herself that the world was so much bigger than her problems.

A servant entered the chamber where Gilyan stood at the open window and approached.

"Lord Braedyn wants to see you in his greeting

chamber, my lady," she said in a soft voice.

"Thank you, Meryla."

Gilyan smoothed her overdress and checked her head-scarf with her hands. Technically she was in mourning for her betrothed, though they'd scarcely known each other an eight night. She wore black in deference to that, but still kirtled her dress in Llyr blue and yellow and her underdress was in the rich blue she favored. Of middle height and athletic build, Gilyan possessed a strong face with high cheekbones and a bold mouth coupled with large blue eyes and shining hair the same shade as honey. She would never be judged beautiful, but she was handsome and intelligent. At 21 she'd already been married and widowed and lost a child to fever, but she still enjoyed laughter and found life worth living. This unexpected pregnancy by a man now dead was not a tragedy, just a complication in her life.

The halls of Dun Llyr were their usual bustle of activity as she made her way down from the tower to the main broch where her father's greeting chamber could be found on the third floor.

Braedyn ap Umhall of Llyr dismissed his councilor as soon as his eldest daughter arrived.

"I received a message from High Celdrya yesterday," he began as soon as the door closed to leave them alone together.

Gilyan's heart skipped a beat. Her father ordinarily was a pleasant fellow with a ready smile; today his lips hid within his dark beard and his eyes didn't meet hers.

"Tell me the truth, lass. Did you and Maryn sport with one another when he came here at Beltane?"

She felt her cheeks grow warm, not with the idea of what she had done with Maryn, but with the notion of discussing it with her father.

"We are not children to mince about these issues," she replied, mayhap a bit more curtly than she intended.

"Nay, and I do not fault you or him that. Unfortunately, Celdrya does."

Gilyan's heart fluttered in her chest.

"Whatever for?" she asked. "Do they think it's not his?"

"Precisely. I quote King Perryn's message. 'She may be your daughter, but she is a liar. I have on good authority that no such coupling occurred, that Maryn was still mourning his wife and child and only marrying to please our father. I recognize this is a delicate matter for you, Lord Braedyn, but I must insist you put a stop to your daughter's unfounded allegations. The Umhall has always been a trusted ally of the throne, but scandal such as this so early in my reign does not bode well for continuation of that."

"But it is the gods' honest truth!"

"Is it? Do I take your word or his?" Gilyan opened her mouth to point out that she knew whom she had slept with and that there had been no others, but Braedyn cut her off. "You know what King Perryn did upon his father's death -- burned an entire village just to put an end to the poisoners' guild. How could you have risked writing to him without consulting me first?"

"I - I - It was my problem and my solution. I thought he'd acknowledge the child as bastard and set lands upon him. It's what's been done in the past."

"By another king," Braedyn reminded her.

An uncomfortable silence ensued. Braedyn stared at the table top before him. Gilyan stared at the rich tapestry behind him.

"What must I do now?"

"There is only one choice," Braedyn replied with cold resignation in his voice. "Nalyna will take care of you."

Nalyna had been Gilyan's nurse as a babe and was still a trusted servant, for all her age now.

"I don't mean my physical comfort, Da. I mean the legal status of my child."

Braedyn frowned at her.

"Gilyan, there will be no child."

She felt that admission like a blow to her white belly and instinctively put a hand over that area to protect the tiny life within.

"I can't," she said.

"You must. The message was short, but clear. He wants this scandal ended or he'll have my head."

"Surely not."

"Gilyan, not every king is as fair-minded as Vanyn was and he clearly raised a man who will not see his will thwarted."

"It cannot be as bad as killing my baby. I could retire to the hunting lodge for a time, not name Maryn as father."

Braedyn stood abruptly, his face darkening behind his beard.

"You will do as you are told! Nalyna will take you there this afternoon."

"No!" Gilyan replied firmly. "I cannot lose this child. I will not kill it!"

Braedyn came around the table and caught her shoulder in one hand and drove his other fist into her belly. Gilyan collapsed to the Morikan carpet with an exhalation of air and stayed there. For a moment she couldn't think, could only feel pain and fear. Her father had never hit her. As far as she had ever heard, he'd never hit any of his children. He reared back a foot and kicked her, again in the mid-section, sliding her across the carpet.

"You will end this pregnancy with medicinals or you will end it with a beating," he hissed. Gilyan choked out a sob as answer. He grabbed her arm and dragged her to her feet. "You will go to Nalyna's chamber now. She's already been tasked." Gilyan grabbed the edge of the table to keep standing when he let go and strode from the room.

My father has gone mad! What will I do?

Gilyan swallowed bile and held her stomach with her free hand, wondering if she would start bleeding soon. Pain roared through her hip as she took a step toward the door. She caught the door frame. The worst of the pain was easing. The time she reached the spiral staircase, walking upright was possible, though she feared for her baby.

Nalyna met her at the entrance to the stairs. The old woman had grey hair and wrinkles aplenty, but she was still spry and tart-tongued. She enveloped Gilyan in her arms and held her while the lass wept sorely. After a bit, she drew her away to her own small chamber in a distant half-broch.

"Take off your dresses. Let me have a look," she ordered.

Gilyan wept while she removed her clothes all the way down to her skin. There was a bruise starting on her ribs and another on her hip. Nalyna probed her belly with practiced hands.

"You may not lose this child from the beating," she announced. "This one, at least. There's somewhat amiss with your da, though I'm not carrying surprise news to you, I suppose. This is a bad situation."

"What should I do?" Gilyan asked as she pulled on her small breecs.

"Well, a noble woman would go to the darkwife with me and take care of this inconvenience."

"No!" Gilyan clipped out.

"I thought as much. Don't bother with the underdress, love. Where you're going, women don't wear such confining clothes."

"Where I'm going? Where am I going?"

Nalyna opened a chest and brought out a set of brown dresses, which she laid across her narrow bed. They looked pretty much like what every servant girl in the dun wore.

"If you've got coin, I think you should try for your mother's folks in Fyrgal."

"My uncle might take me in," Gilyan agreed. "I've a little silver and my jewelry. That should be enough for a carriage there."

"I'll go get it. You should rest. I'll be a bit."

Nalyna patted the bed, put the dresses on top of the

chest and left the chamber. Gilyan gently fingered her stomach and wondered if her baby was okay. It was too early to feel it move, so there was no way of knowing.

I'll never forgive you, Father!

Gilyan let tears fall unchecked down her cheeks. Nalyna returned almost a watch later, carrying a small bundle which she set upon the bed.

"Your father has your chamber guarded, so I couldn't reach your jewelry or coin," she announced. "But Lord Caedyn provided me with some silver and I've a sack of food." Caedyn was the heir, Gilyan's eldest brother. "It's not enough to hire a carriage to Fyrgal, but he gave me information that was useful like. There's a inn in the Bog, called the Golden Unicorn. Go there. Ask after Alyssa. It's a sort of home for noble women who have bedded commoners."

"But, I didn't …."

Nalyna thrust the brown dresses at her.

"It do not matter what you did or did not do, my sweet lass. It only matters the options you will have if you choose to keep this baby. Your father may forgive you in time and set lands upon the child. Bastards are useful like to the nobles, it seems. Caedyn says he'll act honorably himself once he's vyngretrix. But you must keep the child alive if you are to raise it."

Gilyan wiped a brief scatter of tears from her eyes and resolved to dress. Her child meant more to her than it had when she stood in the tower seeking the harbor's soothing rhythms. She would do what was necessary to protect it. Nalyna patted her shoulder and smiled.

"There are worse things than this in life, lass. The

noble-born do not know the underbelly of life and I pray you will not learn it, but there are far worse things than being made to find your way in the world without a patron."

"Aye, Nalyna," Gilyan said because this was her nurse, the hand that had rocked the cradle, and she knew far more than Gilyan did about the world beyond the walls of her father's dun.

Founding Year 1028
High Celdrya

Padraig spent the morning asking after westbound caravans looking for herbmen and freeswords, but he found none. He finally decided that he was looking in the wrong place and went for an idle walk through the city, wondering what the Lord wanted him to find.

As he traveled through the city, he climbed toward the dun and noted that the rot had entered the core of the city. The stately homes of the higher strata wanted white washing and some were missing window glass that had been there before. In the markets, Padraig listened to the talk and knew that the merchants were close to leaving for the countryside themselves. The constant cycle of siege and abandonment made it hard to make a living in Dun Celdrya and the merchants were starting to look toward Duns Llyr and Galornyn. The craftspeople were leaving this summer and the merchants would have to follow or they'd have nothing to sell.

About mid-afternoon he happened into an area of the city that he'd never been in before. There was a collection of round houses on a plateau about halfway up the market hill. There was naught to set it aside from any other neighborhood except mayhap that all the buildings were in a good repair and the cobbles seemed cleaner than in most of the other parts of the city. Padraig had noted the suspicion and isolation of the city folk, but somehow these folks seemed a bit friendlier. He won a smile from one man who passed by carrying a bucket and a child waved at him. Padraig rounded a neat yard and found himself in an alley between two round houses. He was about to turn round the way he'd come when he saw the apothecary's sign hanging above one of the doors. The mortis and pestle were clearly prominent against a background of sworls and braids like the Celdryan nobles favored, but cleverly worked into the patterns were elven symbols. Curious, Padraig approached the door.

Typical of most shops in the kingdom on a fine spring day, the door stood open in welcome. Within a generous section of the round house's main floor had been sectioned off with a wicker wall and set with shelves and barrels. Near the door to the rest of the house, a board set across two barrels served as a desk and counter for the proprietor, a tall, slender man with dark hair and strongly-colored blue eyes. He smiled pleasantly and asked if Padraig needed anything.

"A passing herbman, just looking about for the moment."

"By all means. I'll just continue with my accounts.

Let me know if you need somewhat." The man's speech rang with the timbrels of the Denygal.

Padraig noted, as he pretended to look about the shop, that the proprietor was an uncommonly handsome man with the fine features that spoke of a lot of elven blood. He had long slender hands and a grace in the way that he moved of which Padraig knew that he should be interested. He sensed the proprietor watching him as well. Padraig had made sure that his elven boots with their lovely engraving were visible to him.

Padraig selected a few jars of things he was running a bit low on and he approached the counter, still a bit wary of the situation.

"I hear the tones of Denygal in your voice, herbman," the propriety began.

"Aye. Yours as well."

"My name is Andyr." There seemed to be somewhat missing in the way that he said that, as if he'd grown up saying somewhat more or differently.

"Padraig."

"Were you an herbman in Denygal?"

"My family are all fishermen," Padraig replied.

To those who didn't know Denygal, the reference to fishermen would mean little. There were no seas nearby, but some folks assumed there might be an inland sea or great lake for fishing. Among Believers, though, the fish stood for Jesu and Believers were called fishermen.

"I have done a fair bit of fishing myself," Andyr said. He drew a seemingly random, curved line in the wax of the tablet he was using to tally supplies, then set the stylus he used on the table beside the tablet. "It's what brought me to Dun Celdrya." Padraig picked up the stylus and drew a second curved line that intersected the first – creating a simple fish.

Andyr grinned briefly.

"I'm going to close up early," he announced. He went to close the door and turn the shingle. When he returned, he and Padraig embraced. Though they had never met, they knew each other as brothers.

"Let us break bread," Andyr began. He ushered Padraig through the door in the wicker wall into the kitchen of his home. Occupying about a third of the main floor, it had a hearth similar to the one in the front room and a table with a wealth of three chairs as well as some benches. Andyr took a teapot and two wooden tankards from a cupboard and set them on the table.

"I've received a prophesy for you," Andyr explained. "Do you want it now or after we eat?"

Padraig did not question how Andyr had known the prophesy was for him. It was a given among the elves that when one received a prophesy God would reveal the recipient.

"Now would be fine."

Andyr continued making tea, preparing his own mind. Elven prophesies were a thing of the everyday, not grand pronouncements from the mountaintops, but that which was given over bread and tea.

"It's too hot for a fire already and there's little wood, so I'll get water out of the pot in the central yard. Wait here a moment."

Andyr went out of the back door, carrying his tea

pot. A bit alarmed, Padraig looked out the window and watched him dip water from a small caldron in the backyard. Five round houses clustered around a central area, rather unusual and more so to see them cooperating like that. Beyond the fire, there were chickens and garden plots.

Andyr grinned as he came back in.

"There's quite a few Believers in this area. We do what we can to help one another and to be a light to those round us in darkness." He continued with the tea, speaking in a normal voice.

"The dragon will rise from the mountain and he will fall to the ground. The dragon will die, but be reborn. When the dragon flies he will not be alone. There is one on the other side, preparing.

Go west, and hither and to. Keep the sword close even as it is broken, for swords can be mended and reforged stronger than before in the fires of refinement. Wait upon the Lord for the king will rise on dragon's wings."

Andyr breathed out.

"That's it. When I received the prophesy our group prayed for interpretation, but we didn't receive any."

"Are you sure it is for me?"

"Oh, aye. Gly was certain of it when I scried to him. He knew you'd be coming this way."

"You know Gly?"

"Aye, he's my da."

Padraig stared at Andyr, honestly confused. The apothecary laughed.

"Well, he's the man that raised me. It's certainly

obvious that my seed-father was a Celtman, I suppose."

"Oh, aye. Then Barana is your mother."

"Aye, and Gly raised me as his own. He's never been one to cast aside what the Lord has a use for."

"Nay, he's not. And the elves do have such a fine honor about children, even the unfathered. If I ask a painful question, please tell me to mind my own business, but I'm assuming Barana was not a willing participant in the mating that produced you."

"She was raped," Andyr replied coldly. "And, you're not causing pain. A bit of anger at the wolf who would do that to another man's wife."

"Aye, even I feel anger for such an insult, though there must be many years since."

"I'm forty and seven," Andyr informed him.

Andyr looked to be a young man in his early twenties, with the usual youthful appearance of an elf or half-elf. Padraig knew by his age that his mother would have been raped during the last purge of Denygal, when the priests of Lugh had convinced Tyran ap Riordan, father of Cunyr, to scour the land free of all elven folk, a fair number of whom were living peacefully in the high valleys of Denygal, close to their children and grandchildren. Gly had mentioned spending time in Denygal, but Padraig had never thought to pin him down on an exact time frame.

"My father's people are often wolves," Padraig commented, trying not to sound bitter. "'Tis a pity, that is certain. Andyr, may I ask you somewhat?"

"Mayhap."

"I've never known an elf to whelp the unfathered,

but I know of at least one half-elven child this side of the border and it occurs to me that his mother wouldn't have put horns on her husband's head. Would an elf ever – well?"

"I've never known one to rape a woman, but I know that one of my older brother exacted some sort of revenge on the Celtman for what they'd done to his mother. I've never known the details because he went into goi'tan. How long did you live among the Kin?"

"Four years."

"So you know that we never hold someone's past sins against him. Once my brother was released from his penitence, his crimes were never mentioned again."

"I know that. I just wondered."

"I would think that even elves are capable of baser actions if they are outside of the will of God. Certainly the histories say that we were as a nation out of that will when the Celtmen fell upon us, so mayhap there are some whose hearts are not pure."

Padraig nodded. He could imagine his own feelings if his mother or sister had been raped. While he didn't think himself capable of such vengeance, he knew that he might feel the desire for such.

Padraig and Andyr sat down at the table for a scant meal of tea and bread. Andyr apologized for the lean fare.

"It's been a hard winter and there's not much left for us to eat. I was able to win free last summer before the siege and take two deer. It sustained us and our neighbors over the winter, but we'll be needing grain and the like soon enough."

"Truly. Why do you remain?"

"Because so many lost remain. Someone must be salt and light here."

"How long have you dwelt here?"

"Hmm, more than 10 years now. I was sent as a spy, more or less, when they began the program of infiltration. You know about such?"

"The half-elf Fanadargilyn's idea? Oh, aye, I've heard of it. Not a bad idea on the whole. Can't defend from what you know naught of. Do you miss your home?"

"Aye, I miss the company of elves, but the Believers here have become a family of sorts. I'm the only Kin here, mind, but we are brothers and sisters at another level."

"True-spoken. Where did these become Believers?"

"Well, I'm not exactly certain. The story goes that there's been a group of Believers in this city for at least two prior generations. They don't completely believe as the elves do – or I should say – they don't worship as we do. They believe in Jesu and they have the same basic theology, but they have different ways of expressing it."

"Descendants of some who did not come north to Denygal, do you think?"

"Aye, that's my thought. Came with the Celtmen, fleeing the Rhwmanes. Mayhap their grandfathers were more crafty than the ones who came to Denygal. They escaped notice by being more careful of what they said and to whom. It's hard to know, but they are here. Only one that I've met so far has traveled east. He got as far as Dublyn, then felt the Lord drawing him home."

"Curious. Well, I'm sure the city is better for your presence here."

"You're welcome to join us for worship if you'd like. I've carved out a meeting room beneath the house."

"I doubt me that I'll have the time. I'm seeking a caravan to take me and mayhap a friend west on a errand for the Lord."

"Here's a bit of news you'll enjoy. I've heard there's a westerner gathering a band for a caravan. He's to be found at the south market gate every afternoon."

"Truly? Do you know his name?"

"Nay, but I've heard he has rather conspicuous banners."

"Thanks to you, Andyr. I'm afraid I should be off, as I must meet this caravan master."

"I'm glad I could help. If you have time, we meet for praise and worship every night at sunset in the cellar."

"I'll keep it in mind."

Padraig let himself out the front door and hurried to the southern market square, which was a fair distance from Andyr's apothecary shop – far enough indeed that the sun touched the walls as Padraig approached the spot. Many of the merchants and craftspeople were starting to close up their stalls and roll up their mats. Padraig hoped he wasn't too late. Just as he thought he was, he saw a man sitting on a bench near the postern gate, a yellow banner emblazoned with the mule and prod of the muleteer and the sword for guards. Padraig approached, seeing that the man who waited was a barrel-chested fellow with a fine set of mustaches and well-made common clothes.

"Are you still seeking hires?" Padraig asked.

The man looked up at him, appraising him with sharp brown eyes.

"Aye, I'm seeking guards and muleteers," he said in a tone that suggested he didn't think Padraig was either, though Padraig wore a sword.

"I'm an herbman, actually."

"An herbman!? Now, I could use the likes of you. We always need physics on this caravan. Do you know how to use that sword?"

"To wear a sword you don't know how to use is to be a paper target that will be knocked over."

"Well-spoken," the caravan master said. "I'm Duglas of Glenconyn. Do you know where that is?"

"West and north. I'm Padraig of Denygal."

"I'm taking a caravan into Mandorlyn. Have you heard of that?"

"Aye, that's a true adventure. Have you done such before?"

"Aye, many times. Why aren't you off looking for a war?"

"Tired of war," Padraig replied, which was true enough.

"I'd be willing to pay you two silvers for your hire, 50 coppers per week, and two silvers for each scrap."

"Those are fine wages. Are you still seeking guards?"

"I'm always seeking guards. Do you know someone interested?"

"Aye, I've been traveling with a young soldier."

"A freesword?"

"Just become."

"Not given to incipient drink?"

"Nay, not that I've seen."

"Fair enough then. I pay guards less well than herbmen, you understand. Silver for the hire, 30 coppers a week and a silver for each scrap."

"I suspect he'll be interested. Where do I report?"

"Dawn on the morrow, right at this gate. We'll be traveling fast west. I've a schedule to keep."

"Well and good. I'll see you then."

Padraig hadn't expected Tamys to be angry over the deal he'd struck, but the lad was.

"I sold my sword to you, but I don't recall giving you the right to sell it to another," he snapped when Padraig told him the news.

Bewildered, Padraig watched Tamys stalk back and forth in the low-ceilinged chamber. He thought mayhap anything he said would make it worse, but he had to try – he couldn't say why.

"The pay is excellent, it's a guarding hire so you won't be selling your sword – merely renting it out – and it's going to Mandorlyn, a very rough and unsettled place, the sort of place that doesn't ask many questions about a man's past."

Tamys kicked the wall by the window hard enough to crack the daub and stood staring down at the street for a while. Padraig waited.

"I know I don't have much choice, but I don't have to like it," Tamys admitted.

"Nay, I should have asked, but the opportunity

might have passed, so I didn't."

"I apologize. I'm just not happy with the dice the gods have tossed in my lap. I shouldn't take my anger out on you."

"I'm not holding it against you. I chose to leave page, but I remember feeling a bit angry when I realized that decision meant I wouldn't eat. I can imagine it's all the worse when you didn't make the decision yourself."

Tamys turned from the window.

"If I've got to sell my sword, I guess this is a better way than what I am facing. I can delay the inevitable a bit longer, aye?"

"It's only inevitable if you think it is and you allow it to be. There are alternatives."

"I'd have to sell my sword still to afford a prentice fee."

Padraig didn't truly feel it was the right time to suggest that there was a tradesman who would train him without a fee. Somewhat kept him silent, though he could not have said what. Sometimes the One said "wait". Mayhap that was it, spoken more softly than Padraig would have liked.

"The day's nearly ended," Padraig said instead. "I'm for bed if we're to wake before dawn."

He began to undress. Tamys continued to stand by the window, staring down at the dark street below. Padraig allowed him time to think, did not intrude upon his reverie with idle chatter. That subject had been broached, what more was there to say. Just as he was about to doze off, a thought came to him.

"I didn't pay a prentice fee," he murmured sleepily.

"There are alternatives."

Tamys answered by blowing out the candle lantern. Padraig took that to mean the subject was closed.

Founding Year 1028
Dun Galornyn

Gregyn stared into the candle lantern, sweat stinging his skin. Everyone else was still at the evening meal and he was atop of a half-broch overlooking the kitchen garden, trying to scry in the stifling heat of a coastal spring night. From long practice, the image of Talidd in his mind quickly formed into the man's facsimile in the flame.

Ah, it's about time you've scried to me, lad! Talidd thought with a hint of irritation in his voice. *What have you been about?*

It had been over an eightnight since Gregyn had sought out Talidd.

Didn't Werglidd tell you? he asked. *There's illness at the dun. Some sort of plague.*

And that affects your ability to report to me in what way?

Gregyn considered pretending someone had come upon the roof and breaking the communication. He had used that excuse before. Tonight he was too tired to make the effort.

They've used the riders to carry away the dead and even work in the infirmary. Werglidd said not to risk scrying when people are talking of curses and the like, so I had to find a time to get away when nobody was looking.

Talidd's face in the flame might have been irritated or thoughtful. The pain he was capable of sending down the link was absent, which Gregyn took as a good sign.

Werglidd told me of this plague. He was to show you the enchantments to keep it at bay.

Gregyn listened to voices drifting on the wind, floating up from the kitchen garden. He was four stories up, however, so not terribly worried about them hearing him.

Aye, I've been working them. The whole city was in chaos when we got back here from the north and then the sicknesses started sweeping through the dun. Teddryn fell ill this morning.

Talidd's image narrowed its eyes.

I would recall you, but I continue to hope your time there at Galornyn will be fruitful.

Gregyn was tired and the scrying link was wavering. He didn't want to risk annoying Talidd further, but he knew he should be in bed.

Some of them sicken and then get better, he thought, mouthing the words at the same time, as novices often did. *Especially the babies get better, but many of the adults and older children die and some who live are left palsied.*

Talidd's image now looked annoyed, but before Gregyn could say anything more, the door to the roof slammed. He looked up to see Taryn of Galoryn, so far from the rule it wasn't worth figuring, stumble forward, then stop and stare at Gregyn.

The link with Talidd disintegrated as Gregyn focused his mind to this problem. Pity to kill such a talented potential, but his life was worth far more than

Taryn's. Then Gregyn realized that Taryn was drunk.

"Hallo, whatcha doing here?" the young lordling asked. He was scarcely more than 14, still without a beard, tall and slender, with light brown hair and captivating blue eyes with multiple shades in the iris. His potential for mage work was strong, but the wine jar in his hand was one reason Gregyn had decided not to pursue him.

"Looking for some peace and quiet," Gregyn replied. "I spent all day in the infirmary."

Taryn nodded absently and then slunk around the roof to slide down a parapet to continue with his wine. Gregyn could not just leave him there. He might remember this conversation and tell folks somewhat that Gregyn didn't want them to know. Gregyn went over to sit beside him.

"How's Teddryn?" he asked.

"Fevered and in pain. So far he's no weaker than a man with a fever. The chirgeon thinks he'll recover."

"Some have," Gregyn said by way of agreement.

Suddenly Taryn's eyes overflowed.

"What is it, lad?" Gregyn asked.

"My da is sick now too."

For Gregyn's purposes, that was a good thing. If Lord Daryn died, he'd be replaced with his eldest son, Egoran, who was much more like his mother than his father -- not an honorable man. Turmoil within the family meant a potential profit for Gregyn and his guild. He merely had to know when to exploit it.

"I'm sorry to hear that," he murmured without meaning it. *Don't smile. People with parents care what happens to them.* He stared up at the stars, tracing the constellations. "Mayhap he will improve as others have."

Taryn nodded, swallowing some wine. The drink might weaken Taryn's defenses.

"We should get you inside, in bed. You need your rest so you don't get sick also."

"What does it matter?" Taryn slurred. "Nobody would notice if I died."

"Your grandmother would notice," Gregyn assured the lad. "Come on. Up you come."

He rose from the roof and dragged Taryn to standing, leading him to the door. The winding stairs proved hazardous, but he got Taryn down them and to his room with neither of them breaking his neck. Taryn didn't ask how a rider knew the way to his room and Gregyn hadn't actually prepared a believable lie, but they didn't meet anyone on the way there and Taryn fell onto the bed without protest.

"Thank you, rider Gregyn," Taryn intoned, turning over and sitting up. *You either have to kill him or make him forget.*

Gregyn captured Taryn's gaze easily enough and said "You won't remember this in the morning. Go to sleep now and in the morning, you will have forgotten seeing me."

He let power aplenty flow into those words. Ordinary people would turn and snuggle into their blankets and awake the next morning with no memory of meeting Gregyn on the roof. Taryn stared at him, perplexed.

"I'm not that in my cups," he announced. "But I am

tired and it's been an exhausting day. Keep yourself clean, Gregyn. We need men like you round the dun."

Gregyn seriously doubted that to be true, but he nodded and fled the room, because no matter how much good sense said to kill this witness, he just couldn't waste that awesome potential, as evidenced by the fact that Gregyn could not ensorcel him under any circumstances.

Hurrying round a narrow curved path between the main broch and the servants quarters, Gregyn pulled up as a pretty young serving lass smiled at him. Her brown hair hung in a single braid down her back and her blue eyes held mysteries he would like to solve.

"Hallo, Gregyn," she greeted. "Can I get your strong shoulders for a moment?" she asked.

"Aye," he grunted, inexplicably feeling shy.

"I've these baskets of laundry to take to the infirmary, but they're too heavy. Could you carry one?"

"Well and good then." Gregyn swung one up to his shoulder and grasped the handle of the other so she could carry half the load.

"You look done in," she remarked. "They had riders working in there today, didn't they?"

"Aye. Put a cloth over three men's faces today," he announced, actually remembering that he'd felt sad over one of them. Only for a heartbeat, but it must have showed on his face.

"Tis sad when so many die so young," she said. "You don't remember my name, do you?"

"I'm sorry. I'm very tired tonight."

"Naryna," she told him. "You smell like a man who bathed after the shift."

"I did."

They bent to lower the basket to the ground next to similar baskets. A large tent had been erected in the middle of the ward and a small booth outside the door was where the baskets were held until they were needed. Gregyn lowered his basket to the ground as well. As they turned, a couple of riders came out bearing a stretcher between them with a cloth-wrapped body upon it.

"I'm wanting to feel alive," Naryna announced, staring at him boldly. Her blue eyes locked with his and her breasts heaved slightly under her bodice. He felt his body respond to the sight and when she held out her hand to draw him toward the stables, he took it willingly enough without any thought of what Talidd might say about it.

Shadow Brothers

The Ammonyts assembled and camped in Gilead; the Israelites gathered together and camped in Mizpah. The leaders of Gilead said to one another, "Who is willing to lead the charge against the Ammonites? He will become the leader of all who live in Gilead!"

Jephthah the Gileadite was a brave warrior. His mother was a prostitute, but Gilead was his father. Gilead's wife also gave him sons. When his wife's sons grew up, they made Jephthah leave, saying to him, "You are not going to inherit any of our father's wealth, because you are another woman's son." Jephthah left his half-brothers and lived in the land of Tob. Outlaws joined Jephthah's gang and traveled with him.

Some time later the Ammonites attacked Israel and the leaders of Gilead asked Jephthah to come back from the land of Tob. They said, :Come, be our commander, so we can fight with the Ammonites." Jephthah said to the leaders of Gilead, "But you hated me and made me leave my father's house. Why do you come to me now, when you are in trouble?" The leaders of Gilead said to Jephthah, "That may be true, but now we pledge our loyalty to you. Come fight with the Ammonites, then you will become the leader of all who live in Gilead." Jephthah agreed, saying, "All right! If you take me back to fight with the Ammonites and the Lord gives them to me, I will be your leader." The leaders of Gilead said to Jephthah, "The Lord will judge any grievance you have against us, if we do not do as you say." Jephthah went with the leaders of Gilead. The people made him their leader and commander. Jephthah repeated the terms of the agreement before the Lord in Mizpah (could this be the Foundation Stone?).

From the Scriptos of the One, Writings of Judges

Recorded by Blethry, Priest of Bel, Moryn
FY 941

Founding Year 931
Dun Llyr · the Bog

The streets of Llyr were filthy and crowded. Gilyan held her cloak about her as she stumbled over broken cobbles, head down, face smudged with dirt and dried tears. She'd been wandering all day. The small bag of food Nalyna had provided had been spent last night. and she'd had naught a morsel this day. The day's heat seemed unbearable as she stumbled along, yet last night she'd huddled down in an alleyway, teeth chattering from the cold.

A group of young men, street toughs by the look of them, brushed past her. She tried to hold herself away from them. One of them muttered something vile and shoved her toward the wall of a building. She stumbled and fell to her knees, the paving piercing her skin. People walked by as she dusted off her hands, picked pebbles from her stinging knees and climbed to her feet. Nobody offered to help.

She could not live like this! How did the people around her survive from day to day, much less to have children and conduct business? She felt beset and chased, hungry and thirsty and incredibly grubby. What must she do to find a safe place?

The Golden Unicorn was supposedly in the infamous slum known as the Bog. She'd heard all manner of fantastical tales concerning wicked men and women in that section of the city. All cities had such a neighborhood. Yet she'd never seen it. The buildings round her looked rough enough for this to be a slum and certainly the people she'd met were crude enough, but she feared to ask for directions and expose herself as an innocent among wolves.

The babe within her stirred, or mayhap it was her imagination. The small swelling in her white belly that represented Maryn's child was more precious to her than her own life and yet its life depended upon hers. What must she do to protect it?

Her da's behavior yesterday stirred rage within her once more. How could he act that way? He'd always been kind and loving. Did he fear Perryn so much? And what of Perryn? Although she'd never met him, even Maryn had called him honorable and forthright. What had changed him so that men like her father, twice his age and with a warband as strong as the Celdryan force, feared him?

Anger won't fill your belly, lass.

True-thought. She had been sorely treated, but tears and anger would not save her babe or put food in her belly. She had to find a place of safety. Looking round her, she thought that very unlikely.

Llyr was a vast city, actually larger than Celdrya in its population. Nalyna had walked with her to the end of the rich houses built against the dun walls, making it seem as if they were obeying Braedyn's orders. Nalyna never asked if she'd changed her mind about the darkwife. She said she'd tell Braedyn that Gilyan had balked at the door and backed away into the crowd of the market square before Nalyna could stop her.

"The Bog is that way," she said when they reached the market square where, presumably, a darkwife could be found. They were in the merchant neighborhood, surrounded by large homes that were nearly brochs sheltered behind high walls. Gilyan's feet now ached more than her ribs. She'd never walked so far in her life. She wanted to sit down and rest.

She turned to Nalyna, who turned to her.

"There is so much I would say," she fumbled. "Now I can't think of the words."

"Thanks would be enough, child. I wish I could do more. The Bog is that way," she announced firmly, pointing down into the city. "Walk until you get to the docks and then go west toward the fortress. When you reach the merchant square above the Hanolan dock, start asking after the Golden Unicorn. Someone will know it. I'll have to raise an alaram soon enough -- I'll wait for the watch call. You need to be far away from here by then."

They embraced, then Gilyan shouldered the small bag of food and turned toward the docks and Nalyna disappeared into the crowd. That had been nearly a day gone.

Gilyan had felt hope this morning when she'd come upon the docks. She'd turned west and entered what she supposed were the slums known as the Bog. The narrow streets here, hemmed in on both sides with walls of brown stone, were filthy and the smell of sewerage was everywhere. Men brushed past her, bumping her arm and laughing when she reeled away. Aye, this had to be the Bog. She'd heard tales of this place where the dregs of society eked out a living by beating each other to death and all other manner of horrible activity.

Overwhelmed with the knowledge of how far her life had fallen, Gilyan stopped walking and stared about her. She had yet to find the market square and the afternoon was growing late. She could not spend another night in another alley. She screwed up her courage and turned to a passing woman who carried a large basket of laundry.

"Excuse me, but I'm seeking an inn in this area. It's called the Golden Unicorn."

The woman, dressed in ragged, but clean dresses, paused and stared at Gilyan as if she'd grown two heads.

"What would a pretty young thing like you want with the Golden Unicorn?"

"I'm meeting someone there," Gilyan replied. "You know it?"

"Aye," the woman said, sounding reluctant. Truly, she was about the age Gilyan's mother would be if she'd not died having her last child. She looked around the neighborhood, eyes upon the rooftops. "It's in that direction," she said, pointing in the general direction of the fortress, but more upslope. "I've never been myself, but it's right round there. There's a bell tower by the market square. People there will know of it."

"Thanks to you," Gilyan said.

The woman grunted, shrugged her shoulders and moved on. Gilyan started in the direction she'd indicated with renewed hope and vigor. That buoyed her forward, but the market square was nearly deserted by the time she reached it. She stopped where a man and woman were closing up their stall and asked after the Golden Unicorn, but they didn't know of the inn. She rounded a group of shuttered stalls and saw the bell tower at the end of a row and hurried to it, until she saw that there was a squad of town guards gathering there. She stepped back into the stalls, realizing this was a guard station. She might have known -- a bell tower for ringing alaram.

Gilyan hurried down the row and found a man shuttering his leather shoppe.

"I'm looking after the Golden Unicorn," she said, made bold by urgency. She would not spend another night out in an alley.

"Are you now?" he said, eying her oddly. "Well, I guess I shouldn't be asking. You know the bell tower?" He apparently saw somewhat in her eyes. "I'm not saying go up there and introduce yourself. It's a landmark, you see. Think of it like a sun dial. If the sun were behind it, go as if the shadow were pointing to the 4th watch. Go four streets in and look toward the left. You should find it easily enough."

Gilyan listened as the squad marched off down the street. She peeked out to find the ground before the bell tower to be deserted. Reviewing the man's instructions, she set out once more.

This area might still have been in the Bog, but the buildings seemed a bit better maintained and the streets didn't smell nearly as bad. She actually smelled flowers from the other side of some of the outer walls. That there were outer walls spoke of a higher class neighborhood than most she'd passed through today. And then she saw the sign.

Like all inns, taverns and businesses in a nation of largely illiterate folk, the Golden Unicorn had a sign that gave its name pictographically. The brightly painted wooden sign showed a golden unicorn rearing on its hind legs, pawing at a blue sky. Oddly, the sign also had the words "Golden Unicorn" worked round the picture. Rarely did the inn owners read and write themselves. This gave Gilyan hope that her brother had the right of it. It looked a fairly prosperous inn -- three stories tall and surrounded by a high outer wall. The front doors were barred, but there were lights glowing inside the windows. Gilyan walked round the side and saw a gate in the outer wall A man of middle years with a sword at his hip waited on a stool by that gate. Gilyan's mouth went dry.

To come so far and find that it had been a cruel joke would be too much. Why would an inn send patrons round the side and post a tough at the gate. Gilyan did not know. Still, the sun's heat was rapidly leaving the stones beneath her feet and she was determined not to spend another night out in the cold.

The guard looked up as she approached.

"What you be seeking, lass?" he asked in a pleasant enough voice. There was a cudgel at his belt as well, but his hands stayed well away from them.

"I was told by someone to come to the Golden Unicorn."

"Were you now? And who would be telling you somewhat like that?"

"My brother."

"Does your brother have a name?"

"Caedyn."

The tough gave her a shrewd gaze from top to bottom and back up to her face.

"A moment, please," he said. He rapped lightly on the gate. A small door, just large enough for a face, opened and he spoke to someone on the far side in low tones so that she could not understand what he said. The message door closed and he turned back to her. "You can sit on my stool, lass, while we wait."

Hesitantly, Gilyan smoothed her skirts and sat down. The guard was dark and his speech was spiced with some accent she didn't recognize. White teeth flashed when he smiled. He didn't seem threatening, but the whole area of the Bog was threatening, so she remained wary.

Many heartbeats passed while they waited. A man in a fine set of stripped breecs came to the gate and the guard, whose name appeared quite foreign, ushered him in like someone he'd known his whole life. The gate, she surmised, was barred from within and only opened when Manoa signaled.

The message door opened and a younger man's face appeared.

"She can come in and wait in the garden," he announced.

"That's Gwin. He's a nice enough fellow," Manoa assured her, as if they were long friends. He handed her through the gate. Gilyan found herself in a gatehouse of sorts where the young man, Gwin, apparently waited.

There were three doors in the other walls and Gwin, a hard-muscled man with reddish hair, pointed to the one on Gilyan's right.

"There's the garden. Bradlyn says you can sit on the bench outside this door and wait. It's more pleasant than the alley."

The garden outside the indicated door was a kitchen garden, fleshly turned for the most part, but with herbs growing near the out-kitchen. She could hear the clatter of pots and the call of female voices within the hut. There was a board fence separating the kitchen garden from some other garden, where she could hear music and pleasant voices and see the reflection of torchlight along the top. She looked up and to her left to see the three-storied inn's back wall with large pleasant windows lit from within.

She somewhat lost track of time after that. It was growing chill and the bench she sat upon was stone. She'd begun to contemplate making demands when the guard hut door opened and Gwin gestured for her to follow him. They entered the building itself this time. A tall, imposing man dressed in fine clothes waited in a somewhat dark hallway that smelled of flowers.

"Thanks to you, Gwin. I'll take her from here."

The young man withdrew, leaving Gilyan with this stranger.

"I'm Bradlyn. Come, Shyralan awaits."

They climbed a curving set of stairs to what might have been the third floor and he ushered her into what could have been a ladies' greeting chamber in her father's dun. Morikan carpets cushioned a clean floor and tapestries, albeit of a floral nature, adorned the stone walls. A pleasant, but low fire twinkled at the hearth, which drafted nicely.

A woman rested on a divan, her silk skirts of shimmering blue arranged for their best effect. Her dark hair was arranged in a fashion favored by Hanolan -- loops and braids and without a head scarf.

"Gilyan of Llyr nee Umhall, I presume," she said in a throaty voice. "Please, be seated. You may eat if you wish."

Gilyan saw the platter of meat, cheese, bread and fruit then. Hesitantly, but driven by hunger, she popped a spring berry in her mouth and then filled a pewter charger with some of the variety available and sat down.

"I take it you're pregnant," Shyralan said. Gilyan gave her a startled look. She laughed. "Why else would a noble woman come here? You were betrothed to Prince Maryn. Is it his?"

Gilyan hesitated. Shyralan swung her feet down from the divan and sat forward.

"I'm Shyralan and I own the Golden Unicorn. If you're to stay here, you must be honest with me." Gilyan nodded stiffly. "And I take it the family did not react well?"

"P-perryn accused me of lying and my father took his side."

Shyralan nodded.

"Maryn's bastard would be a threat to Perryn's heirs," she explained as calmly as any noblewoman might. "I daresay it's likely Perryn had somewhat to do with his brother's death."

That had not occurred to Gilyan. Her heart beat a little faster.

"It would explain your father's reaction. Fortunately, your brother recognizes that a bastard child may have power in the future." Caedyn had surely been trained in political intrigue as he was to take the rule at her father's death. "You understand why you had to come here alone, unaided?"

"Nay. Do you know why Caedyn sent that I shouldn't spend coin on a carriage?"

"Your brother gave you a purse?" Gilyan raised an eyebrow. She might be noble, but she did understand the value of a silver. Shyralan eyed her with eyes the color of her dress for a couple of heartbeats before laughing lightly. "The Golden Unicorn and the noble women of Celdrya have had a long history, almost as long as the Temples of the Moon, but the dun must appear not to know of us. At least here, we let you keep the child. That studied ignorance is why you can keep your child."

"What is this place?" Gilyan demanded.

"You haven't guessed?" Shyralan waited a moment, but Gilyan continued staring at her, waiting. "Noblemen, wealthy merchants, city officials, they have the same needs as a common laborer, but they want company that raises to their level."

Gilyan opened her mouth and then snapped it shut. Shyralan waited.

"This is a brothel?" The madam nodded. Gilyan took a deep breath and let it out slowly. For a moment she took in the opulent surroundings. "I apprehend that this is not a common brothel."

"That would be true."

"Has my brother sold me as a harlot?"

"Nay. The purse you carry, if it has the correct amount of coin, will buy your stay here until the end of your confinement. You may choose to remain or go out on your own when that time comes. Mayhap Caedyn will have resolved your situation by then. That is the usual way of it. If not, well, there are worst places and more distasteful occupations for a woman with no skills and an inconvenient bastard within. If you think differently, you can go out into the night and see how long it is before someone lifts your purse and you have to sell yourself for far less than you're worth. If you want what protection your brother can offer, I'll take your dowry now," Shyralan said, holding out a strong, but lovely hand. After a moment of thought, Gilyan drew the purse from her bosom and handed it over. Shyralan did not open it, just hefted it in her knowing hand and then slid it into her own bosom. Then she rang a bell on the table next to the divan.

"I'll have the steward show you to your room and provide you with a bath and a meal. While you are here, you are simply Gilyan. It's unlikely anyone will ask more than that, but if someone does become curious, it's best to say you come from a merchant family, let's say from Galornyn. Discretion is one way the Golden Unicorn serves its patrons. You understand, of course."

Gilyan started to shake her head, but then realized that she did understand. The Golden Unicorn protected the identities of its customers and its courtesans and continued to be useful to both because of that secrecy.

"Aye, I think I do."

"Good then. We will talk more tomorrow when you've rested. I know that the prospect of this life does not often occur to noble women, but often, by the end of their confinement, they see the advantages."

Bradlyn entered the room once more.

"You may take Gilyan to the room prepared for her. See to a bath and a meal and a fresh change of clothes for the morning when she will start her new life."

Gilyan hesitated only a moment, then stood and followed Bradlyn out to what would be her home for several months, if not the rest of her life.

Founding Year 1028
Dun Celdrya

Duglas, it turned out, had hired quite a few guards for the caravan. They all met at the postern gate, which opened bare inches from the Rock of the Founding on the road that lead south and west round the Rock. Padraig had to admit that Duglas was prepared. He had hired guards late in the season primarily because the wars were leading many away from him and because he'd expected to find more in Dun Celdrya. He'd prepared for a speeded journey by providing a string of horses to share the weight of the men. An army without a baggage train might manage thirty to thirty-five miles in a day, but Duglas wanted to manage fifty miles a day and he set the sort of pace that accomplished such. By the end of the first day, only Joy and the pony, mountain-bred as they were, still had energy for more travel. Duglas explained that he needed to leave for Mandorlyn in one week's time and that meant they needed to reach Dun Wllean within five days. They rode from shortly after dawn, took their midday meal in the saddle and stopped traveling just before dusk. Duglas provided rations of flatbread, ale and cheese, but there were no campfires and no cooked meals. He apologized for that and said it would be made up on the actual caravan journey. Padraig wondered how many of the men believed that. They were a hard lot, cold as a winter day, nearly every one. A couple were younger than Tamys, probably not having been pushed out of a warband onto the roads, but looking for adventure more than a place to settle down. Others were freeswords, the sort of men who had left the warband just shy of the end of a rope. They were dangerous men, and almost as dangerous to those they might call friend as to those they called enemies. All of them would switch sides in a scrap if the pay were high enough. Padraig trusted none of them.

On the way to Dun Wllean, Tamys kept his distance from the others, weighing his options. Padraig thought it a wise choice. Whatever had pushed these men onto the roads, the road had shaped them into somewhat less than honorable.

Galconyn lay west and north of Dun Celdrya, a wide stretch of prairie with a deep forest at its south. To reach it, the band traversed Fyrgal territory. Padraig remembered farms and towns that stood in neat prosperity reminiscent of Dunmaden. This was good farm country. At its eastern edge it was bounded by the Avergal, which was one of the great rivers of the kingdom. The Avergal, though a great river, flowed into the Avercelt about 20 miles before it reached the sea, which lead to Fyral's historic conflict with Dun Llyr. Dun Llyr wanted to control the trade to and from Fyrgal and did. Fyrgal resented it, knowing how rich their land was. There'd been several middling wars fought over this situation during the last 50 years, and these had increased after Fyrgal's vyngetroi in Dun Blaedd had asserted a claim to the kingship. Until recently, until the change in the Maille, Dun Llyr had claimed allegiance to Dun Manahan and the vyngretroix of east Mulyn. Padraig wondered little to see farms and towns near the Avergal burned, for Dun Manahan had raided this area just the autumn before. It seemed the civil wars grew in scope with each passing year.

Farther west Fyrgal remained prosperous. They crossed the Averglas, a slow, wide river that nevertheless was too shallow to be considered a true great river, and entered into Galconyn. Things were rougher in Galconyn where settlement was still rather new. It had only been 120 years ago that the last king had opened Galconyn to settlement. At the time the population of the kingdom had warranted it, but now people mostly lived there because it hadn't been ravaged by war yet. There were few towns in Galconyn, mostly just villages with farmsteads surrounding and only two large towns -- Dun Praedd, the vyngretrix's city, which lay just beyond the river crossing and Dun Wllean, which sat at the far west and controlled the road to Mandorlyn. Dun Wllean was Duglas' city.

Dun Wllean had been built in the foothills of the Mountains of the Western Portal. None quite remembered why they were called that and some suspected it had been borrowed from an elven name. Elven tradition had it that it was a dwarven name. Padraig wondered if the dwarves would attribute the name to another source. The foothills seemed middling compared to the mountains behind them, but they stood above the rolling prairie of the rest of Galnconyn. Dun Wllean been built tight against the cliffs that the Portal spilled out of and that was at once its greatest weakness and its primary salvation.

Fifty years ago, Dun Wllean had been a prosperous town without a wall, enjoying a lucrative trade with the dwarves who inhabited valleys far back in the mountains. Far from the kingdom proper and with no near neighbors, Dun Wllean had never felt the need to protect itself, though it had been in existence for about 50 years by that time. Then the horrible day came when the dwarves spilled out of the Portal, chopping everything with their double-bit axes and laying waste to the town. The noble family had been killed down to the last infant, except for the youngest son, a lad of 16 who'd gone hunting that day with his retinue and had returned to find devastation. Enraged by the murder of his family, he'd raised an army like none had ever seen before and he sent them through the Portal to exact revenge on the dwarves. When they'd reached Mandorlyn, however, they'd found it deserted. The mining works were still there and there were many signs that the settlements had been recently inhabited, but they'd found not a single soul alive. Lord Wllean had rebuilt his town and dun with fine defenses that rivaled those of Dun Celdrya before its continual devastation. He'd allowed any freemen who wanted to travel to Mandorlyn to take over the mining works. He controlled the trade with Mandorlyn with an iron fist, Duglas said.

"He was a fine lord and his son has proved most capable since he's died. Aye, those of us who live there find him most generous, so long as the gold keeps flowing," Duglas explained.

"Is there any chance it won't?" Padraig asked.

"Mandorlyn's gold seems endless, lad, but 'tis a long way from Dun Wllean. I pay so well because 'tis a dangerous thing, the Mandorlyn Pass."

"Thought it might be," Padraig murmured.

They arrived at Dun Wllean two days before Duglas' planned departure. The east wall of the town was lightly armored, though the gate could have held against siege and the walls were well-built. The heavy defenses were toward Mandorlyn in memory of the dwarves. Occupying the highest of the three hills of the city, the dun itself was said to be built as a killing-field with murder-holes aplenty and traps that no man would escape from. They wouldn't be having a chance to see the dun, however, as the preparations for the caravan were already underway when they arrived.

Duglas' estate occupied a large area of the town, a veritable small dun, with barracks for his men and stables for his horses and warehouses for his goods. He turned the newly hired men, Padraig included, over to his captain and strode off toward the three-story broch that was his home.

"Welcome," greeted the captain, Braeden, a tall blond man with dark brown eyes who looked every inch a swordsman. "I'm Braeden of Llyr," he introduced himself. "I'll be in charge of every one of you baseborn bastards this trip and don't be thinking I'll be letting you off easy. We've a caravan of food and goods to see safely to the people of Mandorlyn and then we've a precious cargo to return with. I'll not have any incipient drink, no lifting of the village lasses' skirts, no swinging your swords at one another. Any man who draws cold steel in this caravan against one of our own will face me."

Several of the older freeswords nodded solemnly and moved off to find themselves bunks in the barracks. The younger ones laughed, but Tamys' ice blue eyes narrowed and he elbowed one of them.

"That's Braeden of Llyr, lads. We want to pay him the honor he's due," he said.

"What's to honor about an old guard?" asked Aethan, one of the young freeswords, a laugh bubbling in his throat. He was dark-haired with deep blue eyes. Though slender, the muscles in his forearms suggested practice with his sword.

"Braeden of Llyr is considered the best swordsman in Celdrya," Tamys explained calmly. "Certainly he's the most famous freesword in 50 years. He was hired once by the Lord of Manahan and it's said the lord offered him an honor position to stay on."

Aethen and the others looked at the middle-aged captain a bit more respectfully at that. Padraig wondered yet again just how close Tamys was to the rule to know the doings of the pretender's court.

"You're a wise young cub, aren't you?" Braeden noted of Tamys. "Have we met?"

"Nay, you would not have known me," Tamys assured him.

Braeden seemed to weigh and measure Tamys, then shrugged.

"Mayhap not," he agreed. "And I certainly won't be asking why a Mulyn man might be on the roads. None of my business, you understand. I'll be going along now. Herbman, if you'd rather, there's a nicer bit of barracks across the way."

"This is fine, my thanks. Finer than one expects for guards."

All of Duglas' broch compound seemed fine. His walls were high and thick enough to hold off an army if it were dying of hunger in a siege and inside the ward was paved and kept cleaner than many a dun Padraig had seen. The barracks were fresh swept and the bunks all had new ropes and ticking stuffed with fresh straw. The windows were flung open to let in light and air and there were new blankets folded against one wall for any who did not have enough.

"Duglas treats his people well, even if the hire is for one journey, or for a summer, or for many a year," Braeden explained.

"Is that why you decided to stay on?"

"Aye. I hired on for one caravan three years ago and I decided to stay. Pay's good and Duglas treats me like I'm not the honorless scum that I am. When he's looking for guards again, you remember that. Some of these youngsters won't be able to see the good in a place like this, but you seem a wise young lad." He spoke to Tamys, not Padraig, probably knowing that Padraig's skills would be honored anywhere.

Tamys shrugged, keeping his options open. Padraig thanked Braeden for his time and let the man go. Padraig turned toward arranging his gear under his bunk as Tamys was already doing. As they worked, Padraig became aware that Tamys seemed less at ease with this process than he'd ever seemed uneasy about anything. He stole peeks at what Padraig was doing to find the best way of doing this. Noble-born, for sure, Padraig thought.

With the preparations for the caravan underway, there was plenty to do. Padraig spent the day asking after the ills that had been encountered on previous trips. The men mentioned "the bowels" and Padraig checked his stock of teas and the like. Reasoning that they would be climbing over the mountains, he thanked the One True God for causing him to buy ginger at Andyr's shop. He'd been unable to reason out why he wanted such, but he'd felt a strong compulsion to do so and now he understood why. It was sundown of the second day, the day before departure, before Padraig felt his preparations were in hand.

The sun was setting to the west when Padraig climbed the town wall to look into the Portal. The canyon came out of the cliffs at the postern gate and this time of evening looked like a throat of some great long-dead creature. Padraig shivered despite the warmth of the late-afternoon. He did not have eyes for the future, but he knew that danger lay along that road to Mandorlyn. His skills would be needed beyond his herbcraft. With that, Padraig began to pray, but he received no answers and the militia were beginning to give him the odd look, so he climbed off the wall to check his other supplies.

Tamys was in a foul mood that night at the evening meal. Padraig rather wondered why since Duglas set a fine spread for his men and the dun had sent its own bard for the entertainment. The priests of Lugh came for to give the caravan a blessing, which might have had somewhat to do with it, Padraig supposed. Tamys stopped short of walking out on the blessing, but he downed his ale fast and left as soon as the prayers were finished. Padraig followed him. The lad was uncommonly sure of himself in the dark of a compound he'd never been in before, but Padraig finally found him atop Duglas' walls, staring toward the west.

"Somewhat the matter?" Padraig asked.

Tamys didn't answer right away. To Padraig's elven eyes, there was light enough to see him grimace and chew the inside of his lip.

"I'm truly selling my sword and while I may have to do it, I don't have to like it."

"True-spoken. What are you thinking?"

"That I have a future as cold as a winter night and not half as long," Tamys admitted.

Padraig nodded, looking down into the ward. For some reason his stomach jumped at the height, the like of which had never bothered him before. For a brief moment, on the edge of his consciousness he heard a scream and saw in his mind's eye a body laying on the ground. Then it passed, evaporating like fog in the sun.

"There are alternatives," he reminded Tamys.

"Oh, aye! Prentice to a farmer. Sounds a good one to me," Tamys mocked.

"There's more than that, if you'll but open your eyes and have a look round."

"I was raised as a soldier. It's what I know."

"So was I," Padraig reminded him.

"I've had a few more years along that road, you know." Tamys spat, then stood up from the rampart and stared down into the ward as Padraig had done. "The alternatives don't tempt me," he said softly. Then he turned and strode away to the ladder that would lead him down.

Padraig shuddered. For some reason he couldn't be sure of, he'd felt as though Tamys might jump. Surely not! An honor-bound man did not do such, considering suicide tantamount to hanging. Yet, there'd been that instant. Padraig shuddered again and fled the wall. By the time he reached the barracks, Tamys lay rolled in his blankets and seemed asleep. Padraig decided his imagination was playing tricks on him.

Founding Year 1028
Galornyn, the Bottom

There was plague in Galornyn and Sawyl wished he had time to do somewhat about it. He'd heard of infant's palsy, though why they called it that when it was mostly adults who lost use of their limbs was curious making, but he had never seen it. It had devastated Hanolan when Sawyl had first left the island for the later stages of apprenticeship. There'd been plenty of ships coming to Galornyn from the islands carrying news of fever and palsy. Sawyl's instructor in herb craft had been most interested in the palsy, mostly in how to transmit it so that he could give it to people and then hoping to cure it, to ingratiate him with the right sorts of people. As far as Sawyl knew, Melchior had not achieved his goal. Galornyn's bout with this illness had no doubt come as bad humors from off a ship.

Fog shrouded the Bottom at midday. Sawyl sniffed the foul smelling air as he ducked under the lintel to the Black Crow tavern. The standard passerby, probably raised in the southern coastal city, would not recognize the bird on the sign as a raven and those who frequented the tavern were careful to call it "the Crow". Most folk would never guess that this was the portal to a society of black mages like Sawyl himself.

The tavern man, polishing tankards, didn't act as if he knew Sawyl, but the boy washing dishes at the back of the tavern room slipped out the back door. Sawyl tossed two coppers in the jar and dipped himself a tankard of dark. Custom was slow this early in the morning. A couple of men spoke in low terms in the shadows; otherwise Sawyl had the tavern to himself.

He'd just seen the bottom of the tankard when the lad returned and signaled subtly that Sawyl could go forward. He set his empty tankard on the board, thanked the tavern man and slipped out into the fog.

There were various ways to the dark chambers; Sawyl took the journeyman's route, fading into a alleyway that opened to a door that led down dark stairs, through a series of store rooms and then into a long winding corridor of ancient witch stone. There was somewhat about it, even buried where only the light of candle lanterns touched it, that creeped a man's soul. Sawyl tried not to think of the magicks required to create the luminous rose colored stone.

Eventually, he reached a plain wood door of inch-thick walnut and spoke an incantation that was the only way to open it. Beyond were three more doors requiring different incantations. And then another long corridor, leading forever downward, until Sawyl knocked on a door deep set in ancient walls. The voice within intoned an incantation that ended abruptly. Sawyl completed it and the door unlocked.

Naranddal waited within, seated at a dark wood table on the only chair. Sawyl could stand or sit on a stool. He chose the stool.

"What are you sent here for today?" Naranddal asked. He had a thin face and graying hair. His eyes were a deep dark brown. His accent suggested central Celdrya. Sawyl tried to ignore the shimmering image in the alcove behind him. The master of this guild looked to be in his middle years, but like Talidd, Sawyl suspected he was a great deal older. Talidd said he was not a true dark mage, but Sawyl thought anyone who could capture an ethereal spirit had superior magick.

"My master has requested these items in exchange for these vials," Sawyl reported, opening the bag of poisons and spreading them on the table. Then he began writing the order on a wax tablet he'd brought with him for the purpose.

Naranddal inspected the vials carefully, opening each to sniff them. He restoppered them and set them aside so he could read Sawyl's list.

"I won't provide the last item," Naranddal announced. "That is a forbidden item."

Sawyl turned that over in his mind before replying.

"You do not say that you haven't got it, only that it is forbidden."

Naranddal smiled subtly, his thin lips curving ever so slightly upward.

"I provide what I am able and willing to provide."

The delay was not insurmountable, but Sawyl did not wish to remain in the city any longer than absolutely necessary.

"A full payment should buy a full request."

"I provide what I am able and willing to provide."

The shimmering image, previously a translucent silver, began to radiate with red threads and to take on a more solid visage.

"Aye," Sawyl said, not showing his alarm. "I can find such elsewhere. Do you have incantations to ward off this plague?"

"There are some, but your master is the only one I know of who has effectively resisted it. Mayhap you should go see one of your fellow journeyman in the city."

"Mayhap," Sawyl agreed.

"Sawyl, do you know this spell?"

"Aye, I've read of it."

"Then you know what it is for?"

"For killing specific people."

"For killing specific people who are protected by the gods," Naranddal corrected. "Has Talidd found the king, then?"

"Not to my knowledge. Mayhap he wishes to be prepared."

"I would hope that is all he wants if he hasn't found the king. Talidd knows better than any of us what may happen if a mage works this spell when he doesn't know where or against whom it will be directed. It's been a long time, but surely he still bears those scars of his own master's ill-considered haste."

"I am unfamiliar," Sawyl admitted.

"Truly? Think of what happened to the last king and then you may be more familiar."

"And this final item?"

"I will provide what I am willing and able and that will never be given." The spirit floated away toward a door at the back of the oddly shaped room. The corners creeped Sawyl's soul. The elven murals turned his heart to ice. "Wash well, Sawyl. That is as likely to keep the bad humours away as incantations."

The spirit returned and four jars appeared on the table before Sawyl.

"The requested items that I can provide. A century ago, Talidd might have averted disaster, but he did not act when required. You are now tasked to consider what you will do." Naranddal then stood and strode to the door. "I've duties to attend. I'm sure you know your way out."

With ice-water running down his back, Sawyl packed up the potions and fair fled the chamber. He'd always been curious about Naranddal and once had wondered if he'd be a better master than Talidd. Now, as he strode into the light of the fog-enshrouded day, Sawyl knew with a cold certainty that Naranddal held what Talidd lacked -- a soul of compassion and a caring for his pupils. Sadly, that knowledge would do him no good now. His life was not his own, as Naranddal well knew. To betray Talidd was to die and above all else, Sawyl valued his own life.

Founding Year 1028
Near Dun Llyr (Five Cycles Past)

L lyr had the best port in all the kingdom and her rigs knew it. They well-protected the deep estuary mouth of the Avercelt with fortresses on both headlands and a net of chain that could be lifted to block the entrance. The city had stood attack by Morikan pirates during the Troubles and more recently after the desolation of the Trevellyns, but it had never fallen because of its impregnable harbor. All who had attacked the great city had been repulsed.

Until now, Gilyn thought with a smile. A part of following the goddess was trusting her guidings, but he had wondered this time. Surely the rig of Llyr would know of a portal within the perimeter of his defenses. Nay, his father's people were not so wise as that.

Tucked into a crevasse not much wider than two

longboats abreast, there lay a fissure in the stone that led into a deep pocket where a wide shingle of rock would allow long boats to be easily staged for a push into the city. Across the water, the city climbed the cliffs of the ancient Kin city. Gil wondered that the Celts never wondered about the broad avenues that gracefully climbed the heights to the ramparts protecting the city from land attack. They apparently thought themselves safe. He smiled.

"If any vik had known of this, the city would have fallen a long time ago," Jarl was telling Erik. "They are defenseless within their defenses."

Erik had not immediately warmed to the idea. Behind his young face rested a kong's mind. He knew a city was not as easily captured as a village in the Northern Isles.

"We should find out what their military strength is," he announced. "Dress some of the men in Celdryan clothing and send them to the shore. They are to listen and observe and return here three days hence with a report. They are not to fight and they are to not drink the ale except watered. Understand?"

Jarl smiled like a father hearing his son take charge of the herds for the first time.

Erik unrolled a map they'd picked up in High Celdryan and studied it.

"This river is the key to taking the center of the country. It joins north and south. Is there a portal here?" he asked, pointing to Dun Galornyn.

Gil smiled and nodded.

"With enough ships and men," Jarl said.

"Jah. And the Vik are hungry, waiting for the next great conquest." Erik put a big, callused hand on Gil's shoulder.

Do not kill him now. He will be useful for what we want ... for now.

"You've done a great thing, Gil, and you will be well rewarded for your service. Can you teach my men to operate the portals?"

"Nay. Only one of the Kin may activate them. It will require planning, these attacks. I've not seen so many long ships in your father's fjord."

"Nah, but he is building more and we will build more for the future. This will happen. Let's go to see the portal at Galornyn and then return to my father with the news that we only need men at arms to strike."

The two vik turned toward the portal. Gil glanced back at the harbor. All looked so quiet and calm ... for now.

Sanctuary

The wild goats live in the high mountains; the rock badgers find safety in the cliffs.
From the Scriptos of the One, Songs of Ysrael

Recorded by Blethry, Priest of Bel, Moryn
FY 943

Founding Year 931
Galconyn Mountains ·Kylly Mines

The horses labored up the rise to the point where Pedyr ordered the band to dismount and lead them before they foundered. There were tall trees to either side of the road, thick-trunked evergreens with moss growing on the uphill side. It had been two days since they'd left the foothills and it began to feel as if they had been climbing for years. A steady drizzle of rain added to the misery. It wasn't enough to make the road muddy, but enough to dampen clothes and make joints ache. Donyl's weak leg throbbed when he'd been riding; now it pulsed with every step.

He'd begun to wonder if Nedd had somewhat to do with the rain. The lad claimed not to possess the powers his parents wielded, but the rain had begun shortly after Donyl had asked him if it was true that rain disrupted ethereal powers? He'd claimed not to know what Donyl was talking about, but if Donyl knew of it, the son of a druid and a grania had to be aware of it. Still, Donyl didn't push the lad on the subject because it wouldn't do for the other riders, already on the verge of panic, to mark Nedd as a mage. Donyl expected they would not treat their fellow, whom they liked well-enough in ignorance, with gentleness should they come to suspect.

Pedyr, walking at the front of the column, raised a

hand for halt.

"Do you smell that?" he asked in a low voice that carried.

"Wood smoke," Nedd noted in the same sort of low voice.

Donyl led his horse to join them, then pointed out a wisp of fog that was a bit too dense to be fog.

"Might be a village nearby," he suggested.

"Nedd, take Remry and Stegyl to see what's what," Pedyr said softly. Nedd obeyed without question. Pedyr dolled out journey bread and someone passed an ale bag. Donyl leaned against a tree, exhaustion weighting his limbs. Nedd and his companions returned a bit later than expected with a man from the village just over the nearest rise.

"This is Marstyn," Nedd explained to Pedyr. "He's the village headman."

Marstyn was a tall red-headed fellow with a barrel chest and dark blue eyes.

"You're welcome at our hearths so long as you will peace-bind your blades," he explained.

"Why ever for?" Donyl demanded.

"We are of the Way of Peace. We've no quarrel with how you conduct your lives outside our village, but here we expect you to honor our ways."

Pedyr drew Donyal a bit away.

"I've heard of these. I met some during a traverse of this mountain range as a young man. It's safe enough. There's not that could come against us so far up the mountain."

"Naught but the raven bitch," Nedd said. "The

good of it is that iron is said to ward her and they're miners of iron ore."

"Our horses want rest and the men are spent," Pedyr added. "I think it's safe enough. They're a variety of Believers, so I trust their word as bond."

Donyl wasn't sure if he entirely agreed, but truth be told, he was not the captain of this band. He could overrule Pedyr as any lord might a commoner, but wisdom instructed that Pedyr knew far more about these situations than he did.

"Let us at least spend the night," Donyl agreed.

The mountain believers lived in half-buried homes of logs piled one upon another and notched to hold them together. There was no inn in the village, but the headman found beds for all of them. Donyl bedded with Pedyr and Nedd as guards in the home of Bandar, a loquacious fellow with a smiling wife and several children. They were given a comfortable chamber just above the main room outfitted with a mattress and metal hooks for clothing. The window looked out at ground level since this was the second floor.

As they prepared for bed after a pleasant evening of music and laughter, Marstyn brought his eldest son to them in the chamber. The lad had his own family now, just across the way, Marstyn had explained earlier in the day.

"You must listen to my son, for he is a seer. Jeryd, please to speak with these men as you would with me."

The lad looked a lot like his father, except that his hair was dark, mayhap from his mother.

"I have no certain knowledge, you understand, but I

believe you are stalked by daemons." What could they say? Their faces mayhap expressed it all. "You carry somewhat on you that they want," Jeryd said, looking right at Donyl. "That is all the Lord has given me to say."

"Thank you, Jeryd," Pedyr replied. "I swear by the One, whom you call Lord, that we will find answer to this."

Jeryd and Marstyn both nodded and departed to allow the three conversation.

"What have you kept from us?" Nedd demanded.

"Only what my brother charged me to keep secret," Donyl replied reluctantly. He limped to his belongings and brought the haversack to them. One by one, he pulled out the objects and laid them on the blankets for his guards to view.

"These are Kin work, mayhap," Pedyr noted. "Royal jewels, you say. Hmph!"

Nedd picked up the amulet. Outside, they could hear the drizzle immediately increase to a downpour.

"I knew you were not sharing the whole of it," Donyl said. The rider smiled.

"It's a small gift not worth mentioning until it comes in contact with the right sort of talisman. I rather thought we had somewhat among us when the drizzle started right when we needed, but I couldn't be sure. These are part of legend -- the treasure of the Fey. Do you know of it?"

"I did not, nay." Donyl glanced at Pedyr.

"I wasn't raised in Denygal, so I always thought them stories my mam told to amuse us, but aye, she may have told stories of these."

"So what do we do with them?" Donyl asked.

Pedyr and Nedd were quiet for so long that Donyl feared they'd leave the decision to him, but then they spoke at the same time.

"Get them as far from these good people as we can," they said, "and hope that is enough," Nedd added.

Another long silence ensued.

"How do we do that?" Pedyr asked at last.

Founding Year 1028
Dun Wllean

Duglas' caravan had many wagons and horses and mules and was indeed longer than Dun Wllean was wide. The town guards threw open the Celdryan gates at dawn so that the caravan could form up before the Mandorlyn gates. Padraig and Tamys had been assigned a squad about halfway back in the column, almost to the Celdryan gates.

Padraig watched as the men sorted themselves out, watched as Tamys made tentative friends with some of the freeswords in the caravan. The freeswords, being young, were boasting of their exploits, of the wars they'd fought and the places they'd traveled. Padraig noted that Tamys seemed circumspect, holding his resume to his chest. While this might just be reticence in an unknown situation, it occurred to Padraig that he'd never asked an important question. After a bit of thought, he called Tamys to help him check Earnest's panniers, giving him excuse to draw him away from the group.

"I never thought to ask, for clearly you've been well-trained in arms, but there's naught for it and you need to answer me truly right now. Have you ever ridden to war?"

Tamys cut him an odd stare and then stood silent for several heartbeats. Padraig's own heart contracted, realizing that upon this answer much rode. Presently Tamys began to laugh somewhat maniacally, causing Padraig to stare at him in confusion.

"You might have asked a good deal sooner," he chortled.

"I made an assumption and now I am checking my facts. Answer my question."

Tamys laughed a moment longer, shaking his head, but eventually he recognized that he owned Padraig somewhat. Drawing a calming breath, Tamys glanced around him.

"I'm a Hawk," he whispered, then walked away laughing to himself, leaving Padraig to mull that information over.

Clan Manahan of Mulyn claimed the hawk as their device. Corbryn of Manahan was a principal claimant to the throne. If Tamys were a son of his, and that seemed likely, he'd likely ridden to war his first summer out of page, which likely meant he'd killed a man or a dozen. It was hard to gauge how old Tamys was, for he acted much older than he looked, but Padraig guessed 18. He'd ridden to war as many as five times then, which would likely make him the most experienced of the young freeswords. Assured that he need not worry about Tamys in a scrap, Padraig returned his attention to his hire and let go his concern somewhat.

Leaving the Mandorlyn gate was quite something, for the road to Mandorlyn had been cut into the living rock of the mountains. Above the gate, to the outside, were ramps hung upon the walls, set with boulders and buckets that likely held tar to be set afire if needed. Dun Wllean remembered well the attack of the dwarves and stood prepared for what might come.

The caravan took some time to clear the town, with stops and starts and long waits for those behind the first ones. Thus, the air turned warm as they got underway and mid-morning found them within the canyon, which was no natural canyon. The walls seemed chiseled from the very rock. Although Padraig had seen similar dwarven highways in the East, he'd never seen one so long and it intrigued him that the canyon seemed to stretch into the mountains forever.

As the day wore on, the path climbed steadily upward and the men and animals labored. The mules set their shoulders to their heavy wagons and the horses started fresh. Yet, as the day wore on, Padraig noted that the altitude began to affect some. He thanked the One God for reminding him of the mountain sickness and providing him with the means to treat it. Personally, having spent the past four years in the Eastern Mountains, Padraig felt no effect. He noted that Tamys also didn't seem affected. Although Manahan sat in the southern part of Mulyn, it was near to the mountains and Tamys might have spent a good bit of time there.

"What made these walls?" Tamys asked, whispering

in awe.

"The dwarves," Padraig told him.

"How?" the lad asked.

"That I do not know. I have seen such in the east, but I don't know how they built them."

Tamys reached out to graze his fingers along the stone.

"It's actually smooth like glass in some places."

"Aye, though this is for rude outdoor use. Their interior work is finer still."

Tamys gave Padraig a skeptical look, but he didn't argue. Mayhap it was due to his awe of the workmanship.

Toward mid-morning the caravan stopped and a barrel of water was hand-carted along the line. Braeden rode the line, checking on everyone.

"When will we stop to eat?" Padraig asked. "Duglas did mention the bowels affecting previous caravans and I have medicinals for it, but it wants boiling water."

"We'll not stop to eat until the evening meal. This canyon does grow very hot during the day and there are few places to camp, so we rest where we can, some at midday, but we don't cook except at night, so as to spend as little time as possible in the canyon."

"Well and good, then," Padraig said. He filled his water bags and smiled as he watched Braeden take Tamys' measure. He said naught, but Padraig knew that Tamys had been marked like a prize stallion. He supposed it was safer to be marked by the former freesword than by the younger men in the company.

The canyon grew painfully hot toward mid-day as the men passed bread and cheese from saddle to saddle.

Padraig tied a rag around his head and let it fall over his shoulders to protect his neck, then wet it with a bit of water to comfort himself. It helped him a bit. In the afternoon, as heat wavered off the walls of the canyon, Padraig watched other men following his example, including Tamys.

The canyon didn't end by evening and the caravan ground to a halt long before the heat dissipated. Padraig rode ahead to speak with Duglas.

"There's just this small caravanserie," Duglas explained. "There's water here, but we sleep strung along the canyon and hope for the best. Tomorrow night, we'll camp out in the open."

"Near those mountains ahead?" Padraig asked, noting the snow-covered peaks he could see above the canyon.

"Aye. It's after that we usually get the bowels," Duglas admitted. "Other caravans have been hit by brigands on the second day in the canyon, but mostly they aren't trekking as quickly as we do. I think that's the secret, sure enough."

Padraig hoped he kenned rightly. Clearly, this was not a safe place for the caravan to spend the night if brigands knew they were about.

"What's on top of these cliffs?" Padraig asked Braeden. "This is no natural canyon. The dwarves would have carved it out of the surrounding landscape. What's up top?"

"This part's the big mountains behind Wllean. You can sort of see them. But, tomorrow we'll enter an area of hills with forests, similar to what's on the Wllean side.

We'll spend tomorrow night out in the open, on a high plain."

"That explains why the brigands hit on the second day," Tamys said. "There's little in the high mountains for such as them. It's too cold and barren, rocky. A hard living that. Hills with forests, though, they could live there nicely betwix raids."

"This band here's most likely wanted men," Braeden agreed. "They can't go back to the kingdom without going through Wllean, so they live on what goods they can steal. I've heard they let the caravans live, just so long as they leave their goods behind. Naught is left when you follow after."

"And, if the caravans resist?" Tamys asked.

"I've naught heard that one has," Braeden admitted. "They're all smaller parties, though, with the usual caravan guards. Duglas hires true men at arms. I've little worry for getting us through."

Padraig held his counsel at that point. Tamys seemed ready to question Braeden more, but then he sat back in his saddle and lapsed into silence.

"Duglas pays well," Braeden noted. "And brigands are just part of the hire."

"Aye," Padraig agreed. "These brigands have never been put to the test, then?"

"Not that I know," Braeden said. "Well, I'd best continue with my inspection. These louts need a little booting now and again."

He rode off down the line, stopping to speak with some young freeswords and then moving on farther out of earshot.

"What didn't you say?" Padraig asked Tamys, who hesitated a moment.

"Not my place to question the war leader," Tamys reminded him.

"Braeden is clearly an experienced freesword and Duglas has trusted him with more than a few caravans. What are you not saying?"

Tamys sighed, eyes on the rim of the canyon.

"He's right that smaller caravans with louts for guards are vulnerable, but a caravan this big would be tempting, I'd think. And, our size – while protecting us a bit – is also a hindrance because we draw attention to ourselves by our very passage and we have such a long train to protect."

"Do you think Braeden's more worried than he pretends?"

"Braeden hasn't lived this long by being anyone's fool," Tamys remarked. "If this canyon makes me skittish-like, you can wager it makes him more than a bit nervous. And Braeden is not the sort to wear his feelings on his cuff."

"Aye, my thoughts as well," Padraig agreed. He scanned the rim far above. "This is bad terrain for brigands."

"For now," Tamys agreed.

Evening was still a bit off when Duglas called the halt. The tuck wagon had gone ahead and started a fire, so that they had a bit to eat. Duglas apologized for the closeness of the caravanserie, as wagons, mules and horses were staked out along the canyon. The warmth of the day still radiated from the canyon walls, but Padraig knew that it would be cold that evening. He found his winter cloak and made his bed warm. There were few fires. The men who had come before knew that this was merely a rest stop and that there'd be no sitting up after dark. They pitched tent and turned to their blankets for the night as soon as soon.

Founding Year 1028
The Tongue

With another acolyte dead and an apprentice drooling, Talidd stared into the ink for long hours, willing an image and seeing naught. The aether closed to his vision. Sawyl reported naught on his excursions. *Is he lying to me?* The bright power that was Gregyn waned as the illness swept Galornyn. Gregyn was distracted, exhausted, not alone, every time Talidd reached out to him.

The tiles said the king lived, but the silence of the ink frightened Talidd. He needed power and Gregyn and Sawyl both seemed to be thinner reeds than he supposed.

There's another option. When Sawyl returns ….

Talidd shuddered, remembering the destructive tide that had flowed through him once before at his own master's bidding. His apprentices and journeymen were of better quality. There'd not been a mage in his lifetime as strong as Gregyn's raw talent. That only lived in legend. It would be worth the risk, if he could make it work.

I must learn the identify of the king. If the Bel or Lughan get to him first ....

The Lughan had destroyed the kingdom once before, leading the king astray. It was absolutely necessary to bring the young king round to their position before he was too old to understand its importance. There were enemies afoot and ....

A window opened in the ink .... A child of seven or eight skipped across a stone yard – mayhap the ward of a dun? – singing a nonsense song to himself. The child turned and Talidd caught full view of his face, but then the window dissolved and there was naught.

Talidd slapped the flat of his hand upon the table, growling, causing ink to splatter

The ceremony cannot happen soon enough!

Founding Year 1028
Highway to Mandorlyn

Padraig awoke stiff from sleeping on rock all night and fumbled in the early morning grey to pack his animals. Joy snipped at a stray bit of hay from the meal Duglas had provided the night before. Joy, mountain-bred as she was, did not care for hay and would have preferred her head to find her own pasture.

There are pastures? Padraig asked.

Above and ahead, near where we travel, she answered.

How can you ...?

Are humans born without a sense of smell? she asked.

Padraig didn't dignify that with an answer as Tamys

stood scratching tangles out of his hair.

"Warm enough?" Padraig asked.

"I've good blankets," Tamys replied, for indeed it was good northern wool in his bed roll. "I could use with a bit softer ground," he admitted, rubbing a shoulder.

"No doubt," Padraig agreed. "If I were ever to do this again, I'd bring straw matting."

"I'm going to be sitting my saddle ginger this morning."

They were given chunks of bread and cheese for breakfast and promised that the evening and morrow meals would be worth the wait. They ate in the saddle and marched up the mountain pass, breathing heavily. Soon the wagons began to stir up dust and mix with the sweat to cling upon faces and run into the eyes. Bugs began to buzz and the mules began to complain. The heat of the day grew more intense and the water in the bags became warm and distasteful. Padraig, refusing to gag on dust, wet a rag and wrapped it around his lower face so that now he looked like a desert dweller. Tamys quickly noted the improvement in Padraig's breathing and tried the same. Then the young freeswords who had marked Tamys followed suit. The other horsemen began to do the same. The muleteers, a strange lot as a profession, merely tucked in and refused to complain, driving their mules forward with the stalwartness of men who knew no other life.

Lunch was eaten in the saddle again, though water breaks were frequent. The levels in the barrels were getting lower and some of the riders asked anxiously about when there would be replenishment.

It was in the early afternoon when they encountered the rock fall. It looked as if a slab of rock had broken free from the mountain the canyon was cut through. The rocks did not block the road so much as slow the train. Padraig and Tamys were riding near the front of the caravan, talking with Duglas, when they met the obstruction. Padraig's stomach twisted, because he'd never seen a dwarven road compromised. They rode round the next bend and saw that several more slabs of rock blocked the road enough to prevent wagons from going through. Here, on one side of the canyon, a previous blockade's stones had been roughly stacked, leading to a natural draw at the top of the dressed wall.

Braeden took one look and wheeled his horse to race down the train, but he was scarce round the bend when a rumble sounded. They waited anxiously until Braeden came thundering back.

"They've dropped logs into the canyon behind us, and it looks like there might be a pot of rocks up on the rim. We're trapped for sure."

Padraig made a heartbeat decision then and, releasing Earnest's lead from the saddle hook, pointed Joy in the direction he wanted her to go. Mountain-bred, she responded with perfect coordination, leaping to the first slab and then to the next, until she reached the wash and scrambled for the rim. Tamys, Braeden and Duglas stared in awe as the sorrel mare disappeared from view.

"I'd have not taken that man for a coward," Duglas remarked, just as their "hosts" came to light on the opposite rim of the canyon.

"Who's the leader here?" a tall man asked. It was hard to tell from so great a distance, but he looked young. He and the rest of his lot were dressed in an assortment of clothes and armor and carried a ragtag bit of weaponry.

"I am," Duglas replied. "And, you are?"

The brigand raised his hand and hurled a rock straight for Duglas' head. Duglas dodged it and the rock shattered on the wall behind him.

"First lesson, merchant. I'm the leader here," the brigand hissed. "Yours is the caravan we've been wanting. Lots of food and other goods that we need. So hard to find a market out here."

Irritated by the mockery, Tamys wondered if he could hurl a war dart at that angle, then remembered that he didn't have any. He had only a sword and that wasn't much good against folk more than an arm's length away.

"Here's the offer, merchant," the brigand explained. "My men and I are going to sit up here drinking water and ale and enjoying the cooling breezes while you and yours bake in the road. At anytime, any one of your men who wants can walk on down the road in either direction. We'll let him take his horse and bedroll with him. All he has to leave behind are his saddle bags and weapons. The wagons stay, of course, and all the goods in them. You're not so far from Wllean that you'll starve before you reach help."

"So we leave the caravan?" Duglas asked.

"Oh, aye, down to the last mule."

"No treaty, brigand," Duglas told him.

"Big talk from a man who isn't out of water yet,"

the brigand noted. "Well, we'll give you some time to think about it."

The entire band faded back from the rim as if they had never been there. Then the leader appeared again.

"Ah, don't think that it would be wise to clear the blockage," he announced. "I'll only hurl more rocks down upon you while you work," he explained cheerfully before disappearing once more.

"Braeden," Duglas said after a moment of staring at the rim. "Tamys, aye?" Tamys nodded. "Padraig and you are mates, aye. What do you think he's about?"

"I don't think he'd abandon us," Tamys replied. "I've never been in a scrap with him, but I have not seen a coward in his character."

"I don't know what an herbman, even one who wears a sword, could do from the wrong side of the canyon," Braeden answered. "He's not important as he is not here. This one – " he indicated the rim with his eyes. "He's a smart lout, I'll give you that. He couldn't have picked his place better. There's absolutely no way out with a wagon and he knows our water supply is fading."

"I'll be damned if he's taking the caravan!" Duglas muttered. "The muleteers won't leave their animals. We can't leave them defenseless against this rabble."

"Then we'd best make these louts pay dear. They have the upper hand with the water, though."

"Is there naught we can do?"

"Do you have any men who are good at climbing?" Tamys asked.

"Why?" Braeden asked.

"Once it's dark, we could scale the walls and catch

them by surprise. There must be rope within the wagons somewhere."

"Aye, that's a good plan," Braeden told him. "If we live, I'll see that you get credit for it."

"Aye, if I must lose a caravan, I'd rather go down fighting," Duglas said. "And I will not leave the muleteers to this lot."

"Have muleteers been killed before?" Tamys asked.

"Aye," Duglas grunted. "Caravans have left the wagons and the mules and their muleteers. The mules belong to the muleteer, so they will fight for them. They've been slaughtered, we assume, because naught has been found of mule or muleteer, wagon or good."

"They may be louts, but they're efficient," Tamys quipped. "We'll see if tonight ends their reign."

They hunkered down to the uncomfortable afternoon heat and the buzz of flies all over them. After mayhap a watch, the band appeared on the rim again.

"Thirsty yet?" the leader asked. He must have been watching as water had been drawn. He knew that they couldn't make it past the morning without water.

"I'd rather die than give you what you want," Duglas answered.

"You've already had three guards head back toward Wllean," the leader announced. "Do you truly think the rest won't desert you if you try to fight me?"

"I think I'll fight you and that will be enough."

"Truly? A merchant with skill at arms? How novel! And, you, old man? Are you ready to die for your hire?"

"I am Braeden of Llyr and I have always been ready to die for a hire," Braeden snapped.

His announcement caused a bit of a tremor to run through the brigand band, but they had the upper hand, so they were merely impressed, not swayed, by Braeden's fame.

"I'd be scared if this were a stand up fight, but I hold all the dice – or is it rocks?"

The brigand bent and picked up a head-sized rock that he hefted aloft with two hands.

"I think you'll be the first to die, leader," he crowed and moved to throw the boulder. Before he could let it go, an amazingly long arrow raced across the canyon sky and sunk into his shoulder. He dropped the boulder with a scream and might have pitched into the canyon if his mates hadn't grabbed him.

Tamys drew his sword and shrieked.

"Padraig of Denygal!"

The brigand leader was dragged back away from the edge while half his band disappeared. Another young man stood wavering on the precipice.

"We'll find your man and kill him!"

"Can you outrun an elven arrow, lad?" a voice echoed down the canyon. "Impressive."

Another arrow shot across the canyon and struck in the soil right at this new leader's foot. He didn't hesitate to run. A third arrow buried itself in the dirt behind Tamys. A white flag fluttered in its fletching. Tamys saw it and muttered as he retrieved it.

"Just tell the whole world that I can read. Good way to draw attention to me." He unfurled the note and read it: DON'T WASTE MY ARROW AND JOY WANTS HER PONY BACK. Tamys sighed, but saluted to the rim with the arrow to show that he understood. Braeden was ordering the closest guards to begin clearing a path for the wagons and Duglas was mounting to ride the train to make sure everyone was alright. He was a bit slow in his return, but rumor reached Tamys that two of the three guards had returned with him. The third had decided to return to Wllean.

"The young dolt doesn't realize that he'll not find a hire if the town guards do let him back in the walls," Braeden told Tamys as they were helping to move the last boulder to the side so that the wagons could start moving.

"Duglas has that much power?" Tamys asked.

"Oh, aye! The town guards will likely let him sit at the gates for a few days and then they'll let him in, but he'll not find a hire even among the other caravaners. Nobody treats them so well as Duglas, so the others'll wager he'll shirk his duties. Nay, Wllean's done for him."

The caravan moved swiftly forward as soon as the blockages front and rear were cleared. Nobody seemed anxious to spend another night in the canyon and Duglas promised fresh water and nice pastures were near at hand.

Founding Year 1028
Dun Llyr

The Umhalle was dead and the rumors in the streets of Galornyn were that the chirgeon of Dun Llyr had killed him. Mayhap by error, but still … such was an opportunity. Since his meeting with the shadow mage, Sawyl had been deep in thought as he traversed the city on Talidd's business and he'd come to a conclusion.

Talidd was planning one of the greatest rituals ever performed and he would leave Sawyl out. That might be a blessing, but to an ambitious man, it was also a warning. Gregyn's strength of gift made him valuable beyond measure to whomever controlled him. Sawyl could not control that. He could only wait until Talidd died and then dispatch Gregyn as soon as soon. Yet he could make himself more valuable to Talidd in other ways. Gregyn was too young to put in a position of prestige. Sawyl, however, could replace the chirgeon of Dun Llyr.

It would take some doing – forging letters of recommendation. He was by trade an herbman, but he'd studied enough to be a chirgeon. The young heir of Llyr was a bastard son with less than sophisticated views. All that was needed, now that the Umhalle was dead, was to scatter the seeds of rumor, fertilize with intrigue, and be ready for the fruit to fall off the tree.

He would have to return to Talidd with the ritual supplies, of course, but after … there would be the mourning time and the vetting. There was time.

A harlot called from a doorway as he walked by. Draped in diaphanous purple, she left little to the imagination and naught to desire. The whores were everywhere in this city and the sort he preferred were few and far between. There was a brothel in Dun Llyr that catered to his ilk, but that was an eight-night journey that he had naught time for at the moment.

Return to the island, give Talidd his supplies and then travel to Llyr. Aye, that will suit me nicely.

A dark mage sought power beyond all else, but a devious mind served him well.

Founding Year 1028
Highway to Mandorlyn

It was almost dark when Tamys rode into the caravanserie with the tuck wagon. He'd been given this honor for his willingness to raid the brigands at night. He found Padraig sitting at a bonfire while a deer roasted at another. Joy came immediately to claim her pony and Tamys knew her well enough not to argue.

"It's almost as though that horse can talk," Tamys muttered, dropping from the saddle. "Good caravanserie. Aren't you worried the brigands will see these fires?"

The canyon had topped out. On the far side of the canyon, the walls remained somewhat high, but opened into an amphitheater of sorts. On this side, the mountain side fell away into a pleasant valley with a stream nearby. There were still larger mountains ahead, but for now, they camped in a mountain meadow.

"Wrong side of the canyon and I daresay they will be licking their wounds for a bit. The leader may die of his wound, though I tried to hit soft tissue. The others are more frightened. They all seemed young. Most likely wanted men, or thrown from a warband for some petty breach. They've naught else and they must survive by what they can get from the caravans."

"They could try hiring themselves out like honest folk."

"Aye," Padraig agreed. "I got the deer on my way here. It seemed a fitting way to help. You might want to get washed up while I see to my duties."

"And, those two?" Tamys asked, indicating Joy and Earnest.

"They're fine. I'll unload Earnest after a bit. There's a stream down that way."

Padraig found Duglas detailing guard duties for the evening.

"Ah, herbman! I was coming to thank you for saving our lives back there."

"It's not a problem," Padraig assured him.

"I will pay you scrap pay for this. I suppose I should throw in wages as a guard for the day."

"Not necessary. I'll take the scrap pay and call it even. You say this is where you get the bowels most trips?"

"Aye. Must be foul humors this far up."

"Mayhap," Padraig murmured. He wasn't about to explain to Duglas that foul humors were actually small bugs that people ate or drank. He scanned the area with his elven eyes. "I've a tea for the bowels. I'll give it to the cook to distribute to the men. Make sure they understand that it will keep them from getting ill. It doesn't taste worse than most medicinals, but I wager they won't like the taste. Bit of honey will help, if you'll tell the cook."

"I'll do that," Duglas assured him.

Padraig excused himself at this point and went to

talk to the cook, who was skeptical of teas that might treat bad humors, but agreed to make up a dose for everyone. It was truly dark by then and, after unloading Ernest, Padraig set out to find Tamys. He found his companion at the stream, naked and swimming in the cold mountain water.

"Bit cold for that, isn't it?"

"I'm from Mulyn. Our rivers are never much warmer," Tamys protested. He dunked his head and Padraig saw bubbles floating away on the current. Tamys came up, spitting water out and shaking his head violently. "It's refreshing, actually. I haven't had a bath in – well, forever. My brothers always thought me crazy, but I would swim as soon as the ice was free in the rivers and until they were iced over in the fall. Tis a cold clean, but it is a clean."

Tamys walked naked from the water and began to scrub off with grass pulls. His well-muscled body glistened in the waxing moonlight. He started to shiver at this point and sought warmth in his breecs and siarc, followed by his cloak.

"Meal's about ready. I've some tea for you to drink," Padraig announced.

"Tea? Another of your tinctures?" Tamys asked, stamping on a boot.

"Aye. If you've been swallowing this water, you need to have some tea for your bowels' sake."

"Why?" Tamys asked. "What does the water have to do with it?" He drew on the second boot.

"Animals live in the water and defecate there. The beavers especially make one ill."

Tamys gagged.

"I truly wish you would just talk of bad humors and not mention such to me."

"How will you learn, lad, unless I teach you? Come. The tea will fix all and then we'll have a spot of venison and a snooze by a true fire – on ground, not rock. Aye, it will be a well-deserved night."

Tamys made a face at him, but didn't say anything, covering his consternation by stamping the boot to full. As they approached the camp, Joy and Ernest came trotting up to them. Padraig scratched Joy's ears and she and the pony disappeared toward the picket line. Tamys approached the fire where Padraig's gear had been laid out and tossed a stick on to the flames.

"You were able to gather all this wood while hunting deer?" he noted.

"The deer came across my path while I still had my bow out. The wood was already here. I suspect Duglas plans ahead for these expeditions."

Tamys nodded, keeping his counsel to himself. Padraig handed him the tankard of tea and excused himself to get their rations. He returned to find Tamys staring into the flames.

"What do you see?" he asked.

"I don't know," Tamys answered. "In places it's almost as though you could look into another world if you stared hard enough," he murmured, sending a shiver down Padraig's back.

"I have experienced the same," Padraig told him. Truth be told – and he wasn't – he wasn't good at scrying, but occasionally had moments of seeing beyond the flames to those near and dear. He handed Tamys a trencher of bread with venison and a stew of dried fruit. Tamys set the empty tankard aside.

"How was the tea?" Padraig asked.

"I've tasted worse," Tamys replied, setting to his food. Padraig joined him. "Why are you drinking it?" he asked, nodding to the tankard Padraig set aside. "You didn't drink the water."

"Nay, but the cook does use it for washing the vegetables and cooking the food. Nay, it is best to treat that which is most likely to occur."

"Why not tell him not to use the water?"

"How do I explain it, Tamys? You believe me because you know I'm not mad, but he doesn't know me."

"It does seem to run against good sense," Tamys replied. "Why would bugs live in water?"

"Just trust me when I say that they do."

Tamys shrugged and ate some more food. Padraig decided he could believe it or not. He needn't argue it any further.

After eating, they rose to return their trenchers to the tuck wagon. On the way back, Duglas hailed Padraig from one of the fires. The two entered the circle of warmth.

"You did some fine work with that long bow today," Duglas acknowledged. "Mayhap you'd let me look at it sometime. I haven't seen an elven long bow in a good age."

"That was a pretty weapon," Braeden agreed. "Why do they call it elfin?"

"Not elfin, elven," Duglas corrected. "As in the elves. I'm thinking that our herbman here has spent some time among them if he knows how to use the long bow so well."

Padraig knew he tread on shaky ground even mentioning his association with the elves, but Duglas noted his hesitation and laughed.

"I'd not be too concerned this far from the kingdom, lad. There's no one to call you to task and most of these men are dishonored anyway."

Padraig worded his reply carefully round the truth.

"We Denygal live closer to the elves than any other. We've adopted some of their ways. I studied herbs among them and picked up the bow as well."

"The elves are a marvelous people!" Duglas announced, surprising not just Padraig in that estimation. He sounded downright enthusiastic about a people most folk thought a myth. "My father was a horse trader in Dublyn long years ago, during the time of the settlement at the Southern Confluence."

"You mean where the elves massacred the townsfolk?" Aethyn asked, his voice awed, his accent branding him as from the east.

"Weren't no massacre!" Duglas dismissed. "Folk told it wrong, to incite hatred of the elves, but it weren't their doing and the ones who lived know it."

"I heard nobody lived, the elves killed them all," someone said.

"Only one Celdryan townsfolk died," Duglas insisted. "You must know this story, herbman."

"From the other side, aye. I heard the stories while I

was training. I know someone who was there, but I've never met a Celdryan who was."

"Aye, well, I was about 15 winters then. We'd lived there a few years. The elves have marvelous horses and at the Southern Confluence they were helping us to breed better horses for our own herds. The elves and the Celdryans lived side by side there, working together for somewhat better than what we'd had before. I think the adults hoped it would be much like Denygal, but if we didn't intermarry the priests wouldn't get involved." He stared into the fire for a moment.

"So what went wrong?" Braeden asked.

"A woman," Duglas announced. "Isn't it always about breeding? This elven girl – ah, but she was beautiful! Utterly alien, but totally fascinating."

"I thought the elves crop their babies' ears. How can that be beautiful?"

"That's not true," Padraig told Aethyn. "I've attended birthings in the elven lands. The babies are born with peaked ears. And, you can't explain the eyes on cropping."

"Eyes?"

"Cat-slit," Duglas explained. "Vertical pupils. Quite somewhat to see. Despite that, they are the most beautiful people you will ever see. For myself, I think this girl was more beautiful than most of her kind. And, she of course, attracted attention from men – namely, the mayor's son."

"If your folks were trying to avoid coupling, this wouldn't have been good news," Braeden noted.

"Nay, and her parents were clear that they wanted

him to stay away from her. His father told him to do just that. I heard it. Then she came up pregnant. The elves are very clear about such things. They insisted the boy marry the girl and that he serve a period of penance for his error. His father was most upset with that arrangement, but was considering it when someone killed the boy."

"What?" Padraig gasped, for he had heard another version of this story.

"Not the tale you quite heard?"

"Not quite. Elves are not pacifists. They will kill when they must, but it is uncommon for them to widow a woman carrying a child."

"I know, but the story round the village was that the elves had killed the boy in revenge for bedding one of their women. Anyway, I don't think anyone knew exactly what had happened and the mayor was inclined to believe that the elves were being painted as villains. But, there were others among the village who stirred up still others and they started burning the elven houses. Some died then, trapped. Others ran. As they climbed into the mountains, a garrison from the nearest dun came upon the village and attacked them with crossbows. It was then that they turned and fired with those long bows. I'd never seen a man spitted from the saddle before. Those arrows can go through mail."

"Aye," Padraig grunted. "That's the story I heard, except for the murder of the mayor's son."

"What do the elves say?"

"That he killed himself in cowardice. He died of hanging, aye?"

"Aye," Duglas agreed. "Funny how different people remember things differently."

"The elves live much longer than men, so I tend to believe their memories more," Padraig announced.

"Well, what you say may well be true," Duglas told him.

"Then how did the town folk die?" Aethyn wanted to know.

"They didn't. The mayor's son died by hanging. Mayhap the elves did that, mayhap they didn't. The mayor's wife killed herself – slashed her wrists with a dagger. The mayor himself died shortly after the incident, my father said of a broken heart. Plenty of elves died in the fires and as they were shot down running away. I would not have thought there were more than a couple of archers in that company, but someone must have relieved them, because the arrows just flew."

"Two archers," Padraig told Duglas. Duglas blinked at him. "Just two."

"They took out eight of the 15 riders who rode out from the dun," Duglas explained. "I suppose we could say that was a massacre, but it were more like self-defense. The mountains had been acknowledged as their land. We were pursuing them into it."

"And, since, the elves have been training to defend the mountains," Padraig added. "They won't countenance an attack there. They have stayed out of Celdrya – they've no wish to fight us – but they will not allow us to attack them again," he explained.

"Who'd want the mountains anyway?" Braeden remarked. "Cold and desolate. How they survive up there, I'll never know. How would anyone survive hereabouts? Same sort, I think."

"Aye," Padraig agreed, not mentioning that the elves lived in relative luxury because the dwarves had gifted them with their old played out mines. "They're a hardy people, no doubt."

"And, but for the God they serve, I thinkme they'd be a desperate people," Duglas added. Padraig felt his heart skip a beat.

"God?" Aethyn asked. "Which of the gods is that?"

"Not one you know, lad," Duglas said. "They call their god the One True God and they only have the one."

"Only one?!" one of the young freeswords scoffed. "Can't they afford more than the one?"

"They believe there is only one god," Duglas reiterated.

"How could one god take care of all the plantings, birthings, deaths and wars?" Aethyn wanted to know.

"They seem to think He can," Duglas said. "Padraig, do you know of this god?"

"Aye. You can't be a member of elven society without hearing of Him," Padraig said. "The one God is sufficient for them, Aethyn. They feel that the one God shows His power."

"If there is only one true god," Tamys asked. "How do they explain the others like Bel, Lugh, and Kernos?"

"They say those gods are merely what we created because we didn't know the One True God," Padraig replied, hoping that none noticed how truly scared he was to be speaking out so clearly here.

"Created? Like we made a pot or a table?" Aethyn asked.

"Aye," Duglas said, nodding. "I remember how much their god meant to them. They weren't shy of telling the Celdryans at the Southern Confluence that their gods had no power. One summer there was a drought and the priests of Bel did come and pray and sacrifice, but naught for it. It remained dry as a bone and the crops were failing. Then someone asked the elves if their god would bless the crops and bring the rains. They didn't have priests special-like as the priests of Bel, but they had men they called the Wise or the Knowing. They all stood in the center of the village praying, heads down in reverence as is their way. And, clouds did blow in and it rained that very day. My father said it was coincidence, that Bel had finally heard that we needed the world humors balanced, but I always wondered at that. Seemed convenient like, since our priests had prayed for days with nary a drop."

Padraig hoped that he might get Duglas alone on this journey and ask him if he believed what he was speaking of. A cold wind guttered the fire and sent a cold draught up Padraig's back.

"I'm for my blankets," Duglas announced, tossing the remains of his tankard into the fire. "Aye, morning will dawn early enough and it gets cold up here on the heights."

Padraig and Tamys went back to their campsite to roll in. Tamys seemed to be shooting odd glances Padraig's way as they prepared their blankets, but he said naught and they went to sleep without discussion.

Under the Mountain

I was a child when King Gwin brought us to Daermad. We fled the Rawmaynes, who had deemed us expendable because we would not submit to slavery. As we fled to the east, mist shrouded the road through the forest. We had not time to turn about; we were driven forward as the Rawmayne armies pursued us with their chariots. I remember we were climbing into forested mountains when we entered the mist, but then cold water splashed round my knees and the air tasted of salt. As the last of our number ... some 2000 ... stumbled onto the shingle, the mist dissolved and we found ourselves upon a wide harbor surrounded by low land with mountains in the distance. Behind us, we heard horses screaming and looked back to see the chariots sinking in the deeper water. Some of the Rawmayne soldiers did cut their horses free and they did swim to shore. The Rawmaynes were not so fortunate. Encumbered by their breastplates and swords, most perished. The few who reached shore were near-death with cold and easily disarmed.

Ryla, Druidess of the Krystan Celts, FY 39

Founding Year 931
Galconyn Mountains · Kylly's Mine

This is a dream, Donyl thought as he walked along a corridor that seems to be the dun at Celdrya, but built of logs like the walls that surrounded his physical body. He could hear rain pounding on the roof above his physical body, though he knew logically that he could hear no such thing in the high dun. *Be wary! Dreams are tricky things!*

The thought caused him to stop walking and look round. The dun at Celdrya was a complex of brochs, half-brochs and connecting corridors, so that he could not be absolutely certain of where he was, but he thought himself near the chapel where the priests of Bel attached to the royal family plied their ministry. As dreams do, the wall beside him dissolved and he found himself standing beside the new priest, Perryn's brother-in-law by now, Blethry. When Donyl had met him a matter of a month ago, he'd just had his head shaved as part of his induction into the priesthood, but in this dream he had a full head of hair as if many moons had come and gone. That his tonsure was not shaved reminded Donyl that this had to be a dream as that was a symbol of status among the Bel.

Blethry dipped his quill in a pot of ink and scratched somewhat on parchment. Donyl recognized that he was invisible to the priest, but as this was a dream, Blethry wasn't really there either. Knowing this, Donyl walked round to Blethry's right elbow and watched what the man wrote.

I will remain here and continue my study of the culture, he wrote. *I know the Lughans have requested we convert them by force if necessary, but I do not see this as a feasible course of action. The Denygal are like the Old Faith and will not bow quickly to what they consider sacrilege.*

Donyl's thoughts stumbled. *Denygal? This must be a dream for Blethry is in Celdrya. I must be anticipating my destination.*

Donyl turned from Blethry and recognized the room had changed. They were not in the priestly library at all, but in an odd room he'd not seen before with a low ceiling and, shudder, square walls.

This does not have the feel of a nightmare, yet do not daemons lurk in corners?

Blethry suddenly appeared before him as they walked down a corridor that lead to his father's chambers ... not his father's chambers anymore, but Perryn's now. A fresh wreath of flowers hung upon the door handle.

This is his wedding night then, Donyl thought. He continued to follow Blethry, curious as to why the young priest, now with a short stubble of hair appearing on his scalp round a small tonsure, was going into Perryn's chambers during what was meant to be a private time. Blethry stopped just inside the door, so that Donyl nearly ran into him. If the young priest felt his presence, he showed no sign. Donyl could hear the low tones of a young woman talking with Perryn through the partially opened door, but somewhat of greater importance seized his attention.

This is a nightmare! This is not happening!

Blethry stared at the man who stood with his left hand upon the door to the bedchamber. Deryk was unaware of his observers as he pushed the door open enough to gain passage to the room. The wall dissolved before Donyl so that he could see Perryn and his bride upon the bed. Perryn nuzzled her neck and she giggled. Deryk raised his right hand as Perryn spotted the shadow spreading across the blanket. The knife came down into Perryn's side and sunk deep. Blood sprayed the wall behind the bed as Perryn's young bride twisted and stared at Deryk in horror. With his left hand, Deryk grabbed her throat and lifted her free of the blankets. Her eyes bulged as she scratched desperately at the hand choking her. With incredible strength, Deryk drove the back of her head into the stone wall behind the bed, adding her blood and brains to Perryn's congealing blood.

Donyl could hear himself screaming as Deryk backed away from the murders, mouth working in horror at what he had done. Men rushed into the chamber as Deryk let the knife drop to the floor and covered his face with his blood-dripping hands.

The scene dissolved as Donyl sat up upon his blankets, but he still saw Blethry turn to him and shout *"Flee, you fool! Send them to the five winds and run! She must not be allowed to have them."*

Heart hammering in his chest, Donyl stared around the log-walled room and at the two men who had awakened when he sat up.

"The rain's stopped," Nedd announced, sitting up on the other side of Donyl. He pulled the amulet free of his wrist where he'd wound it. "I think that mayhap not be a good sign."

"Nay," Pedyr agreed, pulling on his boots as he spoke. "What I did just dream did not comfort me in the least and can you not feel what stalks our way?"

"Mayhap ... what did you dream?" Donyl asked, breathless as his heart hammered behind his ribs. Pedyr looked at him, then slid his gaze aside. "Did you dream that Deryk of Cenconyn did stab King Perryn?"

Pedyr's mouth dropped open.

"I dreamt it as well," Nedd did add, reaching for his boots. "I think there's naught time to waste."

The next half-watch was a rush of activity. They'd planned to send the riders to the winds with the artifacts in the morning, but all three were in silent agreement that they needed to go now. They were not in immediate agreement whether to wake the village and warn them of what was coming. Deciding to keep the secret to their chests, they quietly woke the men they could gain easy access to and explained, in hurried and hushed tones, the need.

"Rogyn can take the amulet," Pedyr told Nedd as the Dunmaden man came toward him with his saddlebags over one shoulder.

"Nay, I think naught of that idea," Nedd replied. Pedyr frowned. "Please listen. I can make the amulet work and surely this thing knows someone in our party can do so. By using it, I can draw that thing away from

Donyl. As he may well be our king now, we must protect him at all cost, which is why I will remain in the dark as to whether you are going forward or returning to Celdrya."

Pedyr thought to argue, but how did one argue with good sense? He nodded and briefly clasped his friend's shoulder with one large callused hand. They left their thoughts unspoken and got about the grim business of surviving evil.

Founding Year 1028
Highway to Mandorlyn

The caravan broke camp before dawn, taking to their saddles just as the sky was turning blue. The night had been cold and the morning was frosty, making the animals prance lightly and the men to shiver in their cloaks. Padraig noted as they rode that he had been missing somewhat on this journey. In the elven lands, women rode herd along with the men, owning animals of their own and pulling an equal share of the care. He hadn't seen a woman since leaving Dun Wllean and the lack was wearing on him. It wasn't that he desired romance, for his heart was secured with one he had left behind, but simply that the sound of a female voice and the thoughts of a female mind were lacking here and he felt the want.

Tamys had chosen to ride with some of the freesword guards this morning, so that Padraig might have been riding alone all day if Duglas had not joined him before the warmth of the sun touched the canyon.

"I haven't heard a complaint about the bowels yet, herbman. Good job."

"I earn my hire," Padraig replied pleasantly. They smiled at one another. Duglas glanced around nonchalantly.

"I hope I didn't make you uncomfortable last night."

"A bit, but only because talk of elves in the east will get you hanged."

"Aye, well, we're a bit more realistic this side of the kingdom. Most acknowledge the existence of the dwarves, so the existence of the elves isn't so hard to countenance. The Southern Confluence was a tragedy that Celdryans ought to apologize for, but won't, I'm sure. I was speaking more of the elven god."

"Another topic that can bring a noose with it."

"Aye, but I have wanted all these years to meet someone who knew about their god. Jesu, they called him, familiarly."

"Aye," Padraig grunted.

"They said that you had only to believe, to confess your disobedience to Him and He would enter your heart and tell you who you are."

"Aye," Padraig agreed.

"I did that as a youngling," Duglas admitted. "Now, I'm trusting that you're not going to tell anyone about that. Over the years, I've not met anyone who would understand it. Do you?"

"Aye," Padraig grunted. Duglas smiled at him.

"Well and good then. I am not far off the mark and I am grateful for you joining my caravan."

"If we could but find some privacy to talk, but alas ...."

"Aye, well, He talks to us both, I think. Thanks to you. I should ride round now, so that folk don't go guessing at what they cannot know."

"Indeed," Padraig replied and they parted company. For the rest of the morning, Padraig rode silently praising God for this brother in Kryst.

By late-morning the heat, the dust and the bugs clung around them as the day before. Relieved only by the abundant fresh water they had collected at the caravanserie, thirst parched men's throats and made mule and horse alike surly. Even Joy complained of the biting gnats. Padraig resorted once again to his mask and saw other men do the same. As before, the muleteers did not complain, for like their charges they lived for hard work and balked only when the pull was off their shoulders. Walking as they were at the level of the road, the dust was worst for them, but they had naught a word of complaint.

Toward late mid-afternoon, the caravan ground to a halt and Braeden came back to ask Padraig to join him. He didn't know where Tamys was, but passed him in the column as he rode forward. Tamys followed at a discreet distance, showing that he was still Padraig's friend. Duglas had pulled the caravan to a stop at the entrance to a cave that ran directly under the mountain that had been looming for quite sometime.

"Another dwarven highway," Duglas told Padraig.

"I have men who panic at this every time. Do you have somewhat to take the edge off?"

"Nay. Ale is as good as we have. Some men just don't like being underground."

"That I know, but it's the only way to Mandorlyn and not as bad as they think."

"I have traveled on such in the east. If you like, I will stand here and encourage the men with my knowledge. I'm not sure if it will assist, but I will do as you like."

"Thanks to you, herbman. I also remain here, but they do not always believe such as me."

The first man to protest going under the ground was Tamys, whose horse also shied.

"Men were not meant to go under the ground, Padraig," he protested.

"The dwarves do disagree and the elves have sheltered in their mines in the eastern mountains. Tamys, there's adventure and possible honor on the other end of this tunnel. Are you going to tell me that you'll turn back to join the brigands rather than follow me?"

"Nay, but .... It is unnatural," Tamys assured him, then schooled his horse and rode under the mountain. There were still many men behind him, but the younger freeswords hesitated only and then followed Tamys. Braeden rode up at that moment.

"You can ride forward, herbman," he assured Padraig. "I've many a trip to this place and not turned back a man yet."

"Thanks to you," Padraig said. He turned Joy and the pony to follow the column. Going under the shadow of the mountain instantly cooled the air and drove the bugs away. The tunnel was dry with a good thick layer of the moss the dwarves lined their highways with. Joy sent him a thought of pleasure and even Ernest's step lightened. The ceiling was high with plenty of room to sit upright in the saddle, somewhat that Padraig had never understood, since the dwarves were short and didn't ride horses, but he supposed they had reasons he was not meant to understand. The holt also had unnecessarily high ceilings. Mayhap they just liked the look.

Two wagons could ride abreast in the tunnel, so the column relaxed a bit. Padraig lapsed into a reverie concerning Blue Iris Holt and the folk he knew there. He could only scry through the fire and then not well, but it was almost as if he saw them working and talking within the cavern of the Wise. At one point, he thought Ryanna was urgently waving her hands before his face, beseeching him to listen, but Tamys interrupted him and the vision faded. Tamys had stopped hunching in the saddle to avoid a ceiling that was not low.

"'Tis an ingenious way to get round a mountain," he noted. He nodded to an air shaft ahead. "Those bring in fresh air."

"Aye. In the east, there are a few of these tunnels. There, the dwarves maintenance some of them – the ones they still use – but leave others to nature. They last a long time. I've heard there are some tunnels in the kingdom, but none of the elves I know knew where to find them."

"Tunnels? That would be a nice knowledge for an army to have," Tamys noted. "I'd wager to guess that if my fa – Mulyn knew of tunnels, he'd have used them a long time ago."

"The high city was a citadel in the days of the basketlands. The dwarves didn't serve the same gods as the elves, so I don't know if they would have built tunnels to it."

"So there's elven ruins under Dun Celdrya?" Tamys asked.

"I don't know. I know there's elven ruins below Dun Galornyn and Dun Cenconyn – I've seen them. I know there's most likely elven ruins beneath Dun Llyr. If I had to wager, I'd say there are – or were -- tunnels between those three. They were major cities that the dwarves would have traded with. Of course, that was a thousand years ago and the tunnels may long ago have fallen in."

"The men of Mulyn don't know these tales," Tamys announced. "Your corner of the kingdom must be well-read."

"Aye. There's not much to do in the long winters. And, we had a good bard as well. Learning's well and good when the bard entertains."

"I'll take your word for it," Tamys said. "How long will it take us to reach daylight?"

"Don't know," Padraig announced after a moment. "The tunnels I've traversed before were not so large. I'm thinking we might be spending the night."

"Spending the night!" Tamys exploded. "But – they say there are trolls in the mountains at night!"

"Lad, there are trolls here in the day if there are any at all," Padraig assured him. "They're naught but dwarves of a different tribe. Now, goblins, those are truly scary, though, in all my wide travels I've not met a goblin and I've seen some wild things. Methinks goblins are a dwarven folktale to scare Celdryans away from their mines."

"Was this a mine, herbman?" Aethyn asked, having drawn to the rear of them.

"I'm thinking it wasn't. The mines in the eastern mountains have many tunnels, not just a straight one through the heart of the mountain. Nay, the dwarves use these sorts of tunnels as highways. I think this is just that."

"Too bad. I would brave a goblin or two for some gold or pretty rocks."

"Aye, well, you'd best be worried about dwarves rather than trolls. As I said, I've met dwarves, but never a goblin and the dwarves are a fearsome people when you go touching their pretty stones."

The travel under the mountain seemed to take forever. Occasionally an airshaft would let in some light, but this became rarer as the day wore on and they went deeper under the mountain. The air remained fresh and the torches drafted well, but light simply couldn't make its way down the air shafts. Finally, the caravan ground to a halt near a huge hearth cut into the living stone where the cook was roasting on a spit and a camp was starting to take shape.

"How many nights will we be spending underground?" Padraig asked Duglas.

"Just the one. There's men who have heard strange noises behind the walls at night, so I set a quick pace to the other side."

"Strange noises?"

"I've never heard them myself and I suspect it's all a dream, but I don't need my guards panicking under the mountain. I've always thought the brigands ought to set up their ambuscades here rather than out in the open, but I suppose that's why I'm a caravan leader and they're brigands."

"Mayhap," Padraig said. He knew from experience that stone was not silent. Sometime you could hear water running behind the rocks or ..., well, he didn't know what all made the noises, but he thought them natural enough.

"'Tis a pleasant campsite despite being underground. There's water, a hearth, fresh air. I can see why the elves live in the abandoned dwarven mines."

Padraig smiled, but did not correct Duglas. The Mountain People had given the mines to the elves. They were, as far as he knew, played out, but they were not abandoned.

"When you lived at the Southern Confluence, did you know a girl by the name of Ryanna?"

Duglas looked sore surprised.

"Aye, I remember her. Pretty little thing. Part-Celdryan. Used to beat us lads at archery. She lived? Or, well, I suppose she must have if you know her."

"We met in the mountains," Padraig explained. Although he thought about her everyday with whimsy, speaking of her caused warmth to spread throughout his body.

"I suppose, them being so long-lived, she wouldn't look like more than a lass."

"By elven standards, she is only an adolescent. By half-elven standards, she's the equivalent of my age."

"Is she now?! That do explain much. The elven lads were not exaggerating about their travels, merely not telling us that they were four times our age."

"Aye." Padraig smiled, thinking about the elves he knew.

"So you met Ryanna and fell in love," Duglas noted a twinkle in his eye. "She didn't marry that half-elf who used to follow her about like she were a bitch in heat. Good for her."

"Which one was that?" Padraig asked, though he suspected he knew the answer.

"Well, I suppose he might have died in the Purge. Lad by the name of Gil."

"He lived," Padraig provided. "And, he married Ryanna. He died about five years ago, though. I never met him. Sounds as if he had an unseemly attraction."

"I did not like Gil, not to speak ill of the dead. He was wild as a green pony and not nearly so pleasant. Oh, he'd show you a face anyone might call friend, but you found yourself checking for the knife in his left hand." The elves had been more polite in their estimation, but that was similar to what Padraig had heard in the holt. "Ryanna was indifferent to him, but he seemed pretty persuasive. I know the elves don't force their daughters to marry, but it seemed like Gil was lobbying his cause heavily."

"I know Ryanna married him in haste and repented in leisure. I always wondered what she was like before Gil."

"Strong-willed, but she loved to laugh. Now?"

"Strong-willed, but she enjoys laughing," Padraig said with a smile. There had been those who had credited him with bringing back her laughter.

"Will you be traveling back for her?"

"Mayhap," Padraig said. "The Commander I serve has orders for me and I must do the will of Him who sent me. Under elven law, Ryanna is not free to marry yet. Mayhap we will come together again. We shall see."

"You're the whole kingdom away from the eastern mountains, lad, and traveling in the wrong direction. I would brave the Avercelt in spring flood for a woman like that."

"Aye, so would I, if not for Whom I serve. Ryanna understands. She serves the same."

"Aye. When we get to Mandorlyn, you must attend me at my house there, so that we may speak in private."

"We shall," Padraig assured him. "I'd best get my camp set up. Thanks to you for talking."

Duglas smiled and nodded and they parted ways.

Tamys found it difficult to sleep in the dark of the cavern. While it was light, he'd been impressed by the high vault and scope of the cavern, but when the torches were doused, he had become aware of the weight of the mountain as if it were the true rock resting upon his chest. While the others around him slipped into quiet breaths, he could feel his heart pounding. In time, he swore he heard voices within the rocks. These kept him awake, on the edge of hearing words, fearing the message contained therein. Just as he was ready to start screaming, he drifted off. Tamys knew he was floating on the edge of sleep for he had been here before many a battle. Yet, even as he knew this, he also knew that a dream was starting – the most vivid dream a vivid dreamer had ever had.

All his life, Tamys had dreamt in color and in great detail. Remembering his dreams, he'd shared them with his brothers who had told him this was unusual. In time, he'd learned not to share them any longer, for it only made them nervous, though he'd never really understood why. They were just dreams. Very vivid dreams and sometimes they seemed almost to come true, but dreams all the same. Like the dream he'd had of this cavern. He'd dreamt about it two winters ago and awakened trying to remember if the bard had sung of trolls the night before. Why else would he dream of caverns and hands reaching to grab him in the dark? Thinking that in his semi-sleep, Tamys tried to sit up, to avoid the hands, but he couldn't move. The voices whispered louder now and Tamys wanted to wake Padraig, to tell him what he heard, but he couldn't get his voice to speak.

Mist swirled round him and resolved itself into a castle with a spiral staircase ascending up into clouds. Tamys knew that his dream body could move, even as his physical body was palsied with sleep. He walked around the base of the staircase, trying to see round him. The castle seemed to be in shambles, with blocks of stone scattered across the mosaic floor. Wind lifted his hair and he could see grass growing at the edge of the surrounding mist. He looked up the staircase, which seemed intact. Curious yet wary, he eyed it, unable to see much beyond twice his height. He heard a raven call and evaluated the stair once more. One step, two steps .... He cautiously climbed higher.

Tamys paused, unable to see forward, unable to see back. He had only the step in front of him and the one he was standing on. His heart thudded with fear. The voices grew louder still, speaking from the mist that surrounded him. Then a scream rent the air and a body fell from the sky to the earth lost somewhere in the mist. A raven feather as long as his arm drifted down to the step above and then the staircase collapsed under him.

Tamys woke with a scream, flailing out, grasping for anything that would hold him in a tumbling world. Voices exploded all round him and a candle lantern flared to life. Padraig's worried face was the first he saw.

"Are you all right, lad?" Padraig asked.

Tamys panted, staring around him, surprised to see all the men staring at him. Duglas came padding over in his bare feet, holding a candle of his own.

"Happens every time we camp here," he announced. "As I said, men think they hear the rocks talking and, next thing you know, they're having dreams and seeing visions. You will be aright, lad, in a minute."

Tamys had faced many battles and knew how to calm himself, so that it only took a few moments. Yet, the dream lingered even as he forced it back into his deep mind.

"I guess being under the mountain affected me," he admitted to Padraig.

"Aye, it does take some men that way," Braeden assured him. "Lads, we need our rest if we're to start out fresh on the morrow. Back to your blankets."

Padraig stared at Tamys, who didn't know what to say.

"You're a strong dreamer, aren't you, lad?"

"Aye," Tamys agreed. "Why?"

"It's just an observation. Can you sleep?"

"I doubt it," Tamys admitted.

"I've a sleeping draught if you need it."

"I don't think I want to sleep here any longer," Tamys admitted after a moment's thought. "I'd wager there's somewhat about these walls that do talk."

Padraig scanned the cavern, the elaborately carved walls, the grand hearth.

"I think it was a great hall," he decided. "Somewhat like the great hall of any dun. I don't know why it would affect some as it has you. I never knew anyone who experienced the same in the Eastern Mountains. You'll likely doze off after the torches have been doused."

"I wouldn't count on that," Tamys replied grimly.

"I'm for leaving a torch or two up," Aethyn said nervously. "It creeps a man's flesh to hear someone screaming in the dark."

"The sand glass says we have a bit more until dawn," Braedyn announced. "We could leave a torch up."

Tamys put his back against his saddle and sat with his blanket round his shoulders. He didn't close his eyes all night, but still he thought he heard voices in the rocks. Mayhap because he was awake, he was also aware of the sound of water running somewhere in the walls. He supposed the cistern had to be fed from somewhere. Still, he thought somewhat else stalked behind these walls, somewhat with a mind and a plan to do humans harm.

Kin Cycle 24578 / FY 1028
The Dragon's Back

Marnmara pounded the mound of dough, trying to direct her frustration toward it rather than her daughter. It had been four five-cycles since she'd been able to affect repentance in Ryanna with the sharp edge of her tongue. She should have learned by now that her strength would not overpower the lass's will.

"I'll be voting for you to remain here," Marnmara replied quietly. Oh, how difficult it was to remain quiet!

"Madi', please, this is important."

"It's always important," Marnmara said. "Important and necessary and urgent."

Ryanna sighed. She sat on a stool next to the kneading table. Marnmara loved how her daughter resembled her father in a much prettier way. Her features were entirely human, so unlike Marnmara, who had catslit purple eyes and honey blond hair, the peaks of her furled ears peeking out. Aware that humans found her kind eerily beautiful when they weren't afraid of them, Marnmara had never considered herself particularly attractive. She supposed that's why she'd been drawn a Denygalman with his odd round eyes and ears. No, her Sion was not a pretty man. He made beautiful, if frustratingly hasty, children, though.

"Madi', dragons are coming to me."

"And Padraig was sent forth by prophesy mentioning dragons. It does seem connected. You're still married to Gil and I will be voting for you to remain here until your contract is up."

Ryanna snapped the wood paddle she held in two. Marnmara ignored her destruction and continued kneading.

"Why do you feel that way, Madi'? You've said marrying Gil was a mistake. You supported my decision to leave him three five-cycles ago. Why are you resisting me now?"

"Because you chose not to leave him then and he's not legally dead. The Lord requires patience and consideration in these things. And, you very much should not go from one husband to another."

"Gil and I have not been together as husband and wife for 12-cycles, Madi'."

"You've practiced patience enough to be good at it, then," Marnmara observed calmly. Ryanna tossed the two halves of the paddle in a waste bucket and stalked out of the bakery. Sion would say that exchange had gone about how he'd expected.

Ryanna seethed as she crossed the holt toward her chambers in the Hall of the Wise. Her irritation with the entire situation was such she did not pay attention to where she was going and brushed shoulders with Shanara. The weaver dropped the blankets she was carrying.

"My apologies!" Ryanna said, immediately bending to help pick up the mess she'd made. Shanara's super-aura briefly became visible to Ryanna's Knowing. It read brief and mild irritation followed by amusement. Ryanna stopped in her ministrations to stare at the weaver as the super-aura dissolved like gossamer in the rain.

"Yes, you saw it," Shanara assured, as she handed some blankets to Ryanna. "We can bang these off at the storehouse. Come along."

Ryanna had little choice, since she now bore half of Sharana's burden. She followed after the weaver with long-legged strides. With the warmer weather, she'd donned a sleeveless dress that ended just below her knees and leather sandals. The flowing skirt did not impede her in the least while Shanara's tunic and leggings were probably warmer than necessary for the season.

"I'm sensing great agitation from you, Morynsionryanna. What's caught in your liver?"

Ryanna knew of few even among the Wise who could have sensed anything from her with her shields clamped closed, but somehow it didn't surprise her that Shanara was an exception.

"My mother plans to oppose my request to travel with the Avalirad caravan."

"Does she not realize that Padraig did not return to Cenconyn?"

"She does realize, but she believes that I won't keep my word to return to the holt after I've met with the lord of Cenconyn."

"Hmm," Shanara grunted. The storehouse doors stood open to take advantage of the warm weather. The squire glanced up from a ledger, but Shanara merely waved and led Ryanna deeper into the complex of shelves and bins. History taught that the elves had once lived lives separate from their fellow Kin, but since moving into the mountains, they held a great deal in common so as to maximize their efforts. Shanara would tell the squire how many blankets she delivered and receive credit for food and other items. Every adult had to work for the necessity of life and work harder for the luxuries. As Shanara wove blankets and rugs, Ryanna hunted and drove stock.

"You and I are not close, but I sense that you will keep your word," Shanana announced as she accepted the stack of blankets from Ryanna. "You are not the same foolish girl who married a dangerous young man without thinking of the consequences."

"Thank you," Ryanna said. "Were that Madi knew me so well."

"Perhaps you should speak with her as you do with me instead of always seeking an argument."

"Why do you assume that it is me seeking the argument?"

"Is it not? Marnmara is known as a strong-willed woman, but she has consistent conflict only with you."

Ryanna sighed. Shanara had her weighed and measured sure enough.

"What do you suggest I do concerning the caravan, then?" she asked.

"Let the Lord decide that one. You can only do what you can and then, as always, it's up to the One to make the decision. Your mother has reason to worry, based on your past folly, but those of us who watch you with clear eyes know that you've moved beyond it." Shanara wrote her tally on the board hanging on the end of the shelves then they turned toward the entrance. It was chilly in this cavern, a reminder that summer was still new.

"Thank you," Ryanna said as they neared the light-filled exit.

"My estimation of your character won't win the day, of course. I only judge the tenor of the holt and I believe you are the only one truly standing in your way to going on this journey."

Ryanna blinked and then laughed.

"I'm always the one standing in my own way," she admitted.

"I have also been known for my strong will and sharp tongue. Eventually I had to leave my holt and come here to be respected as the adult I had become."

It was impossible to tell Shanara's age, but Ryanna thought that the struggle to be deemed mature was somewhat every half-elf dealt with, though truly Shanara was something altogether different.

Outside the warm summer day was subsiding into mist as scudding clouds moved into the high mountain valleys. The two women paused to survey the darkening sky.

"There's a storm coming," Shanara said in a low voice. Ryanna meant to scoff, for it was obvious, but then an icy hand ran down her back so that she shuddered strongly. Shanara glanced at her, her silver eyes seeming to glow with untapped energy. "We may have time, but it grows shorter than we can know."

Without so much as a farewell, the two women strode off in separate directions, each with apprehension in their heart.

Founding Year 1028
Road to Mandorlyn

On the morrow, they set out briskly and won free of the mountain mid-afternoon. Although he had traveled under-mountain before, Padraig felt grateful for the sun on his back and he noted Joy's step seemed lighter. The band camped in a caravanserie just outside the tunnel's end, in another area where the highway's walls gave way to mountain meadow. Duglas seemed wont to rest that evening and truly, the men seemed tired. Most had probably not slept well after Tamys had awakened them. Padraig commented to Duglas on this.

"We always camp here," Duglas said. "The next caravanserie is a full day's journey, so even though tis an early camp, tis a wise one."

"What's the rest of the journey like?"

"This is the high point. We'll be wending downward starting the morrow. The highway itself falls off and there's more of a true road. There's villages to stop at and a pleasant caravanserie or two."

Padraig wondered what sort of land Mandorlyn was.

"The flora and fauna are most different from the rest of the kingdom," Duglas told him. "Odd trees. Odd animals."

"Hmm," Padraig mused. "Well and good then. Sounds like a curious place. I look forward to the adventure."

"A man of learning such as yourself will no doubt

find much to interest him," Duglys assured.

Padraig found Tamys dicing with a group of young freeswords. The lad proved uncommonly good at guessing the roll, yet also careful not to guess too often right. That he was deliberating guessing wrong spoke loudly to Padraig, who had done much the same himself.

"Curse you, but you've got Lugh's own luck!" Aethyn complained. "Let's play again to see if I can get my losings back."

"Aethyn, it's late and I don't think you're going to get more luck in the next few moments," Tamys replied. "We've days on this journey. I promise you another chance."

Aethyn and the other lads wandered off. Tamys pocketed their coin.

"You might want to guess a bit more roughly," Padraig suggested. "They don't suspect you of cheating yet, but luck like yours is a bit to wonder."

"I'm not cheating," Tamys assured him. "They were Aethyn's dice, so how could I?"

"I'm not saying you're cheating. I'm saying they will suspect it in time if you don't guess more roughly."

Tamys stared as if Padraig had kicked him, then turned away to stride off toward the squatting pit. What was Tamys not telling him? Padraig wished he knew more about the lad so he weren't conjecturing in the dark, but Tamys still didn't open up fully about his life before the Green Giant and Padraig knew better than to tread where a man had set wards. Still, Padraig wagered there was an interesting tale back of those skills with the dice.

Light

Lord Deryk does not seem to know why he killed King Perryn. He tells a tale of eating at the banquet and arising to go to the privy only to find himself entering Perryn's chambers, drawing his dagger and killing them both. He remembers not slitting the throat of the guard. So, he claims.

That cursed priest of Bel, Blethry suggests he's been ensorcelled and certainly there's enough afoot that's curious-making that I'd suspect black magery, but one must remember he was with Maryn when he died as well and all the witnesses are scattered to the wind, dispatched with Prince Donyl (crown-prince Donyl) to Cenconyn. There will be a malover before the priests of Lugh by the moon's turning. It mayhap be that the dispatches will reach Donyl in Chenyn's court by then. The gods help him. The lad's doomed if he sits the throne.

Dumyr, Chief Councilor to Court Trevellyn, Summer FY 932.

Founding Year 931
Galconyn Mountains

The morning dew dripped from the trees in the silent forest. Donyl, Pedyr, and the remaining six of the original 15-strong warband followed the young mountain boy along a barely discernable track. Kylly Mines had its own seers, who had alerted the villagers to the daemon stalking their guests. Marstyn had insisted that his son Faryl escort them as far east as he had knowledge. He was reported to be the best woodsman in Kylly Mines. Donyl feared the village doomed, but Marstyn said they'd pray and the One would protect them. Faryl seemed unconcerned with the fate of his home and family. These Believers were truly a remarkable people. Mayhap foolhardy, but remarkably faithful.

The world round them was aswirl with pearly fog broken by an occasional dark tree trunk. They could neither see upslope or down, east, west, north or south. The sun must be somewhere before them, given the early hour, but Donyl could not spy it. The forest hummed eerily in its silence.. Though not a hunter like his brothers, Donyl knew enough to recognize the forest creatures were on alert -- holding their breath for somewhat Donyl could not hear.

Faryl, barely visible at the head of the column riding

a work-horse, halted the line of march with an upheld hand, staring down the mountain. The warband jostled to a stop, tack jingling oddly within the silence. Men with nerves stretched taut eased their swords in the scabbards. All rode with mail, even Donyl, whose shoulders ached with the unaccustomed weight of it. Faryl was the only one ill-equipped, though what good mail would do against a daemon was uncertain. As if to highlight that concern, Faryl wore a leather jerkin stripped with metal like a corset. Donyl doubted it would turn aside a spear, though it might dull a sword. The metal might ward a daemon, Nedd had said. It was iron and iron was said to repulse daemons.

A sudden wash of fear roiled over Donyl from downslope. He saw the men react to it as if slapped by an icy wave. Cold like a winter night caused the horses to shy and dance. Sound rolled up the hill like naught Donyl had ever heard before -- several rhythmic thudding beats wound together, moving rapidly toward them. The horses rolled their eyes and blew out their noses. Then Donyl's horse reared and tossed him to the ground.

While he lay gasping on the ground, large brown bodies hove into sight, leaping and bounding amid screaming horses and cursing men. Donyl's attention was only for his horse's hooves and the large shapes that sped past him. He rolled away and scrabbled toward a tree trunk. Somewhat caught his sword belt, lifted him free of the ground and flung him closer to the tree. Donyl crawled rapidly toward the shelter and then turned to view the fog-shrouded chaos behind him.

Deer bounded upslope and scattered the warband,

sending horses bucking and men screaming. Dozens, if not hundreds, of deer raced past Donyl. One lowered its horns to hook Donyl's horse in the side and then sped on with the horse upon its head. Another ploughed into a rider's horse, sending it and its rider tumbling. The pounding thud of their travel drowned out all but the closest shouts. Donyl could only stare in awe and terror.

Out of the swirling mist, a deer headed straight for the prince. Seeing his death riding him down, Donyl did the only thing he knew. He drew his sword and swung at the deer's head. His inexpert slice caught it right cross the nose, causing it to swerve and run off into the mist on the other side of his tree. Another deer headed his way and Donyl twisted to meet its charge. The hot breath of the animal warmed his arm as it careened past him with one eye hanging out of its socket..

How long this went on, he did not know, but his arms shook with the effort of keeping the sword aloft and swinging by the time the thundering herd flowed uphill and away from him. Not knowing if it were truly the last, Donyl leaned against the tree, panting. The analytical part of his mind noted the real blood dripping from his sword. These deer were apparently more real than the wolves had been.

In the following quiet, men moaned in the mist. Hesitating, Donyl feared to leave the safety of the tree, where at least he had its bole for partial protection, but he could not leave the men who protected him alone in the fog. Cautiously, he set out toward the nearest voice, holding his sword with both trembling hands. As he did, a bit of the fog began to lift and weak sunlight filtered down to him. Donyl found a rider crushed beneath his horse, a leg bent at a bad angle and blood running from his mouth.

"I'm sorry, sire," he whispered as Donyl bent to him. "I'm done." Then he let go his spirit, eyes growing dim and glossing over. The smell of urine rose to Donyl's nose as he closed the man's eyelids. He felt tears trickle down his cheeks. He'd seen men dead before, but he'd never witnessed a death.

"Sire," Pedyr said, kneeling beside him, his drawn sword dripping with blood. "Are you injured?"

Dumbfounded, Donyl looked down at his body. Blood soaked his breecs.

"I think it's deer's blood," Donyl said wearily. The fog blew off uphill, so that he could now view the scene about him. He struggled to his feet. Men and horses littered a mountain meadow that was broken by occasional trees and large rocks. A quick count showed three horses down. A slower count found four men dead and another dying. Young Faryl stood silently at the edge of the killing field, knowledgeable eyes scanning the trees, the reins of his work horse clutched in one hand. In keeping with his people's ways, he carried only a staff. He'd sunk his spear deep into the chest of one deer … the only one Donyl could see, now dead at the hunter's feet.

"We should bury these men," Donyl said after their inspection. They had no horses beyond the work horse, a few bent arms, some water in bottles and some food.

"We haven't time," Pedyr protested. "It's already past midday and the dark of the moon approaches. We can't remain here. That's what she wants."

"Then what do you suggest. Faryl, can we make it back to your village by some secret way?"

"I'd not be taking you back to where my mam does live, sire," Faryl told him plainly. The lad showed no anger in his speaking, merely a resignation and the clear knowledge that death stalked Donyl. "The way forward is thus." He pointed east. "We should be about it."

"But these men …."

"Are beyond caring," Pedyr told him. "Sire, we must flee. There's a citadel that overlooks the Dengyal valley. Faryl hasn't been there, but I think I remember the way. We wager it's an eight night's hard run there. I believe we'll be safe there."

"An eight night? We won't live to see the other side of the coming night," Donyl scoffed.

Faryl and Pedyr exchanged glances.

"We've lived this long, sire. No use giving up just yet," Pedyr assured. "We've got to be away, sire. Now … if we wish any hope to live."

Donyl looked over the desolate scene and near wept for the dishonor of leaving good men to rot in the sun, but he had naught else for choice. He turned to young Faryl instead. The lad was about his own age and this was not his battle.

"You should give Pedyr directions and we'll be on our way. Go back to Kylly Mines."

Faryl stared at him. Like many of his people, he was dark haired and blue eyed with skin ruddy from outdoor work.

"Begging your pardon, sire, but I'll not be leaving

you. My da did task me to take you at least to the top of the pass and that's two days' ahead. And, you'll be needing the horse to carry your supplies and I'd only have to fetch it back."

"'Tis not your fight, lad. You're risking your life for matters you know naught about."

Faryl narrowed his eyes and then smiled at some inner thought.

"We've not much contact with the kingdom, sire, but we've lots of contact with the Heavenly Host. Tis the name of the village, is it not? Kylly Court. And, God do command us greater than your family and He do command that I take you as far as I'm able."

Donyl knew naught of this god, but he sensed Faryl would countenance no disrespect of him. That decided, he nodded to Faryl, who helped Pedyr swing a pack upon the horse's back, turned his back on the bloody scene and set off up mountain, ghosting through the trees. Donyl limped along behind with Pedyr bringing up the rear. They had a long way to go and hell on their trail. Best to not think about what happened if it overtook them.

Founding Year 1028
Highway to Mandorlyn

Tamys had heard of Mandorlyn as a legend for most of his life. Bards sang of it as an adventurous place with high mountains of gold and bewitching lasses of hardy stock. Thus, he was surprised when they exited the mountain canyon and began to descent into Mandorlyn. It was clear that they had entered the fabled valley because the canyon was gone and a true road, much like the dwarven roads of Mulyn wended through dusty red hills of jagged rock where scraggly stunted plants struggled for life. There were rushing streams in some places and there the plant life seemed less precarious, but certainly not lush. Somehow this was not what Tamys had expected and he felt cheated of his dreams.

For three days they traveled down the mountains until Duglas called a halt at midday. It took a moment of looking around to realize they were just outside of a mining village. The village climbed a narrow side valley with a high rock wall at the bottom by the road and a gaping hole at the top of the valley – the mine.

The men stared at the first sign of civilization in ten days and they began to smile to one another.

"Listen carefully, men," Duglas called. "This is a peaceful village, but they will defend themselves. These are my stock and trade and I'll ask you to be about the business I hired you to do. You'll not be lifting any skirts of their daughters nor fighting with their sons. I'll turn you over to their tender mercies if I catch you at it. Now, the village will be providing us with a meal out here. You're not to go into the town at all. There'll be guards soon enough to keep you from it anyway. Then we'll be setting up a market faire right here. We'll camp by a lake up ahead tonight and we'll move on in the morning. Accept that schedule or find yourself fed to the ravens."

Duglas moved on to speak to the men who had come to the gates of the town. These sturdy farmers carried flails and cudgels and Tamys marked that they held them as the muleteers held their quarter-staves. He would not have bet coin on his sword against their farm implements.

"He means what he says," Braeden told Tamys. "You're a handsome lad, but it's best you turn aside any interest you draw because Duglas means what he says and the miners are cruel with those who touch their shinier goods."

Tamys had learned this lesson in Dunmaden, but he knew Aethyn and some of the others would learn more slowly. He did not doubt that Braeden could teach it to them. He knew for a fact that Braeden could best him with a sword and he'd had many a master-soldier praise his skill on the field.

The miners' wives supplied a delicious meal of stew thick with vegetables that Padraig would not have thought the soil could grow and some meat that he wasn't able to identify, but did not find unpleasant. They brought baskets of real bread and a hearty dark ale of which they were each allowed only one tankard. As soon as the meal was cleared, the market faire was begun. Duglas gave Padraig permission to set out his own shingle and before Padraig had even thought of potential profit, he was surrounded by miners' wives with needs he'd somehow suspected would exist.

Padraig found himself impressed with the knowledge of the women who came to him. Far from midwives, granias and herbmen, they had trained themselves to be knowledgeable in what their families needed. They told him what they needed, not asked his advice for their ills. They paid in bits of unminted gold that they had weighed, so that Padraig had only to check it and agreed to the price.

"You'll want to trade those in Mandorlyn, herbman," Duglas told him. "They know its value more than they do in Cenconyn."

Padraig thanked him for his advice and raked in his profits. He quickly lost sight of the people in front of him and saw only a sea of faces. Then there was a woman asking after red raspberry leaves with a boy of about eight clinging to her dress, his eyes the milky white-blue of the blind.

"Mayhap I ask, good woman. How did your child become thus?" he asked, for he felt a burden for the child.

"It was the red fever," came the answer. "Last summer it was. I tried all that I knew, but he still came blind."

"I've not heard of the red fever. What are the symptoms?"

"Fever, rash, sore throat. It caused blindness and deafness."

"Truly? I thought my knowledge vast, but I've not heard of this. Did nothing seem to help?"

"Nay. I tried all the local remedies, but it seemed relentless. I don't suppose you have anything that would help this late."

Padraig asked for permission and felt the power of God flow through him. Wanting to live, he decided on a canny course of action.

"I might have somewhat for you. If you will meet

me after dusk near the lake. I have a tincture I'd need to create."

"Thanks to you," she said, smiling. "Should I bring the lad?"

"Nay, I'll have no need of seeing him. If your husband wants to come, that would be fine, for the propriety of the thing. Where along the lake shall we meet?"

"There's a peninsula that juts out just east of your camp. I'll be checking the fish traps tonight. I'll meet you there."

"Well and good then."

She parted. When the market faire was finished, the caravan moved onto the lake where the tuck wagon and a crew had already been at work. Tamys seemed distracted and irritable at the evening meal and Padraig reminded himself to speak with the lad after his meeting with the woman. Dusk found him sitting on a boulder on the peninsula waiting for her. She came out of the deepening purple evening, a dark shawl hiding her from view. She set aside her heavy basket before approaching him.

"What have you for my lad, herbman?"

"Naught. He's already healed."

"Wh-at? You jest, certainly."

"Nay. The One God healed him this afternoon."

"He is as blind as night!" she scoffed.

"He will see the morning light," Padraig assured her.

"Truly?" she asked, sounding like a child hoping against hope.

"You will know when his eyes are opened. Then remember that the One God, the True God, worked this in your son."

"What do you or your god want for this healing?" the woman asked reservedly.

"Naught, only that you acknowledge to yourself and your family what was wrought here today."

"That's all?"

"I promise you that, good woman. When your son sees the light, praise the Light from heaven, for He is the one who healed your son."

She left with a skepticism that Padraig knew well. Though he'd been a Believer from his early years, he'd seen unbelief at every turn. The night was deepening into true darkness as Padraig made his way to the tip of the peninsula where large boulders provided a comfortable leeward location to watch the stars come out. There was no moon, but the black velvet sky provided a perfect backdrop for stars that seemed far closer than he'd ever thought possible.

Padraig dreamed of stars and other mountains when he noted a flash of starlight winking off metal as someone came toward him. Padraig's Denygal eyesight recognized Tamys and Padraig was dutifully impressed with the lad's ability to navigate so gracefully in the dark. He wondered mildly at that, though he wondered more about Tamys' ability to target right on him.

"Somewhat you want to discuss?" Padraig asked as Tamys neared.

"Aye," the lad said. He sat down on one of the boulders and looked up at the sky. "Lovely, how the stars seem to make a road across the heavens!"

Padraig agreed in silence. The Wise Ones taught that important decisions were made in silence. The lad seemed to think so as well, for it was several fistfuls of heartbeats before he spoke.

"You healed that lad this afternoon, didn't you?" Tamys asked.

Padraig shot him a look of surprise. How could he know that?

"Aye, though truth be told, my God did the healing. I was only the conduit."

"I knew it!" Tamys insisted.

"Aye, well, clearly you did, but how? Wise Ones say they can sometimes sense it, but not always."

"I know naught," Tamys replied. "I was guarding that wagon near you and wondering how you could stand the chatter of all those women when suddenly I felt – somewhat like it feels in the mountains just before a lightning strike – like there's power being held back in anticipation like a whip. I looked your way to see if there were clouds on the horizon and I knew the lightning would strike at you. Before I could say anything or move, it struck, only you were fine and – and somehow I knew that somewhat had changed. I did not know what until I saw the woman walk away from you tonight. Then I knew, truly knew, that you had healed her son."

"He'll see come the morrow light. I asked her here so that I might tell her whom deserved the praise."

"Your god, you said." Padraig nodded. Tamys shook his head in the near-complete darkness. "I don't believe in your god," he admitted. "I'm not sure I believe in any gods."

"Not even those of your people?"

Tamys shook his head. Padraig found he was not surprised by this revelation.

"Will you tell me what you're thinking?" he asked after Tamys grew silent again.

The lad licked his lips nervously. Padraig waited.

"I wasn't raised to believe in the gods, truly. My father cautioned us to pay the proper respect to the priests of Bel and Lugh and to pay the proper coin as well. The nobles rule because the temple supports them. And, of course, a nobleman sponsors feast days and pays proper homage to the gods, just in case someone might take lack of interest askance. I grew up with that politic sort of religion."

"Aye, tis the religion of my father. I know it well."

"I never questioned it," Tamys assured Padraig. "Not until Galen was struck through with a spear at the siege of Dun Celdrya and I knew that there were no gods. For months that's how I felt. Then I heard the name of your god and – . Mayhap I tell you of this and you'll keep my counsel?"

"Of course, lad. I've trusted you with my life often enough these many weeks."

Tamys took a deep breath and let it out slowly.

"Winter before last I was raiding Lord Tren's lands. We do that frequently, as somewhat of a sport in winter." Padraig nodded, taking for granted that Tamys could see in this light, as apparently the lad could. "I fell captive. Lord Tren noted that I was the youngest of three sons and decided to hang me rather than ransom me. He thought my father wouldn't pay the coin, which was likely true. So, I waited in the donjon to meet my fate. A rider let me free, smuggled me out through a bolt hole with a rider's cloak as cover. I asked him why he'd risk his life for me and he said 'So you'll know that the One God loves you.' I hadn't time to ask more, but I wondered – through that night anyway – what he meant by that. Never thought I'd find out. Never expected to see that rider again."

"Nay, of course not."

"Then Galyn died in summer and I – I think I went a bit mad there for a while. Certainly I acted mad. I couldn't remain with the army. My father sent me home where I spent, for the first time in my life, long hours by myself, walking the heath and riding the forests and trying to forget. Winter came and I fair drank myself into forgetfulness. Until we captured one of Tren's riders. There was no talk of ransom this time, of course. He was just a rider. My father ordered him killed on the morrow. It was the rider to whom I owed my life."

Tamys lapsed into silence.

"So, did you return the favor?"

"Aye, and I hope he got clean away. I think he must have. I was caught, however. My father and the priests of Bel ordered me flogged, but the priests of Lugh arrived and said that I must be hanged, that I was a Believer, that I had the second sight, that I was possessed of a daemon."

"Second sight? Why would they bring that up?"

"I do have a touch. I'm very good at guessing dice and I always could sense things – like storms and the like. I didn't think they should know about it though, since I've never been stupid enough to bet on all my guesses."

"Hmm, so they accused you of this and ..."

"My father refused to have me killed. He pointed out that he might someday need me, since he had but two sons left. He agreed to exile me, however, until such time that I make myself right with the temple. He ordered me whipped, but Galryen threw himself before me and pled for mercy, so my father turned me out with the clothes on my back. Galryen met me on the road with a horse, my sword and a purse full of coin or I surely would have died." Tamys stared into the darkness for a bit. "I thought the priests of Lugh liked those with the second sight, made them into druins."

"Aye, but somewhat about it must have alarmed them. I'm not sure what."

Tamys nodded soberly.

"I wondered a lot after that, about why the rider would risk his life and what was the One God. Then I met you. I wanted to know, but I didn't want to know, if you know what I mean. But, the other day, you saved our lives when you didn't have to. Then today – that lad. Tell me about what it is that you believe, what sets you apart from everyone else."

Padraig answered slowly, not because he didn't know what he wanted to say, but because he wanted to give Tamys an opportunity to clear his mind for the answers. It had been Padraig's experience that the answers were not easy to hear and harder still to grasp. A wrong word without the Lord's guidance could cause a man to close his heart and Padraig never wanted to be responsible for that.

"What do you think about Believers?"

"I haven't thought much about them. When I did it was sort of to think they were like the Old Faith. It wasn't until I knew you that I began to think it was somewhat more."

"Aye, it is much different from the Old Faith. The Old Faith is much like the religion you grew up with. It believes in the same gods. It's more focused on personal sacrifices to appease the gods rather than letting the temple priests do it. Folk of power become druins in the cult of Bel, a separate sect kept well-clear of those they serve, but in the Old Faith, they're called druids and they are the leaders of the worship, not constrained servants. Nay, the Belief is very different."

Padraig mulled his thoughts , knowing Tamys was listening without judgment which was always a good sign.

"When the Celdryans came here, they were probably more like the Old Faith than the Bel system. Among them, though, were a handful of Believers. Even in Gael they were separate, but they fled with the Celts to Rune because the Rhwmanes did not see them as different. At first they probably were needed. We were few in number and if they were quiet, the hands were what counted, not what the heads believed. But, the Celdryans grew more numerous and as they pushed the elves out of the land, they began to distrust any talk of a belief in one god, which the elves held. The Believers may also have brought some of the distrust upon themselves by helping the elves escape the predations of the Celtman. At least among the elves there are stories that indicate that they did. Five hundred years ago, the priests of Bel and the priests of Lugh issued a proclamation that Believers were anathema and ordered that they be exiled. The Believers fled north into what would become Denygal. They found the elves who saw in them no threat and the two became one people. The elves had always believed in one god who required that we love our enemies and do good to those who misuse us, but the Believers taught them that His name is Jesu."

"And Jesu, he is god of everything?"

"Aye. A very powerful God, but also a very personal God."

"How could one god handle it all?"

"I can't answer that," Padraig admitted. "He created the world, so He's not tied to the cycles of it. He's outside of space and time."

"The gods rule from another realm, I've heard. What do you mean by personal?"

"The gods of Bel are – shall we say, uninterested in you as a person. Fate is set not only at birth, but in the lives lived before this one. The gods needn't be concerned with our little problems. They might do us a favor if we offer enough sacrifices, but they really don't care otherwise. And they'll act as capriciously as they feel like. Raise you to the throne, or turn you out onto the roads."

"True-spoken," Tamys whispered.

"Jesu isn't like that. He seeks to be a companion, a friend. He cares if a blind child sees. He cares if you're hungry or fed. Not that He'll do what we ask all the time. Sometimes there are higher goals to be accomplished than our petty requests, no matter how important they may be to us, and He'll always make the decision that is best for us and those around us."

"And how do you pay homage to this god?" Tamys asked.

"You believe in Him, which is as simple as it sounds, and more complicated than it might seem. In order to believe in Him, you must first admit that you're not perfect, that you've disobeyed him, even without knowing it. Then you must accept that He offered Himself for you and that He and He alone can take away your disobedience. All He asks for that is that you ride at His command, not the command of any other."

Tamys' pale eyes flashed in the dark. Padraig had surprised him in this. Tamys had sworn fealty to Lord Corbryn and Padraig could see that he wanted to hold true to that.

The lad stood up abruptly.

"That's why the rider released me?" he inquired. His voice echoed strangely in the dark.

"Mayhap. The Lord required that he obey an order contrary to the warleader's edict."

Tamys looked across the lake toward the sounds of the camp.

"You've given me much to think on, for now." With not fare-the-well, Tamys started back along the peninsula to the main shore, ending their conversation that evening.

The caravan moved on the morrow before the day

dawned. The dust of the caravan's passing had scarcely settled when the lad who had been blind looked at his mother and said her red shawl was lovely. She dropped the jar of milk as her family clustered around. As she mopped up the pool of white liquid, she remembered the herbman saying that this healing came from the One True God. In the privacy of her awe-struck family, she thanked this god she had never heard of before, but wanted to know more about.

Founding Year 1028
Dun Cenconyn

Ryen ap Chenyn, rig of Cenconyn, lounged upon his bed with his wife, Lillirygga, nestled into the crook of his arm. They'd spent a pleasant morning enjoying one another's company and now merely rested in contentment. Lilli was his greatest advisor, the finest mind in all his dun. Bed sports were a side benefit toward their relationship.

A knock on the door startled both of them. They stared at the door, thinking to remain quiet. Of course, a second knock followed the first. Ryen sighed. Lilli buried her lovely face in his shoulder to hide her laughter.

"Aye?"

"My lord, Duncyn of Denygal is back from Clarcom."

Lilli raised her face to smile at Ryen. Both of them enjoyed Duncyn and had missed him during their sojourn in Cenconyn.

"Tell him to make himself at home. We'll be down soon."

"Aye, sir." Footsteps retreated from the door. Lilli sat up wearing only her long dark hair.

"Come back here, wench," Ryen demanded, dragging her back onto the bed. "Duncyn of all people would understand our delay. We've discussions left."

"Discussions?" she giggled. "Is that what you call it?"

"Nay, we did far too little discussing this morning. I need to make a decision about Nigyl of Somerhale."

"We can discuss while dressing," she reminded, her blue eyes twinkling.

"Or we could lie here naked and finish our discussion," he said merrily. They kissed briefly and then rolled apart to sort out their clothes.

"It seems to me," Ryen said as he donned his small clothes, "that we don't actually need a steward. You've been doing the job with intelligence and insight."

Lilli turned, her long lean body a marvel to behold.

"I thank you for the compliment and truly, I could continue doing it until we have children and then … well, the mistress of a great dun, the steward and mother to children … this may be stretching even my extraordinary abilities."

Ryen caressed her cheek with a callused finger. Her skin felt like silk as he traced the curve of her jaw bone.

"I know," he said solemnly. "I don't suppose the vyngretrix council would accept it either."

"How inappropriate to allow your wife such power!" Lilli intoned in a mocking voice. She drew on her small breecs and reached for the chemise.

"Mayhap Duncyn has good news for us on that front. If he's found someone acceptable and not recommended by Cunyr, it will sit much better with me."

Ryen pulled on his breecs, tying the drawstring.

"Aye, that does feel a bit of manipulation," Lilli admitted. "Mayhap Lydya has insight into why her husband wants to install his own man in our dun."

She pulled her underdress over her head. Ryen found his siarc.

"I am so looking forward to an evening with Duncyn entertaining us. He's better than a bard any day," Lilli said, smoothing down her dress and shaking out the overdress.

"I'm more interested in his report on Clarcom," Ryen admitted, tightening his belt.

"You have grown much too serious since taking this dun, my lord."

"Aye, my lady, but I do feel a responsibility here that I did not entirely appreciate from Denygal."

Lilli carefully tied her kirtle, obviously thinking. Ryen appreciated her insight into court affairs so much that he didn't interrupt her thoughts.

"It is very different here than at home," she admitted, gathering her thick hair together to plait it. "The One has a plan, my love, and there's naught for us to do except puzzle it out and wait upon His command."

Ryen stood so quickly from pulling on his second boot that he nearly spilled face-first upon the Morikan carpet, but he quickly righted himself and caught her in a final embrace.

"I could not, would not, do this without you, my lady. You are my best advisor and worth a dun full of old men with stuffy ideas of how to do this and that. It's all well and good, their experience and knowledge, but your wisdom far outshines any I've ever known."

Lilli laughed pleasantly, kissed him on the nose and broke the embrace.

"I must be about the business of the lady of this dun, my lord, or else my skills may come under scrutiny of an ill sort." She spoke as she moved, winding her braid up and securing it with combs as she headed toward the chamber door.

Ryen chased after her as she scampered down the corridor, but she was much quicker than he and already gone before he reached the stairs. Sighing, he walked down the stairs with dignity. His cousin Duncyn, wearing the traditional orange and green of Denygal, turned from the honor hearth where he was talking with another nobleman. Before Ryen could question this stranger, he felt a push on his mind as Lilli registered her concern.

"Duncyn, mayhap you will introduce your companion."

"Of course," the broad-shouldered young-looking man replied. Duncyn was not a typical Denygal in that he enjoyed a good tankard of ale, but he was also not at all like a Celdryan noble. He always had a cheery smile and a ready jest for one and all and he loved to tell stories and go on adventures so that he would have stories to tell. "This is Nigyl of Somerhale."

Ryen felt his face freeze as his breath caught in his throat.

"I'm sorry. Did you say Nigyl of Somerhale?"

"Aye, my lord," Duncyn assured. "Cunyr insisted that you would be so taken with his recommendation that you would retain Nigyl immediately.

Duncyn lacked the gifts of many Denygal ... or at least didn't acknowledge them ... but he had very expressive hazel eyes and these conveyed that it was not his idea, but he had been compelled by Cunyr, who could compel anyone who valued their life to do anything he wanted.

"I see," Ryen said, accepting the situation. He would have to retain Nigyl or explain why not and that was becoming increasingly difficult to entertain. "I suppose you brought letters of recommendation."

"I did," Nigyl said. He was younger than Ryen had expected, thin and reedy, with a hawk nose and narrow eyes. Typical of many younger sons of minor nobles, he wore solid breecs of blue and a blue cloak trimmed in the blue and red plaid of his father's dun. Ryen had researched Somerhale in expectation of an examination of Nigyl's credentials and had found it a smallish dun just outside of Clarcom. Nigyl would be loyal to Cunyr, which was problematic in itself, but he was also likely very inexperienced.

Nigyl produced a message tube sealed with Cunyr's seal. Ryen took it and felt the resonance of Lydya's sealing spell on the knot. He wondered if Nigyl had worried the knot a bit and found it impossible to undo.

"As I am caught surprised by this, I will ask you to rest the evening and allow me to review these in private. I'll speak with you on the morrow. A page will settle you in guest chambers. The meal should be a bit after sundown."

Nigyl's grey eyes widened in surprise, but there was not much to be done as Ryen had said it all. To assure no protests, Ryen asked Duncyn to report on his journey as if Duncyn were his vassal. They were in Ryen's second floor greeting chamber before Duncyn started to chortle.

"I do so wish you could send that officious little ferret packing," he explained upon closing the door behind them. Ryen moved to speak, but Duncyn raised a hand and smiled all the wider. "I know you cannot do so, but I would so love to see his expression when you did. What does your fair sister have to say about all this?"

Ryen sighed and unwound the simple knot that had no doubt confounded Nigyl. He broke the wax seal and opened the tube to slide out the messages. In addition to the letter of recommendation, there was a second message from Cunyr and an envelope bearing Lydya's seal of Denygal.

Duncyn waited patiently while Ryen quickly scanned Cunyr's message concerning taxes and levies. The lord of Cenconyn set aside the letter of recommendation to break the seal on Lydya's envelope.

Dearest brother, there is pleasant news to share. Padraig has turned up, hale and hearty, and headed for the heartland. He has promised to keep in touch better in the future. I have tracked him as far as High Celdrya.

I must apologize for my husband's insistence that he send his man into your dun. I counseled against it, but he has not the high opinion of me that you have of Lilli. Please do give her my kindest regards. There's naught to be done with Nigyl, I'm afraid. Lilli can tell you the color of his character, but it is not a good one in my learned opinion. Again, I wish I did not have to lay pen to parchment and say you have little choice in the matter, but there you have it.

God's grace be upon you and yours. Your faithful vassal, Lydya of Moryn

"She doesn't trust him anymore than I do. Do you have anything to report about him?"

"Just that he's as ignorant as he is inexperienced. Cunyr doesn't even think highly of him, so he's likely a spy."

Ryen sighed. He'd known that, of course, but it pained him to hear Duncyn's assessment because it confirmed his own.

"There's naught for it. I'll give him lots of irritating tasks in hopes that he'll want to return to his father's dun as soon as soon. Did you note any weaknesses on the journey? Incipient drink? Likes the lasses … or the lads?"

"Nay, not either of those. He's judgmental, narrow-minded, gossiping, and less than honest, but naught that would disqualify him from being a steward besides lack of experience."

"Sad," Ryen said with a sigh, then replaced his sadness with a smile. "Well and good then. Life in Cunyr's county is no different than it was a watch ago. Let us gird our loins and partake of a lovely roast beast and you shall tell humorous stories about the board tonight and then on the morrow I shall retain myself a steward … and count my pots and table daggers because

I believe my steward's fingers may be coated with sap."

Duncyn laughed heartily and the two men departed to the great hall.

Solstice

We marched south for an eightnight, following the scouts riding ahead. The Rawmayne soldiers became useful, though they chafed under their bondage. If it weren't for Da, the Celts would have killed them, but he spoke wisely as a scribe will of the usefulness of the horses and of men who could speak some other language besides Gawlish. In a strange land and likely to encounter strange peoples. We might need these men who could wield swords. It was the Rawmaynes' idea to travel south away from the wind-swept moor where we'd first come ashore.

In the high mountains, we found an odd roadway driven through the rock. Most curious! The walls seemed polished and the road bed was spongy with moss that did make our feet laugh.

On the third day, we encountered daemons, short beings with dark hair and eyes who seemed to spring from the earth itself. Some of them men from the eastern tribes did call them trols. I suspect they are but one variety of peoples in this strange land.

Ryla, Druidess of the Krystan Celts, FY 39

Founding Year 931
Dun Celdrya

The donjon stank of piss and vomit. Cold seeped into Deryk's bones as some of those fluids slowly soaked his breecs. He scarce cared, barely noticed. He kept replaying the night of murder over and over, unable to block it out.

He'd liked Perryn! Truthfully, he'd scarce known him before Maryn's death, but he'd found himself admiring how the young prince had handled the sudden ascension to a throne he'd been ill-prepared for. Why, then? Why would he leave a convivial atmosphere of mead and fine foods to plunge a dagger into his liege's heart?

The blood remained on his hands where they lay in his lap, wrists held secure with iron manacles. He'd heard tales of men rubbing their wrists raw trying to get loose, but he'd scarcely moved since they'd thrust him in here. He'd not desired to eat the food they hadn't yet given him or missed the water that wasn't in evidence. He hardly noticed the weak sunlight shining through the high and small barred window. He'd killed the king and it no longer mattered to him what his body went through.

Why had he killed Perryn? It made no sense. It was if someone else were in control of his body, but that was impossible. Why kill a man he admired, a man who he might one day have called friend? Deryk leaned his head back against the stone wall and stared into the gloom.

He stepped from the stairs into the hallway and paused a moment before walking forward. He entered the antechamber where a guard dozed in a chair. The dagger slid like butter through his windpipe. Soft laughter filtered through the door.

Why am I here, he thought. The dagger dripped with blood. He eased the door open and watched the two upon the bed. The dagger skittered on one of Perryn's ribs as he plunged it in, but Deryk knew killing as well as any warrior and the tip found the heart. The girl screamed and he killed her for it, her brains flying back into his face ....

Deryk jerked awake, chains rattling, heart pounding! The weak sunlight was even weaker. Night was coming. How long before the priests of Lugh would gather and let him die? How long before Donyl would know of his treachery? They had trusted him because he'd been Maryn's bosom friend, yet he'd been there when Maryn died and that would seem suspicious. Mayhap he'd had somewhat to do with Maryn's death, somewhat that he'd not known himself.

Why would you kill Perryn? You had naught against the man. He'd have been a fine king and he treated you with honor. Why would you kill Maryn? Nay, I did not kill Maryn!

Outside the cell, Deryk heard the guards changing the shift. He supposed it was the dusk watch. He knew who was on duty this time of night for he had detailed the guard.

Perryn trusted you and you betrayed him! I don't know why I killed him!

Truth be told, it didn't matter if he knew or didn't. The Lughans would meet, they would discuss and they would find him guilty. He'd been caught with a bloody dagger standing over the king's body. There was naught to debate. He'd killed the king. He deserved to die. The only question was whether they would release him from his guilt and anguish on the morrow or wait for Donyl to return from the wilderness. Deryk found himself praying to every god he knew of that the Lughans were feeling blood-thirsty and would let his at dawn's light. He did not wish to face Donyl with guilt choking him and no explanation as to why he'd done such a horrible act.

I know not what gods control such … I suppose Lugh is judge … but I pray you hear my prayer and let me die without fanfare as soon as soon, for I am a worm and deserve no less.

Deryk closed his eyes and felt tears trickled down the grime on his face. Death would be a release.

Founding Year 1028
Mandorlyn

The rest of the trip into Mandorlyn proper was relatively uneventful. There were a few mining villages to stop at along the way, but they never lingered longer than a half day. They stayed at campgrounds between villages. It took another week to reach the only city in Mandorlyn, which was called Mandorlyn.

The settlement occupied the first real valley they'd seen since leaving Celconyn. Clustered around the east side of a large lake, the town was actually larger than a new town in the kingdom might have been. The houses were larger on the whole than homes in the kingdom as well. Yet the streets were unpaved and there was no town wall, though the repository occupied a well-guarded location in the center of town.

Duglas directed his caravan in the public marketplace where merchants he'd already arranged came to take their goods. Once the main part of the merchandise had been parceled out, Duglas set up a pay table and began to pay out the coin he'd promised.

"Will either of you be returning to Glenconyn with me?"

"I think I may," Padraig said. "I'd like to look about before I make a decision, but I think I will be wanting to return and I might as well make coin while doing it."

"Show up an eightnight from now and you'll be welcome. I won't find an herbman with bow skills this side of the Portal. What about you, Tamys?"

"I might be interested, but I want to look about a bit here, see if I can get hired on as a rider for the local lord."

Duglas stared at him blankly for a moment, then looked sympathetic.

"Lad, there are no lords in Mandorlyn. It was founded by freemen and so far no lords have come to where they don't appear to be needed. There's lots of money to be had here, but the lords would have to own some of the mines to make it worth their time and there's no king to give them titles patent, so ... I am babbling. Lad, I'm sorry. It's a long journey to undertake for a disappointing end."

Tamys stared at the ground, disappointment clearly visible on his usually court-trained face. Padraig drew him away from the line to express his own regret.

"I apologize. I might have investigated that a bit before I dragged you all the way here."

"You didn't know. How could you know? Even Denygal has lords, aye?"

"Aye, after a fashion Well, lad, there's still time when we come back to Glenconyn. Summer won't be over." Tamys nodded. "Let's see if we can find an inn to sleep in and then see what's about to see."

Tamys followed Padraig to an inn where the innkeeper didn't question them, only gave a short speech about how he didn't want his furniture broken or his walls damaged. He was already nearly full, having only one dormitory left. The dormitory, well up under the eaves of the three-story inn, consisted of two sloped roof-walls, a wall with a small window and a entry door that had to be entered in a full stoop. There was enough space for three men to sleep shoulder to shoulder, but since they were only two, they had room for their gear.

Right after spreading his bedroll and stowing his gear, Tamys announced he was going to "drink myself blind" then disappeared into the dusty streets of the town. Padraig sighed and let him go, knowing that he couldn't force Tamys to do what was sensible.

Padraig spent some time looking about the town. Despite the unpaved condition of the streets, the unfinished appearances of many of the buildings, the town looked prosperous and well-kempt. Yards were neat, excepting timbers and building stones, sewage was taken care of discreetly and wells were far from midden heaps and privies.

Padraig found a tavern that sold the most delicious stew he'd tasted in a long while. A minstrel of middling abilities held forth in the public square as Padraig made his way back to the inn. The streets were filled with strolling families in good quality clothing. Padraig's Denygal eyes noted the dirt beneath the fathers' nails and sometimes the mothers. These people could afford the fine clothes and probably a nice house because they worked in the mines. It appeared it was a good life.

Padraig started his search for herb lore and spiritual direction at dawn on the morrow. Tamys had not returned and this concerned his friend, but Padraig knew that worry would not solve the problem. He left Tamys' in God's hands and went on the search he'd set before himself. He found the local herbfolk to be closed-mouth. They didn't trust he was seeking lore in exchange for lore and he was taking what he learned back to the kingdom. It was late afternoon of that first day before he found Trynia, an older woman in a neat brown set of dresses who wore the black head scarf of a widow. She occupied a neat two-room cottage at the north end of town, one room stuffed to the rafters with every herb imaginable and a few that boggled Padraig's.

"I'm willing enough to show you about in exchange for some of that elven lore," she agreed. "A body can never stop learning, in my opinion. Don't suppose I'm the first you talked to, though."

"Nay, you are not. Whatever I can do to earn what

you have to teach, I'm willing."

"Oh, I can find plenty enough for a young, strong lad like you to do. Meet me here on the morrow."

Padraig did just that, though he'd lost a bit of sleep over the fact that Tamys had not come in until just before dawn. The lad fell immediately into his blankets and Padraig didn't have the heart to awaken him. Trynia waited for him on her porch, a stack of homespun sacks beside her. She smiled at him, showing strong teeth only slightly stained. Overall, this woman seemed quite strong and vigorous for her age.

"Let's be off," she began. And, thus began three days of hard work and much learning. Trynia knew much about the herblore of Mandorlyn, which was a new and growing area of knowledge. She'd heard of the red fever. "Aye, there's some that think the dwarves left something in the soil to pay us back. It blinds and deafens, sometimes it palsies. But I've not found anything to treat it."

"What about willow bark tea?"

"We've no white willow here."

"You have shrub willow, what we call black willow in Denygal."

"It's a poor plant."

"We make willow bark tea from it. It's not as effective as the white, but it's better than nothing. Mayhap you might mix it with feverfew. It's worth the effort."

"Feverfew has provided some relief, though not enough to make it worthwhile. Mayhap the two together … Aye, well, I'll try it next time."

The third day brought them to a farm a bit away from the town where Trynia had helped birth a baby four days before. The farmwife, her golden-red curls caught back in a headscarf, sat on the porch with the baby in her arms. She quickly covered with a shawl when she saw Padraig following Trynia from her wagon.

"She's so much better, Trynia," the young lass enthused. "You're a marvel!"

"Let me see her, lass. Beryna, this is Padraig of Denygal, who is visiting to learn a bit of our lore. How be you, Rhodda?" she asked an older woman with grey hair pulled back in a widow's scarf.

"I am well, though short on sleep. The fool girl won't listen to me."

"She wants me to feed the baby cow's milk so she'll sleep, but you said to nurse her and I want to do what's right for Liatha."

"Aye, as you should, lass. Let me see her and I'll have a bit of a look. Beryna, wasn't your da from Denygal?"

"Aye, mayhap Padraig has news of your folks," Rhodda suggested. She bustled after Trynia who took the baby to a basket to examine it. Beryna looked bereft, but tried to focus on Padraig.

"They're just trying to keep me away in case there's somewhat more wrong than jaundice."

"Jaundice is bad enough. I'm glad to see Trynia knows about nursing in the sunlight."

"Rhodda thought I would kill the baby that way, but she does seem less yellow."

"Rhodda is your mother-in-law, then?" Beryna

456

nodded, stopping short of rolling her eyes.

"She means well. I think I have somewhat for you, Padraig of Denygal. Do they do much fishing there?"

"Aye, much. And have you done any such yourself?"

"Aye, my husband and I enjoy putting our line in the water."

Padraig crossed his fingers and placed them on his belt. She smiled, crossed her fingers as well, laying them against her kirtle.

"My mam and da came from Denygal, though I was raised all over the kingdom. My da won my husband to the Lord. As I said, I have somewhat for you. Do you know Morglen?"

"'Tis south of Glenconyn, isn't it? On the sea."

"Aye. When you return to Glenconyn travel direct south. It's not the usual way, but I'm sure you're supposed to go the direction."

"Thank you. You've given me the direction I've sought."

Trynia returned with the baby and handed her back to her mother.

"She's a fine strong lass and the yellow's just about passed. A few more days nursing in the sun and she'll be fine."

"They'll catch their deaths!" Rhodda protested. "Herbman, tell them this is folly!"

"It's naught but a treatment for jaundice. We know it at home as well."

The old woman's annoyed look would have made Padraig laugh if it had any chance of being taken humorously. As it was he smiled at Beryna and left it at that. Trynia and he parted at her house for the last time.

"I want to thank you, lad, for your interest in the ramblings of an old woman. I've been out here since the beginning and I think I may know more than any other herbalist in the area, but the young ones don't listen."

"That's their mistake. I wish I could remain to help you for a bit, but I have plans for the winter."

"Aye, well, Mandorlyn's a hard life. I'd not have stayed if I'd had the coin to return when my husband died, but now my children are here and I ... Well, a young man like you probably wouldn't understand such a womanish thing."

"I understand it well enough. This became home."

"What about you? Do you have a home?"

"Aye, I do, far to the east."

"Denygal must be a beautiful place. Why did you leave it?"

Padraig knew he must be careful here. Although Trynia seemed a wonderful old woman, she was faithful in the ways of Bel. Padraig had noted that on several occasions. It would not be fair to give her the burden of such a secret as his beliefs. It would test their friendship greatly.

"Lore," he said. "The Denygal learned much from the elves who have their own system of doing things. They send a new journeyman out into the world to learn what there is to learn. He's supposed to return with a body of knowledge to add to the existing lore."

"Truly? What a novel and sensible idea! Do women have much say in Denygal society?"

"Aye, though less in Denygal than in elven society. Women are equal there with men."

Trynia smiled at him in such a way that said she thought that a pleasant fantasy. Then they made their final goodbyes and Padraig returned to the inn. Tamys was asleep in his bedroll for the first night in three. The dormitory smelled of sour ale. Padraig crawled over to the window to allow fresh air to enter. Tamys burped loudly and opened a blood-shot eye to look at his friend.

"Mind if you blow out that light. We've an early leaving in the morn."

"Aye, but I need to get some dinner before I go to sleep. What are you doing of the evening?"

"Laying here and listening to my head pound."

Padraig might have offered willow bark tea, but he felt that Tamys would learn nothing from avoiding the consequences of his actions. He did put one of his water bottles next to Tamys' bedroll and suggest the lad drink it all.

"You want hydrating, lad, to restore your watery humors."

"You don't believe in humors, remember?"

"It explains it well enough, doesn't it?" Padraig blew out the candle lantern and crawled back to the door. "Do you need more ointment?"

"Nay, I did not – leave me alone," Tamys said, rolling over and hiding his face in his arms. Padraig wished the lad would talk to him, but he knew better than to push in where he had not been invited. Besides, the inn they lodged at at had a good bard and arguing with Tamys wasn't worth missing that.

Founding Year 1028
Dun Cenconyn · Summer Solstice

Reyn, rig of Cenconyn, leaned upon his elbows atop the parapet wall and looked upon the orderly chaos of the elven camp far below him. Truth be known, an ordinary man would not have seen too much at this distance, but Reyn of Cenconyn was not wholly human and his elfling eyesight was far better than that of the man who stood to his left. Reyn looked human enough with black wavy hair and strongly colored blue eyes common among the Denygal and handsome features that could turn any lass' head. In Denygal they would have known him for a quarter elf by his tall and slender form and high coloring, but here in Cenconyn they were not so knowing.

"Rabble," Nigyl, his new steward, muttered. Less than a moon on the post and already he had opinions and not ones that agreed with his new overlord. Reyn walked a thin line, though, for his mother's blood marked him as cursed among his father's people, of which Nigyl was one.

"Those rabble bring a lot of coin into the rigdon," Reyn said pointedly. "Fine horses, the best wool in Dublyn, that coton you enjoy sleeping on, and Morikan goods as well. Nay, but they are the lifeblood of Cenconyn."

"Why do you not simply ride into the mountains and seize their petty villages and take what is rightfully ours rather than being forced to pay for it?"

"Because it is not rightfully ours. The elves have built their communities, bred their horses and sheep and established trade routes with the Morikan, who are known as a fierce people."

"As a subject people, the Fey could fill your coffers rather than line their own purses."

"I do not wish to be a slave-trader," Reyn remarked. "Indeed, I've learned you get more from merchants than from serfs," he explained. "Come, let us walk out and make a bargain for the dun."

Reyn wished fervently that convention did not dictate that he take Nigyl with, but he knew naught for it. When Wrmyll had died of lung congestion last winter, Reyn had been without a steward or a foreseeable replacement. He'd sent out dispatches as soon as the roads had been traversable and had received word from Clarcom that Nigyl was available. Young, fresh from his father's knee in a minor dun near Clarcom, he had much to learn. He'd been raised in a world where elves were scarcely more than a myth and hated beside, so it would take time to train him in the ways of Cenconyn. Reyn's father had had little love for the elves himself, despite marrying a woman who was half of one, but he had used them to his advantage and Cenconyn had prospered. Reyn intended to be a bit more even-handed, but he expected the rigdon would not suffer for it.

The Cenconyn horse faire – held during the traditional mid-summer gathering of the elven and dwarvish clans at the ancient crossroads where an elven citadel had been established – took place in unbelievable heat, but it was as lively as any latter faire elsewhere in the country. There were some tender crops available, but mostly goods and animals were sold during this time and lords from all over Dublyn and Galconyn came for the horses, for the elven horses – called Eastern Regals by men – were the stuff of legends. Tall and leggy with unbelievable stamina and intelligence, Regals were worth their price at any cost. Cut stock were used for a variety of purposes, but breeding stock were almost worshiped. The elves didn't often sell breeders outright and then the price was more coin than a rich rigdon saw in several years.

Thankfully, Reyn did not seek breeding stock. His groom had already bought the horses he wanted from this faire. Reyn's foray into the elven camp had more to do with politics and love than things equine.

Reyn felt encouraged as he walked through the faire grounds, hearing folk calling his name and seeing smiles upon their faces. Due to a series of unfortunate deaths among the males of his family, Reyn had become a secondary heir and folk often feared that "the second spare" would not have been trained to rule. Truly, Reyn experienced deep doubts about his ability to rule when first he inherited the rigdon, but he'd apparently passed some sort of test among the folk over the last four years. Nigyl followed him until they reached the bridge that led across the trickle of a brook that the river had become in the summertime heat.

"I think this a poor idea, m'lord."

"It is a necessary journey, lad," Reyn assured him. "Come. You're perfectly safe with the rig of Cenconyn."

They crossed the bridge and came under the cooling trees along the far bank, entering an utterly alien world. The elven camp had its own order that seemed like disorder to human eyes, with tents here and there and facing all directions. The elven tents were conical, supported by a frame of poles tied in a bundle at the top. In the heat, the leather sides of the tents were rolled up to catch the non-existent breeze and folk lay upon the floor clothes, sweating freely, until they saw the two humans at the entrance to the camp. Activity hesitated for a heartbeat and then resumed. The elven way did not show rudeness, even when confronted with what made the Kin nervous. A male disengaged himself from some work nearby and approached.

"May I inquire of your business among my Kin?" he asked in flawless Celdryan.

Reyn answered in his worst Elvish. Truly, he didn't speak it often enough, but much of his slowness was for Nigyl's benefit. It wouldn't do for the lad to know that Reyn shared more in common with elves than he did with the steward. Humans could become so testy about such subtleties as birth and blood, even among the noble born. Especially among the noble born!

"I am Reyn, rig of Cenconyn, son of Barantha of Denygal. I wish to speak with your squire."

Nigyl's eyes narrowed. Like most humans, he didn't know Elvish, but he did know that word "squire." An Elvish word, that, borrowed by the Denygal. Some of northern Dublyn knew the word, though they thought it a quaint word for "lord" when it meant so much more.

The elven male's eyes – huge with purple irises and

cat-slit pupils – rested upon Reyn for a moment. He'd know that Barantha was his mother's Elvish name – she'd been known as Andda in Celdrya – and this meant much for Reyn's pedigree, even if this particular Kin didn't know Reyn's family history.

"That would be Cai," he said in Celdryan. "He's in the storage floor. Come, I'll take you there." He looked over Nigyl. "Does that one know how to use the sword?" he asked in Elvish.

"He is a human noble, so yes, but not as well as I do. The Kin have nothing to fear."

"I didn't ask out of fear," the Kin assured him. "Come," he announced in Celdryan. "Cai is nearby."

They walked through the camp to a tent with multiple peaks built over a makeshift floor. The sides were down and a half-dozen Kin, some male and some female, guarded its entrances.

"I've a visitor of the squire," the Kin said to the guard at the main entrance. He turned to Reyn and spoke in Celdryan. "Wait here." He ducked under the tent flap and left them waiting.

"How rude!" Nigyl hissed to Reyn.

"We're on their territory now."

"A man of your position –"

"Is merely a dweller of stone tents to them," Reyn replied. "Not to be honored or even dignified. Theirs is a society different from ours."

"Shameful!" Nigyl growled.

The Kin guarding the door said naught, but Reyn was fairly certain that she understood the conversation. Elves were good with languages, most especially the females.

"You may come in, rig of Cenconyn," their guide stated, stepping out of the tent. Nigyl moved to follow Reyn. "You must stay out here," he told the steward.

"The steward is always involved in affairs of commerce," Nigyl protested.

"My squire wishes to deal rig to rig," the guide said, his placid face hiding his undeniable humor over Nigyl's discomfiture.

"I'll be fine, Nigyl," Reyn assured his servitor. He stepped through the tent flap into the coolness within. Light filtered through the leather to the interior, so that he could quickly make out the two young men sitting upon a bale of cotan in the middle of the tent. He'd learned this bit in previous years. They would hold back a bale for him until the last day of the faire, when they could easily sell it to a desperate northern rig. He approached the two there. He recognized the one – a half-elf who looked human except for the peak of an ear pushing its way through his curly sand-colored hair. He had been the squire of the caravan for two summers now. His name was Cai. His companion was new to Reyn and looked even more human with curly chestnut hair and large eyes the color of jade. She was also the most beautiful half-elf he'd ever seen, excepting his wife.

"I am Reyn, son of Barantha of Denygal," he greeted solemnly, in Elvish.

"I recognize you from previous summers," Cai replied in Celdryan. He drained a stone cup of water and rose from the bale. "Do you wish to join us?" he asked, still speaking Celdryan.

"Yes," Reyn answered in Elvish.

"Do you wish to speak in Celdryan or Elvish?" asked Cai's companion in a rather dark voice that was accented with the tones of Denygal.

"I can speak in either," Reyn assured.

"Then let us conduct our business in Elvish," Cai said. "I suppose you want the bale of cotan we're sitting on."

"My wife wants it, truly. I want what her weavers make with it."

"You have always paid well for what we have," Cai noted. "Do you have coin or iron?" he asked.

"I prefer to give coin as iron is becoming short in the kingdom."

"We hear that the basketlands are riven with war," the companion acknowledged.

"'Tis true, though not in Dublyn yet."

"Does that mean their attention will be away from the mountains?"

"They turn westward, true enough. And, Cunyr in Clarcom may be aging. His son, an elfling, will rule once he passes."

The two Kin looked at one another as if communicating silently. Mayhap they were.

"This speaks well for the Kin?" the female asked.

"I cannot say certainly, but Bryan is a Believer who would not harm the Kin by his own design."

"But he might by the design of others? He has no overlords, being rig of Clarcom," Cai noted.

"He is not vyngretroix yet, not until his father dies." Again there was the look between the two. "I believe that

Bryan will do as well as he can to avoid conflict with the holts," Reyn assured them. "I cannot promise that no incursion will happen."

"What do you think, Ry?" Cai asked his companion.

"I believe that the humans are ever treacherous and that we should consider elflings raised among humans with skepticism." Ry's eyes never wavered from Reyn's face as she said this.

"Fair enough," Reyn told her. Tall and strong, dressed in the garb all elves wore outside of the holts -- leather trews with a colorful tunic over -- her beauty was not lessened by the sword she wore belted at her waist. "Does either of you have the ability to read auras?"

Ry smiled slightly with her eyes.

"I do," she told him. Reyn relaxed his shields to allow her to read what was there. Her touch was light as a feather and exceedingly brief, no more than a glance. Her look grew less guarded. "You are truly an elf – fully a quarter."

"Officially an eighth," he explained. "My mother was from Denygal."

"So was our father," he was informed. She pondered somewhat for a heartbeat before standing, proving to be quite tall. "I believe you are the nobleman I seek."

Ryen's heart thumped. *She's as lovely as Lilli. Were she not a stranger ….*

"I have been given a prophesy," she said in Celdryan. "It affects both our lands and the solution can only be found through our joint strength."

Reyn poured a cup of water and waited for her to

continue.

"One of our holt received a prophesy that sent him seeking the One's True King in the basket lands," she explained. "He had already left when I saw a vision -- I flew upon dragon back over sea and saw a navy that can strike at our northern shore in devastating numbers. The Kin could not mount a defense. Can the Celtmen?"

"Doubtful as there is no king in High Celdrya and the ones who would be king are busy spending their vigor on killing one another."

Ry's eyes were deeply sad as she gazed at him.

"Would your father's people join with your mother's people if the need were great?"

"I cannot say," he replied, slowly, soberly. "I am the rig of a great dun, but I am not vyngretrix. I do not control the people of any but my own rigdon. I can mount a small army, but I do not command more than a few thousand. How large is this army you envisioned?"

"Tens of thousands. It was the largest army I've ever seen. I do not think a dragon would visit Kin again if the need were not great."

"Nay, I believe you. You must understand, however, that the Celts will not. Even presented by one they think is of them, they will be skeptical."

Ry turned to Cai and they seemed to speak silently again, then Ry turned to Reyn and asked a final question.

"Is there naught we can do?"

The world seemed to stand still a moment as her words rang like bells in the tent.

"There's always somewhat a Believer or three may do," Reyn assured her.

Cai grinned and Ry breathed a sigh of relief.

"I will find a way to make them listen," Reyn added. "First, let us three pray to the One that I might find soft hearts and wise ears." They linked hands to pray. As the initiator, Reyn started the prayer. "Dear God, One Who loves us all. We seek Your guidance and protection and ask that You will open eyes and soften hearts long hardened." The image of the rulers Reyn knew flowed through his mind's eye, interspersed with Duglas and, unexpectedly, Ry. Cai was murmuring a prayer in Elvish when Ry's grip on Ryen's hand grew stiff and then words began to flow from Ryen's mouth, unbidden, in Elvish.

"The Knowing must choose to be wise. Do not let the staff of mission pass before you. Take it up and walk in the ways of your Commander. Take My words into the world for I move to meet them wherever they may go."

Reyn opened his eyes and looked at his new companions. Cai stared at Ry, who stared at her feet.

I'll not ask, Reyn thought.

"So be it," Cai said and his words sounded in the tent like a temple gong.

Ry pulled her hands from theirs and rounded on her brother.

"No!" she said. "I do not choose to take up this cup."

Cai grinned like a fiend and her face darkened, then went white as parchment. For a moment, Reyn wondered if he'd need to draw his sword, but then she turned on her heel and swept out of the tent. He heard Nygil yell. He'd probably gotten in her way and she'd sent him tumbling. Cai and Reyn grinned at each other, but then both sobered. Reyn shuddered and then felt a touch on his mind, lighter than a feather. Lilli reached out to him. Mayhap this unusual touch of prophesy did not arise from him.

"Much rides on her decision, I think," Reyn told the squire.

"Aye, it always does," Cai admitted laconically. He listened to Nigel arguing with the guard. "Tell me what you can give us in coin or iron for the bale. It will be yours. Too bad cotan cannot hold back armies."

Reyn felt his heart contract painfully.

"True-spoken, squire," he said as another shovelful of snow seemed to slide down his back. Cai shuddered with him.

"Evil's afoot,' Cai assured him. "Even men like us who deal in what can be seen and touched feel it."

A dark cloud permanently covered the sun. A good time to mourn the old world that would end, but Nigyl was demanding entrance into the tent and there was much to do before the world ended.

Bastards Book

Before destruction the heart of a person is proud, but humility comes before honor.

From the 18th Song of King Daffyd of Ysrael
Recorded in Scriptos

Founding Year 931
Mulyn

The servitor known as Talidd pulled the brush hide over the low mouth of the cave before channeling fire into the wick of his lantern. The resulting light illuminated the low ceiling and rough walls and the rougher wooden table toward the back of the cave.

Talidd set the lantern on a natural stone shelf on the right hand wall and set his haversack beside the brazier to unload the contents. He spread the black cloth with its numerous sigals over the top of the table. The large bronze vessel was careful centered upon it and the two stone cups were arranged to the sides. He placed the bronze knife across the top of the right-hand cup.

Talidd paused in the preparation and sent to the raven who sat high in a pine tree. None approached. Talidd had a moment to think before moving on in his preparations.

The mind that he meant to contact was frighteningly powerful, so that he wanted his own mind well-ordered for his protection. Talidd had been Balyster's apprentice and then a journeyman under him for more than half his lifetime. A lot of animosity had been earned in those years. Masters like Balyster somewhat expected hatred concealed under dogged devotion, but it never paid to allow them to see what you really thought. Thus Talidd built up his psychic shields to prevent any breaches and then built up a glamour to conceal the strength of his hiding. The raven would tell him when he needed to start the ritual. He had time. Multiple layers of shielding might seem unnecessary to one who had not been schooled by Balyster's ministrations, but Talidd had seen others destroyed utterly because they had been careless.

The raven's mind touched his. Midnight approached. Talidd took a deep breath and channeled fire into the brazier. The charcoal there caught. Talidd drew bags of herbs out of the haversack and tossed the appropriate handful of each on the coals. Smoke drifted into his face and he moved away so as not to become intoxicated.

He unstoppered a bottle and poured the contents into the bronze bowl. The pungent odor of blood rose to his nostrils. He intoned the first spell and then stirred the blood and thought of Balyster. Because of their close affinity and long acquaintance the image built up very quickly and the old man with the mad eyes appeared in the surface.

"I've come for my instructions, master," Talidd began.

"Tariq al Najeb of Morikan clan Nuss, you will obey me."

Upon hearing his true name as a beginning, all of Talidd's careful preparations were for naught. He had protected his deepest thoughts from Balyster, but he was bound to do or answer whatever Balyster requested.

"Aye, my master."

"The gates ritual, fourth stage."

"Aye, my master," Talidd said, though his heart started beating faster. "That's a major spell. Is that why you asked me to gather items from the families?"

"Aye. You know how to use them. The quarry is Donyl ap Trevellyn. I've sent lower strengths against him. You join a circle of power that will bring him to the God of Rusks this night."

"Aye, my master."

The part of Talidd's mind that was still his own wanted to panic. This ritual ranked levels above anything he'd done before. There were few who had power enough to open these gates and pass on the knowledge gained and still fewer lived beyond the ritual.

Talidd advanced the ritual, speaking the words of power, invoking the spirits, pouring the blood and mixing the family's hair and nail clippings at the appropriate times. Increasingly, he felt the presence of Balyster's mind in the cave with him and then, as he cut his palm with the dagger, he felt the god come. Power like few could hold rushed into him, filled him to bursting and spilled across the link he shared with Balyster and some 10 others of near-equal strength. Bright yellow filled his inner mind as fury rushed through him like fire, searing his nerves, drowning out all sound, all concept of time, all sense of self. He tumbled in the maelstrom, seeking his way to some quiet, some stable ground. A window cleared and he saw the army below, a multitude of soldiers clad in furs and bits of leather, carrying bronze instruments. Beyond them stood a road of darkest night and then a forest of tall trees. With his mind, he commanded them go and then the yellow fire rushed back at him and he tumbled back into it, helpless to control himself.

The floor of the cave had cut his shoulder and left large bruises. The taste of coppers in his mouth revolted him. He rolled to the side to vomit and lay there limp as a wet rag until a seizure shook his body. Then he lay stiff as a board waiting for the rigor to subside.

The pain finally eased so that he was able to crawl to the table and nudge the scrying bowl. The lantern burned low, but the window in the scrying vessel didn't require light for Talidd to see into it, only light at the other end and there was enough there to see Balastyr collapsed amid a group of others in similar condition. Not one of them moved.

FoundingYear 1028
Mandorlyn

Oddly enough, the return journey with Duglas was considered the safer one. Braeden explained that the caravans had had little trouble when taking the gold out, though it was not unheard of.

"The baseborn bastards are usually too lazy to turn their hand to honest work and they'd have to work to transport the gold. Still, it's not unheard of. The year Duglas began the caravan another caravan was beset, but they haven't tried since. Duglas hires too many guards to make it worthwhile."

"The quality of his guards would also make it a poor wager," Tamys noted. They were arranging the gear and goods for the journey, which would commence the next morning. The wagons with the gold were still locked safely in the repository. They would not roll forth until dawn when the caravan would set out.

As they were outside of the repository, Tamys looked at the walls, which were as high as any dun in Celdrya and thick as well. The gates, of which there was only one set, looked stout, the oak bound with iron, then covered with more iron to make it difficult to burn. There were guards aplenty on the catwalks at the top of the walls and Tamys thought he would not want to stand siege under those walls. It seemed to him, though, that the construction differed from what he might expect, though he couldn't quite place his unease.

"The dwarves left that behind," Braeden announced, as if reading Tamys' mind. "There are a number of strong buildings about the valley that are used as repositories and arsenals. They're the best built forts I've ever been in. Walls seemed built of solid rock."

"Solid? Nay, man, that's impossible!" Tamys replied.

"Actually," Padraig corrected. "It isn't. The elves in the eastern mountains live in old dwarven holts and much of what is there was carved from the living rock."

Tamys looked from one man to the other, uncertain of their veracity. The older men laughed at his uncertainty.

"When you've lived as long as I have, traveled the whole kingdom many times over, you will believe the impossible," Braeden assured him.

Tamys wondered if he'd live that long and then shoved the thought aside. There was much to do for the journey.

The Mandorlyn town militia saw them through the settlement and into the hills before turning back round to continue their protection of the town itself. The first day proved a pleasant journey through the farms that fed the people of Mandorlyn proper. They slept in a caravanseri and continued on to a drizzling rain the next morning, leaving the truly settled areas behind. By late morning, they'd neared the river and the rain had been replaced with fog thick as wool. The men grew restive, trying to see into the swirling mist. They could hear the river somewhere to their right, but not see it and for fighting men, what could not be seen was dangerous. Their nerves played out in short tempers with their fellows.

The odd exception to this state of heightened emotions was Tamys, who seemed blithely unaware of the danger they might be in. Padraig wondered if his "touch" of the second sight might not have somewhat to do with it. Certainly Tamys had shown signs of sensing danger before and if he did not now, mayhap there was naught to worry about.

Padraig's own nerves drew tight as they traveled into the fog. Surely this was the sort of situation where brigands might lay ambuscade. With the river to their right and a cliff to their left, it just seemed a precarious position.

Tamys was in the act of handing Padraig a water bottle when he hesitated, eyes suddenly scanning the fog.

Padraig forgot the water bottle as it dropped to the ground and he reached for the hilt of his elven long knife, which he'd donned this morning. Suddenly there was movement in the fog.

" 'Ware!" Tamys hollered and reached for his sword as two brigands mobbed his horse, trapping him in the saddle.

Padraig saw a brigand headed his way and kicked the man in the teeth as he kicked free of the stirrups. He dropped to the ground, elven long knife in one hand and sword in the other. He had a moment to realize that the brigands had trapped most of the riders in the saddle before he was beset by a big, strong brigand with the long arms of a swordsman. Padraig dropped to a crouch with his back against Joy and parried the man's first strike off the long knife. Knowing that this was a fight to the death, Padraig brought his sword round, but the brigand expertly blocked with his shield and the fight was on.

In the back of his mind, Padraig felt the tug of Joy's mind on his.

"Your friend's in trouble," she remarked.

"Busy now. You can handle it."

"You might need my help."

"I'll call you if I do. Help Tamys."

Joy left his back then and Padraig used the change as an opportunity to use both blades to

good advantage. Chopping, striking, swinging, parrying, he began to drive the brigand back toward the river. Padraig could sense the man was not used to fighting two blades at once and certainly not someone who could use both arms to equal measure. The brigand fell back, overwhelmed by the attack and forced to retreat.

Joy and the pony charged up against one of the two brigands who had hold of Tamys' legs and saddle. Joy used her deep Eastern Regal chest to slam the brigand into Tamys' horse's shoulder. The bay sidestepped into the second brigand, but a consummate Mulyn warhorse, he didn't panic or dance at this behavior. Joy nipped the brigand's sword arm, causing him to drop his weapon. Fearing for his life, he fled the field.

Tamys brought his left fist round into the remaining brigand's face, which was inadequately protected with only a mail hood. The brigand staggered back, giving Tamys the opportunity to kick free of the stirrups and drop to the ground, drawing his sword as he was in the air. There was no time for his shield, which hung from his saddle hook, so he slashed the remaining brigand across the face and took his.

Though unused to fighting any real fight on foot, Tamys had been trained in the technique. He charged into the fray, battering unsuspecting brigands in the heads with his borrowed shield as he slashed and parried with his sword. Behind him, he heard the sorrel mare rearing and snorting. He glanced back to see her kill a man with her hooves. The pony bit another brigand who got too close.

Padraig drove his brigand backward off a bluff into the river, where he dropped 20 feet with a scream that ended in a splash. Padraig then turned his attention to rescuing the riders from their saddles, a work that Tamys had already set-to with an efficiency that amazed Padraig. Somewhere in the press, Braeden laughed and howled in the cackle of a berserker while Duglas screamed orders above the din. Not that anyone could understand what he was saying, but at least the man still lived. As riders began to drop from their saddles to enjoin the brigands, Padraig fought his way toward the nearest muleteer, who was using his quarterstaff as efficiently as any swordsman might use his weapon.

Dust rose from the road and fog clung to clothes and skin. The men and horses soon began to sweat in grey gouts of perspiration, sending up an acrid smell that was wholly unpleasant. Padraig began to doubt his ability to fight on for much longer when the brigands suddenly withdrew, disappearing toward the river as easily as they had appeared. A few of the riders pursued them, but soon drew back when Braeden and Duglas yelled at them to return. The resultant quiet echoed with the winded gasps of men at arms following a fight.

"You young louts don't go haring after the scum!" Braeden ordered. "They'll sneak back round and take our guard out. Stay with the wagons, lads! Hold!"

Padraig called Joy with his mind and the mare came trotting, pony beside her, her hooves and legs covered with blood. There was no time to ask her if she'd enjoyed herself. He grabbed his scrap bag and hurried through the caravan, looking for what needed his skills.

Two brigands were close to death, one with his head caved in by one of Joy's hooves. Sensing no guidance from God, Padraig drew his dagger and slit their throats. Beyond God's power, there was naught that he could do for them, and herbcraft on the battle field required nothing less than full mercy and a huge dollop of moral courage. A true healer did not leave a man to suffer in the vain hope of healing him.

There were a fair number of serious injuries among the muleteers and riders. Duglas and Braeden had both received cuts in the fray, though neither was deep enough for more than a few stitches. Tamys' leg pour blood from a cut in his breecs, but he waved Padraig off when the herbman came his way.

"I can staunch the flow myself. You can take care of it when others have been bandaged."

"It might turn septic," Padraig warned. "Wash it with some ale." Padraig lay some bandaging nearby.

Tamys nodded, grimly reaching for the ale bag that hung from his saddle hook.

Padraig did not get back to him for a watch or more. As he approached Tamys, who sat on the ground taking a long draught from his ale bag, he was explaining to Duglas why they couldn't move on yet.

"I've one muleteer with a broken arm that I can't set until the man is well drunk and I've still got to check Tamys' leg. If we toss the muleteer into a wagon after I'm done, we'll be able to move on in a watch, most like."

"I like this spot not at all, herbman. Even with the mist blowing off, it's a ill-begotten location."

"Aye, I hear you, man, but we'll not be helped by more death or sepsis. All right, lad, let's see what we've got here."

Tamys had staunched the flow with a clumsy, but

clean and serviceable bandage. When Padraig unwound the strip, the wound proved a wide gash across Tamys' muscular thigh. It still seeped sluggish brown blood, but on the whole it was a far healthier wound than Padraig had expected.

"You drunk enough for some stitches?" he asked Tamys. The lad nodded. Padraig prepared needle and thread, using ale because there was no time to build a fire. "All and all, you heal pretty well. It'll be a few days though before you'll be sitting a saddle."

"You really don't know me that well, yet, do you?" Tamys replied, taking a slug of the medicinal Padraig had offered him, a mixture of mead, opium and herbs. "My father didn't raise men who couldn't handle pain. I'll be all right."

Padraig shrugged. It wasn't for him to argue with a rider about whether to ride or not. His hire only said he should say somewhat about it. Ten stitches closed the wound, then Padraig put a clean bandage on it and went to set the muleteer's arm. When they rode out, Tamys grimaced mightily gaining the saddle, but he managed and without a whimper of complaint.

The men were tired and some were woozy from wounds, thus Duglas called a halt at a caravanseri he hadn't planned to stay at. They were all worn out from the day's excitement, but there was stock to tend and fires to start and meals to prepare, all with fewer hands than they'd previously used.

Tamys, despite his pain, offered to take care of their stock while Padraig saw to his patients.

"Joy won't let you ...," he began.

"If she won't, she can wear her saddle until you come back. I'll take care of the pony at least."

I'll let the worm remove the saddle if he'll brush me down and wash off the blood, Joy announced.

"She saved my life today, so I'm minded to give her a good rub-down," Tamys announced, causing Padraig to blink at him in surprise. There was no time to pursue how Joy had placed that thought in Tamys' mind, for Padraig had patients to care for and daylight was growing short. It was well after dark before Padraig returned to their campfire. Tamys already slept, but he'd left a bowl of stew for Padraig with bread and a cup of well-watered ale. Padraig smiled. He sought Joy and found her nearby, her saddle off and her coat gleaming as though she'd been properly pampered.

Did you somehow ensorcel the lad? Padraig asked her, as she nipped tiredly at some grass at her feet.

Horses can't ensorcel humans, she protested sleepily. *He's able to hear my thoughts when I want. Must be the company he keeps.*

She rubbed her nose against his arm. He could tell that she had no more to say on the subject. She wanted her sleep and he wanted his evening's meal. He left her and the pony to drowse and nibble grass and returned to the fire to eat and think.

As Padraig was drowsing to sleep, he began to wonder about the day in general and Tamys in particular. The lad admitted to a touch of second sight, and it had been clearly evident before the ambuscade had been sprung that he'd sensed somewhat. Certainly his wound had staunched easily. He'd told Padraig enough that the herbman knew that Tamys' grandmother had haled from somewhere to the east of Mulyn, possibly Denygal. If that were the case, he might have a fair dollop of elven blood running in his veins, enough to account for the second sight, the quick healing, and the ability to pick up on what Joy was thinking. Mayhap. Padraig decided, as he drifted into darkness, that he ought to pursue that investigation sometime during the journey back to Cenconyn. Suddenly, a thought occurred that jolted him awake, fully upright on his blankets.

Have I missed it all along, Lord? Could Tamys be the True King?

Founding Year 1028
Dun Galornyn

Gregyn extricated his arm from Naryna's weight and slid free of the straw pile they shared. She'd sleep until he returned, he was certain. He'd been borrowing ethereal power from her for weeks now and knew her replenishment cycles well. Because of what he had planned, he left a strand of ethereal attachment between them so he could draw more power if needed.

Sucking the power of another left him feeling a bit drunk, similar to what he experienced from the blood of animals. He began to understand why the black mages favored a mixture of sexual excitation and fear, but he thought they were missing the pure raw power he experienced from Naryna. Fear gave another flavor to it altogether and he wasn't sure that it was any better.

Gregyn wrapped his aura tightly round him, so as to be virtually invisible in his trek through the dun. Guards looked at him, but didn't really see him, unless they were looking for him, which was not likely at this time of night. It allowed him to slip down the stairs to the cellars and the unused one he had appropriated for his own purposes. He'd found this cellar months ago and outfitted it for what was needed to work the ritual Talidd had planned. The murals bothered him a bit with their elves and mythical creatures. He supposed that was one reason the dun used this cellar to hold items they never cared to find again.

Since the first night with Naryna, Gregyn had been stretching his abilities after every session. It coincided with Talidd's desire to perform a ritual of high order. Talidd had been encouraging him to push his limits as often as possible. He cautioned Gregyn not to draw more than he was capable of and had suggested using his acolyte, but Gregyn found Naryna more than enough supplement. Gregyn had chosen to keep his relationship with Naryna to himself. He allowed Talidd to think what he wanted.

I'm here, he said as soon as Talidd appeared in the scrying link. *What is your command?*

Hello, Gregyn of Llyr, son of none, Talidd said. Gregyn felt the power flow down through the link and knew that he was supposed to obey every command now, but it had never seemed to affect him the way it affected others. He pretended it affected him, but his free will remained his own.

Aye, master. What is it you command?

We seek the True King, Talidd announced. *You will open the stations and we will locate him and draw him to us.*

Aye, master, Gregyn said. The Stations Ritual was powerful. Even at a low level, it sometimes killed acolytes. Gregyn had been party to the Stations Rituals many times; his strength of gift was favored by many of the journeymen. Pretending ensorcelment, he could not ask the question of his role in the ritual. He assumed they would be drawing his power across the link. His body sang with the glory of sexual energy that he'd drawn from Naryna. There would be no want of power in this bond.

Gregyn and the others in the circle worked the ritual of opening the stations and calling upon the god of Rusks. Talidd guided them in focusing on the True King. Gregyn felt his consciousness slid into an alien mind. Talidd had explained long ago that most mages could not channel another species' consciousness. It was a sign of great power. Talidd had the raven. Gregyn had ... he didn't know. Something that could fly, but he had only been aware of it for a matter of weeks. He watched the ground glide beneath him, circling a lonely dun in a distant copse of trees. Nay, it was a Temple of the Moon and those mountains behind it must be ... Galconyn, mayhap Then the consciousness flowed away to the north and east. Naught but forest flashed beneath his flight and then a tiny dot of light surrounded by a scattering of other lights. The king might be found in Denygal? Curious.

Suddenly, Gregyn was racing at incredible speed

across the breadth of the kingdom, to Llyr and the Bog and then away toward the northwest to a city he didn't recognize.

The taste of coppers came to the back of his mouth. A powerful hand gripped him and he came awake to the feeling of power coursing through him down the link as he started to shake uncontrollably. His nerves felt as if fire coursed through him and not for the first time, he remembered what happened to mages who drew more power than they ought … and he broke the link and fell to his knees, arms and legs spasmodically flaying against the smooth stone floor. He couldn't breathe, couldn't stop jerking, couldn't feel Talidd in the link anymore. Fear gripped him. *Is this death come for me?* Abruptly, Gregyn lost consciousness.

Founding Year 1028
Dun Llyr

Randoff of Llyr rather enjoyed his life in the dun for all the complications it caused him. His brother's strict belief that they need not forget their common beginnings had him spending a portion of every eightnight at the Golden Unicorn while maintaining a chamber in Dun Llyr. He didn't object that much. The Golden Unicorn might have been in the Bottom, but it was a fine inn with the very best of clientele and his mother set a fine board.

There were times, however, when being his

brother's aide grated upon him. Today was one of those days. Howedd had insisted he go to the dun library and ask after Gillian of Llyr.

The library occupied a generous crescent wing along the back of the main broch. Hearths were set at regular intervals along the curving floor to keep the place warm in winter. Now, at almost Lughnasda, the windows were propped open to allow freshening breezes. Scribes worked diligently at lecterns throughout the room. Randoff would much rather have been out-of-doors enjoying the pleasant weather, but here he was amid dusty scrolls and codices seeking answers to questions that were a century old.

"My brother asks after Gillian of Llyr, who lived about a century ago," Randodd explained to the librarian, a stuffy man with a slender face and yellow teeth.

"Hmm," Brechsys hummed. "Well and good. I've a couch for you over there. I'll return eventually."

Randodd sighed and took a seat. He had been trained to read and write, so the library held some interest to him, but he still lacked confidence to set forth without permission. He was the rig's brother, but he was not noble-born and he'd spent his life knowing that there were consequences for any who dared to rise too far above their station.

Nearly a watch passed before Brechsys returned with a codex which he set upon a low table just in front of the couch. Brechsys flipped open the codex, examined a leaf and then flipped another leaf. Randodd leaned forward to try and see what he was reading.

"These are the genealogies from the last century. Ah, aye, there's a Gillian. She married to Fargyl -- Dun Loch -- and had a child in FY 929."

"What does that mark and date mean?"

"The child died. This refers us to another book. Oh, my!"

"What?"

"It's a book known as -- and forgive the vernacular -- the bastard's book."

"Why would that upset me?" Randodd replied calmly. Brechsys looked even more nervous. "Truly, it is what I am. Let us see this book."

The bastard's book was quite difficult to locate, so that the afternoon had faded to evening dark, heavy with the perfume of flowers, before Brechsys set it before him.

"It would seem the Umhall line was given to sexual indiscretions," Randodd said with a laugh. Brechsys gave him a sour look. "You might want to ease up a bit, old man," he said with a whisper. "Remember who your rig is this time."

Brechsys swallowed audibly, but he nodded and flipped open the book.

"Here she is. Gillian nee Umhall. She had a bastard son in FY 933. Oh, my!"

"Another book?" Randodd asked, heart sinking a bit.

"Nay. Surely this cannot be. She was betrothed to Maryn of Celdrya."

"Prince Maryn?"

"Aye. And, the birth of that child is ... well,

curious."

Randodd stared at the writing himself. This book was different from the other genealogies in that it didn't just show relationships. It included snippets of narrative, explaining the situation. Gillian's bastard had been adopted privately by her brother, rig of Llyr. He'd been married to a younger daughter of a small dun that had needed the bride price. He'd served in Dun Llyr as a servitor. Their children had been married to other minor duns, except for one -- a girl --who had gone to the Golden Unicorn and bore another child -- this one the child of her cousin, rig of Llyr. The child, a girl, had been adopted and raised in the dun. She'd been married to a noble servitor and their children had been married out, except for one girl, who had born her cousin's child and retired to the Golden Unicorn. Then Randodd's mother appeared. Rhodda had born Howedd by design. Randodd sat back on the couch.

"They were keeping the line alive," Brechsys said. "But they've never claimed it. I'd have seen it in the histories if they had."

"But they maintained a genealogy," Randodd added. "It's a direct line through the female. I must take this to my brother, so that he may know."

"Aye, of course, lad. I'll get a carry sack for it. Please do treat it as important."

"Of course," Randodd assured him. "I think this may be the most important book in all the kingdom."

As soon as Brechsys delivered the sack, Randoff slung over his shoulder so that no one would guess how important the item he carried might be and hurried off to his brother's chambers to turn his view of the world upon its head.

Willow Branch

We know that all things work together for good for those who love God, who are called according to His purpose.

This curious statement is found in a letter by Pwl, who was a learned man from the before world. He wrote this letter to the Rwmanes, which is still a matter of deep confusion to me, as we know they were the conquerors and enslavers of the Travellyn tribe. The Believer's religion is most curious, for it would seem that they found friendship among enemies.

From the Scriptos of the One, Letter to the Rwmanes

Recorded by Brethry, Priest of Bel, Moryn
FY 933

Founding Year 931
Denygal Mountains

Donyl's lungs burned. He felt light-headed and heavy-limbed as if he were laboring under a burden far beyond the light pack and water bottle he carried. It was as if there just wasn't as much air here as elsewhere. Surely that could not be the truth. It was merely that he was exhausted from days of hard travel and the unaccustomed mode of his feet.

Pedyr looked as exhausted as he, with dark circles under his eyes and his face slick with sweat. Faryl seemed completely comfortable, legs eating up the vertical slope as if he might run all day … as indeed he had. To take his mind off the pain in his legs and ribs, Donyl wondered if mayhap Faryl and his horse had adapted somehow to the altitude. Kylly Mines was two ridges below this one, but with ups and downs might only be a little below in altitude. Could people mayhap adjust to living in the mountains over living in the valleys? Could the exhaustion Pedyr and Donyl labored under have somewhat to do with the altitude? He would need to ask wiser heads when he arrived in Denygal. If ….

Nay! He would not allow the possibility of failure! They'd eluded the daemon thus far. There was hope they might make the citadel at Denygal on the morrow. The thumbnail moon in the darkening solstice sky harbingered disaster, but the longer northern day meant they could travel much farther twixt sunrise and sunset.

Faryl came to a stop, chest barely heaving. Pedyr stumbled up beside him, hands on his knees, sucking air. Donyl labored up the last slope, recognizing that they were completely free of the tree line now, with only waist-high brush surrounding them. He dropped to his knees and fumbled for his water bottle.

"We're there," Faryl announced, pouring water into a bowl for the horse to drink. They'd encountered a small spring this morning, but there was little water this high up.

Pedyr stared at him, still breathing hard. After taking a long draught of water, he straightened and looked where Faryl pointed. He signaled for Donyl to look as well, but from his position on his knees Donyl could see only brush and sky and looming mountains. He struggled to gain his feet.

Across a gorge, they could see a collection of buildings clinging to a mountaintop at a lower level. Faryl's instinct that the path they'd taken two days before led to the citadel had been correct. Donyl and Pedyr smiled at one another.

"Good job, lad," Donyl said to the mountain village boy.

"We're not there yet," Pedyr reminded. "We've got that gorge to cross."

"There's a bridge," Faryl explained. "You trek down this path," he indicated the cairn-marked path that Donyl had not seen before, "and it comes to a bridge. The bridge takes you to the citadel."

"We can't traverse it by sundown," Pedyr told

Donyl.

Donyl nodded, drinking another slug of water. His heart no longer galloped, but his throat felt wind-burned. He walked to the cairns and looked down at a narrow footpath cut into the side of the gorge. It seemed to switchback many times before it disappeared into the gloom.

"We've a trek of it, to be sure," he agreed. He turned to Faryl. The lad's eyes were averted as if he expected the conversation ... or mayhap had intended to initiate it. "The agreement with your father was that you take us to within sight of the citadel. Unless you have an overwhelming desire to see the citadel, I suggest you return home."

"The horse ...?"

"You may take him with you. There's little left of our supplies once we give you enough to return with, so there's no reason we can't carry it in backpacks."

Faryl glanced toward Pedyr. Far more than the men of the warband, he had deferred to Donyl as liege on this journey, but he recognized that Donyl often deferred to Pedyr, who now frowned and stared at the clouds for a bit.

"We've no cause to hold you, lad," Pedyr agreed finally. "You've fulfilled your commitment and with the moon just about at dark, we need to let you go. I wish we'd been able to release you earlier, so you'd not be upon the trail at this ill-omened time."

"I'll be fine," Faryl assured. "I've the Light of the World to guide me."

He opened a pannier and began to lay out what few

supplies they had left. Donyl and Pedyr shed their packs and took a bit of journey bread, some cheese and a bag of the sour ale the Kylly Mines folks used to cleanse their water.

"I must say this before we part," Faryl said as he and Donyl faced each other over the goods. "I've the Light of the World to guide me and Pedyr does as well, but you are in darkness. Listen to his counsel and cling unto the One."

Donyl stared at him. What little breath they'd had to spare since the stampede had been spent in speaking of the One God and how Donyl might know him. Donyl had listened respectfully and he recognized the earnestness with which they held their beliefs. That they believed the same though one had been raised in a mountain fast and the other just outside High Celdrya resonated with him somewhat. Donyl nodded soberly. Faryl rose and put his supplies in the pannier.

"I'll be going then. I'll pray for you now."

He placed his hands upon each of their shoulders and lowered his head.

"My God, You know the powers and principalities that are coming against these men. I pray Your hedge about them so that no power on earth or below may come against them. In Jesu's name."

"So be it," Pedyr whispered. There were tears in the man's eyes as he embraced the mountain lad. "Fly swiftly home, lad."

"Fair fortune to you," Donyl added. "If we survive, I'll remember this and the loving care of Kylly Mines to its potential king."

Faryl nodded, gathered the horse's reins, leapt into the saddle and rode off downslope the way they'd come. Pedyr and Donyl stood a while, quiet in the gusts of wind that swirled through the pass.

"We'd best make for that bridge now," Pedyr decided. "We can bed down on the trail as well as here on the mountain."

Donyl nodded, barely caring that he was exhausted beyond measure. Pedyr gestured for him to go before him down the trail. It seemed an odd path, one side sheer cliff, but the outer edge trimmed with a low rampart that rose to waist height.

"Is this a dwarves' road?" Donyl asked. He'd read of such and this seemed to fit the description.

"Mayhap. Seems like their sort of work, true-spoken."

The air was still thin, so that they didn't speak much as they walked the downward trail. It grew shadowy not long after the first sharp bend in the path. After so long trudging uphill, Donyl had expected his legs to welcome the change of exertion, but it didn't take long for them to start screaming again. Oh, how he wanted to rest.

They hurried along into the deepening gloom until they came to a wide spot off one of the bends and Pedyr called a halt. Besides the path they had come down on, there were two paths off this wide ledge -- one going down toward the bridge and the other -- well, from somewhere to the south.

"We can't see and a torch would only be a beacon in this chasm. We'll camp here til dawn and then push on."

They wrapped themselves in their cloaks with blankets over those and settled with their backs against the cliff. A chill wind blew past them. Donyl thought he smelled incense at one point, but he decided he must have been wishing. Exhausted from days of running, he quickly dozed off, head drooping onto Pedyr's shoulder. Within heartbeats, he was beyond embarrassment.

Waking from a dead sleep caught him by surprise and he sat for a moment, unsure why he was awake. Then the ground beneath him trembled and he nudged Pedyr to wakefulness.

"Hmm?" the soldier grunted.

"Do you feel somewhat?" Donyl whispered.

Pedyr cocked a head as if listening and then laid his hand upon the stone before them.

"God in Heaven, I pray this is not what I think it is," the rider breathed. Then he stood up, dragging Donyl with him. They could see the path to the south now, lit by a long string of torches, still some distance from their bivouac. The path from above was also lit by torches. The ground trembled harder now as those two forces descended upon them.

"Run," Pedyr ordered, drawing his sword and pushing Donyl toward the path that supposedly led to the citadel. Donyl stumbled and turned to obey. He could see something moving along the path that descended that way. The thumb nail moon had been replaced by a gibbous orb like a golden charger that made is easier to see their destruction closing in.

"I don't think it will do any good," he announced. Pedyr glanced the direction he indicated and growled.

"What do we do?" Donyl asked, drawing his own sword.

"We die here," Pedyr told him. "We can die well, but we will surely die."

The thought, oddly, held no terror for Donyl. He nodded as if this were the most ordinary conversation he'd ever had. After days of fighting to stay alive, he was comfortable with death when no other options existed.

"Back to back. Keep swinging and we'll take some hell-spawn with us."

"Aye," Donyl agreed. The ground truly rumbled now beneath his feet and the torches were growing close enough so that he could see the man-shapes that carried them. He drew the sword Perryn had given him, put his back to Donyl's back and took a deep breath, letting it out just as the first daemon reached him. He heard the clang of steel on bronze from Pedyr's sword and then he swung his own. A being fell, but another took its place. These were not men, for all their shape, but hideous creatures with distorted faces, though their swords seemed real enough. As soon as Donyl killed one, another or two or three came forward. The narrow path and the ledge meant that there was room for only that many to assail him at one time, but it was enough and soon Donyl's whole body felt afire from the effort of defending his life. He could hear Pedyr breathing heavily behind him, feel his shoulders working as he cut his own assailants down. Soon it became clear that they would not win because their foes would not stop and Donyl despaired for a moment and thought *Does Pedyr's One God care what is happening here?* A good man, a Believer of His, will die fighting evil. *God, please, help us now.*

A heartbeat later, an air-rending roar filled the gorge and the daemon host ducked as if expecting attack from on high. A dark winged shape glided out of the moon light and swept low. Donyl screamed as the enormous claws reached down and lifted him free of the ledge.

Founding Year 1028
Dun Wllean

The journey back through the Mandorlyn Pass was largely uneventful. There were no signs of brigands. The spring weather had turned to summer in a mere eightnight and that kept Padraig busy doctoring the wounds of the injured, preventing infection and gangrene. Tamys was the only one who didn't have Padraig worried. He healed quickly, without sign of infection. He even stopped limping after a few days. His only complaint was that the stitches itched, which Padraig took care of on the eightnight by removing them. If it weren't for Padraig's growing interest in his parentage, he'd have been no concern at all.

How could I have missed what was standing right before me, God? If I'm right, he's both human and Kin. He's courtly and court-raised. He has an ancestral claim. He's a warrior of mythic aspect. He doesn't desire to rule. He's a younger son. How much more of the prophesy does he fulfill?

The consuming thought for Padraig was how to broach this subject to Tamys. He'd always had this consideration. How did one convince someone who was the One's True King that he was indeed the One's True King? Padraig did not fear to face ridicule, but he could not force Tamys not to think him mad. Then, upon convincing Tamys, there would be the harder task of acquiring the throne for him. Padraig believed that the One could accomplish all things within His will, but it had yet to be clear how He intended to do this. How did an herbman and a dishonored nobleman's son convince anyone of God's will?

That's getting very far ahead of myself, Padraig reminded himself sternly. *I first need to explain it to Tamys.*

Yet, he had not come to any decisions as the caravan drew near Dun Wllead. A day shy of the city, the scouts noted movement on the heights and the men drew swords. However, the movement never materialized into anything, but at the early morning of the day they would reach Dun Wllead, the caravan drew to a halt when a young lad in ragged clothes stepped into the canyon. Muleteers growled, riders drew their swords, but Duglas rode forth with Braeden beside him and they surveyed this novelty in the track.

"Lad, you're a long way from the town, in a dangerous place," Duglas greeted.

"I'm not from the town," the lad explained. "My brother is a brigand. We came out here thinking we'd get a caravan and go back with lots of coin, but I'm tired of starving. I can't get back through the gates on my own. I need a ride."

Duglas tugged on his mustaches and looked at Braeden. The freesword weighed and judged the lad without passion.

"He's just a child. He can't carry off even one of the bars of gold."

"True-spoken," Duglas agreed. "We'll give you a ride, lad."

"Thanks to you, merchant," the lad said with a smile. Braeden swung down and helped the lad into the wagon. Padraig and Tamys, who'd been riding further back in the column, came riding up then to ask what was going on.

"We just found a brigand's whelp who's decided an honest life makes more sense," Duglas explained to them. "We'll give him a ride into the city."

Padraig glanced at Tamys, who looked suddenly pale under the tan that he'd developed since leaving Dun Celdrya a month before.

"Somewhat the matter, lad?"

"Wha – ? Nay, geese walking on my grave, is all."

They fell into the forward movement of the column.

"Lad, I've been meaning to ask you of your plans," Padraig said.

"Aethan and some of the others say they're headed to Dun Llyr to find a hire. I'll likely be traveling with them."

Padraig's heart contracted painfully. Did he dear risk missing this opportunity? What if his suspicions were correct?

"You don't need to, lad," Padraig insisted. "There's no reason to sell your soul."

"It's what I know, Padraig," Tamys explained. "I can't see taking up a trade or becoming a farmer. I'm no farmer, Padraig."

"Neither am I, Tam, lad. I found another way, that incorporates both the warband training I received as a child and a trade that's honest and supports me quite nicely."

"Padraig, I thank you, but I'm not a herbman. I am naught but a lousy freesword and you know that. There's no stopping what was set in motion when my father turned me out."

"There is, if you'll but decide to stop it."

Tamys shook his head and they said no more about it. For Tamys, silence was a means not to destroy a friendship. His mind was made up. For Padraig, it was to avoid Tamys' becoming defensive, for he knew naught but the power of God could dislodge the lad from his chosen course.

The entry into Dun Wllean took most of the day. The gates would only allow one wagon through at a time and two riders at any one time. Duglas set up his pay table as before. He asked Padraig and Tamys if they would be remaining in Dun Wllean. He had a second caravan going through the Pass in a month.

"I'm journeying south. I still can find lots of work along the way and I need to put in an herb crop for the winter."

"And you, Tamys lad?"

"I need to find a hire for the winter," Tamys explained. "Winter is coming."

"Aye, true-spoken. I'm sorry there were no lords in Mandorlyn. You might want to try Morglen, or Denygal, if you've got your heart set on a warband. I hear the lords there are less particular about points of honor and such."

"Thanks to you," Tamys said. He and Padraig turned to leave. The town of Dun Wllean stretched before them.

"Will you be staying at the caravanseri?" Padraig asked, hopeful for one more chance to persuade him.

"Nay. I'll find an inn with some lasses to dance with," Tamys admitted. "I'll stop by on my way out, though."

They paused. Padraig held out a hand to his friend. Tamys took it.

"I can't say I agree with your decision, but I'll be praying for you. The Lord will open your way, I believe, if it's His will."

"Thanks. I'll keep my ears open for an herbman with an Eastern Regal. Mayhap we'll see each other again."

"Aye. Lad, remember, just because it seems the only course, it isn't necessarily. The One has a great path for you, if you will but open to it."

Tamys nodded, then shook his head. They clasped hands again and parted. There was nothing more to say. Padraig could only hope that somewhat opened the lad's eyes before he rode down the road with Aethan and the others, because truth be told, he suspected this was the king of all Celdrya riding away from him.

Founding Year 1028
Dun Wllean

Aethan seemed determined to spend all his wages on getting his mates drunk. He'd already bought three rounds for Tamys and the other two young freeswords who had formed a unit out of Duglas' larger troop. There were some of the other men from the caravan at the Blue Goose and all were singing and laughing. The serving lasses returned their friendly chivvying with banter of their own. Tamys had already had a bowl of quite excellent stew and fresh brown bread, so that Aethan's coin was not having the desired effect as soon as might be expected, but after the third tankard even he was starting to feel a bit off-kilter.

"Which one do you want?" Aethan asked him, indicating the harlots who were intermixed with the men and serving wenches.

"I think I'll pass this night," Tamys replied.

"Surely not."

"I wish not to spend my coin. Winter's coming sooner than we think and the price of a harlot will pay for an eightnight in a dormitory."

"You jest!" Aethan insisted.

"Nay, I do not."

Snorting, Aethan got up to fill his tankard, grabbing Tamys' off the bench. The two others had already found their pick for the next little while and gone off to the sporting stalls. Aethan and Tamys had rented a room on the third floor and Aethan rather thought he could have it for a while.

Truth be told, Tamys was weighing going to talk with Padraig. He was headed south to Morglen, mayhap, and the lords there were less strict about history and honor. Tamys was tempted to see if that were really true. He rose from the bench, preparing to catch up his cloak from the peg by the door and set out for the caravanserie outside the walls.

The door opened to admit a woman and Tamys froze in mid-movement as the chaos of the tavern room dropped away. She turned toward him -- tall and shapely with black hair that ripped over her shoulders, dressed in a purple dress with gilt threading the bodice. She seemed to see naught but him as she wove through the crowd to stand before him.

"Tamys ap Manahan of Mulyn, I would have sport with you this evening," she said and her words seemed to bind him with iron chains cushioned with velvet.

"I would gladly sport with you, lass," he agreed.

She held out a soft hand that was surprisingly firm and they walked up the stairs to the third floor where Tamys unlocked the room he shared with Aethan. He did not think that Aethan would mind a night in the hay loft. The room was not large and only had one bed, but it smelled more of bread than piss and had a nice window over the innyard. Tamys and the woman kissed and he felt heat like warm honey flow through his entire body. He undid his sword belt and lowered the weapon to the floor. Now she was all over him, fingers working his siarc free of his belt, fumbling to remove the belt itself, moving him back across the room until he felt the windowsill at the back of his thighs and … then naught but open air at his back. He grabbed for her with one hand and the window frame with the other, but both hands missed. He screamed as he fell and then knew naught more.

Founding Year 1028
Dun Cenconyn

Ryanna sat up in the darkness of the tent she shared with Cai, heart pounding, sweat slicking her breasts, breath harsh in her chest. Her hands closed on nothingness and she expected to feel her back slam into the pavement.

A dream? Yes, but a dream of deeper stuff. She channeled fire and lit a lantern. Cai rolled to bury his face in the leather pillow formed by a saddlebag. Ryanna drew on a shift and left the tent. Outside, a gibbous moon shone when none should be and she was not the only one to note this.

"There's something amiss in the spiritual," Jotham, one of the guards, noted.

"Yes," Ryanna agreed. She walked into the shadows and stared into the flame of her lantern, thinking of Padraig. She saw him curled in the dark of a tent somewhere far to the west. He seemed fine. Yet, she could not shake the fear she felt. She probed through the flame and felt a responding mind, so turned her thoughts that way.

You are needed, elf-girl, the dragon asserted. *Destruction is at hand and the world cannot wait for you to decide if you want to serve the One. There is only need. Want must wait for a another time.*

Destruction? she thought-asked.

Of course, child. Did you think I would be called back into the world of men for anything less?

What must I do?

You must follow the path that is shown and do so immediately.

Then upon the wall of the tent before Ryanna, she could see a map of Celdrya, only with the ancient Kindred names upon it. A golden line stretched from Avalirad -- that which Cenconyn sat above -- to Lindanmadan.

Commit it to your soul, child, and march at the orders of the One.

Ryanna knew she could refuse. The One never commanded blind obedience. Her will remained her own and she'd promised to return to the holt; she'd meant to keep her word. However, she also knew that when the One commanded, you obeyed or you stood the consequences. Sometimes you stood the consequences even when you obeyed. She hesitated for only a moment and then put her hand upon the tent side and let her gifts absorb the vision into her soul.

There is hope, the dragon announced and then its presence faded from her mind. Ryanna turned to view the camp, seeing the people she loved, who gave her strength and acceptance. She stood stalk-still for several heartbeats before turning to gaze up at the dun. She would need assistance from Reyn and his people. Good that he was a Believer.

One step at a time, hasty one! Gly's tutoring came to mind. Truth be told, she had a more difficult task to accomplish before going to the dun. She must needs tell her brother that she would be continuing onward without him, but with a far more powerful Companion than even Sabre.

Destruction is afoot, but so is hope, the dog spoke into her mind. *We will find God's will together and bring it to Him as I might a fine bird or a polished beaver stick.*

Something lay across the ground before the tent flap and she bent to pick it up. When the winter people had brought the prophesy to Padraig in the winter, their leader had carried such a stick, a six-foot-long willow branch that had been worked and polished until the natural jewel-shaped furrows had formed decorative elements all long the twisted length. Ryanna felt power flow through her into the walking stick. Holding it before her, she felt it would make a fine fighting staff and took it with her as she went to wake Cai to tell him that "destruction is afoot, but the One intends to use me to provide hope."

Ryanna smiled, assured she was exactly where she was meant to be and through absolutely no agency of her own.

To Be Continued ...

A Word About Language

This is a fan's nod to Katharine Kerr, writer of the phenomenal Deverry series. I tried as much as possible to render the writing of names in keeping with her linguistic guidelines from that series. Any errors are my own.

Celdryan is a Celtic language, which is closely related to languages that exist in our own world, principally Welsh. However, it is not identical. The Celdryans left Gaul a millennia ago. Of course, their language has drifted. The following guide might be helpful in pronunciation.

DD is voiced "th" as in thin or breathe. There is also a hard form of TH, as in The or breath.

Y is never a consonant. When long it is voiced as the "i" in machine or the "ee" in teeth, when short it is voiced as the "e" in butter.

DW, GW, and TW are single sounds as in Gwendolyn or twit.

Wmgleadd would be pronounced "um – glath", for example.

Ll is a breathy l sound, somewhat like combining l with an h.

Some terms to know –

Daermad – derived from Gaelic for "forgetting" or

"mistake" It is what the Celdryans call the world they live in. It's the equivalent of Earth or planet.

Kin – Daermad native race of elven type. They tend to be tall, slender and long of limb, with large cat slit eyes and furled ears. When they mate with humans however, these resulting "elflings" can have a mixture of features. They are naturally psychic, though some are more gifted than others.

Celdryan – the descendants of Celts who arrived in Daermad a millennia ago.

Denygal – a mixed race of nominal Celdryans who share ancestry with both Celdrya and Kin.

Basketlands – the former home territory of the Kin, it has been under Celdryan rule for centuries. It is the fertile lands of the valleys between the great mountain ranges and the Stormmor.

Aver – Celdryan for "river"

Temple of the Moon – women's religion dedicated to the worship of goddesses, principally the Morrigan. Psychically gifted priestesses are called domas.

Cult of Lugh ¬– a sect of the Celdryan religion that has done away with personal sacrifices and relies on political power to control society. They oppose all magic and reject diversity of religious beliefs.

Cult of Bel – a sect of the Celdryan religion that emphasizes academics and charity. Their druins are ecclesiastical-approved mages.

Old Faith ¬– a sect of the Celdryan religion that performs personal sacrifices and emphasize honor and community. Their priests are known as druids and have the gifts of mages. Their granias are herb women who also work in psychic gifts.

Mages – there are various sects from various traditions. Sometimes they work together and sometimes they work against each other.

Goi'tan – a voluntary period of servitude in Kindred society for the purposes of repentance. It involves a public acknowledgment by wearing grey robes, shaving one's head and keeping silence. After a period of goi-tan, a Kin's transgressions are never to be mentioned again.

Cotan – a soft fabric similar to our cotton that is cultivated by the Kin and highly valued by the nobility of Dublyn.

Breecs – baggy woolen pants worn by Celdryan men. Nobles wear plaid breecs that distinguish their clan.

Trews – form fitting pants worn by Kin and others

Siarc – a linen shirt worn in Celdrya. The yokes are often embroidered. The nobility adorns theirs with the clan symbols.

Dun – a fortress including the main keep and outbuildings surrounded by a wall. The city that supports a dun is often called Dun also.

Broch – a dun tower, a round building preferably built of stone.

Companion – another Kin term indicating a sentient non-human animal that has a psychic connection with a human.

Lumina – a type of translucent building stone used by Kin in former times to build cities. The art of working it has been lost.

Excerpt from

Murklin Wood

Thus says the One Whose Name We Are Not to Know, hear Me, Kindred, and know that I am One God.

The raptors fight over the aviary, but only one can rule and no bird of a feather will mount the throne. The dragon stirs and the One's King will arise. Go you then to find him and win him free of those who would exploit him. Who shall go? One who knows both worlds and can heal both the body and the rifts of men, one whose brothers rule, yet who would walk barefoot himself, one whose Companion shines like the sun.

And how shall you know the One's King? He will be obscure -- near the rule, but not of it. He will be of the Kin, but not know the Kin. He will pass through tribulation. He will be plain of speech, heroic and thoughtful. The dragon will claim him.

The raptors fight over the aviary, but all will bow before the dragon.

Know this and hear the One speak.

Navaransen, Sentinel, Kin Cycle 17602 Old Calendar

Founding Year (FY) 931
Denygal · Summer · A Century Ago

Gravity dictates the fate of a dragon dancer. Miss a handhold and gravity wins.

After spending all of yestermorrow climbing the ropes on a sheer cliff face, it would be ironic if a sliding bit of shale on a scree slope sent her tumbling to her death.

Janara jerked her downslope foot off the treacherous slab, dropping to her upslope knee with a teeth-jarring thump and slapping her hands hard on the solid rock. The slab clattered off down the slope, launched into the void with an avalanche of similar stones headed to the river far below.

Janara pretended she'd meant to do that. Settling the pack straps more comfortably on her shoulders, she reached for the water bottle at her side. The late summer sun sent trickles of sweat meandering down her back under her sleeveless linen shirt.

Haste will kill you, girl! A dancer works with the mountain. Forget that at your peril!

The hard blue sky arched above her, wide open to the south all the way to the green valley of Fairhaven and disappearing over the crest of the gray mountain in front of her. Not far now, truly. She'd reach the ridge by noontide. She splashed a little water in a slender, long fingered hand and wiped it across her face and the front of her braided hair. She longed to dump a bit down her back and wet her shirt, but this was not a situation for extravagance. Securing her water bottle in the pouch on the pack, she rose from her knees and began laboring upward once more.

Put one foot in front of the other. Step, breathe in, release, step, breathe in, release, ….

What was that? She scrambled up the last few steps of inclination to kneel panting upon the warm stone. A dark shape flew along the crest of the next highest ridge. A large bird, perhaps? *A dragon?*

She'd seen a dragon flying once, a long way off. It had been a rare sighting, deemed auspicious by her parents, reason enough to train in the Dragon Corpse. She'd dreamt of dragons since, but she doubted to have the privilege of true sighting again, even as she hoped to be granted it. The Denygal rarely found Companions these days and none had Touched a dragon in half a millennia. Why would the One deny such a blessing to one who loved Him utterly? Why would He grant it, either?

It was an eagle, she decided, riding the thermals at the edge of the ridge. There'd been an eagle in her dream, the one that had prompted her parents to send her northward at daybreak two days ago. Lowering her pack to the stone, she knelt to pull out a cloth-wrapped bundle of sharp cheese and thick bread. She took her lunch sitting tailor-fashion on the ground, looking west.

Mam had encouraged her to trek here when she'd awakened from the dream. It did no good to ignore a Prompting. Da had wanted her to wait for her brothers, but none of them were dancers. They'd only have taken her to the base of the ropes. She'd still be alone here, contemplating the vast wilderness beyond the Milk. Janara washed down fruit leather with tepid water and considered the deep valley before her.

The Dragon's Milk scoured down the side of the Dragon's Head mountain, an enormous waterfall fed by a glacier. It stopped halfway down in a churning lake, then spilled on downward, finally becoming a mighty river that carved a canyon through the Roof of the World into Denygal to the south. Few could cross the Milk this far north because there were no bridges up river of Fairhaven, but dancers like Janara had a way ... if she chose to use it. She had to be sure of the Prompting because following her heart meant a long dangerous walk back. Stowing her tuck bag, she stood on the verge, looking far down at the gray-brown streak of the Milk and waited for the One's Spirit to speak to her.

A warm breeze brushed her face and dried her lips as she scanned the dark-green forest on the other side of the river. Something pulled at her heart, but she waited for confirmation. *Never trust your heart. Wait for the One to lead.*

She prepared to step back from the verge when a rustle of feathers shuffled past her ear. The eagle paused for a moment before her astonished eyes, hovering in space as if frozen in time, and then dropped into the void. For two heartbeats it streaked downward, then opening its wings, it kited off toward the north, swooping low over the evergreen forest.

Janara's breath caught in her throat as she followed the eagle's flight. Perhaps a day's walk from the river, on a ridgeline likely formed by on of the active glaciers that came down from the roof of the world, she saw a plume of smoke. *The One speaks!*

Decided, she wasted no time in pulling the faery suit from the pack and donning it. Wide bands of cloth stretched from her wrists, along her arms and sides and down her legs, then between her legs to form a kite that gave the dancers their gravity defying abilities.

The suit does not define your courage.

Securing everything within the pack, which she tied tightly to her body beneath the suit, she stepped once more to the verge and waited, arms half-stretched-out, feeling for the updraft. It started as a gentle feeling of being nudged, followed by a growing sense of being pushed back toward the rock. She leaned into it, stretching her arms further, feeling the fabric between her legs catching and flagging. She wanted to step back, to avoid the danger inherent in dancing. She looked toward the ridge line once more and saw the long slitherin shape leave the ground, wings flapping. *Dragon?* The updraft caught the suit full, her feet left the shale, and she became the eagle, headed west toward the fire on the ridge.

Founding Year 1028
Galornyn – The Present

Rain fell in sheets from a sullen sky, filling the streets of Galornyn with fetid streams of mud that oozed toward the harbor in thick brown ropes like excrement loosed from a cesspit. The unnatural downpour had kept the city enthralled for three days now. Folk spoke of Hanaloran witchcraft while the merchants of the Southern Isles stood off the jetty awaiting a favorable wind for home.

In the markets, there was news that three academics from the collegiate had died as if strangled by unseen hands the night before the storm broke. Fear was palpable in the streets and taverns where every man, woman and child saw plague and sorcery round every corner.

Gregyn stood in the shadows of the dim interior of the temple of Bel, watching Naryna's parents mourn over their daughter, the whole of his saved wages arranged about their daughter. He'd been unable to persuade the priests to provide this time of mercy for Naryn's parents, but the priests of Bel in Galornyn liked coin as much as other men, though they pretended not to.

The failure of persuasion gnawed at him. A symptom of Talidd's murderous spell, no doubt. Gregyn had not eaten for three days and his hands shook when he didn't will them not to. His head ached and every muscle of his body throbbed as if he'd labored for days in a mine.

His gift was as exhausted as his body. It would be some time before he could work magic again, though he could still feel its power on the edge of his awareness. He'd been fortunate. Others had not been. Naryna had died in his stead as other familiars had died in the place of their journeymen. Wrgyn had explained it to him, he who had not been included in the ritual, but who recognized its aftermath.

"I know it was you, lad," he'd said that first morning when he'd found Gregyn sliding back into the dun after taking Naryna to the town hospital to be found by her family. He'd barely been able to stand by that time and hadn't tried to protest or defend himself when Wrgyn had dragged him up to his tower apartment and barred the door.

The middle-aged sorcerer fair sparkled with excitement as Gregyn sunk exhausted onto the divan.

"I knew Talidd was about to work a high-level ritual. My eyes-and-ears told me that Sawyl had been here purchasing supplies. And, of course, for a ritual of that magnitude, Talidd needed his strongest people. Even an apprentice would do when possessed of your power."

Gregyn let his head fall back on the divan, allowing Wrgyn's words to wash over him as the chamber spun round him.

"Who were you linked with?" Wrgyn asked. Time had passed. Gregyn sensed he'd slept. He felt worse than before. Although Gregyn normally was much stronger than Wrgyn and therefore immune to his magicks, today was an exception. Gregyn felt scoured out and beyond the flows of power that had been at his fingertips for most of his life. Wrgyn had ensnared him at his weakest. "Who were you linked with, lad? Lying will only cause you pain. I know you were linked, else you'd be dead. How'd you learn that trick? You're only a Level 2, so you've not been taught it. Who were you linked with?"

"Naryna," Gregyn whispered, lips moving over their own volition.

"A lass?! Now that's very interesting! Shouldn't have worked. You're the interesting one, now aren't you? Well and good then. I'll keep your secret and you'll keep mine, if I tell you any. Do you understand what you did?"

"Sexual effluent," Gregyn said. "I stretched my gifts using her lust." He was slurring; his need for sleep was paramount.

"Aye. Females have lust, but not like men. The lads are so much more powerful, you see. Somehow you've stumbled across what's been lost to the Guild for centuries. You should not have been able to use her as your familiar."

Wrgyn wanted more from Gregyn, but Gregyn's physical weakness dragged him down into the darkness and further questioning only resulted in a seizure ... his first not triggered by an awen. Gregyn woke sometime in the night, covered with a blanket, still on the divan. His clothes stank of vomit and his body felt like he'd been stomped by a horse. Wrgyn snored in the bed chamber. The man had not pulled off his boots or removed his sword belt. It would be so easy ... except that he had all the strength of a wrung-out washrag and doubted he could raise his sword and bring it down with sufficient power to cleave Wrgyn's chest.

He'd left the sycophant sleeping peacefully to stumble out of the tower toward the barracks. His legs weighed stones. He wanted simply to sit down and sleep wherever he was. He crossed near the privies and nearly fell down when one of the doors swung open, revealing Taryn fresh from dumping this night's wine from his system.

"Are you ill, lad?" Taryn asked.

"Aye," Gregyn whispered and passed out clean then and there. He supposed Taryn had seen to his return to his bunk, but he had no memory until the next day when he'd awakened to the black rain that matched the state of his soul.

Naryna's mam held her daughter's cold dead hand as the priest spoke the words that would commend her to the Otherworld. Gregyn knew it should be him departing this world's realm. If he'd only known, he'd ....

What would he have done? Volunteered to die? Used his apprentice as a familiar? The alternatives were limited and unpleasant. Black mages could not afford the luxury of love or caring? Everyone was a playing piece in a massive game of hounds and hares and black mages meant always to be the hound. He'd not meant to kill Naryna, but he'd learned a valuable lesson from her death. Wrgyn would keep his secret for reasons of his own, so the power Gregyn now wielded was somewhat Talidd need not know.

The priest placed the wreath of flowers Gregyn had provided across the chest of the dead lass. Gregyn sighed and turned, striding out into the liquid darkness that held no redemption. He'd gone three steps from the door before he saw the wild folk standing in the street, oblivious of the poisonous rain. They stared at him with sad eyes, shaking their warty heads, their mouths drawn in silent anguish at his decision.

Intent upon the spectacle that only he could see, Gregyn ran up against a tall, thin man dressed in a sopping grey cloak. Instinctively, Gregyn reached for his shields, but the mental prowess that normally set him apart from other apprentices was lacking in his exhaustion, so that the man's eyes touched his soul as they came face to face.

It's a dark path you trod, lad, the man thought to him. If I may suggest, there are better treks to choose.

He disappeared into the crowd of huddled cloaks, leaving Gregyn gasping and quaking, staring at the wild folk who nodded their heads solemnly as if they too had heard the unheard advice and thought quite highly of it.

Shuddering, Gregyn hurled the contents of his stomach into the gutter. The crowd bent around him. In this time of plague, no one offered to help. Gregyn hunched with water running down his neck, soaking the inside of his cloak as much as the outside. When the worst passed, leaving him cold, wet and aching, he set his face toward the dun and his black future.

Founding Year 1028
Wmgleadd

Dun Wmgleadd sat under a dinner plate full moon, the streets bright as day. A caravan had arrived earlier in the day, so the night sang with the great merriment that accompanies hardworking men with coin in their purses after a long job is accomplished. Every inn of any reputation spilled over with light, laughter and frivolity, harlots plied their trade and ale flowed like water in a stream. At the Blue Goose just off the market square, the gaiety was shattered by a scream and the dull thud of a body hitting a grassy yard.

Far from the celebrating throng, Padraig slept soundly, luxuriating in a morrow with no commitments. He'd been on the move constantly since leaving Clarcom two moons hence and a single night without concern for the morrow was a rare luxury that he meant to savor until dawn. When the dream of the eastern mountains began, he though mayhap it was a melting of the blockage he'd labored with for more than a moon, but this had the flavor of vision more than of dream.

The majestic sunlit peaks soared behind Gly as he shouted at Padraig from a great distance. The elven master's words shredded on an unfelt wind so that Padraig recognized only the word "sword". Sword? What sword? Gly gestured, so that Padraig looked behind him, flinching back as lightning rent a storm-black sky. An unnatural raven unfolded enormous wings to launch itself into the storm, somewhat clenched in its talons. Just as it threatened to disappear into the clouds, the raven dropped what it carried and Padraig stared as a sword flashed past his perch to fall broadside upon the grassy yard Padraig suddenly stood upon.

A large fat goose with blue feathers honked at him and waddled off into the darkness. A falcon lifted its beak free of the shelter of its wing in a tree in Mulyn and launched itself into the sky, pushing southward. Ryanna picked up a walking stick of honor willow. A Kin woman he knew from the holt told her elfling husband she was with child. Lydia watched Danyl as he slept. A dark and forbidden forest stretched toward unknown mountains. Gly's voice echoed through his head.

"The broken sword has value. Arise, sleeper, and protect it."

526

The dream vision dissolved as loud whispering called his name.

"Padraig of Denygal? Where are you? Padraig?"

Men began to curse the voice that awakened them and Padraig crawled out of the tent in only his small clothes to keep Braeden from being killed … or more like having to kill someone to keep from being killed. Braeden's reputation was no doubt deserved.

"Braeden, over here," he whispered loudly, which brought complaints from the tents round his. Braeden's tall form came toward him in the darkness, backlit by the glow from a fire across the camping ground. "What brings you here, man? Are you ill?"

"Tamys needs you," the captain of Wmglead's largest caravan said. Padraig immediately reached for his boots. "Damn young fools! He's sore hurt." Braeden continued. Padraig handed him his scrap bag and reached for his siarc. "He was still breathing when I left, but …."

"What happened?" Padraig asked as they won free of the caravanserie and walked quickly toward the main gates of the city.

"He fell from a window at this inn, you see. I didn't see it, you understand."

They'd reached the city gates. The mangate stood open. Padraig supposed Duglas' right hand could ask a great many things of the militia of Wmnglead. People certainly cleared a path as he walked, rapidly explaining events as Padraig struggled to keep up.

"Some of the lads had gone to an inn to carouse. I joined them late because I wanted to ask Tamys to join the caravan permanent-like. "He's the best warrior I've seen in twenty years," the best swordsman in all of Celdrya said.

"When I got there, Tamys had kipped off to the room with a harlot. He must have been in the cups good to fall out of a window."

A shovel-load of cold slid down Padraig's back at the news. Had the True King, meant to unite Celdrya and the Kinholts just died because Padraig had failed to speak when called to do so?

Stay Tuned ...

The Story Continues ...

About Lela Markham

Hi. I was raised in a house made of books in Alaska and told tales from the time I could talk. A teacher eventually made me write one of them down. I hated the exercise, but it was the spark that ignited a fire that has never gone out.

My daring husband, two fearless offspring and I live the adventure of a lifetime here on the Last Frontier where the midnight sun encourages wandering the wilderness and the long dark winters favor reading, writing and staring at the northern lights ... hence the moniker Aurorawatcher. We share our adventure with a sentient husky who inspired Joy and Sabre's characters in The Willow Branch and a very dominated, but extremely happy yellow Lab.

Check out my Smashwords interview for more details or visit me at my website. Feel free to drop a comment or ask me questions. Lela

aurorawatcherak@wordpress.com

thewillowbranch@wordpress.com

Or you can reach me old-school at lelamarkham@gmail.com.

We Recommend
Breakwater Harbor Books:

BHB Anthology

Fusion: A collection of short stories from Breakwater Harbor Books' authors

Fantasy

The Ark of Humanity, by Scott J. Toney
Eden Legacy, by Scott J. Toney
Horker's Law, by Mike Lee
The Beholder, by Ivan Amberlake
The Firelord's Crown, by Dee Harrison
Firelord's Heir, by Dee Harrison
Firelord's Curse, by Dee Harrison
Godhead, by Ken Mooney

Sci-Fi

Fey, by Mike Lee
StarFire, by Mike Lee
Dr. Zimm's Elixir, by Mike Lee
NovaForge, by Scott J. Toney

Historical Sci-Fi / Fantasy

Chasing Pharaohs, by C.M.T. Stibbe

Dark Paranormal

Limerence, by Claire C Riley
Odium, by Claire C Riley
Odium II, by Claire C Riley
Odium Origins. A Dead Saga Novella. Part One., by Claire C Riley
Diary of the Gone, by Ivan Amberlake

Crime Thriller

Hazard Pay, by Melissa Simonson

Christian

Lazarus, Man, by Scott J. Toney
The Last Supper: John, by Scott J. Toney
Zacchaeus (Pulpit to Page), by Scott J. Toney
The Messenger, by Mindy Haig
Glory, by Mindy Haig

Visit Breakwater Harbor Books for these and other great titles!

www.breakwaterharborbooks.com